THE CROOKEDEST STREET

THE CROOKEDEST STREET

Joe Strupp

ISBN: 978-1-7330875-4-4

Any references to historical events, real people, or real places are used fictitiously. Names, characters, and events are products of the author's imagination.

Book design by Thomas Edward West of Amarna Books & Media.

First print edition 2020

Amarna Books & Media
Maplewood, New Jersey

www.amarnabooksandmedia.com

DEDICATION

For Claire, Cloey and Cole

For San Francisco, still the best

INTRODUCTION

San Francisco has long been a unique place for politics, culture, people, music, and even weather. For many years, news coverage in the city was like few other places. Battling daily newspapers, deep-digging alternative papers, and some of the first niche publications—on gay issues, the environment, tech, drugs, and even the homeless—spanned the 49-square-mile town and beyond.

For years the *San Francisco Chronicle* and the *San Francisco Examiner* duked it out each morning and afternoon for the educated, inquisitive, and often outlandish readership. Both papers had historic and gritty histories that reflected the city's Barbary Coast beginnings, progressive pioneering image, and groundbreaking business breakthroughs that made it the financial capital of the west, along with HIV and other public health discoveries that drew international medical attention and the first real Internet and wireless explosions in the nation.

The *Chronicle's* history dates back to 1865 when, legend has it, that Michael de Young won it in a poker game. He was once shot by an angry business owner who apparently objected to a news article, but survived.

As for the *Examiner*, legendary owner William Randolph Hearst took it over from his father in 1887 and used it and his famed *New York Journal* to pump up circulation with sensational stories, street-smart coverage, and outspoken editorials.

When I moved to San Francisco in 1990, where I spent seven years working for two different newspapers, the daily news battle was in high form. Hearst Corporation owned the *Examiner*, still a true afternoon paper at the time, and the DeYoung descendants ran the *Chronicle*.

Both papers were booming with readers, ads, news, and a great citywide rivalry. It culminated at one point when a 1996 *Chronicle* story about an alleged alligator in Mountain Lake sparked rival columns and stories that raised the mysterious reptile to Loch Ness proportions.

The *Examiner* followed with its own story, as well as the hiring of a psychic to connect with the beast. The *Chronicle* responded by hiring an alligator hunter to catch the elusive creature.

Things got even stranger when then-*Examiner* Executive Editor Phil Bronstein donned a wetsuit with a reporter and threatened to go diving in the lake to find the creature.

The *Examiner* also got one of its biggest scoops in 1997 when legendary *Chronicle* columnist Herb Caen died on a late Friday evening. The *Examiner*, which had the only Saturday edition of the two, took the story first, leaving

Caen's employers at the *Chronicle* to play catch up on their own writer's demise two days later.

But the daily fistfight of news was only one part of the newspaper war in the 1990s. The alternative weeklies *Bay Guardian* and *SF Weekly* sought to top each other every Wednesday with underground stories, insider news of City Hall, and tidbits and battles the dailies and broadcast outlets would never touch. These tabloid-style papers would also keep an eye on the daily paper gossip and doings.

Then there was the *San Francisco Independent*, the great three-times-weekly free paper where I worked for four years. The *Indy* covered both the neighborhoods and the city government. We held our own in both areas, often beating the other publications to city news and giving a broader perspective. Our publisher, Ted Fang, even took the big boys to court when he sued the *Examiner* for predatory pricing and won.

One of my favorite moments came when *SF Weekly* tried to do a hit job on Ted and the *Indy*. Ted agreed to an interview with their reporter but set up our conference room before the scribe arrived with about a dozen framed front pages and other publications with his own picture to make it look as if he was a narcissistic egomaniac.

In addition, Ted made them agree to allow him to choose the cover photo. When their photographer arrived, Ted had him shoot pictures of him smoking a cigar—which Ted did not do normally do—and demanded that that be the cover shot. When their weak story came out, the cover line with that shot read "Blowing Smoke, Breathing Fire." It also included detailed descriptions of the fake conference room gallery.

Ted had managed to trick them into two wrong representations of himself, all for an inside joke that would have made Andy Kaufman smile. As he once told me: "You have to know how to have fun in this town."

He was right.

Overall, these newspapers set the daily agenda for San Francisco like no one else. Everyone grabbed the latest editions of each—well before the Internet and mobile device updates came along. The local TV newscasts might as well have been named the *Chronicle* front page for how they chose stories. City Hall insiders devoured every inch of the weeklies as soon as they stocked the newspaper boxes on Powell Street.

TV, radio, and other news sources couldn't come close. They did not have the staff, insight, or beat coverage sensibility of the print products, or often the understanding of the unusual nature of news in The City. Back then it was a city whose mantra was "anything goes": groundbreaking gay rights legislation, the first domestic partners laws, the first such weddings, naked people running in the annual Bay to Breakers road race, a retired prostitute nearly winning a seat on the Board of Supervisors, and pioneering AIDS education, research, and patient rights.

I reluctantly left San Francisco in 1997 for a bigger daily paper in Riverside, west of Los Angeles, where I was able to cover even more oddball news, corruption, and crime and courts. But it never came close to San Francisco for its combination of hardline politics, progressive issues and print news battles that grabbed every reader and set the tone for power, viewpoints, and excitement.

Things are quite different 25 years later. The *Chronicle* is now owned by Hearst, at a fraction of its size, and the *Examiner* is a downsized shadow of its former self owned by a Colorado-based publisher. The *Bay Guardian*, *SF Weekly*, and *San Francisco Independent* are all gone. The replacement web products do not scratch the surface of real underground and broad-based news.

The city is also not what it once was. Gentrification and a skyrocketing cost of living—due in large part to the explosion of Silicon Valley money—have driven out many of the city's middle- and low-income folks and ushered in corporate and chain outlets that impact many of the independent and creative shops that made the city famous.

A friend still in town recently lamented to me, "Politics here is so boring." Boring was not a term used to describe the San Francisco I knew and covered in the 1990s. More than two decades later, the memories are strong and the characters fascinating—so much so that I wanted to tell the story of that time and place and the news that it created.

That's where this book comes in. Based loosely on many true (and not-so-true) stories and people from the S.F. of the past, *The Crookedest Street* offers a snapshot of what it was like not so long ago. It was a time when news battles were real, the power struggle was strong, and the wildness was appreciated.

So much of what drew me and many out-of-towners to relocate there over the years—the non-judgment, the creativity, the flavor, and even the weather—is gone or in limited supply.

But here is what the city was really like, the good and the bad, from a generation ago through the tales of my fictional characters: Billy Dale, Jack Callahan, Jimmy Min, and many more...and why many of us miss the real people and stories that inspired their creation.

—Joe Strupp

TABLE OF CONTENTS

You can't get rich in politics unless you're a crook.

—Harry S. Truman

Chapter One

A Big Night for Victory

Rain tapped on the window of the limousine as Billy Dale took a swig from his vodka bottle, wiped the sweat from his stubbled chin, and blew out a puff of smoke. The burning embers of the roach clasped between thumb and forefinger glowed in the back seat's dim light as he cleared his lungs of the pot's incense and began to laugh and cough at the same time.

As the stretch barreled through the showers that were drowning O'Farrell Street on the hazy, wet Election Night, Billy glanced out the window just as the car passed the Swing Top Bar at O'Farrell and Polk.

"Ya see that place?" Billy asked the driver as he attempted to navigate the foggy, wet road. "When I first came to San Francisco, I couldn't afford to go in there. Now they're buying me drinks."

The driver couldn't even respond. He was too busy trying to keep from driving onto the sidewalk.

Billy didn't care. He just laughed, took another drink, and smiled.

Tonight was a big night for him. A big night for his career. A big night for San Francisco. And a big night for victory. You could almost sense it in the air as the Pacific Ocean breezes whirled through the city, crashing with the raindrops and providing a mist into the Bay Area night.

There was a feeling that things were changing. That victory was at hand. That something strange had happened. Billy felt it. The city's political elite felt it. Even the limo driver knew something was happening.

Billy had pulled off what could arguably be the biggest upset in the city's history. With his guidance, determination, and at times downright dirty tricks, he had taken out one of the city's political heavyweights and replaced him with a virtual unknown.

Mayor William Carlson, the former state senator who had ruled as San Francisco's most powerful political boss for 12 years—first as a deal-making genius in Sacramento and then as the city's iron-clad leader—had lost. It was only 10 p.m., but the initial returns already showed that Carlson was being ousted by a two-to-one margin.

Political commentators would blame Carlson's arrogance, his failure to counter-attack Dale's ambush charges, and even his inability to turn the city around for his loss.

The truth was that Billy had turned the voters against Carlson and put his man in office through sheer deceit, trickery, and some good old-fashioned dirty campaigning.

That man he put in was Jack Callahan.

Callahan had served as San Francisco police chief for 10 years. Although he had succeeded in driving crime down and putting more officers on the street, he had not made a big name for himself. He had never before run for political office and had never even been interested in local politics until Billy came to him.

Billy, who took revenge as a serious business, had made it his cause for three years to get Carlson out of office. He got mad after the mayor used a technicality in the 1988 election to keep one of Billy's best clients, then-Supervisor John Gilbert, from running for municipal judge.

Carlson was a longtime friend of Judge Harold Weeds, against whom Gilbert was running, and he'd become nervous when Weeds began slipping in the polls. The mayor owed Weeds a lot of favors for his help in squashing a long list of charges against Carlson in recent years, ranging from arrests of prostitutes that Carlson frequented to dismissing cases involving Carlson's friends and deputy mayors.

Although the judge had never had to intervene in cases involving the mayor himself, Carlson liked having him there just in case.

So when that election began to turn against Weeds and in favor of Gilbert, the mayor took action. He deployed three deputy city attorneys to find a loophole, an infraction, something in the election code that could keep Gilbert out.

The investigation found that Gilbert had been registered in two places for more than five years. In addition to regularly voting in San Francisco, Gilbert had also voted in Oakland, where his cousin, Danny, was on the city council. When Carlson got hold of that information, Weeds's people submitted it to a judge who ruled that Gilbert was ineligible.

The night Weeds won his seat again, Billy Dale vowed to get even with Carlson. "Even if I have to tear this city apart to do it," he said.

* * *

Billy thought about that night three years ago as the driver turned the corner on Hyde and passed Lombard Steet, at the top of the block dubbed "the Crookedest Street in the World" for its twisting roadway that drew tourists daily. Later, at Powell Street, he punched the gas pedal, and roared down the hillside street toward Nob Hill. When the black stretch pulled in front of the Fairmont Hotel, Billy acted like it was his hotel, his palace, his night to shine.

The relentless rain continued as the car came to a halt in front of the hotel known for hosting everyone from kings and presidents to rock stars. The flags of many nations that adorned the magnificent building's front facade flapped in the wind as the driver ran around to Billy's door, bounced his shoe through a puddle, and clutched the shiny metal handle with a wet grip.

As the door opened, a cloud of smoke blew out of the car ahead of Billy, who stumbled a bit as he stepped on the sidewalk, but was able to gain his balance without a fall.

Even before he got out of the car, a swarm of television crews and reporters had surrounded the limo's door, ready with questions and inquiries about what had occurred that night.

"Ain't it great?" Billy asked the throng of news crews, friends, and political hangers-on who listened as he stepped forward. "This is what democracy is all about."

Billy shoved past the reporters. He didn't like to talk to news people unless he was out to complain about a story they had done on him or an attack a political rival had made.

That was his power as a political consultant, as both his critics and supporters know. He could hold back and let his candidates shine by themselves, but jump up and attack others when needed.

"It's our own art of thrust and parry," said Billy, who had, among his varying hobbies, taken up fencing. "You don't attack unless provoked, but you provoke when necessary."

The doorman, who knew Billy well from his many Fairmont private parties, opened the tall golden doors for Billy and ushered him through the main lobby. The hotel's famous oil paintings and brass fixtures towered overhead as he turned right and headed toward the grand ballroom.

Billy's tux was pure Pierre Cardin. But after the night he'd had, it looked as disheveled as any bum's ten-year old suit. He stopped at the nearest mirror and adjusted his tie, tried to tuck in the wrinkled shirt, and even spit-shined his rain-weathered shoes. His gut stuck out as usual and the chubby cheeks he had had since birth pouted out.

Billy had always tried to look sharp, despite the fact that his weight and his health were not good. He'd been diagnosed HIV positive a year earlier and had only recently taken steps to try to eat better. Still, his appearance was rough.

Most of the young guys he romanced acted as if they didn't mind his messy, less-than-sexy look. Most were magnetized enough by his awesome power, both in the political world and in the personal approach to other people. He had an assurance, a self-confidence, and an arrogance to which even his rivals would attest.

His recent rise to the top of San Francisco's power elite also had helped him find good-looking young men during his strolls through the bars on Polk Street or in the Castro District—the city's gay Mecca.

As Billy's mind wandered in a hundred different directions on this night, he began to almost jog toward the ballroom with excitement. Nearing the front door, more television cameras waited, along with political supporters and friends.

Billy's classic smile greeted them.

Fifteen flights up, in one of the Fairmont's most expensive suites, sat the victor who garnered Billy Dale's spoils that night.

Jack Callahan was never much of a drinker. During his days as a cop, and even later as chief, he had stuck to a rare glass of wine with dinner and preferred 7-Up or a Coke over hard booze. Growing up in a family of alcoholics had kept him away from the hard stuff and often frightened him about the dangers it could possess.

But on this night, Jack was in a different form. The champagne flowed and he smiled an innocent grin as he sat on the bed with his wife, Glenda, and watched the television reports.

Channel 4's reporter had just come on and announced that with 65 percent of the vote in, Jack had claimed 55 percent to Carlson's 45 percent in the two-man runoff election. He glanced over at Glenda and gave her a friendly squeeze with his arm. Jack's brother, and deputy chief, Phil, came over to give him a hug and kiss Glenda's cheek.

"Looks like you did it, Jackie boy. Looks like you pulled it off," Phil said, a cigar jutting out of the side of his mouth.

Jack didn't say anything. He just smiled and felt a shiver down his back.

*   *   *

The longtime cop who had grown up on the Mission District's streets in the late '50s, back when it was a predominantly working-class Irish area, had never even dreamed of becoming a politician. The second of five boys, he had strong, traditional values of work and family, despite being the son of alcoholics. His parents had always fought the booze, but still managed to raise their boys properly after giving up drinking when Jack was a teen.

His goal had always been to be a street cop, marry a good woman and live out his days in the city where he was born. He had attained part of that dream as a rising young star in the department. After only five years as a patrolman, Jack became a sergeant in 1969 and went on to a lieutenant's post two years later. After a succession of promotions, he found himself appointed chief in 1980 when former chief Leo Pendelton was killed in a bizarre traffic accident.

Mayor Bella Williams, who went on to become a U.S. Senator, had appointed him because of his family man image and straight-arrow approach. Williams had taken office only a year earlier after the tragic murder of former Mayor Kit Lange. She wanted someone who would not draw too much criticism during her first term.

Jack was the perfect choice. By the time Williams ended her two terms as mayor in 1987, crime was down 30 percent and more than 200 new officers had been added to the police ranks. Williams and Callahan had also orchestrated the hiring of more gays, women, and minorities, as well as appointing a string of new black captains and deputy chiefs.

When Carlson ran for mayor the first time in 1987, after Williams left, Jack had supported him and endorsed him, saying the two could work well together to keep the city going.

But during his time as chief, Jack's personal life had also fallen apart. His first wife, Jackie, hadn't wanted to move into the city, which was a requirement for San Francisco's police chief. The couple, who'd been married since Jack's first year on the force, had always lived in Half Moon Bay, the scenic, quiet, seaside town about 50 miles south of San Francisco.

Jackie had grown up in the small town, knew everyone by name, and despised the big city. After a year-and-a-half-long separation in 1985, the couple divorced.

Jack did not meet Glenda until a year before the mayoral race of 1991 began. Although Jack had not yet entertained the idea of running, he had begun to socialize more with some of the political heavyweights, including Billy Dale and his columnist friend, Mike McLean. McLean, who wrote for the weekly neighborhood newspaper the *Advocate*, had once written a glowing column about Jack's police chief accomplishments.

McLean called Jack "the most honest cop in a city of dishonest cops." While the dishonest reference had irked most of the force, the accolades for Jack turned his head.

The two began to have dinner together often and McLean started taking Jack around to parties with Billy Dale and other political leaders. It was at one such gathering in 1990 at the posh Star's Restaurant that Jack met Glenda.

Glenda Pullman Oberlin had been a banking wizard for 15 years. The chief financial analyst for Krugler Johnson Trust, the west coast's leading commercial bank, Glenda had broken many glass ceilings in her industry and reached a place of prominence for herself in recent years.

But for the social ladder-climber who thrived on status and power, that wasn't enough. She knew that San Francisco's power lay in its political machine almost as much as in its corporate honchos. If she could get her hand in the city government power structure, she thought, her status would rise immeasurably.

So it was not by accident that she had a friend of Jack's introduce her to the popular police chief that night. Although Jack was 12 years older than Glenda, she was still drawn to his potential. Everyone in town knew that Jack would be ripe to run for some kind of office in the coming elections of the 90s. Be it sheriff, assemblyman or a member of the Board of Supervisors—San Francisco's city council—he definitely had a future.

Glenda wanted to latch on to that future and set her sights on Jack. By the end of the night, she had gotten him to drive her home and stay the night. For six months after that, she was with him all the time and at every major social function. The two were married just a week before Jack announced his campaign for mayor.

*   *   *

As the couple sat on the bed in the Fairmont Hotel suite, Glenda grinned at the television set. Jumping from channel to channel to watch all of them announce her husband's impending victory, she wallowed in the excitement and power that it evoked.

As the city's first lady, she would have access to all the social events, the major dinners and parties, and the attention that only the powerful can have. She put her arms around Jack and kissed him hard. As she hugged him, her eyes wandered out the window to the view of the Transamerica building and the dark, rainy streets. In the distance, she could see the dome of City Hall. The thought of that place under her control gave her both an adrenaline rush and sexual excitement.

"It's all ours," she told Jack. To herself, she thought: "It's all mine!"

While Jack and his friends celebrated in their suite and the victory party in the ballroom below got underway, one man across the street in the nearby Mark Hopkins Hotel was not as happy.

William Carlson, who had worked his way up from the son of a grocery store clerk in Oakland to become an assemblyman, a state senator, and eventually the most powerful mayor of San Francisco, was about to meet the political defeat of his life.

Carlson, who had managed to knock down Billy Dale three years earlier, had just been knocked out of his own political kingdom. Through Billy's trickery, deceit, and hardball campaigning, and Carlson's own arrogance and failure to strike back, Carlson had been blown out of an election that all critics one year earlier were ready to hand him.

Carlson sat alone in the three-room suite. He'd ordered everyone out an hour before and was ready to go down to admit defeat. The former Golden Gloves boxer and one-time cab driver had been a master at fighting back. He'd never lost an election, though, and did not know how to handle it.

The incumbent sneered at the television reports as he switched from channel to channel and saw his hopes diminish with the increased returns. Carlson also cursed the reporters whom he had been blaming for digging up dirt on his past, his messy divorce, and his alleged ties to Nevada organized crime leaders.

But, even as he shouted obscenities toward the press as their faces appeared on the television screen, he knew that the man to blame was Billy Dale. Along with McLean, it had been Billy who carefully orchestrated the line of negative press about Carlson. Although some of the stories were stretched to fit Billy's needs, many of the items about Carlson's weekend retreats to Vegas and Reno to meet with underworld figures were genuine.

While most in City Hall had long known about the mayor's side trips to visit some of the casino industry's most notorious bosses, the local beat reporters had not bothered to track down the reports. Since the city's two newspapers regularly backed Carlson and had endorsed him for every election in which he had run, including this one, editors had not pushed their reporters to go after Carlson.

In fact, the daily papers' investigative pieces had been more about Callahan and efforts to discredit him. Most of the stories, however, had little substance to sway people's views in the face of such outlandish accusations against Carlson.

It had been Billy Dale, with the help of Mike McLean and the *Advocate*, who had succeeded in putting out enough dirt on Carlson to steer the electorate in Callahan's favor.

Carlson crushed a beer can in his hand and threw it out the window as he remembered the dirty campaign. His face flushed as he thought about Billy celebrating next door. He continued to rage as more reports came in.

About 20 blocks south, someone else watched the television reports and spouted his own anger. Tim Cross, editor of the San Francisco *Journal*, was watching the news as well and not liking what he saw.

The *Journal*, the city's afternoon newspaper, had been under fire from its parent company, Mack Corporation, to do everything possible to keep Carlson in office. Mack, one of the city's largest development firms, was trying to get approval for construction of the city's biggest retail/residential complex on 600 acres south of the Bay Bridge in the former Hunter's Point Naval Shipyard.

The development would have 3,000 condominiums and apartments, office space, and myriad shops, services, and entertainment centers. The project would be a cash cow for Mack, which had taken a bath on a string of projects in the 1980s and was hanging its hopes on the development.

With Carlson in office, Mack chairman and *Journal* publisher Donald Grossman knew he would easily gain approval from the Planning Commission. Because six of the seven commissioners had been Carlson appointees, their vote was locked in.

But if Callahan came in, he could appoint four new commissioners, all of whom would likely reject the project to get back at Mack and the *Journal* for endorsing his rival. Callahan had been the target of regular attacks from the *Journal* during the campaign, which attempted to paint him as a flunky cop with no leadership ability and a right-wing approach to law enforcement.

"If Jack Callahan becomes mayor, the diversity and liberal values that have made San Francisco a welcoming home to all outsiders will be destroyed and replaced with the Gestapo tactics and military-style enforcement that we've seen in the days of Adolf Hitler's Germany," the *Journal* had written in an editorial just two weeks earlier. "For San Franciscans seeking an even-handed approach to government and law enforcement, Jack Callahan is all thumbs."

Even for the mild-mannered, low-key Callahan, the editorial had been a hard shot.

Tim Cross knew it as he followed the news reports and he also knew it when Grossman himself had come to his office and demanded that the paper "get Bill Carlson re-elected."

Cross realized early on that his position at the paper was riding on the outcome of the election. After overseeing a five-part series the *Journal* had published on a local health maintenance organization's operation, which drew a libel lawsuit costing the paper $750,000 in legal fees, Cross had nearly been fired.

When Grossman relayed his latest order for a Carlson victory, he had also reminded Cross of the financial problems the paper—and Mack—faced due to the HMO lawsuit. If Carlson lost and its big development project went down, the paper's future and Cross's job would be in trouble.

Slamming his fist down on the desk, Cross yelled for a news assistant to bring him coffee. When the young intern left, Cross pulled out a bottle of Malibu Rum and a container of aspirin. He popped the pills in his mouth, slugged them down with a shot of the rum, and settled in with his coffee. He knew there was a long night ahead and he began plunking the keys on his keyboard for the editorial in which he would congratulate Jack Callahan and urge all residents to get behind the city's new mayor.

Next door to the *Journal* were the offices of San Francisco's morning newspaper, the larger, more successful San Francisco *Bulletin*, which dominated the city's newspaper market and was seen as the paper of record.

On the sixth floor newsroom, in the corner office that he'd occupied for 15 years sat *Bulletin* editor J.C. Townsend. About 10 years older than his counterpart at the *Journal*, Townsend was a smaller, calmer man. Still, he was just as upset at the night's developments as the younger, angrier Cross.

Townsend, who was known for the rocking chair he kept in his office for afternoon coffee breaks, tipped back in the pine-framed object while listening to news reports from one of the city's two all-news radio stations—KLSF. Townsend grumbled as KLSF City Hall reporter Jane Leonard reported the disappointing news.

"It looks as though Mayor Carlson's chances for re-election are all but gone," Leonard said. "As of 10:45 p.m., with 55% of the ballots counted, Carlson has only 43% of the vote to challenger Jack Callahan's 57%. KLSF is predicting that Callahan will win the election by a comfortable margin."

With that, Townsend stopped rocking and leaned forward. He flicked the ash off the cigarette that had been burning in his hand and stuck the cigarette in his mouth. The chair rocked back as he stood up and headed toward his desk.

Blowing a puff of smoke from his mouth and glancing down at the rainy streets below, Townsend sat and rifled through the wire copy on his desk. He snuffed out the cigarette in a nearby ashtray and got up to get his raincoat.

Stepping out into the newsroom, Townsend heard the clatter of keyboards, the blare of television, and a distant laugh of a group arguing over what the headline for the mayoral victory should be.

Instead of taking the elevator for the long trek to the street, Townsend headed down the stairs, almost tripping twice. He didn't want to chance running into one of the publishers or owners.

The Ingle family, which had owned the *Bulletin* since it started in 1855 and now ran a media empire consisting of five television stations, four radio stations, and the influential S.F. Magazine, was one of the most powerful families in the Bay Area.

Charlie Ingle, the gambler who won the newspaper's original building in a poker game more than a century ago, had used it for decades to push his political agenda and vision for city expansion. His editorials against crime and corruption had resulted in many of the tightest ethics laws and law enforcement efforts the city ever had.

He had also succeeded in helping to elect some of the city's most powerful officials, who in turn did everything to help the thriving newspaper gain more advertising business, expand related businesses, and maintain a stronghold on its newspaper base in the face of competition from the *Journal* and other smaller newspapers.

So when the newspaper's current chairman of the board, Charlie Ingle's granddaughter, Emily, had pushed the *Bulletin* to support Carlson, Townsend knew it was a necessity.

Emily Ingle had reminded Townsend only a week earlier over a rather caustic lunch at One Market, the upscale waterfront restaurant, that Carlson's re-election was essential.

Everyone in the city's business community knew the link. Carlson's brother, Ronny, was vice president of marketing for Statler Markets, the Bay Area's largest chain of food stores and one of the *Bulletin*'s leading advertisers. Statler Market's ads and inserts were the largest part of the *Bulletin*'s Sunday paper and a major revenue source for the newspaper.

Statler Markets had hinted that they might pull out of newspaper advertising and switch to mail-based ads. Although the loss of one client would not devastate the *Bulletin*, it would put a tight hold on the company's finances, especially at a time when newsprint costs were rising and the competition was growing.

Ronny Carlson had told Mrs. Ingle straight out that if his brother managed to hold on to his seat, the company would gladly remain a client. He even went so far as to say that Mayor Carlson would be willing to give more exclusives to the *Bulletin*, in an effort to boost the paper's competitive edge.

"You don't need to be told how important this is for us," Mrs. Ingle had said during her lunch with Townsend. "I know you understand that we will suffer greatly if this outcome is, well, disappointing."

As he stepped out into the dissipating rain and flung on his raincoat, Townsend recalled that conversation. He also recalled, with disdain, his efforts to go after Jack Callahan. He had sent several investigative reporters to dig up dirt on the longtime police chief. All they uncovered were some details about his divorce and vague accusations that his ex-wife had made about infidelity.

Although there was no proof that Callahan had cheated on his wife, the fact that the allegations had made it into court records was enough for Townsend to play it up.

Using the divorce records, Townsend and the reporters helped paint a picture of Callahan as a womanizing, neglectful husband who dumped his wife and could not be trusted to be honest with residents.

But when the stories became public, they backfired.

Callahan went on television with his children and friends and helped create an image of a victim of a failed marriage, instead of the instigator. Voters learned that it wasn't Callahan, but his first wife, Jackie, who pushed for the divorce and made up the stories of infidelity to try to get a bigger settlement.

During one live television interview, Callahan asked voters to put themselves in his shoes. "What would you do if the woman you loved, supported, and tried to build a life with had made up lies about you?" the police chief asked, with just a hint of a tear in his eye. "Haven't I been through enough?"

After the appearance, Callahan's polling numbers not only soared, but the incident helped put him over the top, some political pundits thought.

Townsend replayed the entire event in his mind while walking the half block to the Deadline Bar, the favorite watering hole of reporters and editors from both papers. The front door's bells clanged as Townsend entered the dark, smoky tavern. Because it was election night, the place lacked the usual swarm of reporters. A handful of writers he knew were scattered about, while the television blared more news reports of the evening's political changes.

The tired editor sat down at the bar, ordered a scotch and soda, and leaned back to drink it.

Two cops were playing pool at one of the bar's two billiard tables, while what looked to be a prostitute and a cab driver negotiated a price. Next to them, an older couple just sat and drank while trying to avoid looking at each other, and two college-aged kids played quarters in the corner.

Townsend looked back at the bar as one of his favorite bartenders, Sammy Dilson, approached him.

"Rough night, J.C.?" the bartender asked as he freshened his drink.

"I'd rather not talk about it," Townsend responded.

But another editor who was gladly in the mood for talking about the night's events was doing just that at the same time that J.C. Townsend began his drinking binge.

About two miles from the *Journal* and *Bulletin* offices, in the quieter, dirtier Tenderloin neighborhood, stood the home of the San Francisco *Reader*—the city's major alternative weekly.

Located in a three-story building that once housed San Francisco's biggest Barbary Coast brothel, the *Reader* was legendary for opposing nearly every major city government establishment policy and machine politics candidate.

Editor and publisher Danny Dugan, who grew up in New York City and cut his teeth as a street reporter for the former New York Herald, went out of his way to bash city politicians and support underdog candidates.

In the race for mayor, Dugan and the *Reader* had opposed both Callahan and Carlson and endorsed the lesser-known challenger, Supervisor Marie Alzeti. Alzeti, whose father, Carlo, had served as mayor for two terms in the early

1960s, was a secondary candidate from the beginning.

Although many voters liked her liberal approach and affinity for the homeless, minorities, the poor, and citizen's rights, her often outlandish statements had irked some in recent weeks. While she had been president of the Board of Supervisors twice, her proposals on two major occasions had made her lose ground with voters.

The first downfall came two years earlier when Alzeti had proposed a 10% city income tax to fund a string of homeless shelters and programs for the poor. The proposal went to the ballot but lost by a close margin. Many observers had blamed the loss on a statement Alzeti made during a television debate on the initiative, in which she bashed voters for not caring.

"If the people of San Francisco are so selfish that they won't give up their expensive dinners, BMWs, and vacations so some downtrodden folks can have a decent life, then I am ashamed of this city."

Since the comments also came on the heels of the 1989 earthquake, one of the city's worst disasters, they hit a major nerve with many voters.

Alzeti also drew criticism when, in the final weeks of the mayoral race, she suggested that she would seek a city charter change to assure that 15 percent of the city's budget would be set aside for funding programs in the city's worst neighborhoods.

When that idea came out, several neighborhood groups jumped on Alzeti, and even some of her staunchest supporters pulled out, worried that she would radically change the city's budget process and might deny the city valuable resources, such as police and fire protection—always hot-button issues in a city election.

Callahan and Carlson also used Alzeti's wild comments and unusual proposals to knock her down. In one debate, Carlson accused Alzeti of "letting your heart take over your brain," and also accused her of a "Robin Hood mentality that will lead San Francisco into a Sherwood Forest of depression, deficit spending, and instability."

Despite her minimal chances for victory, the *Reader* had endorsed Alzeti and even helped her print campaign material on its presses.

As the election night tallies grew, Dugan became more and more upset that another establishment candidate with big-money backing and corporate support would be leading the city.

Dugan recalled the nasty, bitter campaign while watching the returns on the banged-up, black-and-white television in the corner of his small, cramped, third-floor office.

In its effort to give Alzeti even a chance at victory, the *Reader* had hit hard on Carlson's record of inaction for San Francisco's poor and downtrodden, while also attempting to paint a picture of Callahan's police department as a group of racist, homophobic thugs that took every chance to knock down minorities and boost graft.

Although the *Reader* had difficulty proving that Callahan or his officers had engaged in any underhanded enforcement that could be tied directly to the police chief, the paper succeeded in raising suspicions about one incident: the death of a homeless man in Golden Gate Park.

About six months before Election Day, several homeless people living in the park reported seeing three cops beat a fellow homeless man to death. When a rival newspaper wrote a story that a complaint had been filed by a witness and a city park maintenance worker had reported finding the body, the *Reader* took note.

After a three-week search, one reporter obtained a videotape from an anonymous resident showing three cops, including Callahan's brother, Phil, giving the fatal blows to the dead man. Although Jack Callahan had not been chief for more than a year, a video of his brother and other cops previously under his charge killing a homeless man would be devastating news.

Eventually, word got back to Callahan about the tape and he made a personal visit to the *Reader*'s newsroom.

During a conversation with Dugan, Callahan made no bones about the fact that he would "make things very uncomfortable" for Dugan if any word of the tape made it into the *Reader*'s next issue.

As usual, Dugan ignored Callahan's warning and planned to publish the following week.

But the next morning, the tape was gone and signs of a burglary were everywhere. The newspaper's front doors were broken into and the locks on Dugan's office door and desk had been smashed. Strangely, about $20 in the desk drawer remained untouched, while the videotape was gone.

Just minutes after discovering the tape had been taken, Dugan called Callahan and threatened to write the story anyway.

"Go ahead," the chief said. "I'll have a libel suit filed within an hour after the first issue hits the stand." Dugan knew he couldn't write the story without proof, so the entire issue ended.

Still, Dugan remained determined that Callahan would not reach the mayor's office without a fight. But despite his strongest editorials and stories showing police brutality statistics on the rise, the new mayor was on his way in.

With an angry glare, Dugan shut off the television, and sat down at his typewriter. Even though newspapers had used computers for nearly 20 years, he still banged out his editorials on a 25-year-old manual typewriter. He had written his first freelance story on the machine and felt it was bad luck to write editorials on anything else.

Although he gladly edited copy on the computer, his strong superstitions forbade him from writing editorials in any other way. As the clock above his desk hit midnight, he began work on yet another editorial. This one would slam Callahan even more than the previous ones. He considered it his duty to issue a warning to voters about what they should expect under the new mayor. ■

Chapter Two

Road to the Fairmont

The Fairmont Hotel ballroom shook with excitement as returns continued to come in and Callahan's supporters kept celebrating. Billy Dale strolled through the Grand Ballroom, accepting accolades from friends left and right as the night wore on and victory inched closer.

Supervisors, state officials, and even Senator Bella Williams were there to greet him. Billy also caught a glimpse of Ted Fang, former publisher of The Independent, and Bruce Brugmann, who had once run The Bay Guardian. Both Fang and Brugmann had gotten out of the newspaper business in recent years, choosing instead to focus on broadcasting and book publishing ventures.

Just as Billy was about to head toward the podium to take his place among the victors, he felt a slap on his back.

"Billy, you son of a bitch, how the hell are ya?" said the voice.

Billy turned around to see who it was and hugged the man with both arms.

"Jimmy, you bastard, do you believe this shit?" Billy said with a smile. "We got'em by the balls."

Jimmy Min, the skinny owner and publisher of the *Advocate* and one of Billy's best friends, grinned his trademark ear-to-ear smile and sipped the Mai Tai perched in his hand. The city's youngest newspaper publisher at 32, and part of the most powerful Asian family in San Francisco, Jimmy had waited a long time for something like this.

Ever since his father, Sam, had come to the United States from China 40 years earlier, the Min family had made it their goal to take advantage of America's opportunities.

As he hugged Billy and thought about the future of the city under a mayor who viewed the *Advocate* and the Mins as a force to be reckoned with, Jimmy also thought about how far his family had come and what his father had done to give him so much.

Sam Min grew up on the streets of Beijing a poor but happy child. His father, a tailor, and his mother, who cleaned rooms in local hotels, had little to offer their three sons. But they always made sure to instill them with the values of honesty, hard work, and love.

Those beliefs stuck with Sam until he was 12, the year his father was killed by gangsters who demanded that he turn over part of the earnings from his tailor shop to them. When he refused, they set fire to his shop while he was inside, bound and gagged.

When he reached 18, Sam grabbed his first chance to come to the United States, hitching a ride on a cargo vessel bound for San Francisco. Once there, he got a job in a printing shop and worked day and night to print everything from garage sale flyers to restaurant menus.

When he reached 30, he took over the shop, buying out the owner and expanding with money he had saved over the years. Min Printing, which had been a struggling concern at the beginning, grew into a thriving business with Sam's ingenuity, hard work, and when necessary, hardball competitiveness.

He'd call and cancel orders for other printing shops, bribe police officers to tow his competitors' trucks and cite them for minor infractions, and once even convinced some workers at two other printing shops to strike for better hours and pay so that he could get their business.

"Success is about ingenuity, hard work, and when necessary, everything else," Sam once told his sons. "The rules are, there are no rules but winning."

Eventually, Min Printing became the most successful printing shop in all of Chinatown and began to lure business from other neighborhoods in the early 1970s.

Sam Min was on top of his world.

But, to this immigrant from China who viewed the United States as the land of opportunity, just running a successful business was not enough. Sam wanted to be a part of the power elite, have a say in the city, and take control of things.

At that time, Chinatown did not have a place in local government. No Asians were on the Board of Supervisors or the Board of Education and the Asian community's influence at City Hall was minimal.

When Chinese merchants wanted any help for improvements, expansion, or crime problems, city officials ignored them. Sam knew they needed a voice.

That's when he turned to news.

Chinatown had only one newspaper at the time, the weekly Chinatown Gazette. It wasn't a bad paper, but it included mostly small-time news about merchant meetings, parades, and local profiles. It never took on issues or put any heat on City Hall.

Sam knew it could be an outlet for his ideas and a way to force city officials to come to his neighborhood's calling.

After arranging financing and finding some investors from other neighboring businesses, Sam bought the Gazette and turned it around.

The weekly newspaper immediately doubled its audience by adding an English-language edition. That allowed Asians who spoke only English, and other city residents, to find out what was going on in Chinatown.

It also allowed the mainstream press and the television and radio stations to see the issues and problems of Chinatown. Sam soon began sending a free copy of each issue to the print and broadcast mediums throughout the Bay Area.

Then Sam went to work.

The very first issue attacked the work of police in the Central District police station, which covered Chinatown. Sam wrote about how crime in the area was the worst of the Central District neighborhoods and slammed the city for assigning no bilingual officers.

"As residents of this community named for our homeland, we are entitled to equal protection and equal access to that protection," Sam wrote in an editorial for the first edition under his ownership. "We demand it."

The issue took off citywide after three television stations used the item for their own stories and attacked City Hall for failing to provide equal coverage for Chinatown and for ignoring the need for bilingual officers.

In two days, then-Mayor Clayton Barlow was forced to address the issue at a press conference. He vowed to increase patrols and hire at least five bilingual officers, who began work just a month later.

Sam was ecstatic, but he didn't stop there. Over the next year, the Gazette took on every issue known to Chinatown, including rent control, property values, better access for tourists, school deterioration, and local health care.

In each case, Sam's coverage opened up the Chinatown issues to the entire city, forcing City Hall to take notice and causing other major news outlets to cover the topics.

Sam's biggest influence came when he helped elect the first Asian to the Board of Supervisors: Tom Chin. Although he'd held a variety of appointed positions on city commissions, Chin had run for the board only once before. But when district elections came to San Francisco in the late 1970s, Chin found the best chance to join the board.

With strong backing from Sam, Chin won by nearly a 2-to-1 margin, giving Sam more prestige and a fixed ally at City Hall. With Chin's help, legislation was passed giving minority businesses, such as Sam's, preferences for city contracts. In less than a year, Sam got the contracts for dozens of City Hall printing jobs, as well as printing the official Chinese-language public notices for issues related to Chinatown in the Gazette.

In two years from the date that Chin was elected, Sam's profits for his shop tripled and the newspaper's revenue more than doubled. He made enough to move his wife and two boys from Chinatown to the more residential Sunset District and expand his circulation to include all Asian neighborhoods in San Francisco, not just Chinatown.

But that still wasn't enough.

Despite his rise in political influence and substantial wealth, Sam still was at the mercy of Chinatown's gangs. The ruthless mobs that shook down Chinese businesses, paid off Central Station cops, and undercut some businesses with their black market products were taking still more profits out of Sam's pocket.

One of the most powerful gangs was the Lee Ming Crew, whose territory included the offices of Sam's shop and the Gazette. From the first day he opened, Sam had been forced to pay off Lee Ming and its leader, Ted Wong, every month.

Although most business owners paid the underworld boss as just another business expense, Sam had always hated the shakedowns. He looked at them as cheap hoods who were using their strength to hurt their own people.

"I'm sick of these sonsabitches," he would tell his wife, Rose. "As soon as I have enough pull, I'm going to tell them to take a hike."

So, just a few days later, when Lee Ming's collection man came around as usual, Sam told him he wasn't paying up. The collector argued but eventually left.

The next day, Wong himself came by just as Sam was locking up the Gazette offices.

"Hi, Sam, I hear we have a little problem," said Wong, who sported an expensive Italian suit, dark black shoes, and one of his trademark fedoras. "I hear you don't want to do your part."

Sam gave a dirty look and sneered. "I am doing my part, I just don't want to give in to your sleaze anymore, that's all," he said.

Wong didn't move a muscle, he just smiled. "I'd reconsider if I were you," Wong said and then walked away.

Sam sat there thinking for a minute as dark descended on the cold, quiet stretch of Grand Avenue that housed his entire business world. He realized he might be pushing too far too fast, and didn't need to jeopardize his livelihood and family like this. He decided he would continue paying Wong off, but with a side plan in place.

The next day, he ordered his two best reporters to dig up everything they could on Lee Ming and Wong. He knew there had to be something on the underworld leader that could make good front-page news.

For weeks, the reporters dug through tax records, business license receipts, crime statistics, and even immigration papers looking for some scrap of evidence to link to the crime boss.

After a month of investigative work, the reporters had come up with what they wanted. It seemed that Wong had paid no taxes on two nightclubs he owned, and had not paid his own income taxes for three years.

But Sam waited before making anything public. He knew this had to be done carefully and ordered his reporters to go to the nightclubs, which were known as drug dens, to find proof that drug deals were occurring there.

He knew that illegal drug sales would make such a story more appealing, and more damaging to Wong. The reporters went to both clubs every night for two weeks but found nothing.

The drug action was done so secretively and with such protection that they couldn't infiltrate.

Sam was fuming. "Well, then write it anyway," he said.

Sam ordered the reporters to use the tax evasion information, but also write a separate piece about how they'd bought drugs at the nightclubs on several occasions.

The reporters reluctantly did so, and in two days the three-part series was ready.

When the following week's issue of the Gazette hit the streets, the headline "Chinatown's Dirty Laundry" was smack on Page One.

Underneath it, the subhead stated, "How Chinatown's dirtiest gang has ignored City Hall and funneled drugs to your kids."

The series detailed all aspects of Wong's underground empire of drugs and illegal sales of stolen goods, as well as his spotty tax history.

When city officials got wind of the stories, they launched their own investigation, eventually including the FBI and the U.S. Drug Enforcement Agency. In the end, Wong himself was arrested, along with three of his top deputies. All four received 10 years in prison when the trials ended a year later.

Sam became a hero, Chinatown's image as a good place to live and shop improved, and even fellow newspaper editors praised his work. It seemed like Sam was on his way to being a major political force in San Francisco.

Then it all ended.

About a week after Wong and his underbosses were sentenced, Sam received a call from Central Station that the alarm in his store had gone off. He quickly drove to Chinatown to see what happened and found the door locked up as before, but the alarm's loud clang-clang continuing.

As he slid open the front gate and unlocked the front door, Sam noticed that all the lights were out. Whenever he closed up, Sam usually left at least one back light on for the police who toured the area after hours. But on this night, the offices were pitch black.

With the loud clanging in his ears, Sam stumbled toward the back to the heavy iron alarm shut-off switch. Just as he reached the rear, he noticed two dark figures standing in the corner.

He recognized both of them. One was Chad Wong, Ted Wong's cousin, and the other he knew as Simon Pang, one of Ted's top neighborhood collectors.

Before Sam could say anything to the two men, they each pulled out a .38 caliber revolver and pulled the triggers.

The handguns spit sparks and fired as the clanging bells of the shop's alarm continued to sound in the cool, dark Chinatown night. The alarm sound muffled much of the gunfire and drowned out most of its echo.

The first bullet hit Sam in the stomach, causing him to lurch forward, with the second hitting him in the head. He dropped and fell over as the last bullet struck his temple, his right hand still stretched out.

As Sam fell, his arm struck the alarm switch, turning it off, and its clang-clang ended the moment Sam hit the ground. He died almost instantly.

*   *   *

Jimmy Min, who had just finished college a year earlier, immediately took over operation of the Gazette at his mother's request. For several years he used the paper to continue his father's work of slamming City Hall and promoting city issues.

But Jimmy also continued to attack the Chinese gangs, intensely following the trials of any members who were arrested, while putting pressure on Central Station police to clamp down on gang activities.

Police never brought charges against Sam Min's killers, which infuriated Jimmy. He was never sure if it was a police cover-up or just bad investigating.

Years later, Jimmy took the profits from the Gazette and Min Printing and bought the *Advocate*. As he expanded the family's journalism empire, he remained true to his father's mission of promoting neighborhood and minority issues, while also using the publications to gain political advantage.

When Jimmy purchased the *Advocate*, it had been a struggling, small publication that covered mostly the city's wealthier neighborhoods like Pacific Heights and Nob Hill. But, with Jimmy's funding and hard-edged approach, he built it into a political force that brought an alternative view for minorities and neighborhood issues.

By 1990, the *Advocate* had become a citywide newspaper that covered City Hall and neighborhood news. It was also the only free weekly delivered to each home at no charge.

The home delivery idea was Jimmy's and his alone. He realized that residents would more easily read a newspaper that was on their porch than in a news rack near a coffee shop. He was right. Circulation jumped, as did advertising rates.

Eventually, Jimmy gained the same clout as every other free newspaper in

San Francisco, while making his family giants in the Asian community.

His continued support of Tom Chin had elevated the former supervisor to the State Assembly and, eventually, the State Senate. He had also helped get two more Asians elected to the Board of Supervisors.

But despite Jimmy's political marksmanship, the *Advocate* still did not have all the influence it could seek. What it needed to be a real player in town was a mayor. Getting someone elected mayor would be the boost to put the newspaper, and Min's family, over the top.

Jimmy knew this was the key. ◼

Chapter Three

A Night in Reno

For the *Advocate* to play any kind of part in the election of a mayor, it would have to support someone that none of the other daily newspapers would back. If Jimmy's candidate could pull ahead and win, that person would be indebted to Jimmy. But if the *Advocate* just supported an obvious winner that already had backing from the two dailies, his part would be lost.

Jimmy knew finding the right candidate and the right way to make him a winner would take some planning. Where to find someone who could be a viable player, but had not yet received enough support, was tough.

It was late December 1990 when Jimmy's efforts to recruit a candidate began. The mayoral primary election was less than 10 months away and Jimmy needed to act fast.

During their usual Friday morning breakfast together at Tiger's Coffee Shop in Glen Park, Jimmy and Billy Dale discussed the idea of pitching a candidate against Carlson. The incumbent mayor had a strong record, which had been boosted by his leadership abilities shown during the chaos following the devastating 1989 earthquake. Both daily newspapers had published that historic shot of Carlson pulling a child out of a damaged home in the Marina District just hours after the quake.

He had also succeeded in gaining quick federal and state funds that helped the city rebuild the most damaged portions within six months. Still, Carlson had been in office as a state senator and mayor for a combined 12 years and some problems, such as homelessness, had increased.

Billy and Jimmy, who had been friends since meeting at a neighborhood political club meeting in 1984, pondered the idea.

Jimmy sipped his favorite tomato juice and munched on a piece of toast while Billy downed his trademark morning pancakes. The two remained in their own thoughts until Billy had an idea.

"The first thing we have to do is knock Carlson down," Billy said with a mouth full of food. "That guy is popular, but if we raised some issues that people haven't focused on, and found some dirt, it could happen."

Jimmy nodded his head and took a drink of juice as the waitress added more coffee to each of their cups.

"But what?" Jimmy asked. "The guy was a hero in the earthquake, crime is down, and everyone is happy with him. We need something heavy, something that hasn't been touched to become an issue."

Both men knew, and had known for years, that San Francisco politics are like those in no other city. Issues confront a variety of groups, from homeowners to gays to smalltime merchants to corporate giants to liberals to conservatives. No mayor can possibly please them all, so the best anyone can do is feed each one something now and then. In some cases, all you need is the appearance that you have confronted an issue. And if you confront it in a way that no one else has, and appear to satisfy everyone, that wins you votes.

Once, during a supervisor's campaign, Billy had given one of his protégés a key piece of advice. "Don't worry about what your guy actually does, just worry about what voters think he does," Billy had said. "That's what they cast ballots on."

Both Billy and Jimmy were pondering that idea as they ate. While they downed their morning feed inside the grungy-but-friendly breakfast spot, a homeless man knocked on the coffee shop window and pointed to his mouth as if to indicate hunger. Jimmy waved nicely but shooed him away.

Not a moment later, a smile crossed Jimmy's face.

As he looked up from his plate, he grinned at Billy, who thought for a minute and had the same reaction. The two didn't even have to say anything, they just ate faster.

Later that day, Jimmy called Mike McLean. McLean, a San Francisco native who'd written columns for, and been fired from, nearly every newspaper in the Bay Area, was now working for the *Advocate*.

Although he'd been there for less than six months, his columns slamming City Hall on everything from parking spaces to dirty streets had already turned some heads. His latest piece, bashing the supervisors for a midnight pay raise vote, had gotten a protest of 200 people to organize and picket City Hall. While it did not stop the supervisors from keeping the higher salaries, it certainly made it hard for them to go to work.

This time, Jimmy had other plans for McLean. He wanted him to write a front-page column attacking the city's homeless problem and targeting Carlson specifically.

McLean, always game for a good newspaper brawl, was glad to oblige. But he said he needed some statistics and a new effort to get rid of the homeless to make it worthwhile.

He reached several homeless advocacy groups and asked them to give statistics on the increase in homelessness during Carlson's four-year term. He didn't tell them he planned to use the information to attack the homeless. He said it would help their cause by bringing attention to the fact that there were so many homeless on the street.

He talked to the S.F. Homeless Alliance, Catholic Charities for the Homeless, and Street People's Defense, a group of lawyers that had recently formed to defend homeless people accused of crimes.

The combination of statistics showed that the number of homeless people had just about doubled between 1980 and 1990. That meant that it had grown from 5,000 to 10,000.

McLean had his hook. He wrote an editorial slamming the city's elite for ignoring the plight of the homeless, but also ripping into the street people as "withered souls that litter our streets and sidewalks." His column even blamed Carlson, referring to him as "William the Ignorant," for avoiding the problem.

For most people, the homeless had always been accepted because of San Francisco's image as an open, diverse place where pretty much anything goes. And, since the '80s had been so profitable for most residents, the bums and street people had been more of a tolerated nuisance.

McLean's column caused a stir because, for the first time, the diverse, open view of San Francisco that had been sparked by the 1960's flower power movement was being challenged.

McLean was saying that, although the city was viewed as a haven for tolerance and anything-goes behavior, residents were sick of this problem and wanted a change.

As the earthquake's effects continued to linger on the economy and the overall financial health of the city had been dropping since the late 1980s' Wall Street crash, the city's troubles were taking on more attention.

Jimmy Min and Mike McLean knew this. After the column ran, Jimmy took further action, getting Senator Chin to sponsor legislation in Sacramento that would provide additional state aid to cities that formed special police units to monitor the homeless and cite them for minor crimes such as sleeping in the parks, urinating outdoors, and even blocking doorways.

Most people hadn't cared about such petty incidents, but with homelessness becoming a hot new issue, the state law took on more attention.

Once the legislation was introduced, Jimmy ran his own editorial demanding that Carlson not only crack down on the homeless, but direct his new police chief, Kelly Darren, to form the special unit to go after them and help bring in the extra state funding once the new legislation took effect.

It was brilliant.

Jimmy had found a sleeper issue and turned it into the hot topic of the day. Soon, several supervisors picked up the homeless debate and urged Carlson to go after the street people. Although most supervisors supported homeless rights, the pressure that had come from the few who wanted a crackdown was enough to keep the issue hot.

But Carlson wouldn't give in. The mayor and longtime public servant knew that this was Jimmy's game to gain attention and he also felt strongly that the homeless needed to be helped.

Reluctant to react at first, Carlson made no formal response. But when Senator Chin openly criticized Carlson for failing to act, the mayor could not stay silent.

During an unusually candid press conference in front of City Hall, Carlson openly attacked Chin's legislation and vowed "never to arrest someone for being poor, for having nowhere to live, and for trying to keep from freezing."

Carlson said the city should seek to find more places for the homeless to live and get them training and jobs before arresting them.

This played right into Jimmy's hands. The same day the mayor made those comments, Jimmy ordered his top reporter, Tammy Sharp, to check into how many homeless shelters and homeless beds the city had, and how many it had had in the recent past.

Sharp did the research and discovered that, under Carlson, the city had shut down three homeless shelters in four years, eliminating 300 beds. Jimmy howled with delight and made that the *Advocate*'s lead story two days later.

Now he not only could go after Carlson for his reluctance to clear the homeless off the street, but he could blame him for the fact that they were there.

"Mayor Carlson claims to want to help the city's downtrodden by refusing to arrest them, but he himself has done more to harm their existence than anyone," Jimmy wrote in an editorial accompanying Sharp's story. "He is talking out of both sides of his mouth."

The story and editorial drew raves. Soon the two daily papers and the *Reader* took up the cause and even the homeless advocates who'd been backing Carlson for his refusal to clamp down on them began to oppose him when they heard that he had shut down shelters.

Television stations also covered the topic, as did talk radio, which couldn't keep up with the calls from residents slamming Carlson's flip-flop ways. He had real problems.

But the final attack was about to come. And Mike McLean was going to deliver it.

McLean liked to eat out almost every night. With a different friend or woman in tow, he traveled from restaurant to restaurant, downing his multiple martinis and partaking of the best steaks, seafood, and ribs in town.

On one particular night, during the midst of the homeless debate, he ran into Jack Callahan. As the two men chatted at the bar at Moose's, one of the city's newest trendy spots, McLean got around to asking Callahan what he thought of the whole homeless thing.

Callahan, who'd just retired as chief a year earlier, said he agreed that the police should crack down on the homeless who break laws, but also thought they should be given more shelter space.

"I always ran into these guys when I was a patrolman, but now they are everywhere," Callahan said during the conversation in the crowded bar. "You need to straighten them up, but you can't kick'em when they're down. That doesn't make sense."

McLean liked what he'd heard. Callahan had always been popular in the department, but he seldom made his own news. He'd kept order while he was chief and had quietly gone into retirement. In fact, when he left he didn't even have the usual send-off dinner that the police officers' association held as a tribute for retiring chiefs. Just a few drinks with some of his top deputies and friends was all Callahan wanted.

McLean believed that Callahan could help their cause. He asked the former chief to write a special column for the *Advocate*, giving his views on the homeless situation.

Callahan thought a minute and, at first, declined. But after some convincing from McLean, he agreed.

"That's great," McLean said as he tossed back his third shot of Tequila. "And it can be whatever you want. Jimmy'll love it."

When McLean met with Jimmy Min the next day and told him, the publisher was ecstatic.

"We'll kick Carlson's ass," said McLean. "A former chief who never took a stand on issues comes out of retirement to slam this guy, and we got him. That will really stir the pot."

And stir it did. When Callahan's column ran, it got the attention of all the city's news outlets, which considered it a story simply because he had come out of retirement to say his piece.

What made it even more surprising was that Callahan had served as chief under Carlson for many years and had always supported him. For him to criticize his former boss truly meant something.

"Mayor Carlson has the right idea, but has failed to do what is needed to make it work effectively," Callahan wrote. "For him to let homeless people break the law on city streets and in city parks is bad enough. But for him to sit back and do nothing while their shelter space disappears is a crime in itself."

The reaction was startling.

Talk radio shows began calling to ask Callahan to come on the air to fire back at the mayor. Both daily newspapers ran editorials that took the former police chief to task for hitting Carlson when Callahan himself had had the power to crack down on the homeless as chief, but didn't.

The *Reader*, considered the most liberal of the city's newspapers, also shot back, attacking Callahan for wanting more homeless arrests, but also criticizing Carlson for reducing homeless shelter space.

The issue had taken over the city and Jimmy Min was on top of the world.

His paper, which had been only a small neighborhood fluff rag, was now leading the charge on the issue of the day.

Editorials, letters to the editor, and McLean's columns pushed the homeless issue during the first three months of 1991. Citywide, the struggle over whether the homeless should be allowed to roam free, be forced to be locked up, or be given more shelter space gripped the city.

Callahan was on more and more talk shows and news interview programs by the day, while Carlson couldn't get away from the issue. At every public function and news conference, the mayor was slammed with questions about the homeless.

When the Assembly and the State Senate passed Chin's legislation and the governor signed it, the debate grew louder as neighborhood leaders pushed for the special police units to be organized against the homeless, and homeless rights groups threatened to start daily protests if they were formed.

The battle was being waged on all sides and Carlson didn't know what to do.

Then McLean dropped his bomb.

In a special column written on March 1, 1991, McLean and Jimmy took their efforts for an opposition to Carlson one step further, asking Callahan to run for mayor against him.

The column was one of McLean's shortest ever and was headlined simply, "Run, Jack, Run." In the piece, McLean urged Callahan to come out of retirement and take the mayor's post so he could do what he had criticized Carlson for not doing: clear the homeless off the streets with tougher law enforcement, but also expand shelter space for them at the same time.

"Jack Callahan knows what the police can do to stop the nuisance and harm that the homeless have caused," McLean wrote. "But he also has the compassion to do it right. He won't brush them under the city's collective rug. He will take care of them."

The column went on to urge Callahan to run and asked voters to write to the *Advocate* and other papers with their thoughts on a possible Callahan candidacy.

This was part of Jimmy and Billy's setup.

The column didn't just ask Callahan to run, it also asked voters to push him to run. That way, if enough support came forward it would make it harder for Callahan to back out and easier for him to jump in without appearing egotistical.

He could rightly say that he had not had any intention of running, but "felt compelled to enter the race at the urging of others." And that's exactly what happened.

Two weeks after the column ran, Callahan met with Jimmy, Billy, and Senator Chin and announced privately that he would throw his hat into the ring. They set the announcement date for—what else—March 17, St. Patrick's Day. And to show his sincerity to the homeless plight, he staged the announcement inside Golden Gate Park, just a few feet from one of the largest homeless encampments.

"After much discussion with my family and friends and supporters, I have decided to enter the race for mayor," Callahan said during the press conference, as representatives from newspapers and television stations as far away as Los Angeles and San Diego witnessed the event. "I believe that Mayor Carlson has done a good job, but has not seen fit to handle the growing homeless problem that now grips our city."

The crowd of a hundred or so supporters burst into applause, and Billy and Jimmy grinned at each other.

"I also believe that San Francisco is ready for a strong hand, someone who knows law enforcement and can use it to clamp down on not only the homeless who break laws, but every other criminal in the city," Callahan said. "But I also vow to do it fairly, justly, and in a way that harms no one." The crowd and the reporters ate it up.

Just three months after their coffee shop brainstorming session, Jimmy and Billy had not only struck a chord with residents over an almost sleeping issue, but they'd found a candidate humble enough to be trusted and strong enough to appear tougher than the current mayor.

Sure, crime was down, streets were safer, and most people were happy with the way the city was running under Carlson. But show them an issue and tell them that they should believe in it—while finding a candidate who appears more adept at solving it—and you have created a real mayor's race.

Carlson couldn't believe it. Here he had practically owned this town, had become a hero following the earthquake, and had most of the Board of Supervisors eating out of his hand, and these two guys come along and blow it up in his face.

"This isn't going to be easy," he confided to a friend as the two watched Callahan's press conference on television that night. "I have a bad feeling about it."

Carlson immediately increased his campaign preparations, meeting almost daily with his longtime campaign manager, Densly Hutchins, and formulating a strategy to get the campaign off the homeless issue and on to something else.

The two strategized and realized that they couldn't compete with Callahan on homeless concerns, so they needed to find something new; something that could make Callahan's image as a law enforcement genius backfire on him.

Hutchins, who'd effectively created issues for Carlson to win every previous race, knew the best offense was to put Callahan on the defense. And he had the perfect issue.

"Suppose someone linked this guy to a case of police brutality," he told Carlson during a meeting in the mayor's office. "If we can connect him to even a hint of police abuse that occurred while he was chief, we've got him."

Carlson grinned, but then soured. "The guy is squeaky clean and the press has never found a hint of a problem with him," he told Hutchins.

"We'd have to create something."

"Maybe not," Hutchins said.

Carlson never asked Hutchins what he meant by that comment, but always wondered. Especially two weeks later when the beating of a homeless man in Golden Gate Park occurred.

There it was, the issue that Hutchins had wanted. A homeless man had been beaten to death and witnesses claimed it had been done by three cops, including Callahan's brother, Deputy Chief Phil Callahan.

The newspapers were all over it, especially the *Journal* and the *Bulletin*, which were ordered to go after Callahan in any way possible. Homelessness was out and police brutality was in.

Even though Callahan hadn't been chief for nearly a year and had been nowhere near the alleged site of the beating incident, the link of a police beating to this mayoral candidate was enough to cause problems.

And the fact that the victim was a homeless man, the very type of person that Callahan had vowed to rid the city of and find new homes for, made it doubly difficult for him.

As the days went on and the investigation into the homeless beating continued, both daily newspapers put most of their efforts on the stories, talking to homeless people living in the park who claimed to have seen regular police beatings, using off-the-record comments from officers about how the brutal beating had occurred, and ripping the police in editorials and columns every day.

Meanwhile, Callahan had difficulty defending his officers and his brother because all he could do was continue denying that the incident had occurred, despite the mounting evidence. He had no proof that the beatings had not happened, he just insisted they hadn't.

Soon the mood shifted completely away from how Carlson had ignored the homeless and how Callahan was going to help them. Instead, there was only intense scrutiny of Callahan for the actions of his brother and the other officers.

Jimmy Min was concerned. He had not only put his paper's time, money, and support behind Callahan, but he'd gone out on a limb and risked losing every bit of political force he had mustered in the past few years.

Aside from having McLean slam Carlson and praise Callahan in his columns, and having reporters dig up everything they could on Carlson, Min had also put his efforts into campaigning for Callahan.

Although none of it was declared on Callahan's campaign disclosure statements, the *Advocate* had been printing up flyers, signs, and brochures for Callahan's campaign at cost and distributing them. Min also had several workers assigned solely to phoning prospective voters to push for Callahan, often using *Advocate* phone lines and offices after hours.

"We need to get this guy in office so we can be in office," Jimmy had told one of his employees during a long weekend phone campaign. "He is our ticket in."

But the ticket was sinking fast. Every day brought another link of Callahan's brother to the beating. He was eventually taken off active duty, while the homeless began holding daily protests outside Callahan's campaign headquarters on Van Ness Avenue, one of the city's major thoroughfares.

The issue kept raging for the next month. As it spun out of control, Jimmy and Billy tried to do everything they could. Counterattacks in the press, issue papers spouting all Callahan had done for the homeless as chief, and even a lengthy mailer on his 10-point plan for bringing San Francisco back to success were put out.

But none of it could block the beating issue.

At one point, in mid-June, Billy Dale was so upset by the whole thing that he disappeared on a long weekend to Reno. He often went there to stay with his Uncle Simon, who owned the Miracle Hotel and Casino. The two would play poker, drink, and talk about politics. Although Simon didn't dabble in Billy's profession, he'd met a lot of politicians through the casino and his mob connections.

When Billy got there on that Friday afternoon, he met Simon in his private penthouse suite and the two ordered up some drinks.

"Sorry to hear about your problems," Simon said as he poured some brandy. "That bastard has got your chief against a wall."

"Yeah, I know, but we've got to have a way to shoot back. There has got to be something in that guy's history that we can hit," Billy said. "But we've run after everything we can. Nothing can go up against this beating case."

"Well, what about his casino friends?" Simon asked as he blew smoke from a Cuban cigar over in Billy's direction. "The guy has a reputation up here."

"Sure," Billy said as he took a bite of a sandwich. "We all know that he comes up here a lot. I hear he likes Tom Jones."

The two laughed.

"What we would really need is proof that he has associated with underworld people. Rumor won't be enough."

"Well, let me see what I can do," Simon said, coughing as he puffed the last of his cigar. "You never know what you can find until you look."

Billy smiled. After two days of drinking, gambling, and enough buffet food to add at least 10 pounds, Billy went back home. He wasn't looking forward to returning to San Francisco with the whole police brutality mess waiting, but he knew he had to face it.

Two weeks after he returned, he got a call from Simon.

"I got something for you, but I can't talk on the phone, you never know who might be listening," Simon said, as a smile grew on Billy's face. "Just wait for it."

The next day, a UPS truck pulled up to Callahan's campaign headquarters and the driver brought Billy a special delivery package. He took it inside and opened it.

Inside was a videotape and nothing else. Billy took it into his private office and shut the door. He also told his secretary that he did not want to be interrupted.

He popped the videotape in the machine, turned it on, and watched.

What he saw, he couldn't believe.

There on the tape was a recording of three men playing poker in a suite at the El Presidente Hotel and Casino in Reno, just one block from the Miracle. The three men were very well known to Billy and almost everyone in California.

One of the men was John Garligo, the west coast head of one of the country's most powerful restaurant unions, while the other was underworld boss Anthony Marsconi, who controlled mob casino operations from Reno to Las Vegas.

The third man in the video was none other than William Carlson.

Billy beamed. This could be it. Forget about the homeless, forget about police brutality, forget about all of that. They had the mayor... the fucking mayor of San Francisco... on tape with one of the country's biggest mobsters.

Billy immediately called Simon from a payphone to find out what had happened.

Billy and most of San Francisco had known that Carlson liked to frequent Reno and liked to stay at the El Presidente. Some said it was because it made him feel like he was the president by staying somewhere with a presidential name.

While his trips to Reno didn't make him look good, no one could ever associate him with any questionable people. Simon, after talking to Billy, had made a few phone calls to see if he could. After 20 years in Reno, a lot of people liked Simon and a lot more owed him favors. He had gotten a reputation as a good businessman who treated his employees well.

Even when workers had left him to go to bigger hotels and casinos, Simon never held grudges and always kept in touch. Those connections had finally paid off.

The day after Billy left, Simon got on the phone to the El Presidente and talked to its chief day manager, Charlie Coles, who had worked for Simon about five years earlier. He asked him if Carlson had a reservation to visit anytime soon. Coles said he had just made a reservation for the following weekend.

Simon then asked if there were any major political events in the city that weekend. He was told there were not, which meant Carlson was just planning to socialize and might spend a lot of time meeting with people in his room.

He then asked Coles if Carlson had a favorite room he liked to frequent.

"Yeah, he loves the honeymoon suite," Coles laughed. "I'm not sure why, but he always stays there, even without his wife. I think it makes him feel young when he brings hookers up there."

Simon laughed and asked if that room was available for Carlson. Coles said it was and had been booked for him. That was enough for Simon, who hung up.

* * *

Later that day, Simon waited outside of the employee entrance to the El Presidente for another former employee, Dick Greers, the head of the El Presidente maintenance crew. Dick had worked for Simon for only about a year, but they had grown close when Simon paid for his alcohol rehabilitation after Greers' drinking had caused him to lose his job.

Although Simon had fired Greers, he'd helped him get the rehab he needed and later got him a better job at another casino. When Greers saw Simon, he couldn't help but give him a big hug.

After they chatted, Simon took him out for lunch and asked him for a favor. He wanted Greers to plant a videotape camera inside Carlson's room. His hope was to catch him with one of the hookers Carlson often ordered up to the room.

"That's asking a lot," Greers said. "Not only could I get fired, but we could get sued. It's too risky."

Simon asked again. He pleaded and begged. He really wanted to do this for Billy.

Greers finally gave in. He returned the next day to work and carefully placed the camera inside the hotel room closet, where it could peer out through a small hole in the top. His plan was to run it each night for the maximum six-hour VHS tape limit and change it in the morning when Carlson left.

But it only took one night. Although no hookers ever made it up to Carlson's room that weekend, something better happened on Friday night. After a secret dinner with Garligo and Marsconi at Marsconi's house in the Reno foothills, the three had come back to Carlson's room, through a hotel back door, and played poker all night.

The next Monday, Greers gave the tape to Simon who sent it to Billy Dale.

Billy was ecstatic. He called the news directors of San Francisco's top three news stations and told them to meet him in his office. He said he would give them each the tape if they vowed not to say where they got it. He said he wanted to deal directly with them instead of their reporters so that there would be no misunderstanding about who knew what.

That night, all three 6 p.m. newscasts led with the tape and the story of the mayor meeting with a major organized crime figure. Although no one was doing anything illegal, no money changed hands, and no laws were broken, that link was worse than anything Callahan had allegedly done.

And it worked like nothing ever had.

From that July day through Election Night, the polls steadily dropped for Carlson. Callahan, meanwhile, regained his stature when the police beating case died out for lack of evidence. Since the only witnesses for the investigators were homeless people and no direct link to Phil or Jack Callahan ever surfaced, the case was dropped without a charge against anyone.

When Election Day came, Carlson was out, Callahan was in, and Billy and Jimmy were sitting on a cloud.

As the Fairmont Hotel ballroom crowd partied toward midnight, Billy and Jimmy drank, danced, and cheered themselves to victory.

Billy knew that his political power had hit the top and Jimmy knew that his newspaper would now be regarded among the most powerful in the city. He also knew that the new mayor could help him boost that power more by helping him to get city contracts for public notices, have a say in issues that affected his readers and, most importantly, help him wield his position as a city leader.

Just before midnight, as the party hit full stride, Senator Chin got up at the podium. He greeted the cheers of the crowd with just one sentence.

"Ladies and gentlemen," Chin said, his voice raspy and slightly slurred.

"Your new mayor, Jack Callahan." ■

Chapter Four

Taking Charge

Slivers of sun darted through the bedroom window of the 16th Street duplex and poked at the comforter that sprawled across Glenda Callahan as she slept, wrapped in silk sheets, billowy pillows, and a string of pearls that draped her neck.

Outside the Castro District townhouse, swirls of fog snaked through the neighborhood as delivery trucks made their way, joggers bounded up the hills, and two beat cops strolled in the dawn's dew.

On the oak nightstand next to Glenda's bed, the alarm clock stayed silent as she rustled the sheets and turned over to block the sun stream with a pillow.

Peeking out of one eye, Glenda noticed the time as the sunshine streamed through the pillows into her eyes, causing a squint. As she rubbed them and turned her head, a sound from the other room was heard.

"Are you awake, sleepyhead?" she heard the familiar voice calling. "Are you ready to become the most important woman in San Francisco?"

Glenda smiled and pulled the covers down to her waist, then pulled her body up to a sitting position. The window's light caught up with her eyes and caused sudden blindness as she stretched and yawned.

The city's next first lady glanced around the room, her eyes shifting from a rare Ming vase and Van Gogh painting on one wall to a framed photo of New York City's Christopher Street nightlife on another to a closet stuffed with dresses, shoes, and three mink coats.

The morning light partially blocked the bedroom doorway as she looked over to see a silhouetted figure standing in the doorway. A clearer view gave her the full sight of the person's shape. The long, slender legs, the shapely figure and hips, and the dazzling smile filled her view.

Glenda's pulse immediately began to rush as the figure walked toward her, letting a pink silk robe fall from its shoulders and kneeling on the bed. Glenda, never one to hold back where personal desires were concerned, grabbed the body that knelt before her and pulled it on to the sheets.

The two embraced as Glenda began kissing the object of her desire passionately, stroking hair, skin, and fingers, and rubbing their bodies together.

"Does this make me the other first lady?" the person said, with a grin. "I mean, after all, I deserve something."

The two laughed as Glenda thought about what awaited her that day... January 13, 1992, and she was about to be thrust into the limelight as San Francisco's most famous woman.

Just six hours away stood the inauguration of her husband, soon to be San Francisco's most powerful politician. The biggest morning of the biggest day of his life and she was miles away.

Instead of waking up next to her husband of nearly two years, ready to start his morning with loving hugs and smiles, Glenda was in the arms of someone she considered much closer to her heart, and her lust.

Missy King, the rising young blues singer who was 10 years Glenda's junior, snuggled closer to her in the warm, feathered bed as each thought about the day's planned events.

Glenda almost purred with delight as she thought what it would mean to have a husband with such power. Missy, who had been Glenda's longtime secret companion for nearly three years, had hoped that it would make her lover happy, but also worried that she might lose her closest partner to the power and prestige of City Hall society.

"Will you be happy?" Missy asked, as she stroked Glenda's black hair, sprinkled with gray flecks. "Will you still be there for me?"

Glenda, never one to give too many details of her thoughts, just smiled. "Haven't I always been?" she whispered. But Glenda's thoughts were focused more on her own future, with or without Missy.

Although she enjoyed the wild, youthful encounters that the two had shared, Glenda was not planning in the long term where Missy was concerned. The two had run into each other at a blues bar three summers earlier and, when the mood hit, Glenda had taken advantage of Missy's Castro District home on numerous occasions.

But while Glenda was glad to share her lustful needs with her younger lover, she was adamant that the two were not to be seen in public and that no strings were attached.

"We want each other, and we use each other," she had told Missy several months earlier during a heated discussion on a cool, summer night. "But once either of us wants to go, it's ended."

Missy, the product of a broken home in her native Midwest, had agreed with Glenda's rules. But her fragile heart let her go too far. She knew that the whole thing could end at any time, but deep down she had let herself become too close to Glenda.

The soon-to-be-first lady became both a lover and pseudo-mother figure to Missy, whose own mother had divorced her father when Missy was 12 to run off with a lesbian lover of her own.

From her teen years, Missy always searched for someone to comfort her as only a mother could. In Glenda she had found the reassuring, comforting presence that her childhood lacked.

Since the two had met, they'd gotten together as often as possible, although sometimes in secretive, quick meetings. Glenda would sometimes show up at Missy's gigs in the North Beach blues bars that she frequented. Sporting dark glasses and a wig, or often a baseball cap, Glenda would usually hide in the back and give Missy supportive glances as the singer belted out her favorite versions of B.B. King and Janis Joplin tunes.

Sometimes, Glenda would just stop by on a Friday night when Jack was out of town or attending late campaign meetings or functions. He usually got home late and never asked where Glenda had been.

More often than not, however, Glenda and Missy's rendezvous were limited to afternoon love sessions at Missy's place or some of the city's big-league hotels, which Glenda had accessed through corporate accounts or friendly concierges.

The two would order up champagne, chocolates, and strawberries and lounge together in front of the television, lingering before their favorite romantic movies, with an occasional X-rated flick thrown in.

On this morning, however, both women remained unsure of what their futures would bring. For Glenda, it could be the beginning of her rise to the top of power and prestige. For Missy, it might be the end of a lustful ride that she'd enjoyed and needed to help her return to an emotional level of happiness.

Both women ran through their thoughts as the sun rose higher and the morning broke before them.

Several hours later, and several blocks away, Glenda sat smiling and ready as the sun shone directly over the gold dome of San Francisco City Hall. Seated upon the special inauguration platform in front of the city government headquarters, Glenda looked out over the crowd as she grabbed her husband's hand firmly and gave it a playful squeeze.

Next to her sat Jack Callahan, directly beside the podium where he would soon take the oath of office as San Francisco's next mayor. Sporting a simple blue suit, with a red tie and shined black shoes, Jack gave a mild smile as Glenda held his hand.

The city's next mayor knew where his wife had been the night before. Although he'd accepted Glenda's promiscuous ways about a year earlier after catching her with one of their female house employees, Jack had not made any attempts to end their marriage.

He still needed a good, intelligent wife to help him through the campaign and knew that a divorce and a soap opera-like lovers' triangle would not have helped at the polls.

Although his election was over and his place in San Francisco power was assured, Jack knew that a divorce while in office would be hurtful to his attempts at getting his programs and changes completed. The press would have a field day if they found out his wife had been having a lesbian affair, and the attention would spoil his place in city history and his current progress.

Until the two figured out where their relationship was headed, they agreed to present themselves as the happy, newly crowned first couple.

While Jack and Glenda stood on stage awaiting the ceremony's beginning, others in the crowd milled about and found their seats. Dignitaries from throughout California and even as far away as New York and Washington took seats in the front row.

Senator Williams, State Senator Chin, and all the members of the Board of Supervisors were prominently situated in the audience. Former mayors, police chiefs, and several wealthy campaign contributors also were among the honored guests that day.

Two of those who sat directly in front of Jack in the audience below were none other than Billy Dale and Jimmy Min. Both greeted friends and political rivals alike as the crowd grew and the appointed 1 p.m. starting time approached.

Billy laughed his trademark loud laugh, while Jimmy's quiet, wide-mouthed grin greeted those he encountered.

As Billy and Jimmy shook hands, gave hugs, and patted the backs of those they met, someone else found the seat next to Jimmy. Someone few in the city knew, but whom many were about to become familiar.

Benny Min, Jimmy's younger brother, had done little to earn the reputation that his big brother had enjoyed. While Jimmy was making waves with his editorial criticisms, backroom campaign dealings, and hard-edged reporting, Benny stayed behind the scenes as the *Advocate*'s financial wizard.

When Jimmy took over the *Advocate* and launched its rise to citywide prominence, he asked Benny, a longtime math whiz, to handle the money. At the time, Benny had been just three years out of San Francisco University, but his mathematical abilities had already become legendary at the Bay Area's most prominent university.

Upon graduating, Benny had been given a great entry-level position at one of San Francisco's largest accounting firms with the promise of rapid advancement in the future.

But when Jimmy asked his brother to come in and help move the *Advocate* along, he couldn't say no. The two boys had always been close growing up in Chinatown together, playing baseball in the streets, fishing along the waterfront, and picking pockets of commuters on city buses for extra money.

When Sam Min was killed years earlier, the event drew them even closer together. That's one of the reasons Benny had agreed to work at the *Advocate* instead of pursuing a corporate career track. He wanted to help the family.

And when Jimmy started his plans to get Callahan elected, Benny pitched in there as well: helping to organize the campaign's finances, setting up fundraisers, and figuring out the best ways to hide illegal campaign contributions.

So, on this inauguration day, both Benny and Jimmy had reason to smile. But while most in the crowd knew Jimmy's reasons for being excited that day, none were ready for the news that would make Benny Min grin with pride.

Once again, Jimmy had taken his push for power onward and made his backing of Callahan work for him. Sure, Callahan's victory had already raised Jimmy and the *Advocate* up to major influential levels. But that was still not enough.

Just days after Callahan's victory, Jimmy had begun to use that power to his advantage. Three days after Election Day, Jimmy organized a private lunch with Callahan outside the city, in Sausalito.

During the meal, the two gloated over the recent victory and discussed what they could do together to help their mutual causes.

Among the causes was the Min Family's place in City Hall power.

Jimmy made it clear to Callahan that he expected a place for his family in city government, a place where they could wield some influence in return for getting Callahan elected.

"We didn't put ourselves out to win this election for you out of an act of kindness," Jimmy had said over the lunch of Caesar salad and club sandwiches. "We expect to get a piece of the action. If we don't, we can bring you down just as easily as we brought you up."

The demand did not surprise Callahan. He was a bit naive about politics, but his years as chief, and before that as a police union negotiator, had taught him that politics is all about give and take. Someone gives you something, and they will take something else back.

During the lunch, Jimmy was blunt. He wanted a government appointment for Benny and he wouldn't take no for an answer.

"It'll be easy," he said at the time. "My brother is a math expert, a hard worker and Asian. All of those will make him an easy appointment to a place of prominence."

Callahan thought about it, and after realizing he couldn't say no, agreed.

Benny Min would be Callahan's new budget director, with a say over city budget planning and a major influence in which city programs would receive certain funds.

As budget director, Benny could help divert city funds to programs that the Mins supported and have the inner workings of the budget available for the *Advocate* before any other newspaper.

When the inauguration festivities began, both Benny and Jimmy smiled. The ceremony included speeches from outgoing Mayor Carlson, former mayors, and even Callahan's mother, Gina. Then, after taking the oath of office, Jack Callahan proceeded to give his inaugural address.

During the 20-minute speech, in which he vowed to turn the city around through tougher policies, compassionate programs, and hard-line efficiency, Callahan named his choices for each city department.

Some changes were announced for police and fire chief, while other city departments, such as transportation and public works, remained the same. When he got to his personal city staff, he offered few surprises.

Until the name of his new budget director.

"I believe that we need someone who can handle our finances honestly, thoroughly, and with a sharp mind," Callahan told the crowd. "For this, I have chosen someone who knows how to handle large corporate finances as well as smaller, family-owned businesses. That man is Benny Min."

Many in the crowd went silent as the name was announced. No one had heard of this person. Was he some rising, young corporate star? Or maybe an up-and-coming financial wizard from a nearby university?

Then, people started putting the last name together and realized what had happened. A small wave of applause went up, but most people raised their eyebrows.

Jimmy and Benny just gave each other a grin and slapped a high-five.

Jimmy's plans for city power were inching forward and the latest move had just been made. He turned to Benny, who smiled shyly and shook his hand.

"Many of you may not know him, but trust me; Benny Min can do the job for San Francisco," the new mayor said. "We will be fiscally sound, financially wise, and strategically accurate."

The rest of the inauguration continued. After more announcements of staff, speeches, and musical interludes by a youth symphony, the first couple and other dignitaries left the podium and headed the two blocks to Market Street for the inaugural parade.

The sun beat down on the long, wide main drag that connected the city's waterfront with the hilly Twin Peaks area. The Callahans led the stream of marchers south toward the bay, as supporters and others lined the route.

At the end of the street, Callahan and several other guests hopped aboard a large yacht that would sail around the bay into the evening before dropping them off at the Ferry Building for the night's first inaugural ball.

The next morning, the newspapers were covered with stories about the new mayor's speech, plans, and his choices for top posts. Most of the picks for police and fire chief and other top department slots were met with support. But the name of Benny Min got quite a wave of attention.

Editors at both the *Journal* and the *Bulletin* questioned Min's selection. Tim Cross and J.C. Townsend both knew this was payback. Each grew angrier as they read the stories about the city's new budget director.

Their opposition came not only from the fact that Jimmy Min's brother had received a top position, further rubbing their faces in the fact that they'd supported a loser in Carlson, but also from the impact Min could have on their newspapers' business interests.

The *Journal* and the *Bulletin* each faced strong economic problems with the election of Callahan. But with Min in the financial driver's seat at City Hall, any project involving either paper or their parent companies would come under further scrutiny.

Townsend knew that as he sipped his morning coffee inside his office the day after the inauguration. He determined that Min's scrutiny of anything involving the *Bulletin* would be greater than that of anything else he had to review.

"We've got to do something about this," Townsend told his assistant editors just before lunch. "We need to find out what is behind Benny Min."

With that, Townsend ordered three of his reporters, including veteran City Hall scribe Justin Swan, to dig up anything and everything they could on Benny Min. He told them to go through tax records, criminal files, and even his student records at San Francisco University.

"If there is something on this guy, we want it and need it," he bellowed that morning. "This guy can't be all that clean."

Swan had his marching orders and went to work. The longtime reporter, who had started at the S.F. *Reader* and worked his way up to the *Bulletin*, had a reputation for digging up dirt and finding out everything he could about politicians. In 15 years at City Hall, he'd worked up sources in almost every department and knew the city government history better than most politicians.

He even had his own key to City Hall's front door, the gift of a former head of maintenance who'd given it to Swan after being fired in a dispute with the city administrator.

"This is one way for me to get back at them," the former maintenance chief had told Swan when he gave him the key. "Put it to good use."

Swan had rarely used the key, but it was symbolic of the kind of insider status he had in San Francisco government. During his time in the City Hall press room, Swan had exposed corruption among supervisors, pointed out serious budget discrepancies, and even saved one visitor's life when a gunman held a group of hostages in a restroom and demanded that his cousin be released from jail.

Swan had grabbed the gunman's arm during the siege and, eventually, received a medal from the police department for his quick action.

But it was Swan's ability to get confidential files, inside gossip, and personal histories of anyone in city government that made him famous.

In the case of Min, however, it might be difficult. Few people knew anything about this guy outside of his reputation as a financial master and his family links to the *Advocate*.

Sure, the *Advocate* had a sleazy reputation for backroom policies and partisan coverage, but Min's connection was strictly economic. And, as far as anyone could tell, the newspaper's finances were straight.

Swan started with checks through the IRS and state tax boards to see if Min or the newspaper had had any tax problems. The research proved nothing. In fact, Benny Min had an exemplary record of filing tax reports and paying taxes ahead of deadline.

Next, Swan used sources he had at SFU to dig into his past there. He checked with a friend in the student records department who found only that Min was a straight-A student, with no violations of campus rules or other problems.

Swan went on to look at police records, property tax documents, and even computer files Still, he had nothing with which to hurt Benny Min's reputation.

"This is the most frustrating thing," Swan told a fellow reporter over a beer one night. "This guy is too clean to believe."

But little did Swan realize that that was one of the reasons that Callahan and Jimmy Min had chosen to put Benny where they did. Jimmy knew that his brother was the upstanding one in the family, as did Callahan. The new mayor had to give some plums to the Mins for helping him, but realized that the person had to be above reproach.

"Let them look," Jimmy told one of his assistants when he got wind that Swan was digging up information on his brother. "They'll find nothing."

That's what Swan feared. It'd been a week since Townsend ordered him to seek and destroy Min's reputation, but his push had been fruitless. He realized that he was coming up with nothing as he slammed the phone down hard at his newsroom desk after yet another dead-end phone call.

As he got up from his chair to head down to the corner coffee shop one afternoon, he glanced at a picture in that morning's *Bulletin*. It was a shot of Callahan, Benny Min, and some other new appointees during a meeting at City Hall. There was Min, the short, quiet guy whom Swan was ordered to take out.

As Swan stared at the picture, silently cursing Min in his mind, he noticed a pin on the man's lapel. A small, triangular-shaped symbol with the Greek letters Alpha, Beta, and Omega. That, he assumed, meant that Min was a member of that fraternity.

Swan thought little about it at the time, but then sought to see if he could use it to his advantage. Min had been out of college for about five years, but maybe someone in his fraternity would have some way to help.

After jogging downstairs for his cup of java, Swan hit the phones.

He called the Alpha Beta Omega House at SFU and found the current president. He asked if he knew Benny Min, but the student had not been there when Min was a student. Swan then asked him if he could help track down some frat brothers who had attended with Min. He told him the years that Min was a student and the fraternity brother set to work.

The next day, Swan found dropped on his front door a list of Alpha Beta Omega brothers spanning the years that Min had gone to the university. He did not recognize any of the names but set about calling them. A total of 32 people were on the list, although two had died and several were not listed in any phone directories.

Those frat alums that Swan did track down had good things to say about Min. Quiet, friendly, maybe a little bookish, were among the comments Swan found.

"He was a real smart, nice guy," said one former frat brother. "He used to like to go fishing off the pier at Santa Cruz, but he never caught much."

Swan continued to call and interrogate the names on the list. He talked to every person he could get a hold of, but nothing worthwhile was found.

Then, one day, he got a very important message.

After returning from lunch, Swan found a note on his desk from one of the former frat brothers he'd called.

Sam Mullen, who'd been a freshman when Benny Min was a senior at SFU, left a message that said simply, "need to talk."

Swan immediately called the number and got Mullen on the phone.

"Thanks for calling back," Mullen said when Swan phoned him. "I was out of town when you called the other day, but I think we should talk. Not on the phone, though. The phones have many ears. Could you meet me someplace?"

"Sure," Swan said, getting interested. "Where do you live?"

"Let's just say I am in the East Bay," Mullen said. "How about the Coffee Mill in Oakland? Noon on Saturday?"

Swan agreed and, two days later, he found himself sitting outside of Oakland's legendary coffee house, which boasted itself as the oldest coffee house in the East Bay's largest city.

Sipping a cup of the house special on the outside patio, Swan glanced up and down the street looking for Mullen, although he didn't know what he looked like. He had told the SFU grad that he'd be wearing his customary Fedora hat, with pencil in ear.

After about five minutes, a short bearded man with sideburns, shorts, and a T-shirt approached. He leaned over the railing of the sidewalk patio seating area where Swan sat and shook the reporter's hand. After sitting down and ordering a cafe latte, Mullen remained quiet, looked around, and rubbed his beard nervously.

"Hi, thanks for meeting me," Mullen said sheepishly. "Did anyone follow you?"

Swan laughed for a minute, then wiped away his smile when he realized Mullen was serious. "No, no one," he said. "Why would you think that?"

"Well, I know the way the Mins operate," Mullen answered. "They don't like anyone making them look bad."

Swan didn't know what to make of that comment. But he figured this guy had something to talk about, and something that was making him quite worried.

The waitress brought Mullen's drink and his hands shook as he raised the foam-covered cup to his lips, sipping with a loud slurp, and moving his eyes from side to side.

"Well, you see, it's like this," the former frat brother said as he cradled the cup in his hands and looked into Swan's eyes. "This guy is a criminal."

Swan wasn't quite sure how to react. The Mins' strong political and hardball history was legendary and they had long been accused of being crooks. But Benny had been the straight arrow in the family. Good grades, good jobs, and not a hint of scandal had ever come from the second-oldest son.

"What are you talking about?" Swan asked with intrigue. "What do you mean, criminal?"

Mullen sighed slowly and paused for a minute, then he blurted it out.

"He's a rapist!" Mullen said loudly, then quickly quieted his voice. "He attacked two girls in the frat house, over a winter break, and his family strong-armed them to keep quiet."

Swan's first reaction was shock, then his skepticism sliced through the horror and he gave the man a cynical look.

"What, are you kidding?" Swan said, shaking his head in disbelief. "You got me out here to tell me this? You might as well tell me he's a cross-dresser."

Mullen just nodded his head. "Look, man, it's true. You can check it out if you want."

Swan smiled a suspicious smile and said, "Okay, tell me all about it." Mullen looked around quickly to see who might be listening.

Then he went into the story of how several high school girls had come to campus during their senior year as part of a student group that was checking out San Francisco University during a winter break.

Mullen and Benny Min had been staying at the frat house during the intercession to keep up with their part-time jobs, Benny's at a local accounting firm in Mill Valley and Mullen's at the Pint-Size, a local pub in the Richmond District.

One Saturday night, they had a small party with some other frat brothers and a group of assorted girls. One of the brothers knew five of the high school girls who had been with the visiting group and were staying in some unoccupied dorms on campus.

The girls had come to the party with the frat brother they knew, but he'd left at about 11 p.m. with his girlfriend, Mullen said.

"So it was those five girls, about six of us guys, and a handful of college girls, all in different rooms, talking, making out, and drinking," Mullen said, his voice trembling. "So Benny comes up to me and says, 'Look at those two over there'."

"He wanted us to make some moves on them, get them upstairs to his room and have a little fun," Mullen remembered, his voice quivering. "We went over, started talking to them and kept plying them with drinks until they could barely stand up."

"Finally, we took them upstairs, and in his room we started making out with them," Mullen told Swan. "After a while, things got kind of heavy, we started taking their clothes off and...and..."

"And what?" Swan asked.

"And, that's when I passed out," he said with an embarrassed smile. "I woke up about an hour later in my room, with a killer headache and beer all over me. One of the girls, Susan, was sitting at the foot of my bed, in a cold sweat, crying, with her shirt torn."

"I asked her what happened. She said once I passed out, Benny had dragged me into the hallway, and went back into the room to attack both of them," Mullen said. "She said he started by grabbing her friend and then came after her. They were both too sleepy and drunk to stop him, she said, and when they were awake enough to realize what had happened, he was gone."

Swan's face went serious. "What did you do?" he asked

"I couldn't do much," Mullen said. "I eventually found him and asked him about it and he admitted it. He was actually proud of it."

"What happened to the girls?" Swan inquired. "Did they ever go to the police?"

"Well, the next morning, before either one could even get in touch with their parents, Benny and his brother, Jimmy, went to the dorm rooms they were using, and found them," Mullen said. "They took each one aside and vowed to kill them if they told anyone. Benny said he even took a gun along and waved it in front of them for good measure."

Swan couldn't believe it. This was damaging stuff, but it was too bizarre.

"This is unreal," Swan told the man. "This does not sound like this guy."

"If you don't believe me, you can ask them. I've got their names. Susan Thomas and Jane Kelding. They both went to Sacred Temple Academy in San Francisco. If you can track them down, they might... might... talk," Mullen said. "But don't be surprised if they clam up. Remember, Sacred Temple is not exactly for those who are used to dealing with low-life crime and spreading information about themselves around."

With that, Mullen got up, put his cap and glasses on, and hurried down Grand Avenue toward the BART station. Swan just sat there with his mouth open.

Swan knew what Mullen meant. Sacred Temple was a private, exclusive school whose alumni included the rich, the famous, and the politically powerful, including Senator Williams herself.

The reporter surmised that the girls had likely kept the rapes quiet to protect their own reputations, not to mention their lives in the wake of Benny Min's alleged threats.

The next day, Swan went to work. His first stop: Sacred Temple. He asked the secretary in the main office for a copy of the school yearbook from when the alleged rapes took place. Since it was both girls' senior year, their pictures would not be difficult to find.

Knowing that the secretary in this prestigious school would be reluctant to hand over a yearbook to a nosy reporter, he told her he was looking for a picture of his cousin.

A quick scan of the book produced both of them: Jennifer Kelding on Page 15 and Susan Thomas on Page 18.

But that was just a confirmation that the alleged victims existed and that they had, indeed, gone to Sacred Temple. He needed to find them.

Back in the newsroom, Swan quickly logged onto his computer and jumped on the archives. After some fast programming, he launched a search for their names.

After typing in Susan Thomas's name, he found an announcement about her graduation from college that said she was planning to attend law school at the University of California, Berkeley. The announcement was a year old, which meant she was probably still a student there.

Next, Swan searched Jane Kelding's name. The only thing the computer request found was a marriage announcement that said she was to marry someone named Robert Miller the previous April and planned to live in San Jose to work on a master's degree at San Jose State University.

Swan had his start. Now all he had to do was find these alleged victims and hope they would talk.

The January air was a mix of chilly breezes and warming sunshine on the Berkeley campus of the University of California as Justin Swan parked his Mazda Miata convertible and walked along the grounds toward Boalt Hall, the campus law school where he hoped Susan Thomas could be found.

The campus, known to those in the Bay Area simply as Cal, boasted both its tradition of academic excellence as the main campus of the state university system and its reputation for strange and rebellious behavior that began in the 1960s and continued right up to the 1990s.

As Swan checked his watch and took in a deep breath, his eyes scoured the campus for the main admissions office. He approached it, went inside, and put on his best lost-student face.

"Excuse me," he told the woman at the counter. "I am looking for my friend, Susan Thomas? I know she is in one of these dorms. Could you help me?"

The woman, not knowing that Swan was a curious reporter, smiled helpfully and ran a quick directory check.

"She does live here, but we are not allowed to give out the addresses of students. Who are you?" she asked with suspicion.

"I'm her cousin and I came here to surprise her," Swan said, trying to hide his reporter notebook from view. "I know this is out of the blue. But I need to find her."

The woman looked Swan over, thought about it, and gave in. She handed him a piece of paper with her dorm room written down and pointed out the door to where he could find it.

"Thanks," Swan said, heading out on to the campus, trying to hide his grin.

A breeze grabbed Swan's face as he strolled along the college grounds, past groups of chatting students, loners reading or sleeping on the grounds, and the occasional professor hurrying to class.

Following the admissions office directions, he soon found himself in front of the dormitory hall . The place where, he hoped, his answers would be found.

Glancing at the paper, which said "Room 215," Swan entered the orange brick building, which had large windows, but little else in terms of original design. Inside, a half-dozen students sat watching television in a lounge, while several others were parked on one of several couches, reading or talking.

Swan walked straight up to the reception desk and replayed his lost student act for the student assigned to greet visitors to the building.

"I'll ring her room," the short, blonde freshman who sat behind the desk told Swan when he asked for Thomas.

After the woman listened for about a minute, she informed the reporter that no one was in.

"She might be back in a moment, you can wait over there if you want," the student said with a smile.

Swan took a seat on the couch and watched every woman who entered the building, hoping to find the face he had seen in the yearbook. His eyes went from face to face as students came and went, wondering if this alleged victim would even speak with him, let alone detail the story he'd heard.

After about 30 minutes, the object of his search entered. As she passed the reception desk, the receptionist flagged her down, told her that Swan was looking for her, and pointed over to him.

Thomas squinted as she sought to see Swan clearly, then walked slowly over to him. When she reached him, the reporter stood up and reached out his hand.

"Hi, are you Susan Thomas?" he said with a mixture of hope and nervousness.

"Maybe. Who are you?" the woman said with the same concerns.

"Someone who may need your help," he said.

With that, the two sat down on the couch. Swan fumbled with his notebook as he looked her over. She had short, black hair, a thin figure, but pouty cheeks and lips that seemed too large.

She would not bowl anyone over in a beauty pageant, but her smile gave her an otherwise attractive look. Swan took a deep breath and began his questioning. He told her he was a reporter and that he was looking for information about Benny Min.

As soon as he said the name, she lost her smile and worry gripped her face.

"Look, it's nothing personal, but I really don't want to get into that," Thomas said as her feet squirmed nervously and her hands began to sweat. "It took me a long time to get over it and after what those people did to me, I don't want to deal with it again. I'm sorry."

With that, she jumped up, quickly grabbed her books, and started to walk away. Before she could escape, however, Swan stuck a business card in her hand.

"If you change your mind, give me a call," Swan said as he jammed the card in her palm. "If this stuff is true, people need to know about it."

The woman took the card and stuffed it in her pocket before scurrying away to her room.

Swan stamped his foot and whispered to himself, "Damn it!!"

He quickly drove back to the paper and plunked himself down in his chair. At least he had found Susan Thomas and, from her reaction, it looked as though his information was correct. Benny Min may not have raped her, but he obviously did something that made her upset, something she still feared five years later.

That hope that he might be on to something quickly changed his angry grimace to a slight smile. Then he went for Plan B.

His computer search had told him only a few things about Jane Kelding. She was supposed to marry a Robert Miller and seek a master's degree at San Jose State. Swan's first move was to check both names through San Jose information.

The operator had no number for a Jane Kelding, but a Robert and Jane Miller popped up in nearby Sunnyvale. Bingo!

He quickly called the number and, to his surprise, a woman answered despite it being the middle of the afternoon.

"Hello, is this Jane Miller?" Swan asked.

"Yes," the woman said.

"The former Jane Kelding?" he said again.

"...Yes?," the person on the other end responded, with a bit more uncertainty. "Who is this?"

Swan told her who he was and, carefully, told her what he was calling about.

"Please don't hang up," he asked as the woman paused on the other end. "I've heard some things about what happened and I just want to find out if it is true."

The woman remained silent on the other end, but did not hang up. Swan began to sweat and hope. He just wanted to keep her on the phone long enough to find out what she could tell him.

"Look, I know you don't know me, but if this family did what I think they did, people need to know. Benny Min is about to take over a major place in City Hall," Swan pleaded. "If he did something like this, it should keep him out. Shouldn't it?"

Miller just stayed silent but remained on the line.

"I won't write anything without your permission," Swan promised. "I would just like to talk to you about it, somewhere. No phones or notebooks, just a casual talk. Please! It could help out a lot of people and stop this family from doing these things again."

Miller paused again and thought. Swan's heart began to pound.

"Well," she said slowly. "Where do you want to meet and when?"

Swan's hopes soared. "Wherever you want, whenever you want."

"Do you know the Rose and Crown in Palo Alto?" she said, mentioning one of Swan's favorite watering holes.

"Sure," the reporter said.

"Meet me there in one hour," the woman said, worriedly. "I'll be the one in the dark glasses."

Swan thanked her and hung up.

One hour later, he pulled his convertible into the parking lot of the British-style pub. The saloon was a favorite with the nearby Stanford University students and other folks in their early 20's. He was a little early, so he didn't expect to see the woman just yet.

His eyes widened as he entered the establishment. To his surprise, it was somewhat crowded, despite it being just 3:30 p.m. About half the tables were filled, while only one dartboard was in use and six or seven drinkers nursed beers and cocktails at the bar.

Swan scanned the room looking for the woman. All he knew was that she was in her early 20's and would be sporting sunglasses. As he walked further inside, he looked around wondering which could be her.

Just then, a finger tapped him on the shoulder. He was so startled, he jumped, then turned around.

The person who had surprised him stood only about five feet, four inches tall. A slim woman, she wore only a short skirt and leotard top, although it was nearly winter outside. Her red hair glowed in the dark barroom as large gold earrings dangled from her lobes.

And, yes, she had sunglasses. They gave her away since the dark, smokey room held little glare for the eyes.

"I didn't mean to startle you," she said in a whisper. "Are you Justin?"

He said he was and the two took a table in the back corner. After ordering two beers, Swan started in.

"Thanks for meeting me, now can you tell me what happened," he said.

Miller fidgeted nervously and looked around the room. She took the sunglasses off slowly, revealing a bright pair of green eyes, but a face that appeared worn down by worry.

"Well, you have to promise that you won't write anything about this until I agree to let you," She ordered. Swan nodded his head.

Then the woman went into the story. She said she and Thomas and four other girls from Sacred Temple had gone to SFU that weekend just to look around. She remembered being excited about the chance to go to such a big name school and meet college-aged men.

"I admit I was a bit of a flirt, but it was innocent. All we wanted to do was have a good time," Miller said, her voice cracking. "Then it just happened, all of a sudden."

Swan handed her a handkerchief to wipe away her tears as she continued.

"I don't remember a lot, but what I do know is that he attacked both of us," she cried. "I just remember waking up on the floor and knowing that he had been inside me."

Miller wiped her tears again and put her head in her hands. Swan just sighed and crossed his arms.

"But then it got worse the next day," she recounted. "Benny and that brother of his came to our room, the room we were using for the visit, and practically pounded the door down.

"Once we opened it, they came in, grabbed us by the arm, and threatened to blow our heads off if we did anything," she said, tears still streaming down her face. "One of them, I don't know which, pulled out a pistol and said we would get it if we talked. We were both so scared we just kept it to ourselves. After a few months, it was like it never happened."

Miller sunk her face in her hands and cried more. Swan slumped back in his chair, raised his beer, and took a hard swallow.

Neither one of them talked for several minutes as Miller's crying slowed. They just sat and thought.

She thought hard about what had happened and how she had suppressed it for so long, not even telling her new husband the story. Swan thought about the impact this could have and knew that he had to do whatever he could to get the story out there.

"So now what do we do?" Swan asked after the two sat quietly for several minutes. "This obviously happened. You know that people need to know about it and this guy needs to be put away."

Miller's face went red again and shivers ran down her spine. She didn't dare let anyone know about this horrible moment. It's over, done with, in the past. She didn't need to deal with this stuff again. She had a new husband, a promising career ahead, and plans to start a family.

"I.....I can't." she stammered with regret. "I mean, who knows what these guys might do. They are evil. I can't put my husband through that."

Swan didn't show it, but inside he had one thought. He had been screwed again. This would be the greatest way to get the Mins and the *Advocate* out of the way, at least for a while, but these two women were not helping.

The reporter didn't say what he was feeling, just thanked Miller for her time. He also handed her a card but knew it would likely amount to nothing.

"If you change your mind," he said hopelessly. "Let me know."

Miller parked the sunglasses back on her nose, got up with a jerk, and left the pub. Swan just stayed and took out his anger with a punch to the wall next to their table.

Then he ordered something a little stronger, a rare drink for him, a double vodka.

About an hour later, Swan returned to the newspaper. He was glad he'd taken the time to meet those women. At least they had backhandedly confirmed the story. But that wasn't enough. He still needed a real accusation and people to support it.

He went home with plans to begin all over again tracking down information from Benny Min's past. The next day he returned and started his search once more. For the next three days, Swan went through every data search, computer link, and newspaper file he could find in search of dirt on the city's new budget director.

The reporter even talked to members of William Carlson's former campaign crew, but none had ever heard of anything.

It was about five days since Swan had first met with his initial informant at the Oakland coffee house and he was no closer to a story on Benny Min than he had been before. He was ready to junk it all.

That's when the phone rang. The person on the other end was none other than Jane Miller. At first, she talked slowly, then poured out her comments.

"Hi...look, I'm sorry I didn't help you the other day but...I was...you know, scared," she stuttered. "I mean this was something very bad that happened a long time ago and I...we've been trying to forget about it." Swan listened and responded.

"Anyway, after I called you, I tracked down Susan and we had a long talk. We really cleared the air about this and helped each other get a lot of thoughts out," Miller said. "So, then she told me you had talked to her, too." Swan confirmed the conversation in Berkeley.

"Well, so, we decided that we would talk to you, but we wanted to be clear about it," Miller said, choking on every other word. "We don't want our names used."

Swan felt a surge of excitement, but also a stressful worry at the notion of using unnamed sources.

"I don't know about that," Swan told Miller. "They are very sensitive here about stuff like that. This is such a major accusation that we would really need to use your names if we can."

Miller paused and asked Swan again to keep them out of it. "Can't you, please? We don't want to go through a public battle on this," she pleaded. "It would really make it easier."

Swan thought about it and told her he would check with his editors. She thanked him and they hung up the phone. Then he darted into Townsend's office. He recounted the entire journey of the last week to his boss and told him where he was stuck.

"Fuck!!" Townsend said. "That's a great story, but anonymous sources are a pain in the ass. You sure you can't get them to go on the record?"

Swan just shook his head in frustration. The two men then began to discuss the merits of printing such a major story and the fallout of using anonymous victims.

"How sure are you of these two?" Townsend asked.

"Well, I went after them and they both gave pretty much the same story," Swan said. "I think they are sincere but scared."

Townsend went over to his legendary rocking chair and plopped down, kicked the floor in front of him as he sat, and leaned the chair back to rock. As the wooden contraption see-sawed back and forth, so did Townsend's decision.

Finally, he looked at Swan and said, "Fuck it, let's do it."

With that, Swan didn't need to hear anymore. He immediately got on the phone with Miller and set up a time for him to meet with each woman. He not only took notes but tape-recorded each conversation. He promised them that no one would have access to the tapes except him and his editors.

He also interviewed them separately to see if there were any inconsistencies in their stories. After speaking with each for more than three hours, he found no differences in their recounting of the ordeal.

Three days later, the story was ready. It was not long and involved, but simply recounted each woman's tale. No photo, just general descriptions. That's when he went after Min.

It was early on a Friday morning when Swan phoned Benny Min. He got him after just one ring and told him what his story would say.

Min was calm on the other end, but inside he was worried. "I deny all of it," he said sharply. "And if you print it, we will sue. It's that simple."

Swan took the comments, added them to the story, and finished it up. Then he and Townsend carefully edited the final version before putting it to bed.

The editors waited a day, seeking to run the story on Sunday when the largest audience would be reading. They also wanted to give the paper's attorneys a crack at it and were given the obvious warnings from their lawyer about printing an anonymously-sourced story with such libelous accusations. Still, they made sure the article clearly indicated that these were accusations and that no charges had been filed. They also placed Min's denial up high.

On Sunday, the front page blared the eye-grabbing headline, "Callahan Budget Director Accused of College Rape."

The story went into detail about how the two women had told separate accounts of the same incident, with both nearly identical. It included denials from Min and specific elements of each woman's life and why they did not want their names used.

"The victims have requested anonymity and the *Bulletin* has sought to adhere to their requests," the story said. "But the newspaper believes the accuracy of this report and finds it important enough to disclose to the public."

The reaction was huge.

Coming just three weeks after Callahan's inauguration, the accusation that one of his major appointees—and a brother of the *Advocate*'s publisher—had committed such a shocking crime drew both positive and negative responses.

Callahan supporters and Min's friends condemned the report, while community leaders and women's rights groups praised it. Some criticized the newspaper for not revealing the victims' names, while others said they should not be disgraced by having their identities dragged through the mud again.

The new mayor didn't wait long to respond. By 2 p.m. that Sunday, he had set up a meeting with both Min brothers, Billy Dale, and several other advisors. He wanted to get to the bottom of this right away.

The first thing Callahan did was ask Benny Min if the story was true.

At first, the shy man didn't respond; then he admitted it.

"Yes, but it happened a long time ago, and besides they don't have anything more than a couple of unidentified people, this can't go anywhere," Benny Min said.

Callahan still looked worried, as did Billy Dale.

"Proof is not always what you need," the mayor said. "Sometimes just the appearance of wrongdoing is enough. If people think I have a rapist handling the city's finances, that doesn't look good, true or not."

Billy Dale agreed. He knew that Callahan had a lot to accomplish in the next four years if he wanted to get re-elected and this kind of baggage wasn't needed at the start.

"Look, let's just see how it plays out over the next few days and go from there," Billy advised. "But until then, we have to have some kind of response today."

The four men then discussed the best way to react to the story. They didn't want to give the accusations too much credit, but they also knew that they had to respond firmly and decisively.

Eventually, Billy Dale had the answer. They would not hold a press conference but would fax a very firm denial to all media. Billy would then make himself available to give a positive spin comment to any reporter who asked.

Billy and Jimmy got together and created the press release, eschewing the mayor's press secretary. They did not want to take any chances. It was written on the mayor's stationery but signed only by Benny Min. The idea was to acknowledge that the mayor was standing behind his appointee, but not make the message come directly from him.

"Back the guy up, but stay out of the line of fire," Billy told the others.

The denial was simple and straightforward. "I hereby deny the accusations printed in today's edition of the *Bulletin*," the release stated. "I find the accusations offensive and to be completely without truth or substantial facts. I had nothing whatsoever to do with this alleged incident and deplore these allegations."

The release was signed by Benny Min and quickly faxed to all of the radio and television stations in the Bay Area, as well as all the newspapers.

Then Billy got on the phone with the news directors and editors of each media outlet and put his own spin in the coverage.

"Look, it's obvious that the *Bulletin* is steamed because their candidate for mayor lost and the choice of an opposition newspaper won," Billy told one television reporter on the phone. "Jack Callahan is someone who was chosen by the people and his budget director, Benny Min, is the perfect choice to make the city's finances whole. Detractors simply want to take him out before he can do his job and that is simply anti-democratic behavior."

Billy Dale's strategy worked. By the time the Sunday night local news shows were broadcast, the spin changed from the accusations printed in the *Bulletin* to the denials that came out of the mayor's office. Billy had successfully shifted gears away from Benny Min and on to the *Bulletin*.

"That ought to hold 'em for a while," Billy told Jimmy Min.

On Monday, the four men—Callahan, Benny and Jimmy Min, and Billy Dale—planned to meet again over breakfast. They brainstormed ways of knocking the story down even further.

Billy's idea was to push forward at a news conference the fact that the story contained two unidentified sources who claimed that crimes were committed against them, but did not come forward. They were going to demand that the *Bulletin* produce their sources.

The mayor's office faxed out a press release at 10 a.m. announcing that the Mins and the mayor would hold a press briefing on the allegations at 1 p.m. inside the mayor's office. Once the press corps was assembled, the mayor started the push.

"I have met with Benny Min about the allegations printed in Sunday's edition of the San Francisco *Bulletin*, "Callahan began. "After listening to his response and reviewing the story, I have come to the conclusion that it is false. I have full confidence in Benny Min and condemn the story and its publisher."

With that, Billy Dale stepped forward and put it simply. "This story is untrue," he said. "If the *Bulletin* has victims of a crime, let's see them."

Then the press corps pushed for Benny Min to make a comment. At first, he just stood next to the mayor and looked away. Then he walked slowly toward the podium.

The object of all the fuss scratched his head and loosened his tie nervously. After a glance at his older brother for encouragement, Benny spoke up.

"All I have to say is that I did nothing wrong and I have never engaged in such behavior," Benny said as the cameras rolled and flashbulbs popped. "This is all a lie."

With that, the press event was over and the message was out. The mayor and the Mins had denied everything and the ball was now effectively in the *Bulletin's* court. Among those in the press briefing was Swan himself. He quickly got on the phone to Townsend and told him what had happened.

"This isn't good, no one else is carrying the story," Swan told his boss. "All they are carrying are the denials."

Both realized that they needed Miller and Thomas to come forward and support the story. When Swan got back to his desk he immediately phoned them, urging them to appear.

"Look, if you BOTH come forward, it will look better, you can support each other and share the heat," he told Thomas. "Otherwise, he is going to get off."

But neither woman budged. They still insisted on remaining anonymous.

That night, both women sat in their homes as the television news programs broadcast it all, the word of the accusations and the press conference where the denials were spoken.

Thomas huddled in her dorm room at Cal with her roommate while Miller sat on a couch with her husband. As they watched, both felt queasy as the television cameras showed Benny Min's face.

After their attacker came to the podium and spouted his denial, their anxiousness quickly turned to anger.

"How dare he sit there and lie," Thomas thought to herself. "That bastard! That son of a bitch!"

That was it, she had had it. Thomas quickly went to her phone and called Miller. The fellow victim knew exactly what she was thinking as she answered the phone.

"Let's get him!!" Miller told Thomas. "Let's nail him."

The two went to see Swan the next day and said they would gladly come forward, but asked if they could go on television so that any question of their story's validity would be immediately knocked down. Swan happily agreed.

The reporter called KKSF-TV and spoke to his longtime friend, reporter Kim Connor. He told her that he had the victims in his office and they wanted to tell their story on television. She quickly agreed to set up an interview right in the *Bulletin* newsroom.

After the television cameras and lights were set up that afternoon, Connor interviewed both Thomas and Miller about the rapes live and about why they had initially refused to be named.

"We were too afraid," Thomas said. "After his family had threatened us, we didn't want to be put through it again."

"What made you change your minds?" Connor asked.

Before Thomas could answer, Miller jumped in. "It was the way he got up there and lied," she snapped. "I couldn't take it, I couldn't take that kind of lie staying out there when I knew what had happened."

Once the interview ended, the camera crew left and the story was put together at the KKSF studios for broadcast on the early 5 p.m. news that night. Before the broadcast, Connor called Benny Min's office for comment, but he never called back.

Swan, eager to prove his first story correct, also worked on a printed version for the next day's paper, which would most likely include reaction from the mayor and other city officials once the 5 p.m. newscast occurred.

The story led the news and immediately started the Mayor's office phone ringing, as well as those at Benny Min's City Hall office and the *Advocate*. Other news organizations demanded comment, while several women's rights groups that had backed Callahan began calling for him to dump Benny Min.

"This mayor, whom we supported, must keep his word to the women of San Francisco and drop this reputed sex offender at once," said Doris Wills, president of San Francisco Women for Justice. "Benny Min cannot uphold the rights of the city with this kind of past."

Similar attacks came from all over. Even some Asian groups that had praised the choice of Min now backed down, calling him a "disgrace to the Asian people."

Callahan himself also came under fire. A radio editorial on KLSF, the all-news station, said the appointment of Min would question Callahan's decision-making abilities.

"Any mayor who would give such an important assignment to someone capable of such a heinous crime should have his judgment carefully questioned," the editorial blared. "Mayor Callahan, the City is Watching You!"

Billy and the mayor both issued statements citing the fact that no crime had been proven and that these were just simple accusations.

"Benny Min has been convicted of nothing and all you still have are accusations," Billy Dale told a reporter. "Isn't a suspect in this country still innocent until proven guilty?"

That comment quickly turned a spotlight on District Attorney Dennis Haynes.

Haynes, who'd been elected to office only four years earlier, had won his re-election on the same day Callahan won his seat. But Haynes's victory had been far less political. During his first four years, the former member of the Board of Supervisors had managed to increase his office's prosecution rate, successfully convicted more death-penalty defendants than any previous first-term D.A., and set up a string of neighborhood offices to help residents lower crime rates.

But now, this case was likely going to pull him into the limelight. With such strong accusations coming from two separate sources, and the target such a highly-placed public official, Haynes could not stand idly by and do nothing.

The pressure from the public and several news outlets would force him to at least conduct an investigation. He could not appear to be shirking his responsibilities, but also worried about damaging his own political position.

Although Haynes and Callahan hadn't exactly run together in the last election, they had appealed to many of the same voters. Callahan's conservative fiscal view and push toward reducing the number of homeless had fit well with Haynes's overall efforts at increasing prosecutions and death penalty convictions.

Haynes pondered all of this as he watched the news reports about Thomas and Miller's admissions that they were the victims of Min's alleged attacks. He then got on the phone to Callahan.

"Jack," he said in a stern voice. "We need to talk." ◼

Chapter Five

Benny's Backlash

The glinting light of the morning dawn sprinkled through the treetops as Dennis Haynes huffed and puffed during his morning run through Golden Gate Park. The 45-year-old veteran prosecutor looked down at his feet as they pounded on the pavement, then up ahead at the snaking road that his jogging path followed.

The five-mile run through San Francisco's largest and most famous park was a ritual he began each morning promptly at 6:30 a.m. The course was always the same: enter at 30th and Fulton Streets, hang a right down John F. Kennedy Drive toward the Pacific Ocean. Cut a left at the oceanfront, then left back into the park, up Martin Luther King Boulevard to 19th Street, and left on the cross-park footpath back to Fulton.

Haynes, who grew up in the Richmond District, had been running the same course for about 20 years, ever since he first went to work for the city as a prosecutor in the District Attorney's Office.

After 10 years of prosecuting cases, he ran for the Board of Supervisors, winning on the first try. After only one term on the board, he ran again for D.A., winning a landslide over a longtime incumbent.

Part of Haynes's early success in politics was based on a murder conviction he'd gotten early in his career. He successfully prosecuted Chris Raynor, the serial murderer who abducted eight children over a two-year period and killed six of them.

For more than 24 months, Raynor's pursuit of youngsters throughout the city had left most parents gripped with fear. Once he was caught, investigators had difficulty tying him directly to the killings because there were few similarities to them and little material evidence.

Raynor had been arrested initially because he matched the description given by witnesses who saw some of the victims with "a strange man." But police had no physical evidence linking Raynor, no confession, and only one child among those that had survived Raynor's kidnapping willing to testify.

That one child was only four and offered little substantial testimony on the stand because of her fears. She only cried and Haynes eventually halted her testimony at the request of her parents.

But Haynes later won the case. His ace in the hole was a last-second presentation of parking tickets Raynor had accumulated during his crime spree, each one written on his car as it was parked within a block or less of four of the eight abductions.

"It was a masterstroke of criminal science," one law professor had commented to the *Reader* following the trial. "Dennis Haynes leaves no stone unturned."

A jury found Raynor guilty and sentenced him to death, San Francisco's first death penalty conviction in 35 years. The success of that case boosted Haynes on to The Board of Supervisors and, eventually, to District Attorney.

In fact, in his first race for D.A., Haynes had recycled the comment from the law professor as a campaign slogan, "Vote for Haynes: he leaves no stone unturned."

As the recently re-elected D.A. rounded the corner at 19th Street during his morning sprint, his mind reached back to his political victories and legal triumphs. But that morning he was less than confident that he could wrangle through his latest challenge.

The charges against Benny Min that had been lodged by two women had stuck Haynes directly in the middle of the city's biggest news story. If he prosecuted the new budget director, Jack Callahan, Billy Dale, and the Mins would come down hard on him, which could cripple him before the next election.

If Haynes did nothing, the *Bulletin* and almost every other newspaper would attack him on the grounds of being soft, a charge that would be more damaging if it appeared he had backed away from prosecuting Min because of the political realities.

As Haynes finished his run in front of his 27th Avenue house, he kicked a can that lay in the street and pounded his fist against a telephone pole. He knew it wouldn't be easy.

After entering his home, a conservatively-decorated neighborhood duplex, Haynes kissed his wife, Jody, and then hit the shower. He dressed, grabbed a quick bagel, and headed toward the office. His meeting with Callahan was set for 1 p.m. in the mayor's office.

But, before that, he was scheduled to interview Miller and Thomas separately in his office. His chief investigator had organized the interviews just an hour after the women appeared on television. He made sure that his office could not appear to be delaying any inquiry.

When he reached the Hall of Justice's third floor, Miller was already waiting. He brought her into his outer office and listened carefully as she recounted her story. He asked her if she could go through the rigors of a trial, put up with embarrassing cross-examination, and, possibly, have her private life—past and present—dragged through the media and the court.

Miller looked a little startled, but agreed.

Ten minutes later, Thomas showed up. Haynes was impressed that she recounted the attack in almost the exact same way, down to what kind of clothes Min had been wearing and what music was playing in the background.

Haynes then asked her the same questions. Could she endure the difficult inquiries and abuse of a trial? She also agreed.

After the interviews, Haynes huddled with his top investigators and chief assistant and determined that, had this been any other case, they would be able to go to trial. They had corroborating evidence from two separate sources, with no visible vendetta against Min other than the crime. This case would have to be tried.

Haynes shook his head as he planned to meet with Callahan. He knew it would not be easy.

When the appointed hour came about, Haynes found himself inside Room 200 on the second floor of City Hall, which housed the mayor and several of his staff. He found Callahan and Billy Dale waiting anxiously. It had been just three days since the *Bulletin* story had come out, and less than 24 hours since Thomas and Miller had admitted being the women behind the accusations.

Haynes stated his position very clearly.

"Look, we all know what has to happen here," Haynes said. "We all have our positions to keep and images to maintain. For me, that means conducting a full-scale investigation."

Both Callahan and Billy Dale nodded their heads.

"Well, after interviewing these women and checking out their pasts, it looks like we have enough to go after Benny Min," Haynes said, glancing at both men. "I've checked into their backgrounds and they have spotless records. One is a successful businesswoman, while the other is kicking ass in law school. Neither has any criminal history or any other reason to go after Min."

Callahan and Billy Dale just leaned back and looked at Haynes. The mayor crossed his arms, while Billy put his hands behind his head.

"Well, you see where this puts us," the mayor said. "If we dump Benny Min, we admit a mistake and lose our strongest newspaper support in the *Advocate*. On the other hand, if you don't go after Min, we all look like we're avoiding the crime to save our political support."

The three discussed the situation further and agreed on the solution. Benny Min would have to go, the investigation would go forward toward an arrest, and they would try to quickly put the matter behind them.

With four years to go before either Callahan or Haynes had to deal with re-election, plenty of time remained to get the appointment of Benny Min behind them, work on other matters, and forge a record of success that could easily bring them both toward re-election.

But, there was one problem. Jimmy Min wasn't buying it.

Jimmy, who had worked his staff and himself hard to elect Callahan, wasn't about to let his brother's rise to a top post slip through this easily. When Billy called him and gave him the bad news, Jimmy exploded.

"Are you crazy?" he yelled into the phone so loudly that reporters in the *Advocate* newsroom one floor below heard him. "This is bullshit. We practically handed that guy the mayor's office and he is just going to pull out. No fuckin' way!"

With that, Jimmy slammed down the phone, grabbed his coat, and ran out of the *Advocate* office. He jumped into his Mercedes convertible—one of five cars he owned—and zoomed to City Hall. Once parked, he ran up to the second floor.

Not even stopping to ask if he could see Callahan, Jimmy rushed past the receptionist and directly into the mayor's private chambers. Callahan, not expecting to see the young publisher, was dictating a letter to his secretary.

Callahan knew what Jimmy wanted and quickly ushered his secretary out. After the woman left, the two men just stared at each other for a minute, then Jimmy, still panting from the run, dropped down into a chair.

"So, what brings you here?" the mayor said, pretending not to know what had angered the man who sat before him.

Jimmy, known for his wide-mouthed smiles, directed an angry glare at the mayor. "You know exactly what is going on and it ain't going to happen," Jimmy fumed. "This will not take place. You owe us and we own you."

Callahan remained calm, almost understanding.

"Look, I know where you're coming from, but Haynes tells us the case against Benny is practically iron-clad," Callahan explained. "If we don't do this, we all go down. By dropping Benny, we can at least keep our position and, down the line, help you out later. But for now, this has to be down."

"Screw Haynes," Jimmy barked. "This isn't just about my brother's career, it's also about his life. If he gets nailed for two rapes, he could be put away forever."

"I'm sorry, but if I don't remove him and let the prosecution continue, I could be forced out of office and face charges of subverting justice," the mayor said. "I could end up in jail, too."

Jimmy just sat fuming, while the mayor shrugged his shoulders and gave a helpless look. "What else is there?"

Then Jimmy's anger turned to deep thought. As it had always done in his battle for power and respect, his mind worked like a machine. He passed each bit of evidence and fact through his brain until he came up with what he believed could be the answer.

"Call Haynes and tell him to meet us in my office tonight, at 7 p.m., and not to tell anyone," Jimmy said.

"What can we do?" the mayor asked with uncertainty.

"Don't worry," Jimmy said, his trademark smile returning. "This will do it for all of us."

*   *   *

Later that evening, Dennis Haynes found himself behind the wheel of his sky-blue convertible BMW, the one he had treated himself to when he won the D.A.'s race. The one that took him from court to court, from law office to law office, and from political fundraiser to political fundraiser.

Those stops, where he had to glad-hand and cajole for money to keep running for office, were the worst part of his job, he always said. He leaned more toward the policymaking points when he was on the Board of Supervisors, and now seriously wanted to spend his time stepping up prosecutions and putting programs in place to reduce crime, improve prevention, and give the poor a chance to get ahead in law enforcement.

Driving to see Jimmy Min under an almost-direct order was not the way Haynes wanted to spend time. Sure, he knew that political favors and deal-making went with the territory, and never assumed that he could be some kind of white knight in office. But still, the idea of cutting a plan with Min to save his guilty brother was not one of Haynes's favorite pursuits.

The chief prosecutor ran all such thoughts through his head while waiting for a red light to change at an intersection just blocks from the *Advocate*'s offices. The setting sun still peeked out from the Pacific Ocean shores several miles west, while a light breeze whisked by Haynes's face. When the light turned green, Haynes slammed the accelerator and sped forward.

Two blocks later, his car turned into the newspaper's parking lot. Few cars were left at that evening hour. Up in Min's office, Haynes could see that the light was on and glanced toward it just as Callahan entered the room and shook the publisher's hand. He saw the two smile and begin talking as he climbed the steps to the building's beat-up front door. The *Advocate*'s building, which had once housed a meat-packing plant decades earlier, still had worn-out wooden floors from the days when men lined up, side-by-side, to slice up the beef and send it down a conveyor belt to be chopped.

The building had also been the site of one of the city's greatest murders, the 1939 Halloween Horror, when three union officials were shot to death, execution-style, by gangsters after attempting to steal mob money that had been diverted from the city's trucking local and was destined for mob bosses who'd been controlling the union.

The story went that the three victims had agreed to divert the money for mob boss Gino Ventorini, but instead had kept the cash and headed to the airport. Ventorini, whose influence had spanned from local cops to taxi drivers, got wind of their attempted exit from San Francisco Airport and sent some of his hoods to stop them. The mobsters ran their taxi off the road just a mile from the airport, killed the driver, and kidnapped the three union leaders.

After driving them to the meat-packing plant, the legend goes, they were tied to the packing machine and shot just as their heads were about to enter the compressor. No arrests were ever made, but the story grew into a legend of its own over the years.

When Jimmy had sought a new home for the *Advocate* several years earlier, he liked the idea that he would take over a meat-packing house and a legend-ary crime spot.

"Maybe people will think twice about giving me any shit knowing that we have ghosts here," he had told a deputy editor once. "Ghosts can come back to haunt you anytime."

Haynes did not think about the *Advocate* building's history as he rang the after-hours buzzer and Jimmy hit the switch to let him in. Haynes knew his way to Jimmy's private office, having been there about half a dozen times in the past, including several seeking endorsements. As he entered the office, he saw Jimmy sitting and smiling and Mayor Callahan, who extended a hand as Haynes sat down.

Haynes scanned the framed editions of the *Advocate* that adorned the walls, including the largest one proclaiming Callahan's victory and several others from the days when Sam Min oversaw things. He also glanced over Jimmy's desktop, which displayed photos of his tight-knit family, several ornamental Chinese trinkets, and a coffee cup that read "What part of Right Now didn't you understand?"

As Haynes's eyes met Jimmy's, the D.A. began to breathe uncertainly. Jim-my just leaned back and grinned as he spoke.

"Okay, Haynes, here's the deal, I hear you got enough to put my brother away for a while?" he asked. "Is that true."

Haynes shifted nervously in the leather chair while responding. "Yeah, ac-tually, two corroborating victims on the same case is tough to ignore," Haynes said, stammering a bit. "We can't just let it go."

"You sure?" Callahan asked. "Is there any way that we could say there wasn't enough evidence? Any details that could be missing?"

Haynes's nervousness turned slowly to aggravation as he realized what was happening. These two were trying to get him to keep from pressing charges. But he knew that the case was solid and the public outcry would not be worth keeping Benny Min out of jail.

"It is practically an open-and-shut case," Haynes said. "Sorry. Unless you have a better way that won't put all of us on the public's shit list, this is what will happen."

With that, Haynes folded his arms across his chest and leaned back, nearly cracking a smile in his righteousness.

But Jimmy also smiled, with as big a grin as he'd ever had. "Well, maybe we do have something that would work, but we need your help," he said.

Haynes's ears perked up as Callahan also moved forward to hear Jimmy's idea.

"What if you arrested Benny, made a big stink about it, and gave your prosecutors and the cops all the credit in the world for catching him," Jimmy said, much to the surprise of Callahan and Haynes. "You pick him up, book and fingerprint him, and stick him in a cell. You could do it live on TV for all I care."

The mayor and D.A. were almost aghast at the unusual approach. Then Jimmy gave them the key part of the plan.

"Benny is arrested, charged, and makes bail. Then, after about three days, you suddenly discover that the cops who arrested him did not properly read him his rights. All of a sudden, he is out on a technicality, the case is over, and in a couple of days, he is back on the job."

Haynes couldn't believe what he was hearing. Was this guy for real? This could almost be worse than not pressing charges at all. Arrest the guy and have such a screw up that he gets away?

"That would never work and, besides, who would we get in the police department to screw up the procedures?" Haynes asked.

Just then, Jimmy's old friend Mike Berry walked in. The heavy-set, stubble-faced sergeant had been on the force for 20 years, including 15 on Sam and Jimmy Mins' payroll. He had done everything from fixing parking tickets to arresting their political enemies.

Haynes's face flashed a look of revulsion as Berry entered the room. "Hi, Mr. Haynes," Berry sneered as he shook his hand.

Haynes reluctantly put his hand out but shook his head at the same time. "I don't like it," Haynes said. "We could end up in a worse position than we are now."

Jimmy stood firm. "Well, that's the way it's going to be," Jimmy said. "We can do it with or without your cooperation. If you cooperate, we may be able to return the favor down the road when you are up for re-election. Without your cooperation, well, let's just say that Sgt. Berry might accidentally find something in your car someday and we might accidentally have to write a story about it, say, when you run for re-election."

Haynes listened in disgust. Who the hell was this snotty little bastard to try to threaten him? He could have this guy run out of town or locked up on so many political fraud charges that it wasn't funny.

But he also knew that he would end up getting hurt in the end if he pushed back too hard. He agreed to go along with the plan, at least for now.

The next day, Berry and the investigators for the sex crimes unit who were on the Benny Min case met and worked out a surrender with Benny and Jimmy. Benny would give himself up at police headquarters, go through the arrest and booking, and be released on $50,000 bail.

When the arrest occurred, it hit the press like a bolt of lightning. Television, radio, and newspapers—especially the *Bulletin* and Justin Swan—descended on the police department as Benny Min came out after making bail. He made no comments, but his attorney, Arthur Cronin, proclaimed his innocence and vowed to fight back.

Callahan issued a statement that said Benny was being placed on unpaid leave until the legal matter was settled and said he would not make any further decisions about his budget director until after the criminal proceedings had ended.

That night, Benny's arrest was all over television and radio news, complete with several more editorials demanding his firing and conviction. The next day, both daily newspapers played the story on Page One, with the *Bulletin* giving the arrest most of the front page and several inside columns.

"Callahan Budget Director Arrested For Rape" the *Bulletin* headline read. The subhead also proclaimed "Police Nab Min Family Scion After Exclusive *Bulletin* report."

"This is kick-ass," Townsend told Swan the next day as the papers hit the stands and the arrest buzzed from newsrooms to talk radio to street corners. Everyone was waiting for Min to go to trial and face his conviction, a conviction that would hurt both Callahan and the *Advocate*, Townsend said.

"We're finally going to get back at those bastards," Townsend told several reporters. "This could really turn into something. Who knows, with the right push, we could catapult this into a recall election and boot that son-of-a-bitch Callahan out before his first year is even up."

Townsend pounded his fist on his desk in excitement. "Damn straight," he said. "Love that power of the press."

But over at the *Advocate*, Jimmy and Billy Dale also were smiling. Benny had gone straight home after his release, but Jimmy and Billy wanted to prepare for the anger that would come out when the news hit that Benny's charges would not stick.

Both men knew that, although this move would get Benny off the hook, it would also unleash some serious criticism at the *Advocate* and Callahan's administration. Still, if they could make it look as though it had been the police who screwed up and not the mayor or D.A.'s office, Berry would take the heat and they would be able to divert attention with some other issue.

In four years, when Callahan faced re-election, the Benny issue would be gone for good. "It's perfect," Billy sneered. "The only way to operate."

The next day, Billy and Jimmy met Police Chief Steve Brown, who had been appointed by Callahan just weeks earlier, and set the plan in motion. Brown would call a press conference for later that day where he would announce that the case against Benny would be dropped because of an officer's error in reading Benny his rights.

The blame would be placed on Sgt. Berry, who would then be suspended for a month as a punishment. Brown and Berry both agreed, especially when Jimmy promised to give Berry a little token of his thanks for taking the hit: $10,000 in cash.

The press gathered in Brown's office later that day at 4 p.m., the news would be announced just in time for the 5 p.m. newscasts and for the newspapers to get it in before deadline. Brown issued a one-page statement that read simply, "All charges against Benny Min involving the alleged rapes reported this week have been dropped after investigators determined that Mr. Min had not been properly read his rights and, as the law requires, did not receive the proper procedural benefits of legal counsel prior to questioning accorded to other suspects."

"Therefore," the statement continued. "We have closed the case on Benny Min and have no other recourse but to cease all prosecutorial efforts against him."

The statement also disclosed that the officer who made the mistake would be suspended for a month, but did not name him. "That is a personnel issue," Brown told the reporters, "which we are not at liberty to discuss."

One hour later, Callahan's office issued its own statement that said Min would return to his job the following Monday and that the mayor "had complete confidence in his ability and character as an upstanding citizen."

Townsend and Swan were livid. Swan, who'd attended the Brown press conference and had been one of the first to receive the mayor's press release, jumped to the nearest telephone after Callahan's press secretary had given the word.

"You are not going to believe this bullshit," Swan told his boss over the phone, as other reporters at City Hall also grabbed for payphones and cellular lines. "It's the fucking *Advocate* all over again."

Townsend's face went red as he took in all of Swan's reports. But still, he wasn't surprised. He knew the way the *Advocate* had worked itself into Callahan's camp and had a feeling that Benny's arrest would not stick, somehow.

But the fact that Benny had been removed on a technicality made it a bit easier to criticize. Which is exactly what he did. As Swan wrote up the story, complete with comment from Benny's own victims and women's rights groups, Townsend wrote an editorial blasting the mayor, police chief, and D.A., and taking his personal shots at the Mins.

"It is clear that the mayor and police department are bowing down to pressure from the Min family, which made no bones about its support for the administration and has everything to gain from this dismissal," the editorial in the next day's paper read. "Even if the *Advocate*'s influence played no part in this mysterious outcome, the fact that such a heinous crime could be swept under the carpet because of the failure of a single police officer calls into question the ability of the administration to do its job. And, moreover, the mayor's decision to keep an accused rapist on his staff is even more troublesome."

Townsend then clearly called for the removal of Min, Callahan, and Brown, the first time the paper had so clearly moved for the resignation of a San Francisco mayor.

But they were not alone. At the *Journal* and the *Reader*, similar editorials were plastered in the next issues. Although the *Journal* did not seek to remove the administrative leadership or Callahan, it too blasted the move. "One finds it hard to believe that Benny Min could be off the hook through such a careless police department's actions," the *Journal* editorial stated. "It is even more mind-boggling that Mayor Callahan would choose to have someone on his staff with such a cloud hanging overhead."

In the next issue of the *Reader*, days later, Dugan took exception to the move. "While we believe in following the rules of law to the letter with regard to arrest and prosecutorial procedures," Dugan stated in his column that week, "it is clear that this situation occurred through police carelessness and not some sudden innocence on the part of Benny Min."

Dugan knew he had to be careful. While his ambition steered more toward the success of his newspaper as an voice for free speech and underdog opinions, rather than the powerful machine that Jimmy Min chose to create at the *Advocate*, he also knew that he needed Min as an alternative ally, the same way Min needed him.

Still, this instance went beyond alternative versus mainstream newspaper warfare. Dugan had always vowed to cut through the politics and present his case clearly. And in this instance, he knew that Benny Min had been wrongly let off the hook.

"I am worried about this guy," Dugan told one of his reporters the day after that week's *Reader* hit the newsstands. "I know Jimmy Min is having fun with his newfound power play, but this could get ugly."

And he wasn't kidding. Just hours after the announcement that Benny Min was off the hook, protests began to form outside the *Advocate* and City Hall. Women's rights groups called for Benny's case to be reopened, while other liberal advocacy groups protested with demands for everything from Callahan's recall to criminal charges being filed against Brown and Berry.

Callahan's and Min's supporters, including Senator Williams, began to feel the heat and were weighing whether to speak out in support, stand neutral, or take a stand against Min. Williams, Chin, and the others who'd been aided by the *Advocate* were caught in a tough spot. Each knew that if they took a stand behind Benny, public support could shrink. Still, if they came out against him, the power of the *Advocate*, which had successfully killed Carlson's political life, could topple them.

For the moment, each remained mum. But that would not last long.

Inside City Hall, Jimmy, Benny, Callahan, and Billy Dale gathered three days after the charges had been dropped against Benny. They knew that the political firestorm would come if the charges against Benny were dismissed, but none seemed to realize how hard it would be,

"We have to do something to get this issue off the table," Billy told the group. "It's the same as in the election; get something else to divert their attention."

Billy knew how to respond. Just as he had made homelessness an issue during the election, and used it to knock Carlson out, he could do the same thing here. If the city came to find itself in another crisis, their minds would be taken off Benny and, if handled correctly, could be changed to support Callahan and the cops. But the issue had to be serious and real, and not appear too much like it was created.

The four men batted around ideas. Homelessness had already been covered, crime was still down—thanks mostly to Carlson—and the city's budget was looking good. Billy knew that something else had to be done.

Several more days went by following the special sit-down meeting at City Hall, and no one had come up with any solutions, at least not publicly, to the public outcry that had followed Benny's dismissed charges. The weekend found Callahan still dealing with the backlash. Protests had continued outside his office and, on this Saturday, the first of April, a group was planning to rally in Civic Center Park in front of City Hall to stage one of the biggest protests yet against Benny and Callahan. It had been only a week since the charges were dropped, and there was no sign of any support returning for the mayor.

Callahan had tried to deal with other issues and had not spoken to Billy

Dale or Jimmy Min since their meeting. He assumed that any efforts at diversion had proven fruitless. Rather than be caught up in the protest, Callahan planned to join some supporters for a luncheon in the Richmond District, where some of his strongest backing had always been. After getting ready that morning, he went down to the car that sat outside waiting and jumped into the back for the ride. The mayoral limousine, newly purchased and supplied with features ranging from TV to a wet bar and cellular phones, set out for the city's west side without the usual police escort.

The mayor's worries subsided for a brief moment as the vehicle steered down the hill on Fulton Street, zoomed past the Haight-Ashbury sunshine, and nestled next to Golden Gate Park. Callahan peered out the window toward the park as dog walkers joined rollerbladers and parents strolling with their children. He managed a minor smile, but it did not completely hide the concerns that remained.

Callahan's driver, one of his former officers, Dan Schmidt, chatted easily with the mayor as they rolled west, the two-way police radio squawking with the echoes of minor police calls around the city. A fender-bender here, a first-aid call there, and, of course, the usual homeless removals that had become commonplace since Callahan took office.

But just as the car was passing the corner of Fulton Street and 37th Avenue near the park, an emergency call came blasting through the radio. "Code Red, all units in the vicinity of Mount Davidson respond immediately. We have a situation with a lone suspect and possible explosive devices. Repeat, respond immediately to Mount Davidson, Code Red. Keep sirens silent. We have an unstable suspect, keep sirens down!"

Both Callahan and the driver listened quietly, then reacted with horror. Mount Davidson was one of San Francisco's oldest landmarks. It had long been a place of interest for tourists and locals. Not only was it a quiet spot for hiking with one of the city's most scenic views, but it also housed the famous 150-foot Mount Davidson cross, an icon of devotion for many that could be seen several miles away on a clear day.

The cross, which dated back to the early 1900s, was the site of an annual Easter sunrise service and had also come under attack from many groups claiming it should not be allowed on public property as a religious symbol. Although many attempts, including court actions, had been made to try to take it down, none had succeeded.

The cross was an ideal place for someone seeking attention or destruction to make a "statement." The spot not only held a great view of the city, but its symbolism could be used by anyone seeking to make a political, religious, or criminal voice.

Schmidt didn't even wait for Callahan to direct him to turn around and head toward the cross; he knew the mayor would have to be there. Schmidt clicked on the limo's flashing light, installed just for such emergencies, and sped through town toward the cross in the quiet neighborhood near the city's south side. As the stretch climbed up the winding roads that led toward the towering cross and its wide mountain base, the mayor could see police already knocking on doors to quietly evacuate residents. Since the roads that led to the hilltop were narrow and winding, the process was slow.

Officers directing traffic recognized the mayoral limo and waved it through, past other police cars and people trying to drive out of the area. Some were crying, others yelling in anger and fear as police rushed them down the streets.

When the limo reached the mountain base, Callahan saw members of the city SWAT team, some who had served under him as officers, heading through the forest-like terrainl. The mayor quickly jumped out and grabbed the police chief by the arm as he moved up the hill.

"What do we have, Steve?" Callahan asked. "What the hell happened?"

Brown, who was still figuring out the situation himself, told the mayor all that he knew. "Well, so far all we know is that some guy is up there with what he claims are ten boxes of dynamite. Our guys are not close enough to tell what he has, but the boxes are labeled as TNT and look like the same ones that I used to see when they were blowing parts of the Marin headlands to get that freeway through."

"What has he said? Anything?" Callahan asked.

"He said he wants the cross taken down because it's a partisan religious symbol," the chief said. "He has a bullhorn and keeps yelling that unless someone comes and takes it down now, he will blow it up. He also claims to have dynamite strapped to himself and is threatening to kill himself with the cross if it isn't taken down."

Callahan grimaced. This was all he needed. First the Min problem and now this. The last thing he wanted was some nut killing himself in the name of religious freedom.

Up at the base of the cross, the bearded man, about 45 to 50 years old, paced back and forth. He had two backpacks tied around him, along with about ten boxes lined up at the cross's base. In between paces, he called out on the bullhorn indiscriminately, "Remove this sign of Christian blackmail and let religious freedom reign or you will be damned to Hell for persecuting the free-thinking people."

As SWAT team members circled around, Brown and Callahan spoke with other deputies about who the man was. "We don't know anything about him," one deputy chief said. "He won't tell us his name, just that he wants this removed and if we don't, he'll kill himself and take the cross with him."

Just as the police and Callahan were trying to decide what to do, a wave of reporters and television cameras appeared. Police immediately blocked off the mountain at the base, trying to keep the news people at the bottom of the slope. All the local television news stations went live on the air, while CNN also hooked up through its San Francisco bureau. After all, how often does someone take a city landmark hostage, not to mention a spot in one of the country's most famous cities, and with such harsh anti-religious overtones?

On a Saturday morning, this was even bigger news, given the slow news day. Cameramen took up positions up and down the hillside as reporters went on the air to bring the tragedy live into people's living rooms.

An hour had passed since the drama had begun at about 9 a.m. Swat teams were everywhere and the television crews were getting all of it. Callahan, Brown, and several SWAT leaders continued to contemplate what to do.

Just as they were weighing their options, the man raised his bullhorn again. "I want to talk to Mayor Callahan," the man bellowed. "He is the one who is allowing this persecution to continue. Come answer for yourself."

Callahan looked at Brown. "What do you think?" the mayor asked. "Could this do anything to help?"

The chief surveyed the situation. The man was standing with what looked like a detonation device next to him. If Callahan could divert his attention or at least get him to move away from it, the SWAT officers might be able to grab him, or at least take a shot at him.

Brown urged the mayor not to take a chance. "You don't know what this guy might do. What if he pulls a gun or wants to blow you up with the cross?" the chief said. "Let our guys work on him."

But Callahan knew from his own police work that talking is often the best way to calm someone down in this type of situation. "Look, I've done this before with hostages," the mayor said. "If I hadn't, maybe we could try something else. But if the guy's calling for me and I don't at least try to do something, well, if he ends up blowing this place away, how would that look?"

Brown and the other SWAT leaders just nodded their heads.

With that, Callahan ventured out into the open clearing at the top of the hill. The cross towered overhead at the center of the hill, with the open clearing extending out to the hill's edge and the panoramic view of the city. A warm spring breeze wafted through the air without the usual fog of a San Francisco morning.

As Callahan stepped out into the clearing, the man moved suddenly, then stopped when he saw who it was. Callahan put his hands up and opened his suit jacket to show he had no weapons.

"Hello," he yelled, as the SWAT officers moved cautiously around the clearing and cameramen took position for the best angle. "I'm here, what do you want?"

The man stayed in one spot, his eyes shifting to make sure no one was making a move toward him. He lifted the bullhorn again. "I want you to answer for what you have allowed this city to do," the man said calmly. "This cross dictates a religious expression that should not be forced on the city."

Callahan moved slowly toward him and continued talking. "There are ways to do this other than with violence," the mayor said, his voice calm. "If you want the cross removed or the city to give up ownership, we can review it with the proper procedures. This is not the way to handle it."

"I know the way the city works," the man yelled. "Nothing gets done. I have tried and tried, and gotten nowhere."

Callahan stopped as the man raised his voice. "This is the only way," he yelled.

Just as the suspect shouted his last comments, he threw the bullhorn down and ran toward Callahan. The mayor ducked and the SWAT teams moved in. When the man was safely away from the detonating device, one of the SWAT officers opened fire and struck him directly in the heart. Other officers quickly jumped on Callahan to protect him and rushed the man away.

The commotion continued as police cleared the area and camera crews and reporters ran up the hill after hearing the shots. SWAT members quickly secured boxes of suspected dynamite, while the suspect was taken to a waiting ambulance. Callahan received some bruises after being knocked down to safety but appeared to be all right.

Just as he was getting up, the mayor found himself in a sea of microphones, cameras, and reporters' questions. Another group of press also chased after the ambulance. But in the sea of chaos, their vehicles could not get down the hill fast enough as the ambulance sped away.

Callahan, still bewildered by the incident, composed himself and answered the reporters' questions. As he made comments, it dawned on him what had happened. Not only had he helped catch this nut, but he had saved one of the city's historic landmarks, all on live television.

The press and police stayed at the scene for several hours. Later that night, police reported that the man was a drifter with no known identity or address. They also said he had died several hours after the incident at San Francisco General Hospital. An inquiry would be done as it is with all police shootings, but most evidence pointed to the shooting as a necessary action.

Ironically, the issue took the problem of Benny Min off the table. The protest that had been planned for that day ended before it began. Once the Mount

Davidson situation had started, most of the television and news coverage at Civic Center Plaza ready to cover the protest had quickly moved to Mount Davidson. After the mayor's heroics, the tide began to turn and almost all of the editorials in the Sunday papers and on radio and television news turned in his favor.

That Sunday night, Callahan got a congratulatory phone call from Billy Dale, whom he had not been able to talk to during the crazy events of Saturday. Billy asked the mayor to come over to his house for a drink. The mayor gladly accepted.

As he rode in the same limo that had taken him to the Mount Davidson standoff just a day earlier, Callahan thought about this good fortune and the strange way that events can change. "I guess sometimes things just turn around," the mayor thought to himself as the limo drove up to Billy's Noe Valley house.

Callahan got out of the car just as Billy walked out the front door, one hand on a glass of vodka and the other stretched out to the mayor. Sporting his casual polo shirt and shorts, with light-colored sunglasses and a golf cap, Billy shook the mayor's hand and invited him in.

The first person he saw was Jimmy Min, who grinned his usual ear-to-ear smile and wrapped himself around Callahan in a full bear hug. Sure, Jimmy knew that the mayor's actions would make him a hero, but he also knew that it would help Benny. Maybe he would still get some static, but what Callahan did would easily push Benny's troubles out of sight. It's hard to call for a mayor to resign or be thrown out when he is a hero.

"Great job, mayor," Jimmy said, as he slapped him on the back. "We couldn't have done it better ourselves."

Just then, Billy put his arm around Callahan's shoulder and walked him to the back porch. When they reached the deck that shot out from Billy's three-story townhouse, the sun was just setting. In the colored light of the late afternoon, Callahan saw a familiar face sitting in a lounge chair.

The mayor's eyes bugged out and he almost fainted when he saw the man.

"Meet an old friend of mine, mayor," Billy said as he introduced the man who sat in shorts and a T-shirt. "This is Hal Shanks, an old friend of mine from New York."

Callahan just slumped in a chair and shook his head. He knew this man, this "friend" of Billy's.

He was the same man who'd terrorized the city just a day earlier. The man who had held the city at bay, and half the police force, and millions of viewers, was now sitting in front of Callahan, sipping iced tea and wearing an eerie smile.

Callahan looked up at Billy and shook his head. "What the hell did you do?"

he asked. "This is not what I wanted." The mayor's face turned red.

Billy just smiled and said, matter-of-fact, "We had to do something and, damn it, it worked."

Callahan felt a mix of anger, frustration and downright sadness. He had thought that something positive was finally happening. After all the Benny Min static, here he'd gone out and done something heroic. He wasn't looking for it, but he thought it had just happened, one of those acts of faith that would turn things around.

Now to find out that it was all a set-up. Billy Dale and his usual tricks had taken things a step further. Billy and Jimmy just smiled and laughed, as Callahan sighed with a mix of fear and disgust.

"Come on, mayor, what are you worried about? It worked, you're a hero, Benny's off the hook, and no one knows anything about it," Billy said. "Let it go."

Callahan still shook his head. "But how? I saw him get shot right in front of me?" the mayor asked.

Shanks, who had been silent the entire time, reached behind his chair and pulled out a cardboard box. Callahan leaned forward and glared with interest as the man stuck his hand into it and pulled out a bullet-proof vest.

"Works every time," Shanks said. With that, they all laughed. All except Callahan. The mayor just shook his head. ■

Chapter Six

A Perfect Issue

Visitors to City Hall in San Francisco know immediately that they are in a center of government like no other. With a shining dome that is adorned with 14-carat gold leaf and rises higher than even the capitol building in Washington, D.C., the city's political center is truly an awe-inspiring place to both tourists and veteran elected officials alike.

Entering from the grander Polk Street side, those who venture into the stone castle initially meet Beaux-Arts arches and pillars before stepping into the open-air main floor where the view shoots up toward the fifth-floor dome itself and a cascading staircase drapes down to their feet like a gushing waterfall.

Atop the staircase, where centuries of public officials have taken oaths of office, brides and grooms that include Joe DiMaggio and Marilyn Monroe have exchanged vows of marriage, and news events ranging from the formation of a United Nations to the shocking news of a mayor's shooting death have been announced, one senses the aroma of both power and beauty. Looking back toward the preceding steps, one also realizes that the rise to such power is challenging, rewarding, and most importantly, fleeting.

Among the items that remind those who come to City Hall of its history and presence are the busts of past mayors and leaders, paintings ranging from Van Gogh to Picasso, and the smoothed brass and finely carved stone of the building itself.

None more perfectly defines the building, its history, and its future than a photograph of the first Board of Supervisors to occupy the board chambers when it opened in 1916. Few who work here generally bother to give the gold-framed photo more than a passing glance. But if they were to look closer, they would seek to find almost 80 years of history in that single, framed creation.

All eyes stare at the camera in the nearly century-old posed shot, which shows 18 Supervisors, more than the current 11. All stand proud and proper, adorned in dapper outfits and robust smiles. The power of that age ready to take on the needs, wants, and fears of government.

But more noticeable than the date, time, and place of the photograph is the identity of those in it. At the time, all 18 supervisors were white, straight men. No women, no minorities, no openly gay members, and certainly no one who couldn't get up and walk without the aid of more than a cane.

Years later, as Jack Callahan began his dealings with a later generation of supervisors, the mix and political identity of the board had changed. Not only had it been reduced from 18 members to 11, but the pool from which voters now chose their city leaders had expanded to include all of those previously left out. Today's board included four women, one of them gay and one of them black, two black men, two Asians, two gay men, and, nearly 90 years after a board of 18 straight, white men had controlled the city, one straight, white man remained.

The board had been known for both promoting diverse, progressive agendas that went far beyond what most city governments were doing and getting bogged down in endless, divided debate in an effort to satisfy so many divergent opinions.

While most cities had the burden of pacifying conservatives, liberals, labor, minorities, women, and business, San Francisco had more. Known for many years as a strong union town and a place of liberal thinking, the city also had both a major retail and corporate business world vying for City Hall's ear.

In addition, the longtime gay community continued to power ahead with support and leverage, while Asians and blacks could boast stronger political muscle than ever. Religious groups also had a major power play, in addition to a west side affluence and social set that wielded strength, matched with a loud, noisy poor advocate community that had already caused Callahan trouble when he tried to battle against the homeless during his election.

Billy Dale had once said that "politics in San Francisco doesn't mean swimming with the sharks, it means swimming with the sharks, and the dolphins, whales, and goldfish who all have teeth that are just as sharp."

For any politician to find success, he or she had to satisfy all political groups without angering any. Usually, this meant finding a way to keep as many happy and as few angry as possible. No one could serve everyone, so the key was serving those with the ability to help most.

When Jack Callahan and Billy Dale entered the board chambers on a sunny July day several weeks after the Mount Davidson episode, and about six months after Callahan took office, both men realized that such broad political satisfaction would be difficult. Especially with the task that lay ahead of them.

The board was meeting, as it did every Monday at 2 p.m., for its regular session, which could include issues as serious as funding for AIDS care and prevention and as bizarre as naming a street after a former drag queen.

Luckily, neither of those items were on the massive agenda that stood before the elected officials.

On this agenda was an item of particular interest to both Billy and Callahan, as well as to the city's many newspapers.

Since the Mount Davidson Cross scam, Callahan's image had been improved considerably. Although his "heroic" move had not completely removed the tarnish of Benny Min's past, it helped him enough to ensure that Min could keep his job, provided he made no major mistakes, and allowed Callahan to continue in office, provided he made some major improvements.

Being mayor in San Francisco is not just about fake heroic exploits. After a while, voters want results and, if they aren't provided, the next election would mean that opposition candidates, however minuscule and unlikely, would begin to crop up.

It was the only city where a former prostitute, a slew of gay leaders, and even a convicted killer could reach high office. The pro and con of the city's vast, diverse electorate were that it allowed anyone a chance to make their case to voters.

For a newly-elected mayor, that meant an ability to get into office in the first place. But after a while, Callahan would go from newly-elected to incumbent and, eventually, to someone who needed support in his bid to stay.

Callahan had been able to ride the crest of his so-called heroic move, but Billy Dale, Jimmy Min, and nearly every newspaper editor within 20 miles knew that that would last only so long. The mayor had to begin building a list of accomplishments, or at least perceived accomplishments, if he was to continue beyond one term.

Billy Dale was already writing up the next Callahan election brochure in his mind and he knew it needed a couple of biggies. After some long meetings and brainstorming, and a good cross-checking of voter polling, Billy came up with at least the first item that could build a success list for Callahan's first term.

As the two men waited in the front row of the board's visitor gallery, nodding at and shaking hands of those 11 who held their fate, Billy smiled uneasily and ran the different outcomes through his mind.

Next to him, the rookie mayor contemplated all angles in his politically uneducated head. The mayor had seen the way manipulation, lies, and hard work had each played a part in his last year and a half. He had taken a stab at politics without thinking about the risks and, to a certain extent, without realizing the benefits. He had just let the path of events take him to his present-day situation: a man on the edge of both power and manipulation, placed in a position that could lead him to political triumph or failure.

Jack Callahan had not expected events to go where they had in only six months, and part of him had been disgusted by the deception and outright distraction of things like the homeless issue election debate and the Mount Davidson escapade.

But, the truth-seeking side of Callahan also held out hope that if he could hold on to this position long enough, get the political victories and power gains that Billy Dale always talked about, he could position himself to do some real good for this city. A city he had wanted to help from the day he first put on his police uniform through the day he took off his chief's stars.

Just as the mayor pondered these ideas, the gavel of Board President Marie Alzeti struck, the meeting was called to order, and the group began to rise for the reciting of the Pledge of Allegiance.

Both Billy and Callahan stood up and took the oath that most Americans had memorized by third grade. The gallery stood full of political hangers-on, visitors, and interested spectators peering forward as the oath was read. The fact that Callahan was at the meeting was enough reason to spark speculation.

Under the city's bylaws, the mayor and the board were separate entities of government. As mayor, Callahan was not required to attend board meetings and, like most mayors, had visited rarely. His only formal duty with the board was to present a State of the City address once a year and a budget every Spring. Callahan had done both and, following a calm-but-heated debate, had gotten his budget passed.

Today, as the beginning of San Francisco's usually windy summer blew leaves around outside the chamber windows, and the sun peeked through the drifting fog, Callahan sat back down, nodding at the waves from voters and political enemies and friends. Billy did the same.

Precisely at 2 p.m., a rarity for the often-late political body, Board President Alzeti, who had faced Callahan in the previous year's election, pounded the gavel to begin the meeting. The supervisors each stood to recite the pledge of allegiance, except for Supervisor Ken Raven, one of the staunchest liberal and gay members, who had long opposed the flag pledge claiming that the United States government did not offer "liberty and justice for all."

"It's a sham," Raven had said during an in-depth column he'd written two years earlier during his first campaign for office. "I love this city, but my patriotism requires proof."

After getting through the calendar that included funding for a slew of special programs, the extension of a parking ban along Geary Boulevard for construction, and a pay raise for police, the board took a short break at 4 p.m. before coming to the matter for which Callahan, Billy, and many in the audience had waited.

The proposal was simple and harkened back to the reason why Callahan had run for mayor in the first place: the homeless. The mayor had taken on William Carlson with the mantra that Carlson had neglected the homeless and made them live on the street and in the parks because of a lack of shelters.

The issue had been successful because it pleased both liberals, who supported homeless rights, and conservatives, who wanted them off the streets. Callahan had vowed to please both during the election and now, six months after taking office, it was time to put the plan forward.

All the newspapers had been pressuring Callahan in editorials to come up with a plan for his key election issue. The *Journal* had called him "Mayor Mouth-off" for making promises he couldn't keep, while the *Bulletin* wrote that Callahan had "...failed to take, head-on, an issue he waived in front of voters like a butcher holding steak before a hungry dog."

At The S.F. *Reader*, which had not backed off on Callahan since he took the oath of office, editorials and columns—including a front-page slam by Danny Dugan himself—hit the new mayor with everything from statistics on the growing homeless population since his inauguration to photos of Callahan dining at Star's Restaurant, a five-star political hangout, published next to pictures of people lined up for a local soup kitchen.

"Enough is enough," Billy said two weeks before the supervisors' meeting when he approached Callahan with an idea for a homeless plan. "We need to bring something out now."

With that, Billy, Callahan, Benny Min and a handful of homeless and finance officials from the mayor's office had brainstormed over two days and nights and come up with the proposal the mayor submitted to the supervisors a week prior to the meeting.

In a nutshell, the plan would institute a street crackdown by police of minor homeless offenses like sleeping outdoors, urinating outside, drinking in public, and loitering. But, instead of arresting the lawbreakers, each would be turned over to a new team of homeless workers who would evaluate them, find them shelters, and process them into homeless programs to return them to work.

At the same time, the city would reduce its monthly welfare payment—which went to half of the city's roughly 10,000 homeless—from $375 to $275. Conservatives and homeless experts had long complained that because San Francisco's $375 monthly stipend was among the highest in the Bay Area, it lured many homeless people from other cities where monthly welfare checks averaged $300.

And, in the final part of the plan, which Billy called "genius," the city would take the extra $500,000 per month it saved in welfare checks and use it to add 5,000 new shelter beds for the homeless, while requiring those who received the welfare checks to use a portion of it for housing in one of the city's low-rent hotels, where rooms ran $200 per month.

The scheme, Callahan and Billy deduced, would be a key way to help all sides, while giving Carlson a slap in the face and Callahan a pat on the back. And, if it was successful, the administration could give much of the credit to Benny Min, a move that would help take the sting out of his previous troubles.

"It does it all," Callahan had told a woman's club meeting during the week before the supervisors' meeting after announcing the plan at a press conference. "The city needs a compassionate but firm homeless policy to make every person without a home feel at home."

Callahan, Billy, and even Jimmy Min had taken the plan to local clubs, unions, and community groups to pitch it for support during the days leading up to Monday's meeting.

But now they were facing the moment of truth. The 11 people taking their seats in the 80-year-old, stone-carved supervisors' chambers were the ones who mattered. They had to say yes or Callahan's hope for the future—and re-election—would be just a hope that faded.

Alzeti stood up and called the next item on the agenda, the exact title was simple "Mayor's Homeless Plan, Ordinances 1433, 1434, 1435." With that, the board clerk recited the details of each ordinance and the overall legal aspects of the plan.

With each description, some in the audience booed and hissed, even yelling out against the mayor, while others applauded and chanted "Callahan, Callahan!" After the formal descriptions were read, Alzeti welcomed the mayor—a rare visitor to the chamber—and asked him to present his proposal.

Callahan stood up, his sharp blue suit draped over his shoulders, a light blue shirt buttoned up in front, and a Jerry Garcia flower-painted tie—which the Grateful Dead legend had presented at a post-victory breakfast—perfectly in place. The mayor acknowledged all the supervisors as he approached the podium and presented his case.

Opening a loose-leaf binder, Callahan began with a prepared text that he, Billy, and Benny Min had gone over the night before. Billy and Benny kept their eyes glued on the supervisors to see any reaction. The board members showed a mix of stares as the mayor began. Some with smiles showing eager support, others, like Raven and Alzeti, with obvious disgust, but most waiting to hear the facts before deciding the best course of action.

For most of the undecided supervisors, the best course would be determined by how they could use this issue to help their own cause or avoid hurting it with their voters.

"Supervisors, as I stand before you to help lead San Francisco to the next century," the mayor said, "I ask your humble help in ridding our city of one of its most tragic epidemics, the rising plague against those who cannot afford to live and eat in a home of their own.

"Since the day I decided to run for office, I vowed to make sure that this city would be a place where the homeless are cared for, but not at the expense of their dignity, well-being, and safety," Callahan continued. "I propose not to rid the city of the homeless, but rather of homelessness."

As the mayor paused, several in the crowd yelled and cheered, while others offered a collective hiss. Billy smiled and gave Benny a supportive squeeze on his shoulder. Their strategy seemed to be working. Callahan's approach of dividing homelessness as a tragic thing from the homeless who were victims would help show the way. But more needed to be done.

"The best way to solve this problem, as with most civic problems, is through a multi-pronged approach that provides care with strength and firm support. But most of all, with the expectation that every person able to rise up from homelessness to be productive be given that chance and that responsibility," the mayor said.

At that point, some members of the board, who had remained silent throughout the beginning, began to clap and even whistle in favor of the mayor. The audience continued with its balance between supportive cheering and abrasive opposition. Several police officers who had been dispatched by the mayor's office poked their heads inside the chamber to make sure no problems were occurring.

Callahan, meanwhile, continued with his outline of the plan. He pulled out charts and graphs showing the rising number of homeless, but also the studies that showed San Francisco had drawn homeless from other areas because of its higher monthly welfare payments. Another chart pointed out the shift in spending that would be done by reducing the welfare payment amount and, instead, using it for more shelter beds.

Finally, the mayor went over the need to keep the homeless out of the parks and streets and quoted Constitutional scholars who had testified that such actions were legally allowed. After 45 minutes, the mayor closed his presentation and made it clear that the decision rested with the 11-member board.

"So, I say to you fellow city leaders, will you continue to sit back and allow this blight on the city to fester? Or will you join with me in making this the beginning of a new San Francisco that will care for its people, but make sure its people care for the city, too."

As Callahan stepped down, the crowd erupted. Homeless supporters and other liberal leaders hissed and booed, while several of the community groups and business associations cheered loudly. The board itself offered a mix of supportive and opposition displays, while Alzeti pounded the gavel for order.

With Callahan's presentation finished, Alzeti opened the floor to public comments and questions. A line quickly formed with representatives from all sides waiting to give their opinions. Among the first was Homeless Rights Association president Pete Bowden, an outspoken former welfare recipient who'd built his non-profit group from scratch after coming to San Francisco from Virginia as a teenager.

Bowden, who had campaigned for Alzeti and supported her tax increase the previous year, was never one to hold back on his language where serious issues were concerned. And this would be no exception.

"This is a fucking civil rights catastrophe," Bowden said, with cheers from his membership behind him. "The people who live on the street are not there by choice. Many have mental problems, alcoholism, and real emotional depression. To clear them out, take away their money, and tell them how much they can spend is ludicrous. I say increase education, free health care, and social programs first and you will see a difference. This is neo-Nazi rhetoric."

Bowden slammed the microphone as he went to sit down. Others followed, including Tyler Kellman, president of the San Francisco Merchants Coalition, which strongly supported the plan and had endorsed and campaigned for Callahan.

"We do not hate the homeless, but we feel that their plight needs a forceful approach," Kellman said. "For the small business owner, the rows of homeless people sleeping in doorways, on streets, and in some cases in our basements, is a detriment to business. Do we want them criminalized? No! But we do not want them to be left unattended."

For the next three hours, the comments came, back and forth, with every viewpoint ranging from those who thought the homeless should be put on a boat and shipped to Russia to those who said Callahan should let a few live in his $2.5 million Fillmore Street mansion.

Finally, at 8 p.m., the board members had their chance and, as usual, held every view possible. Alzeti and Raven both vehemently opposed the proposal, while others like Lee Ming, one of the Chinese board members and an advocate ally, spoke in favor of the approach as a "tough-love" kind of strategy. Still stronger backing came from West Side Supervisor Mary Menning, daughter of jewelry tycoon George Menning, who'd made a fortune in gems and bankrolled her elections for the past 12 years.

"We can make this city great again if we take the step to do great things, like clear away the homeless problem for good," Menning said.

After all of the supervisors had talked and public comments were heard, the board voted, 6 to 5, in favor of the plan. But one supervisor, Amy Milstein, a favorite of both liberals and small business, had placed a provision that would make the program a temporary step for the next three months. Realizing that she had to walk a tightrope between her two biggest support bases, Milstein wanted to show the business leaders that she was willing to try this approach, but also show liberals that she wanted to make sure it would not unfairly attack those on the street.

With that, the board approved the plan, gave three months for a test, and adjourned. Billy and Callahan sat surprised but victorious. They had at least gotten a start to their efforts, but realized that the program would have to be positive and progressive to ensure that the board would give permanent approval 90 days later.

Outside the chambers, reporters, radio microphones, and television cameras swarmed over the supervisors, the mayor, and supporters and opponents in the crowd. The pro-homeless groups screamed their opposition and even talked of plans to recall Callahan from office. Business and conservative leaders, on the other hand, set their spin with the image that the program would clear the city of homeless, but in a dignified and fair manner.

On the news that night, the story led nearly every major local newscast, while newspapers preparing for the next day's editions gave clear details of the effort and enough opposition comment to push the opposing viewpoint up front.

The *Bulletin* headline read, "Callahan's Homeless Reduction Plan," while the *Journal* presented it as "Jack's Homeless Joust." Each contained editorials decrying the approach, with the *Bulletin* carrying a special column by Bowden ripping into the idea as "inhumane, unfair and, worst of all, political."

As they opened the next day's papers, Callahan, Billy and Jimmy Min set forth to find the best way not only to win, but to make sure that the win was something voters would remember. ■

Chapter Seven

Naked Prey and a Giant Loss

Just minutes after the board had voted to give Callahan's homeless elimination plan a chance, the mayor got on the phone to the police chief, ordering him to send patrols into Golden Gate Park and to some of the worst homeless neighborhoods to begin the assault. Ordering the use of foot patrols, motorcycle cops, squad cars, and even the park's horseback unit, Callahan wanted to make sure that the tone of the program—one of kind, but firm enforcement and aid—was set by the administration, not by the press and liberal protesters.

The cops set up to enter the park at 6 a.m. the next day with patrols that would cite anyone who had broken any of the laws, but make sure they were taken away to health centers and shelters as needed. Billy Dale contacted all local media, told them where the first patrols would go out, and invited them to come along and watch "as San Francisco begins a new era at the start of a new day."

At just after 6 a.m., at the Golden Gate Park entrance of 30th Avenue and Fulton Street in the Richmond District, a mob of television, radio, and newspaper reporters packed around the park. A mild chill whisked through the air. After a short pep talk from the chief, including a reminder to give the utmost respect to the homeless "because we don't need any abuse problems," the patrols started off.

Camera crews and reporters scribbling in notebooks followed as the police went from one encampment to another, explaining to the people living in them that they were violating a specific city code and would have to leave. Citations were written, camps packed up, and people led out of the park. Few scuffles occurred, although one homeless man carrying a knife had to be pepper-sprayed before being arrested.

A group of protesters, including Bowden and Supervisor Alzeti, took up their cause at the east entrance to the park near Haight Street. Waving banners that said, "Help the homeless, don't sweep them away," and "We need jobs, not jails," the protesters yelled and booed as police dragged the street people out of the park.

Photographers took shots of all of it, including one that landed on the front page of the next day's *Bulletin* under the headline "Tough Love?" a direct slap at Lee Ming's comments.

More police were dispatched around town during the late morning to clear the street people from areas near downtown businesses, merchant centers, playgrounds, and the all-important tourist sites like Fisherman's Wharf, Chinatown, and Telegraph Hill.

By the end of the day, police tallied 1,223 citations written; 25 people jailed for more serious offenses like resisting arrest, striking officers, and weapons possession; and the removal of at least 55 encampments housing 10 or more people each.

"We believe this has been a most positive beginning to a very necessary end," the police chief told reporters after releasing the day's totals. "Mayor Callahan has taken the step of active abolishment of homelessness while seeking to keep the homeless alive and safe."

The daily newspapers, however, realized this could be their way to rake Callahan over the coals and took their first shots the day after the effort began. In reaction to the *Bulletin*'s headline and a damning editorial inside, the *Journal* ran a shot of one homeless person being handcuffed, with the headline, "Guilty of Poverty!"

TV news broadcasts carried the story with plenty of pictures and comments of the first day, most focused on the remarks of store owners and neighborhood leaders who backed the plan, leaving opposition views to only a few homeless and people like Supervisor Alzeti.

But while TV seemed to be caught only in the visual and daily news aspects of the plan, editors at both the *Journal* and the *Bulletin* knew that this was a chance to get back at Callahan for his victory over their collective candidate and take new shots at him after he sidestepped the Benny Min controversy.

"This is it," a smiling J.C. Townsend said to his fellow editors at the *Bulletin* after the first-day coverage ended. "We can pummel him with everything until the pressure gets so bad that he'll cut his losses and lick his wounds."

Townsend's counterpart at the *Journal*, Tim Cross, had even stronger ideas about revenge. He sent out about half of his metro reporters each day with orders to find the most abusive incidents and the most troubled people to profile. He also set up a statistics box on the front page tallying how many arrests were made daily, the number of citations given, and the number of homeless shelter beds available.

Under Callahan's plan, the arrests and citations would be made first, then the welfare cutback would start, then the additional shelter space added. Because the shelter space would likely not be made available for another two months, the homeless were being arrested, cited, and swept out before they had any place to go.

"That is the key," Cross told his reporters. "We need to show that this plan is not working and, if they can't prove any positive gains—like more shelter space— before the three-month pilot time period, we know that it won't continue."

Cross also set aside space on the editorial page each day for a specific editorial slamming the Callahan plan, which included everything from bible verses to quotes of Winston Churchill, FDR, and Abraham Lincoln. The daily attacks also sought support from the community to oppose the program, while urging supervisors to vote it down when the three-month trial had ended.

"You can plainly see that Mayor Jack Callahan's homeless aid plan is nothing more than a way to sweep poor people under the rug," a particularly strong editorial proclaimed. "If this atrocity doesn't end, it'll be the voters who will have reason to sweep Mayor Callahan under the rug at the ballot box."

Along with the editorials and daily harsh coverage, Callahan also had to contend with protests in numerous locations each day at City Hall, at his home, and even outside the park.

When Callahan went to Candlestick Park to throw out the first pitch during a ball game, protesters were outside; when he attended a fundraiser to help clear his campaign debt on Nob Hill, banners and picket signs greeted him; and even when the mayor went out of town to Stinson Beach or Napa for a wine country tour with Glenda, some pro-homeless contingent would find them.

"I don't know if this is going to work," the mayor said to Billy Dale during a late-night meeting in his office over Chinese food. "The pressure is big. I know our supporters are liking the cleaner streets and swept up sidewalks, but the pressure from the other side might be too much for the supervisors, they may have to cave in."

Billy saw Callahan's point. The board members were as fickle and as vulnerable to losing their next elections as anyone. Some staunch supporters like Menning and Ming were easy to count on, but with a handful of opposition votes lined up, they could not afford to lose some of the uncertain swing votes.

Billy knew that the key was to get more support out there for the plan. While liberal, anti-law-enforcement factions routinely protested and picketed against almost anything they believed was unfair, most conservatives, family types, and business owners were too busy and, to a degree, subdued to take part in such an action.

Along with the supporters, Billy believed that the police needed to show a unifying force that presented their efforts as both necessary and respectful. If they could show that the cops wanted to help the homeless and the city, and were not out for some kind of Rambo or Old West police-brutality show, some of the undecided might come around.

Billy left the mayor's office with a clear idea of what he had to do and went back to his own office. He immediately got on the phone with Jimmy Min and other community leaders and told them that the homeless plan needed its own protest. He needed to get the supporters together in a full-scale, wide-open rally that would show they were strongly behind this.

Billy began by calling city business leaders and neighborhood organizations. "We really need to bring this together and fight back," he told each one. "Otherwise, the liberals are going to railroad it right out of the Board of Supervisors with fear and pressure."

Jimmy and Benny Min did the same, organizing the event for the following Sunday at the Polo Fields in Golden Gate Park. They also urged the supporters not to dress in the most conservative, business-like attire. They wanted to show that these people were just like most others in the community—real folks who wanted a nice place to live.

When Sunday came, the stage was set in the park with a giant platform above the crowd that began filling at 9 a.m. At noon, the event began with an opening prayer by Rev. Harold Green, who prayed not only for the police and the homeless who were being affected by the program, but "for all San Francisco to join together in a spirit of help and hope."

After that, a school choir sang and several street performers, including two formerly homeless people who had worked their way off the streets using their talents, took the stage to the delight of the crowd.

That's when Callahan came out with the police chief. Neither wore business attire, with the mayor sporting a polo shirt and slacks and the chief in jeans and a buttoned-up shirt. They applauded the street performers and said they were an example of how the homeless can "pull themselves up by their own bootstraps for a change."

More business leaders, community group presidents, and even a few preachers got up to hail the plan. With each appearance, the crowd roared, although a few of those opposed to the plan managed to find their way in and boo at certain moments.

After three hours of speeches, music, and cheers, the rally ended and the groups took to the exits of the park. Billy and Callahan walked out with Benny and Jimmy Min and the police chief with high hopes that the rally had done well to at least balance, if not tip, the scales in favor of the homeless control plan.

As they walked toward the Richmond District exits from the park, the mayor and his aides watched as news crews and reporters put their stories together. Cameras pointed at TV reporters, who summed up the day's activities and painted a somewhat favorable assessment of the rally.

The mayor also glanced over to see reporters from the city's newspapers interviewing local residents, rally speakers, and, of course, the homeless protesters who had positioned themselves outside the park to counter the rally.

Billy wasn't worried. He knew that the backlash would continue. But he also knew that the rally would have an effect. Some of those who'd been on the fence would no longer feel reluctant about choosing the mayor's side. They could see that taking up for a cause, with a group of fellow supporters, did not always have to be anti-government or anti-authority. It was okay, as Billy put it, for people to protest in favor of their politicians.

"That's what makes this such a positive program," Billy said on the news that night when a reporter asked to explain the meaning of the rally. "The ordinary person who doesn't usually get involved in rallies or other protests has taken a stand in favor of what we're doing. When was the last time you saw people out protesting FOR the police? That shows that this is the right thing."

But the newspapers didn't budge an inch. Stories in the *Bulletin* and the *Journal* the following Monday were as partisan as ever. Each paper covered the rally fully with multiple stories, photos, and again, scathing editorials that ripped the rally as a "staged sham!"

"The pitiful show of pro-militant beliefs and anti-civil right rhetoric at Golden Gate Park yesterday makes clear again how dangerous Mayor Callahan's homeless program is," the *Journal* editorial declared. "It's obvious that the mayor's cronies have corralled together a group of supporters and attempted to pass them off as the kind of spirited, free-thinking protesters that made this city great and, in essence, characterize those who are against his plan."

The *Bulletin*, as usual, took a harsher approach, editorializing that the rally was reminiscent of "Hitler Youth forcefulness of World War II." Adding that the mayor should "be working at City Hall, not working on eliminating rights."

The mayor's strategy had backfired. Instead of turning the tide and showing that protests could come from both sides, Billy's rally idea had appeared to be what it was: a set-up effort to counter the real protests of the left. Billy knew the daily newspapers were against Callahan, but he thought that at least they would be forced to cover the event as it happened.

But before Billy was ready to admit defeat, part two of his program to raise support hit on Monday when nearly every off-duty cop gathered in front of the Hall of Justice for another rally. This was to promote the work of police and carefully show that the cops wanted to support the needs of residents, not hurt the homeless. The rally drew about 5,000 cops, their families, and city officials who gathered just after 6 p.m.

Doug Simpson, president of the Police Officers Association, started the program with a speech proclaiming that San Francisco Police were "kind, but firm." He explained that the city can only be great if "police are allowed to enforce the laws and help those in need, two things that can be achieved together."

Again, television cameras and newspaper reporters were on the scene to record the event with interviews of the cops, politicians, and, yes, the few opposition protesters who stood in the back and yelled out against the homeless plan.

But when the first news reports that night described the event as another "staged, pro-Callahan rally," Billy just sunk his head and shook it side-to-side.

"This isn't what we wanted," Billy said, as he and Jimmy Min watched the news in Jimmy's house. "I know we can do this, but it isn't going the way we need."

The day after the police rally, the *Bulletin* and the *Journal* did a replay of their previous editorials and stories, ripping into the rally as a phony event staged to support the police. The *Bulletin* even went so far as to call the rally an attempt to "whip up a frenzy to justify the cruel treatment of the city's homeless using a public building as the backdrop."

Meanwhile, both newspapers, and that week's SF *Reader*, also continued to count the arrests, citations, and sweeps of the homeless as the mayor's plan entered its third week. The *Bulletin* and the *Journal* each ran photos of homeless people being dragged away, while the *Reader* devoted three inside pages to shots of the sweeps and arrests, including one that showed a police officer pushing a homeless man out in his wheelchair.

But the *Reader*'s big hit came on its tabloid cover, which offered a shot of a police officer pushing a naked homeless man into a police car, handcuffed. The headline gave a simple, two-word description: "Naked Prey!"

Callahan began to get worried, then angry. He knew that his program would eventually bear a positive outcome with more shelters and fewer homeless coming to San Francisco for welfare checks. But until the full plan could be implemented, the only press he would receive would be for the arrests, citations, and park sweeps.

"We need to get some pressure on for better coverage," Callahan told Billy at breakfast on Friday. "We have to find a way to cut a deal or something with these editors to back off, or at least be a little fairer about it."

Billy realized Callahan had a point, but he also knew that it could harm them if the *Journal* and the *Bulletin* knew that their press coverage was hurting Callahan's plan. That's what the newspapers wanted and they were not going to back off unless it was in their best interest.

While the two poked at their food and chatted about how they would approach the newspaper, a morning news report came on the television behind the counter at the bagel shop where they were eating.

The anchorwoman had simple, but bad news: the San Francisco Giants were leaving town.

The city's venerable favorites were off for a better stadium in another city, claiming that Candlestick Park was not fan-friendly enough for their needs and, in addition, needed about $100 million in earthquake safety improvements.

The story said Giants owner Vernon Bogart had declared that, unless a new ballpark was built within the next three years, he would leave when the team's lease at Candlestick ended. No one who had ever been to a night game at The 'Stick could argue with Bogart's complaint; night games there were often colder than football games in many other cities. A chilly wind blew and, when fog or rain came down, it frosted up even more.

Adding to the problems was Candlestick's lack of the lucrative luxury boxes that many teams were getting rich on in other markets, as well as the limited parking and in-and-out access from the ballpark, located in the city's southeast corner.

Jimmy and Billy watched the anchorwoman introduce a tape of Bogart at a hastily-prepared press conference about an hour earlier. Surrounded by only a few members of the press who were given warning of the event, Bogart put it straight.

"When I purchased the Giants 20 years ago, I believed that, in that time, we would find a way to replace Candlestick with a suitable home for a baseball team that provided classic looks, warmth, and safety, and a place proud to call home," Bogart said. "Since then, however, with the earthquake and failed maintenance of the ballpark, it has come to my realization that the Giants need a new home. I would have never before considered moving the team out of San Francisco, but for the good of the baseball enterprise, and the team, I will do just that if given no other choice."

Bogart then ended the press conference by passing out copies of the team's annual revenue and expenditure report, which showed that money from new luxury boxes and increased ticket sales from a new ballpark would bring the team out of a fiscal slump that had it losing about $15 million per year. The estimates showed that a new stadium would run about $250 million.

"We will do everything we can to stay in this city, but it's up to the people, the politicians, and the civil servants to help," Bogart finished. "Together, we can find a way to keep the greatest baseball team in the world in the greatest city in the world."

That ended it and, along with most others in the bagel shop, Billy and Callahan just sat and stared.

"That lying bastard," Billy said out loud, almost loud enough for everyone else in the shop to hear. "He's got tons of money. He just wants a nice, new place to show off his lousy team. These fucking baseball guys all cry poverty, but it's bull."

Callahan agreed, although he had not known Bogart that well outside of throwing out the first pitch on opening day and passing him at some campaign stops. He figured that someone with Bogart's background—as the owner of a string of vineyards and wine shops throughout Northern California—was not hurting for cash.

But Billy knew Bogart and knew that if he was threatening to leave town, the threat was real, although it was probably based on his greed and, more importantly, attention. Vernon Bogart had always wanted the exposure and clout of politicians and real movers and shakers, but he could never get it. Sure, he was a success in Northern California, but most of his pull was linked to cities outside of San Francisco. His base of operation was in Oakland and most of his shops and vineyards were out in Napa and Sonoma counties.

When he bought the team, most people knew it was another attempt to get fame and power. He didn't care about baseball, he just saw another way to get out in front.

Now with the team doing poorly and the ballpark in need of repairs and improvements that the city wasn't ready to pay for, Bogart had found another scheme to get his name in the paper and his bad team and dumpy stadium rejuvenated.

Most San Franciscans, however, weren't looking that deeply into Bogart's thinking. All they knew was that the team was leaving San Francisco. The city had never been the baseball town that New York, Boston, or Chicago had become, but it had a fan base and a way to succeed in better times.

As word spread of the team's possible exit, opinions ran the gamut from die-hard fans—who begged the team to stay and urged the city to give the money right away—to non-baseball fans who criticized giving so much attention to "a bunch of men running around a field" when the city had real problems like homelessness, poverty, and crime.

Sports talk radio stations blared discussions of fans and observers who did everything from demand an immediate vote on money to fund a new stadium to slam Bogart for wasting time with such a request for money when schools needed repairs, libraries needed books and, yes, the homeless needed a place to live.

One sports talk host, Jerry Simmons, a former Giants minor leaguer who'd been among the first sports talk hosts ever in San Francisco, summed up many people's opinions when he called Bogart, "a true carpetbagger not worthy of the honor that went with his famous last name."

"Hey, if he wants to leave San Francisco so bad," Simmons said on one show shortly after the announcement. "Let him go, but tell him to leave the Giants behind and not let the door hit him in the ass on the way out."

The comment drew raves from both Giants fans and foes. Since the threat to move was made in the middle of the baseball season, Bogart could hardly show his face at Candlestick during games. Fans, who had hoisted banners at The 'Stick to root for Willie Mays and Willie McCovey, now hung sheets denouncing Bogart.

Signs with messages such as "Bogart should go to Casablanca," and "Let them play again, Bogie" adorned the walls of the stadium. And when Bogart's face could be seen peering out from the owner's box or on the field, boos and an occasional beer bottle or stone might be hurled his way. After a while, Bogart began watching games from back in the box, where he could not be seen, or sometimes in the team's offices.

The Giants team president, Frank Dillon, urged Bogart to resist the temptation to shoot back at the fans or make any kind of angry public statements. Dillon, a former member of the Board of Supervisors, knew that such outward displays of anger or resentment would kill any chance to get a new stadium financed or built.

But Bogart was getting angry.

After three weeks passed since his initial threatening announcement of a possible move and no overtures from City Hall had appeared to help find the funding for a new ballpark, Bogart got mad. He told Dillon that, unless something happened, he would have to further his threats.

Bogart knew that he could easily find a new home for the team in Tampa or San Jose or some other city. But Dillon realized that remaining in San Francisco where the fans and the team's base lived would be easier than moving.

"Give it a chance," Dillon said during a dinner with his boss. "We can work these guys if we play it right."

With that, Dillon called Callahan's office and set up a meeting with Bogart, the mayor, Billy Dale, and Benny Min. The topic was, of course, money: how much the Giants needed and how the city could get it. When the pow-wow occurred, Callahan was in no mood to bargain.

Still mad that his office had not been contacted before Bogart's announcement and threat, Callahan told the team owner and Dillon that he wouldn't care if the Giants moved. The mayor said not coming to him first was such a slap in the face that he would rather see the team leave than help someone who had snubbed him.

That meeting ended without much resolution or progress, but Dillon remained determined to get the deal done. Aside from not wanting the team to go through the troubles of moving and establishing a new home, Dillon also did not want to leave San Francisco, a city where he grew up and where he'd achieved considerable pull in local government, social, and business arenas.

If the Giants moved to Florida, Texas, or even San Jose, Dillon's clout would be well below what it was in San Francisco. For him to keep the fame and muscle he had worked so hard to gain, they would have to remain by The Bay.

As Dillon and Bogart met with the mayor and his advisors, another meeting was taking place in the offices of the *Bulletin*. Emily Ingle, the newspaper's usually hands-off chairman of the board, was discussing the long-term impact of the Giants' departure with publisher Sam Allen. Allen was a bit surprised, since Emily rarely interfered in newspaper business aside from choosing whom to endorse in a number of races. So he made a point of giving his full attention to the newspaper's matriarch.

Ingle was speculating, correctly, that if the Giants left, the newspaper would feel a blow to its subscription and advertising revenues because of lost readers who'd no longer seek the newspaper for Giants coverage, and advertisers who usually filled the sports pages with ads directed not only at baseball fans, but also at the Giants themselves.

"This is not good," she said to Allen, in her calm but firm tone. "This paper has enough problems without losing the one area we know we can count on for reader interest and promotion."

As Allen listened nervously, Ingle explained the dire straits that the publisher already knew about. In addition to lost circulation and ad revenue, the Giants leaving would hit everything from stadium-based newspaper sales, which ran up to 5,000 copies per game, to the economic health of the city through lost parking revenue, souvenirs, and even workers at the stadium refreshment stands.

Ingle had not been much of an expert at newspaper coverage or editorializing, but she had a nose for business, which she learned from a father who made his fortune and his fame by squeezing every penny out of his newspaper—from cutbacks in office furniture to using non-union truck drivers during a long strike. Emily knew that losing the Giants would have too many negative outcomes for the newspaper.

Allen could only agree. "You're right, Mrs. Ingle," he said. "But unless we can come up with $250 million, what is there to do?"

Ingle knew what to do, and Allen had a worried look on his face when he realized it. The newspaper would have to take on the stadium issue in the paper itself. Use its best and most powerful resource to push, prod, and blackmail the city into forking over the money for a new ballpark, even if it embarrassed the newspaper permanently.

"Without that team, we are in trouble," Ingle said directly. "And if we are in trouble, I'm going to have to find a new publisher who can get us out of trouble."

Allen nodded and gave Ingle his assurances that the newspaper would jump on the Giants stadium bandwagon as soon as possible. But he wasn't looking forward to it. These kinds of public fights over public money never made either side look good, and like many other things, diverted the newspaper's attention from covering the REAL news.

But Allen also knew that when the owner made the rare move of dipping her hand into the newspaper's operation, she did it over something in which she had a great interest, and from which she was not going to back away.

Later that day, Allen called J.C. Townsend and told him what had transpired in Ingle's meeting. "You know what we have to do," Allen lamented. "It's a full-court press. Not only do we have to get the city to put together some kind of stadium plan, but we also have to get it approved by either the voters or the Board of Supervisors."

Townsend sneered. "What?" he grumbled. "You know what this usually means: endorsement promises and threatening bullshit when we have real stuff going on."

"I don't care," Allen said. "This is priority number one."

Allen hung up and Townsend called an emergency newsroom meeting. He brainstormed with key editors and reporters and decided that the first move would be a rare, front-page editorial urging the city to get behind a new stadium for the Giants. The push would be predicated on the expected job and economic loss of the Giants leaving and would seek to make Bogart out as the needy owner, rather than the greedy tycoon that he was.

"He will be our friend and focal point, not anyone to blame," Townsend ordered. "That is non-negotiable."

The next day, in the August 1 edition, the *Bulletin* published its first-ever front-page editorial since the end of World War II urging the city to help build a new ballpark.

"The Giants are an institution in San Francisco, as much a part of the city's character as the Golden Gate Bridge or the cable cars," the editorial began. "To allow them to leave would be like tearing down the bridge or blowing up the cable car tracks forever."

The editorial went on to describe how the city would lose its image, economic base, and even morale without the team, while also hinting at a possible crime wave if the team departed. "Summer nights at Candlestick will be replaced by teen violence in the streets," the statement read. "We cannot let this kind of destruction befall our city."

Most in the *Bulletin* newsroom showed disgust at the editorial, but Townsend, and most importantly, Ingle, loved it and played it up big. When the editorial ran, it brought the Giants stadium issue up to a new level. If the stadium push received support from the city's major morning newspaper— which garnered much more respect and influence than its afternoon counterpart—that must mean it was a topic to be focused upon for other news outlets.

Because of that, all the television and radio stations took up the issue with stories on the Giants' threat, as well as some side stories focused on how important the issue must be for the *Bulletin* to give it a rare Page One editorial.

"That was the whole point," Townsend told a fellow editor. "We can't just write in favor of this, we have to show that it is serious. Make 'em think the city will die without it."

After a while, the *Journal* also jumped on the bandwagon. With a little coaxing from Emily Ingle, Donald Grossman, chairman of the Mack Corporation—which owned the *Journal*— realized that the loss of the Giants could hurt his smaller afternoon paper even more than the *Bulletin*.

With a smaller profit margin and more need for Giants fans who often bought the afternoon paper to get scores of day games and snatched up ballpark copies, Grossman realized that his editorial board also had to get moving. Ingle and Grossman, who had long been enemies in the continuing newspaper battle, knew that the two papers could do more in a united fight that would benefit both.

"If our grandfathers could just see us now," Ingle joked to Grossman in their short secret phone conversation two days after the *Bulletin's* first editorial ran. "Well, what would they say?" Grossman managed only a mild smirk. He never liked the *Bulletin* and hated teaming up with them on anything. But he also knew the power of their collective pens was all they had.

That Sunday, the *Journal* editorial page was devoted entirely to the Giants issue with a long diatribe written by Grossman himself, pleading with residents, politicians, and especially Callahan to meet with the Giants and find a way to build a new ballpark. The editorial page also included a letter to Callahan from Grossman and Ingle, an unprecedented show of united support by the two newspapers.

The letter also appeared in the same day's copy of the *Bulletin* and on several billboards. It was a direct move on Callahan, aimed at pressuring him to come up with a plan for a new stadium and get it to work.

"The voters put you in office to keep watch over our city," the letter said. "Mr. Mayor, please do what is needed on your watch and help keep this city treasure here."

Callahan threw down the paper and laughed with disgust when he read the letter and editorial on that Sunday while sitting in his house.

"Who the hell were these sons of bitches?" the mayor thought to himself. "A year ago they were doing everything they could to keep me out of office. Now they want my help so their fucking papers don't lose any money if there's no baseball? Screw them."

Just then Callahan's home phone rang. It was Billy Dale, who laughed. But instead of sharing Callahan's disgust, he showed every sign of joy and victory.

"Don't you love it?" Billy said with a chuckle that sounded like that of a child who'd just gotten away with playing hooky. "This is perfect."

Still smarting from what he'd read, Callahan didn't understand what Billy meant. Perfect? These two newspapers, which had done everything to screw him over a year ago, were putting their hands out for a new ballpark and placing the pressure on the mayor to come up with the money and the plan.

On top of all of his other problems and demands on the way to re-election, now Callahan had to worry about satisfying some stupid ballpark project that the city didn't even need so that two newspapers who didn't like him anyway could keep getting their cash flow, not to mention a greedy baseball owner who just wanted to get greedier.

"What? Are you kidding? This is the last thing I need," the mayor said.

But, as usual, Billy saw the silver lining in Callahan's dark cloud. From Billy's perspective, the mayor now had the right situation to push his homeless plan through. The newspapers, usually the ones orchestrating which issue would be pursued and which would be neglected, were at the mercy of Callahan, Billy said.

The *Journal* and the *Bulletin* had already shown that they wanted the Giants to stay. In Billy's mind, they had acted too quickly, placing their collective hearts on their sleeves with the outward signs of practically begging for a new stadium. The best way, in Billy's mind, would have been for the newspapers to subtly weave a campaign in favor of a new stadium, hiding how much they really wanted it.

But, as usual, the avaricious publishers acted too fast and blew their chance. Because they had taken such a major step with a front-page editorial and a joint letter to Callahan asking for support, that put the mayor in the proverbial driver's seat.

"Don't you see?" Billy asked. "We can hit them in the ass with this. If we go in and tell them that you will push for a new stadium if they support the homeless program, that can put us over the top."

Billy's strategy was key. If Callahan got the newspapers to support his plan in exchange for a promise to at least put a stadium voter measure on the November ballot, that might be all he needed, even if the stadium wasn't approved by voters.

For Callahan to win in this, he only needed the newspapers' support for the next three months, until his homeless plan was given permanent approval by the Board of Supervisors. In that time, he could push to get a stadium ballot measure before voters for the next election. But no vote would be taken until November, several months after the homeless plan needed to be voted on by the board.

So, in reality, all Callahan needed was to get the stadium plan on the ballot in order to get the papers to support the homeless project.

Callahan also would get points for supporting a plan to keep the Giants in town, even if it didn't get approved. Such a position always makes a politician look good, Billy said. People like their baseball teams, and even if they don't want to spend $250 million to pay for a new stadium, they still want to know that their politicians support the home team.

"Will it work?" the mayor told Billy, his skepticism prevailing. "Would the papers really go for this?"

"Are you kidding?" Billy said. "They want that fucking team here, and when push comes to shove they'll sell out for anything that keeps the cash coming in."

*　　*　　*

The next day, Billy set up a meeting with Ingle and Grossman in the mayor's office. It was to be a secret confab with just the two publishers and the mayor. No other press were allowed or were even told about it. The mayor and Billy knew that the television and radio news folks weren't even needed because they just lived off of what the newspapers wrote anyway and would likely follow the lead of the daily papers when it came to both the stadium and homeless issues.

"Okay, let's get down to business here," Billy said when all the parties were in the mayor's private office on the following Tuesday afternoon. "The way we see it, you two need a new stadium to keep the Giants and we need to get the mayor's homeless plan approved after this trial period. The answer is, we will put all our support behind a ballot measure to fund the ballpark if we get firm, strong support for the mayor's homeless program.

"That means," Billy continued as Callahan sat back and watched his friend work the negotiations. "We want at least three editorials during the next two months endorsing the program, along with at least four stories—each angled to support the plan with statistics on arrests, neighborhood and business people happy with the plan, and with the opposition always at the end of each story. We also want the stories to reflect the fact that the reduced welfare payments and expanded shelter beds will eventually come later."

Ingle and Grossman were not as shocked as they were disgusted by Billy's approach. Both knew that they had to do what he wanted, but still disdained his efforts.

"And, if we play this game, what's in it for us?" Ingle asked, tapping her pink-polished nails on the arm of the antique pine chair upon which she sat, breathing easily and silently. "We are not about to sell out unless it's in our best interest."

"You, lady, get it all," Billy said. "After the first editorial is published on

Friday, the mayor will hold a special Saturday press conference with the Giants and Supervisors Menning and Ming to announce a proposed $250 million stadium bond measure that will raise the money over the next 20 years through a combination of naming rights, a 50 cents-per ticket tax, and a property tax increase tied to a separate 15-year bond. That tax would average about $23 per year for most single-family homeowners."

Billy explained, also, that the Giants would kick in another $20 million for low-income improvements to the area around Candlestick and set up a fund for local school sports activities.

"The mayor will put his full support behind the program, which will also be backed by labor, the police and fire unions, and a majority of the Board of Supervisors," Billy said. "That, combined with your papers' own editorial support and news stories promoting the stadium vote, will ensure a victory in November." Ingle listened calmly, taking in all the angles, while Grossman sat nervously contemplating the impact of all of this.

Finally, he spoke.

"How do we know that you will continue backing the stadium after your homeless plan gets the go-ahead?" Grossman asked. "You could just bail out and we're left holding the bag for this new expensive ballpark."

"Well, that's just the chance you'll have to take," Billy said, snidely. "If you want the Giants to stay here and play ball, you have to play ball with us."

Ingle and Grossman whispered between themselves as Billy and Callahan flashed each other two confident grins. Billy knew that they had the two papers where they wanted them. And it was their own fault.

After a few minutes, the two publishers leaned back and nodded their heads.

"Okay," Ingle said, with a half-smile. "We'll do our part. But if you so much as think about pulling out once your side is taken care of, we will fry you but good."

Billy just smiled. "Don't worry, we'll all get what we need out of this," he said. "Just make sure you back up your ends."

With that, the two publishers left and Billy and Callahan celebrated.

*   *   *

Three days later, both the *Journal* and the *Bulletin* ran editorials declaring that Callahan's homeless program was something that needed more time to review. While the opinion page commentaries did not overwhelmingly support the plan, both said it had shown "good promise" by reducing crime and clearing out the homeless from their usual park and doorway hangouts.

"Mayor Callahan has surprised many people by showing that the homeless can be helped with care, while they are removed from areas that should not be home to anyone," the *Journal* editorial stated. "But in order for his vision to be achieved, he must be given further time to allow all elements of his strategy to go forward. We support that endeavor and urge the Board of Supervisors to continue with all parts of the program."

The newspaper also contained a story showing the arrest statistics and giving accounts from merchants and community leaders about how their areas had improved with fewer homeless and less trash and noise since the plan took effect.

The *Bulletin* included a story focused on one person, a former teacher, who had ended up on the street through a series of problems after a car accident left him unable to walk. The story showed how city social workers had gotten him in touch with state disability agencies, given him some rehabilitation, and started him on the road to possible future employment as a teacher of disabled students.

"I have Mayor Callahan to thank," the man was quoted as saying. "If not for him, I would still be sleeping under the stars instead of dreaming about being one."

The quote was classic and Billy loved it, as did the mayor.

And, as promised, the mayor and the Giants held a press conference the next day. Smack in front of Candlestick Park with Bogart, Dillon, and about five members of the team. The mayor had chosen a spot right in front of one of the few cracks that remained in the ballpark from the earthquake to show why the new stadium was needed. With the entire plan laid out on easel charts and in a pamphlet created by the Giants public relations department—with help from Billy—the proposal was put forward.

Billy also added his own touch by arranging for two local high school bands to appear, groups of little league kids in uniform to come by, and even Hall of Famer and Giants legend Willie Mays to show up. The scene looked like something out of a 1930's Chicago political rally.

After reviewing the proposed ballot measure and stadium plan, which included an artist's rendering of the new park, Callahan made his pitch.

"I am convinced that this approach is the best solution for keeping the Giants in San Francisco," Callahan said. "I ask voters to look at their ability to help this city, and in turn themselves, by approving this plan that keeps the Giants here and gives the city some extra funding for school and athletics as well. San Franciscans need the jobs, tax revenue, and national image that a professional team like the Giants provides."

After that, Bogart stepped in. "I believe that this proposal is the best way for the Giants to remain in San Francisco forever and I vow to put the team's entire support behind it," the owner said. "Let's play ball!!"

After that, the bands fired up, the crowd cheered, and the mayor and the others smiled as they waved their hands.

*   *   *

The next month was a whirlwind in the city with editorials and stories appearing left and right, both in support of the stadium plan and the homeless program. The two daily papers took every opportunity to promote both ideas, as did the *Advocate*. Jimmy Min even attempted to combine the two issues into one editorial. Although he hated doing anything that would help his rival dailies, he also knew that Callahan would be aided by a double win of the stadium and homeless plans, and was glad to help that occur.

Jimmy's editorial called the two issues a "double play" for Callahan and urged voters to "give the city this win-win."

But not everyone was winning. At the S.F. *Reader*, Danny Dugan did not like what was happening. A longtime opponent of the daily newspapers' ability to weave public influence for their own purposes, Dugan saw what was happening and despised it.

He had already opposed the homeless program, both in and out of print, and now had worries about the stadium deal.

While Dugan had no specific element of the ballpark plan to target with valid opposition, the idea that both dailies were now getting on the bandwagon with the mayor they had vehemently opposed just a year earlier made him wonder. Sure, he knew that the newspapers wanted the Giants to stay for all the obvious reasons, but their change of heart over the homeless program did not sit well with him.

Dugan wanted to make sure that the other side, in both the homeless and the stadium issues, was given its chance to be heard...for the sake of being a devil's advocate—the role of a newspaper that Dugan most cherished—if for nothing else.

So, two weeks after the stadium deal was announced, and one month before the Board of Supervisors was to vote to extend the homeless plan, the S.F. *Reader* came out with a major front-page story on the stadium proposal. The weekly had already editorialized against the homeless plan and its effort to "rid the city of the downtrodden and underprivileged." But this was the first chance the newspaper had to take shots at the Giants' efforts.

The stories included comments from Callahan, the Giants, and Benny Min about how the new stadium would help the city by keeping the Giants in town and spurring on the city's economy and national image. But they also used quotes from the few community groups that opposed the idea of making voters pay for any of the project, while also incorporating some economists' views that the wording of the bond measure left the possibility for the property tax element to be increased in the future without voter approval.

"Although this is not unusual for bond measures, it is still something voters should consider," said Jason Kinsley, a professor of economics at Stanford, who had studied the measure for the SF *Reader*. "Nothing in this approach guards against future tax increases."

The *Reader* also pointed out that the money to be set aside for the school and low-income athletic programs was not guaranteed to fund them. The bond's wording allowed for the funds to be redistributed at the whim of the Board of Supervisors. When asked about this by a *Reader* reporter, Billy simply turned it back on the voters, saying it would be their job, as always, to keep an eye on the board.

"Nothing at City Hall can be done if voters don't want it," Billy said sternly. "Like all good citizens, the people of San Francisco have the responsibility to make sure their elected officials follow their rules and keep their promises. It's that way with any civic matter."

Billy, again, turned the negative around to a positive. Not only did he deflect the drawbacks of the stadium plan, but he also made voters feel like they had more at stake, telling them, in essence, to keep an eye on city officials, a position that always makes voters feel like they have more influence than they do. It was genius.

Still, the *Reader* piece managed to have some impact. After it ran, a poll showed that support for the stadium plan had wavered slightly. Days after the plan had been announced, a poll taken by the *Journal* showed that 69% of likely voters supported it, enough to make most of the Board of Supervisors ready to place it on the ballot. After the *Reader* story and some follow-up stories pegged off of it for television and radio, that support had dropped to 54%.

"That's not deadly," Billy warned. "But we have to make sure it keeps on the higher side of 50%."

For the next month, the *Journal* and the *Bulletin* continued to write stories and columns backing the stadium plan and the homeless program, with stats, photos, and stories showing all of the possible positive effects of both. Editors knew that they had to show some negative sides, so they threw in an occasional article angling against the plans. But in each case, they were run on Saturdays, which have the lowest readership of the week, and were purposely placed inside the paper.

The *Reader*, on the other hand, put one of the issues on its cover for five weeks straight, with accompanying editorials and photos showing homeless people being dragged away. One *Reader* cover even had a homeless woman in jail with her baby, a situation Callahan quickly rectified with a phone call to the jail. He also lambasted the police chief the day the photo appeared, telling him, "There is no way you can lock up a woman and her baby, don't ever let that happen again."

*   *   *

Finally, the day of reckoning appeared. The Board of Supervisors assembled on September 7 to, ironically, vote on both the homeless plan extension and the ballot measure for the new stadium. If both votes were approved, the stadium measure would go on the Nov. 6 ballot, while the homeless program would be allowed to continue indefinitely, although it could be removed with a future board vote.

The stadium plan had been tweaked slightly to make sure that the money earmarked for school and athletic programs would have to at least be used in the city's recreation department and school system. But the property tax increase remained open for future hikes. The state's bond rules required that provision in case the city could not make payments on the bond and had to raise money to cover it.

"That one is going to hurt," Billy told Jimmy Min at breakfast on the day of the board vote. "But if we push the issue of the people as watchdogs of the city government, that one may slide by. Right now," Billy continued. "All we need to do is get it on the ballot and get the homeless plan going."

Jimmy nodded and crossed his fingers.

Later that day, they entered the chamber again, the same place they had sat just three months earlier when the homeless crackdown was just an idea, and the stadium plan had not even come about. But today, Callahan's entire administration, at least for now, rested on the vote of these 11 people.

Billy knew it and had been lobbying them vigorously during the past week. From threats of future opposition campaigns of those who opposed either plan to promises of support for future programs, and a Callahan endorsement of re-elections if needed, Billy had pushed every button. And he knew which buttons to push.

Some needed a hard hand and blackmail, while others just wanted to know that their vote was needed and were willing to support the mayor if his support was promised down the line.

"You have to know what each politician wants," Billy had once told one of his protégés. "Not all of them take to threats, and not all of them take to thanks. It's a mixed bag."

A mixed bag that Billy had learned to mix at the right speed, and with the right amount of friendly persuasion. The question now was would it be enough?

Several others in the audience also had a stake in the vote. Seated just a few seats away from Billy and Callahan were Donald Grossman and Emily Ingle, the two publishers whose fate rested in the hands of the supervisors along with the mayor's contingent, and who continued to be disgusted by the fact that they had to play by Callahan's rules to win.

Emily Ingle, who had personally directed her staff to keep Callahan from office less than a year ago, smiled kindly toward Billy and the mayor. But inside, she churned with anger and frustration over what she was making herself do. "There is no way I am going to let these men control my future," she said to herself. "This is not what needs to happen."

Next to her, Grossman also vented internally about the situation in which he had been placed. He knew that playing such politics would win approval of the stadium and a solid future for his newspaper, but the feeling that he had to literally be blackmailed to do it did not rest easy. As he scanned the room to observe the crowd, his eyes cringed when they reached the board members' seats.

Also seated in the audience immediately behind the two publishers were Giants owner Vernon Bogart and his team president, Frank Dillon. Bogart, of course, wanted the stadium bond measure put on the ballot, but had actually given little concern to the matter. He would love to stay in San Francisco, but would not mind moving the team to warmer climates in Arizona or Florida.

For Dillon, it was another matter. He had been out lobbying the supervisors and the public support and did not want to leave the city. As he looked around the room, his sweaty hands squeezed a rolled-up copy of the board agenda tightly and he tapped his foot nervously.

The packed board chambers, which were overflowing into the back and outside, hushed to silence as the 11 board members entered and took their seats. The usual chatter and friendly greetings between the supervisors and the public were noticeably absent as the group of politicians sat down.

On most meeting days, the board would enter slowly, little by little, with members waving to friends, greeting lobbyists and fellow politicians, and often hugging those they knew in the crowd. Some meetings started as late as a half-hour because of the pre-meeting glad-handing that often went on, part of San Francisco's lively and friendly political atmosphere.

But today's meeting was different. The supervisors entered quietly, almost in unison, quickly took their seats and said little if anything to each other or the audience. As Alzeti began the meeting, even her usual powerful gavel thumping was diminished to soft taps as she guided the group through the regular agenda toward the two items that were on everyone's mind.

Most in the audience were immediately taken aback by the quiet and orderly demeanor of the board that long had a reputation for loud and boisterous meetings. The mayor and Jimmy Min were so engrossed in their own suspense over the vote, which would affect both men severely, that they hadn't noticed the changes.

But Billy Dale did. He made it his business to know exactly how and when things would play out in city politics and he realized slowly that this was not the usual board conduct he'd known for the past few years; his worries began to rise.

After quickly voting on more than 40 items, ranging from the approval of a fire department appropriation for new gear to allowing the use of Golden Gate Park for a summer soccer league, the board turned to the two issues of the day.

First, the homeless program. After a quick recitation by the board clerk, Alzeti asked for public comment. Nearly the same line of speakers who'd spoken out for and against the program three months ago when it first came to the board rose to give their opinions again over the next two hours.

After the public speaking portion, Alzeti asked if there was any board comment. Not one supervisor rose to address the issue.

Then came the vote.

One by one, the board clerk called off the names. First, as always, Alzeti. "Nay," the proud liberal expressed. Billy and Callahan were not concerned about her. They knew that Alzeti was the last person who would vote to support a crackdown on homelessness, and likely the last person to vote for the mayor on anything.

Next came Ken Kragen, another automatic no, and sure enough, he offered a "nay" as well. But, surprisingly, neither Alzeti or Kragen voiced any spoken opposition. For these two talkative progressive board members to say nothing and simply register their votes was unusual. It was almost as if they did not believe their persuasive comments were needed.

Then the roll call continued, and the biggest surprise of the year slowly unwrapped.

One by one, each board member voted no, without fanfare or discussion. Just "nay, nay, nay." Billy and Callahan just looked at each other, astonished, and sunk their heads in their hands.

Finally, when the roll call reached some of their staunchest allies, like Mary Menning and *Advocate* friend Lee Ming, both men believed they'd at least get some support. But it would not occur.

Neither Menning nor Ming even looked toward the audience when they cast their reluctant-sounding but direct "nays." That was it, the vote was over and the homeless plan had gone down in flames.

Billy and the mayor were stunned, while several others in the audience gasped in astonishment and homeless advocates cheered.

Alzeti went quickly to the stadium plan. Again, the pro and con commentaries flowed during public comment. Grossman and Ingle even got up to speak in favor, giving subtle hints that a vote for the stadium would be remembered by the newspapers during the next election wave. When another two hours of public comment finished, the board again voted, one by one, with almost the exact opposite outcome of the previous round.

As had been expected, the more liberal members such as Alzeti, Kragen, and even Amy Milstein went along with the stadium plan. All three were avid baseball fans and bought into the promise that the stadium would help raise money for school and recreation programs, as well as keep the popular Giants in town.

But as Billy and the mayor watched in amazement, the entire board voted in favor of placing the stadium plan on the ballot, 11-0, with no comment and, outwardly, no sign of resistance or questioning at all. Again, Callahan allies Menning and Ming went along with the vote, despite their support for the mayor and the Mins.

Billy looked over at Ingle and Grossman, who sat quietly, neither gloating over their victory nor showing signs of surprise.

After the vote, Alzeti adjourned the meeting, Grossman and Ingle shook hands, and Billy Dale and Jimmy Min shook their heads. But while Callahan and Jimmy slumped in their seats in defeat, Billy was not ready to go down without finding out what the hell had happened and who was behind it. ■

Chapter Eight

Billy's Revenge

Most of the crowd seemed stunned not only that certain conservative factions had gone along with the stadium measure and against the homeless plan, but also that each vote was a unanimous 11-0, a rarity in San Francisco's mass of diverse and stubborn political opinions.

As the audience filed out, some cheering, others booing, and mostly all wondering, Billy Dale headed straight for the Board of Supervisors offices. One at a time, he went to each supervisor and tried to find out what the deal had been that not only lost the mayor his needed support but handed it over to the Giants and the two newspapers.

First, he grabbed Lee Ming, the right-hand man in many cases for Jimmy Min and someone whom Billy had helped get elected. Shoving past a reporter to get into Ming's office, Billy slammed the door and confronted Ming squarely.

"What the hell happened?" Billy yelled, as sweat appeared on his brow and his face reddened. "Where the hell were you on this thing?"

Ming trembled a bit but remained firm. "Look, Billy, you don't understand," he stammered. "There was a lot riding on both of these things and I just went with what I had to do."

"That's bullshit!" Billy yelled loudly as he knocked over a cup, smashing it against the office wall and turning redder. "You know that this homeless thing was our ticket to stay in office and your people have always been in favor of it. What gives?"

Ming just remained tight-lipped and sat down nervously. As Billy waited for a response, Ming gave none, saying only that Billy would just have to understand his vote. He said that his belief in what was proper had to come first.

"Sorry, Billy, but sometimes I have to do what I feel is right."

Billy didn't believe a word of it. He knew Ming. He knew that he was a staunch conservative who liked less government, reduced taxes, and keeping his wealthy campaign contributors happy, the same wealthy folks who were out in strong favor of the homeless plan.

He didn't care so much about Ming voting for the stadium ballot measure, although that was a bit odd, too, given Ming's penchant for fiscal conservatism. He wanted to know where the votes were and how such a strange turnabout could happen for the homeless plan.

Giving Ming a disgusted sneer, Billy left his office and headed straight for Mary Menning. She was one of the other few votes that Billy and the mayor thought they could have counted on for the homeless plan. She offered the same line of righteous B.S.

"I'm sorry Billy, but this just didn't sound right to me and I had to go with what I thought was proper," Menning said as she leaned over the top of her antique oak desk, which had been hand made in the Marin Headlands and spanned wider than any other desk in City Hall, including the mayor's. "You have to understand."

Billy understood. He understood that she was full of it, too, and he was not getting the answers he needed. His frustration forced him to leave before he felt like taking a punch.

"Okay, I get it," Billy said as he walked out into the hallway. "If you want to play it that way, so can I. But we are going to find out what really happened and take care of it."

On his way out the door, Billy passed Jimmy and Benny Min in the hallway. Jimmy said he'd been talking to other supervisors who had either been wavering on the homeless plan or had registered their support, but to no avail.

"Nobody's talking," Jimmy said as he rubbed his face. "I don't get it. We had the pressure on and should have at least gotten a split vote. Someone did something."

Billy shared his friend's view but wasn't sure which way to turn. He didn't want to start accusing too much before finding out what happened. But he knew that someone had double-crossed him. His mind began to process all of the possibilities.

In San Francisco, as in all places, politics works to the needs of those in power to remain in power and seek more power. Nothing more, nothing less. Billy had learned that as the top priority when dealing with politicians, they liked having it all, they liked keeping it all, and they dreaded any signs that they would lose it all.

As Billy, Jimmy, and Benny walked out of City Hall, they passed Donald Grossman and Emily Ingle being interviewed about the stadium ballot measure, with little discussion of the homeless plan. As any newsperson knows, prospects for a new stadium are more interesting than the loss of a program to crack down on homeless petty crimes.

Sure enough, that night on the news, the stadium bond vote received major attention. Billy could see why even the most conservative, anti-baseball supervisor could view the stadium plan as a solid, voter-positive item. It made it look like the politicians were in favor of baseball, the American game that offers entertainment, community spirit, and escape.

It also held a promise, although limited, that the project could raise money for needed school and athletic programs and create jobs. And the best part was that the final decision still rested with voters. If anything went wrong down the line, like a loss of funding for the stadium or increased taxes to pay for over budgeting, the board could simply say that it was left up to the voters and they approved it, if they approved it.

That was the key to many political items in California that went on the ballot. One of the few states that allowed almost anything to become law if enough voters approved it, California had become the land of the proposition.

From legal marijuana to the end of affirmative action, voters had taken over, leaving politicians to hide behind the banner of "public majority opinion" in a system in which they were supposed to make the hard choices rather than passing them off to voters who often punched the ballot card with their wallets or prejudices instead of fair and reasonable decision-making.

As Billy and Jimmy watched news report after news report that night at the *Advocate* offices, Billy's stomach still turned. He knew that this vote had not gone down straight and he wanted to find out why.

At the same time, things were different in the home of Emily Ingle. The newspaper heiress, who entertained often at her exclusive Sea Gate mansion overlooking the Pacific Ocean, threw a particularly joyous celebration on this Monday night following the board vote. Although the party was not one of her huge catered affairs, it was a pointed celebration. She even went to the unheard-of lengths of inviting Grossman and several editors from the *Journal*, who would not have been allowed within 100 feet of her home in the past. Tonight, however, the two newspapers could share a victory of not only getting over the first hurdle toward keeping the Giants in town, but also of screwing over Billy Dale and Jack Callahan.

As Ingle poured the champagne and passed it around her back deck that overlooked a stunning view of the Golden Gate Bridge, she thought back to the previous week when she put the last piece of her plan into place.

One week earlier, Ingle had been sitting in the offices of the *Bulletin*, watching as the newspaper simultaneously pushed for both the stadium plan and the homeless program in each day's issues. She had known then that the stadium plan seemed assured for board approval, but became increasingly worried about the homeless plan. If the program succeeded in being approved for permanent implementation that would give Callahan more power and more ability to control issues in the city, including those that affected the *Bulletin*.

If Callahan's power became stronger than that of the *Bulletin* and the *Journal*, which had opposed him, the newspapers would lose their pull. Although they had now jumped on board to help with the homeless program, Callahan knew that their backing was only with self-interest in mind and that the newspapers were not truly behind him on any other issues or projects.

Because of that, Callahan could move ahead in the future without any support from the newspapers and, if he got his homeless program approved for good, he wouldn't even need the newspapers' support at all. Without the homeless program, though, Callahan would suffer a sharp defeat, while the newspapers would profit if the stadium plan passed.

Ingle also knew that the stadium plan was almost assured victory at the board level because of all the support it had received, despite the *Reader*'s red flags about financing. But the homeless program remained uncertain simply because the opposition was so strong. In reality, Callahan was the one who needed the newspapers' support for the homeless program more than the newspapers needed his support for the stadium.

At that point, with a week to go before the board vote, Ingle decided that the newspapers did not need to continue the arrangement they had agreed to with Callahan. The dailies had garnered enough support to ensure at least a majority vote to get the stadium on the ballot. They also had gotten Callahan's endorsement.

But Ingle knew that for the *Bulletin* or the *Journal* to do an about-face on the homeless program and withdraw their endorsements at such a late date would do severe damage to each newspaper's reputation. To show a quick change in support, without any real substantial reason other than an obvious opposition to the mayor, would hurt the newspapers' futures.

If the papers launched a new attack on the homeless program at this late stage, that would also give Callahan time to retaliate and switch his support on the stadium plan. No, Ingle decided, if anything was to be done, it would have to be done behind the scenes and at the last minute.

Just as she determined the situation, Ingle quickly called in Justin Swan, the City Hall reporter who had dug up the dirt on Benny Min several months earlier, and asked him who the likely homeless plan supporters on the board were and who were the obvious opponents. Swan, surprised to receive such a question from the newspaper's owner, who barely showed her face in the newsroom, pondered the request and told her that Alzeti and Kragen would definitely vote against the homeless proposal, while Ming, Menning, and Milstein were probably locked into it.

She then asked who might be against the stadium. He quickly answered that, as she had surmized earlier, no one would likely vote against the stadium plan because it held too many positive political advantages and few disadvantages.

Weeks earlier, when the plan was still new and the *Reader* concerns were first raised, some opposition had been likely. But now that changes had been made to make it appear to be fiscally sound, the one or two opposition votes would have to go along with the rest so that, when the stadium was approved, they could be counted among the supporters.

"I think the stadium is pretty solid," Swan said. "People are hopping on board because they know it is a good voter-friendly project with little political risk and big political gain."

That was all Ingle needed to hear. She quickly got on the phone to Grossman and relayed her views to him. She knew that the stadium could pass, but also that the homeless program could be defeated if the newspapers worked things right.

After what Callahan had done to put the newspapers on guard and black-mail them into supporting him, she wanted to turn it around and get him back.

"We need to keep this guy down and get him out," Ingle thought to herself as her face grew red. "My family did not build this paper up for the last 100 years so this son of a bitch could knock us out of power."

After talking to Grossman, who reluctantly agreed to go along with her, Ingle set out to put the final victory crown on the stadium vote, while knocking the homeless plan for good.

Taking the names of those board members who were either solidly behind the homeless program or leaning toward it given to her by Swan, Ingle set out to work. Swan figured that at least three—Menning, Ming, and Milstein—were definite votes for the homeless proposal. Three others, Jerry Gilman, a retired firefighter, Todd Newman, owner of the hip Bayview Restaurant on Union Street, and real estate mogul Jill Thompson, a former welfare mother who had worked her way up from poverty, had voted for it in the past but were unsure about a permanent approval.

Ingle got on the phone that afternoon and made appointments to see those six, as well as the three other undecided members, to make sure the votes were assured.

Over the next day, Ingle met in secret with each one, often after hours and, in some cases, at the board members' homes. She knew it was unusual for one of the owners of the local newspaper to lobby for favors, so she wanted no one—not even her own reporters—to see what she was doing.

Her first stop was Lee Ming. She knew that she had to be careful since Ming was a friend of Jimmy Min's and had long been an opponent of the *Bulletin*. But she also knew that since Ming was up for re-election the following year, he needed money and support. During their meeting, which took place in Ming's City Hall office at 8:30 p.m., Ingle put it straight. If Ming would vote for the stadium and against the homeless program, the newspaper would ensure his endorsement the following year.

"Why do you want me?" Ming asked, puzzled. "You know that the stadium is likely to pass and the homeless program is a maybe. But what do you care? You guys will be way ahead if the stadium goes ahead. Why do you need to knock down the mayor?"

"Because that son of a bitch tried to screw us and we don't take that lightly," Ingle said, her voice rising. "Look, we're going to kill this program, and knock him out in three years and we can just as easily knock you out next year. Understand?"

Ming didn't like being put on the defensive. He had seen enough of this kind of "friendly persuasion" in the past from people like Billy Dale.

But he saw Ingle's point.

"Well, how much is it worth to you?" Ming said. "I need a little bit more than a promise for an endorsement that could easily be taken away at your whim."

With that, Ingle lifted a paper bag and placed it on Ming's desk. She had not wanted to come down to this last resort but knew to be prepared anyway.

Both Ingle and Ming smiled as she pushed the bag forward. "See what this can do to persuade you," she said.

The supervisor felt the contents of the sack, then pulled out several piles of cash, still wrapped in the bank paper wrappers that held them together when Ingle made the withdrawal herself.

The bag held $25,000 cash, in unmarked bills.

At nearly the same time, Grossman sat down with Amy Milstein in her Haight-Ashbury apartment to share a cup of tea. Milstein, who had reluctantly supported the homeless program the first time it came to the board, had said publicly that she was not sure about it for a permanent solution.

"I do want to keep the cleanup of homeless encampments going, but not at the risk of appearing too hard on the poor," Milstein said. "I still have to think about it."

Grossman laid the same offer on her of a future endorsement. She appreciated the suggestion, but, unlike Ming, she felt more of a gut need to preserve the homeless rights.

That's when Grossman went to his sure bet. He quietly pulled out a large envelope from his briefcase and placed it before Milstein.

"Here," he said. "See if this can sweeten the pot."

Milstein opened the envelope and almost immediately became enraged. "How dare you?" she said "What makes you think I would stoop to being bribed? This is an insult."

But Grossman didn't waver. He expected this kind of reaction from someone like Milstein. She had the reputation for being a balanced liberal who would gladly support the rights of the poor, but also bent toward the conservative if she truly believed it was the right cause.

Still, Grossman also knew that she needed money. Milstein, who had made her name as a civil rights attorney, had also made news as someone in financial trouble. Her investment several years ago in a risky development plan that went under prior to her board election had drawn heavy news coverage.

Owing debts on her house and two loans related to the failed condo project in the South Bay, Milstein was teetering on the edge of losing her home if she could not make huge monthly payments. Her legal work was making ends meet, but since her election to the board three years earlier, she had less time to spend on outside cases and therefore made less money.

Grossman calmly reminded her that this cash could help defray some costs, and that her agreement to go along with the newspapers in a vote against Callahan's homeless program would position her well in the future for political support from the newspapers and financial backing.

Milstein sighed with defeated helplessness and silently put the envelope in her purse.

*   *   *

Over the next few days, each of the nine supervisors visited by Grossman and Ingle took the cash given and made at least mild promises to support the stadium and oppose the homeless plan. Grossman, although outwardly supportive of the underhanded effort, remained concerned that either the votes would not be there or someone would find out about this plot, expose the newspapers, and kill any hope of the stadium being approved.

But Ingle did not seem the least bit nervous; she genuinely enjoyed plotting against Callahan and, more importantly, against Billy Dale, whom she continued to despise for his defeat of William Carlson and his bullying ways of blackmailing the newspapers.

So, when the board votes came in on the following Monday, Ingle and Grossman may have seemed surprised, but in reality, they were the ones who were in control.

"Don't you love it?" Ingle whispered to Grossman during the celebration gathering at her home after the board vote. "We are on top again."

But as Ingle and Grossman celebrated their secret victory, Billy Dale and Jimmy Min remained adamant that they would find out what had happened and take action to counter it.

Two days had passed since the board's double vote shook up the city, and Billy and Jimmy were still trying to salvage their political situation. The stadium ballot measure was going to face the voters in just over a month, with a likely passage. True, Callahan had supported the measure and could take some credit if it passed, but deep down he was reluctant given the board's switch on the homeless program.

Billy could have made great political gains as manager of the stadium ballot measure campaign—which was headed for an easy victory—but he was too angry to take on the job. Sure, heading an almost sure winner like the stadium campaign would boost Billy's scorecard. But he was so wrapped up in trying to rebound the homeless plan that the Giants never approached him and, instead, hired Carl Devins to run the campaign. Devins had worked with Billy in the past, but the two had a falling out several years earlier over a minor judge's race.

Still, Billy gave little mind to Devins or the stadium ballot measure and concentrated on finding out what happened with the homeless proposal.

The supervisors who'd been lined up in favor of the homeless plan and switched their votes at the last minute—such as Ming and Menning—remained mum other than to say they had changed their minds.

Something had gone on behind the scenes, but Billy could not get the inside scoop. He even went to Alzeti and Kragen, longtime political enemies, and asked them what might have changed the more conservative supervisors' positions. Neither one offered to speculate and, frankly, didn't care to help Billy Dale after the trouble he'd caused them in the past.

For Alzeti, whose mayoral campaign was partially blocked due to Billy's efforts to get Callahan elected, the homeless program's defeat was such a political victory that she did not care how much it hurt Billy or the mayor. But, deep down, even she was wondering what had happened to the support for the homeless plan at the last minute.

Jimmy, meanwhile, scouted around City Hall and tried to get some insight into what had changed so many people's minds so quickly. He asked his reporters, as well as writers at the *Journal, Bulletin,* and *Reader,* even calling Danny Dugan for some insight. But he got nowhere.

Finally, a week after the board's double-vote surprise, Billy found himself in his favorite Castro Street bar, sipping a rare martini and chatting with one of his former lovers. Larry Cooley, who owned the Out bookstore—named for its devotion to gay and lesbian authors—had remained Billy's friend since their brief fling several years earlier. The two had met in a late-night dance marathon at a local gay bar and had a three-day fling in Larry's loft.

After the long weekend of sex and drinking ended, the two found that they had few romantic feelings for each other, but shared a great mutual interest in music and liked to go out to jazz clubs together.

Lately, the two had spent little time together, but after the board meeting fiasco, Larry figured Billy could use a friend to talk with and share a drink so he had invited him for a cocktail.

The get-together allowed Billy to relax from his anger of the previous week but did not stop him from wanting to find out how his blackmail plan against Ingle and Grossman had collapsed. Larry, not one with much political insight, told Billy to forget about it and concentrate on what he had to do.

But Billy couldn't. It gnawed at him that someone could have gotten away with this. Just as Billy shared his angst and frustration, a small man at the next table was quietly listening to the tirade. Sitting by himself, a row of empty wine glasses in front of him and the breath of an obvious drunk emanating from his mouth, the short, overweight person tapped Billy on the shoulder.

As he turned to see who was bothering him, Billy recognized Gerald Donovon, Lee Ming's former aide. He'd been fired just a few days earlier after Ming found him stealing money.

The firing had not made any news, but those in City Hall knew about it and though many had come to Donovon's defense, Ming sent him packing. Billy was only slightly sorry to see him wallowing in drink, having known about the incident and deciding that Ming was right to remove him.

"Yeah, what do you want?" Billy asked, obviously annoyed.

Donovon said nothing for about 15 seconds, then spit out his words. "B-b-Billy...if you want to know what happened.....I'll tell....you," Donovon stammered as he drank another swallow of red wine and wiped his wine-soaked face with a sleeve. "They....the Supes.....Lee....they, they...sold you out."

Billy's annoyed look turned into startled surprise response. "What the hell are you talking about?" Billy asked, grabbing the man by the arm. "What do you know?"

Then Donovon, although barely able to talk, explained to Billy that he had overheard Ming talking to Grossman on the phone days before the board vote, and had figured out that the supervisors were being paid off to vote for the stadium and against the homeless plan.

"You're fucking crazy!" Billy barked at Donovon. "Where do you get that crap?"

Donovon just nodded his head. "Check it...out," he said. "Ask them yourself."

*   *   *

Later that day, Billy went to several of the supervisors' offices, confronting each one with the accusation. Some, like Menning and Millstein, would not respond, but Newman decided Billy could do nothing to him, so he admitted it.

"It's business," said Newman. "You know the game.

Billy was furious. For him, losing a political battle was bad enough, but to have the newspapers turn on him after they had made a deal, albeit a blackmailed deal, was enough to put him over the edge.

"That's it," he confided to Jimmy during a phone call later in the day. "We are going to nail these bastards to the wall if we have to destroy the city to do it."

That's when Billy, Jimmy, and even Benny Min set forth to make sure that the stadium plan went down to defeat. Billy and Jimmy would deal with resurrecting the homeless program later. This was still the first year of Callahan's term and, after Election Day, they would still have time to bring back the homeless program and make its impact work for them down the line.

But right now, Billy needed to stop the stadium proposal from being approved. He knew that would be difficult with the two daily newspapers supporting the effort, the big-money interests bankrolling the campaign for passage in order to boost their economic interests, and the popular support from voters who wanted to keep the Giants in town for their own reasons.

It would also be difficult for Callahan to switch his stance on the stadium issue and come out against it since he had endorsed it right up to the board meeting where it received approval. For Callahan to flip-flop would be deadly if he could not convince voters that his reasons were genuine. He had to ensure that the stadium plan went down to defeat or else his opposition would come back to haunt him.

"I'm not sure about this..." Callahan said to Billy during a planning session. "Look, we lost the homeless program for now. Why not stay on the stadium bandwagon, take that victory when it comes, and then repair the homeless damage later. If we get into a fight on this and lose, that is a double defeat."

But Billy didn't care. He had been double-crossed by Ingle and Grossman and craved revenge. "This is the way it has to be," Billy told the mayor. "You trusted me enough to get you into office, now you have to trust me enough to know how to keep you here."

That's when Billy went into action. He set up a meeting with Jimmy, Benny, and several other political veterans who had helped him during Callahan's campaign. They knew that the key to knocking down the stadium was not only to seize on the fiscal uncertainty of the financing, but also find something to make the Giants, the *Journal*, and the *Bulletin* look like the bad guys.

"We've got to show that this is a self-serving thing for the dailies that will harm the city and may end up costing the taxpayers money," Billy said. "And of course, we need some kind of insurance policy to make sure it goes down."

By insurance policy, Billy meant some nugget or nuggets of scandal involving the stadium proposal to wave in front of voters. But he would deal with that later. Right now, just setting up a campaign to stop the stadium plan was enough work. And with the vote just a month away, Billy had to act fast to get opposition out there, raise money, and be able to counterattack all of the stadium campaign's propaganda.

The pro-stadium forces, led by Devins, had already been raising money and had about $300,000 in the bank, a sizeable sum for a citywide ballot measure campaign. The group had its strategy pegged to promote the stadium as a winning proposition for the city on two fronts: first, as a way to create jobs and raise money for the city's programs; second, as a needed investment to keep the Giants in town, and thus keep San Francisco's image as a major city.

The campaign even had its slogan already chosen: "Keep San Francisco a Giant city, vote for the stadium." Signs proclaiming the double-entendre message blanketed the area, along with pamphlets showing the specific estimated revenue for local businesses from a baseball team, and for youth and school activities through the portion of the stadium tax.

The proponents even enlisted Bogart and several Giants players to attend community meetings and make appearances, while the two daily newspapers spouted every possible pro-stadium message they could print through stories and editorials.

On the other side, Billy's negative campaign experience proved fruitful as he organized counter-attack pamphlets and signs that extolled the uncertainty of the financial plan, offered opinions from economists around the country about how major league teams don't necessarily help local economies, and detailed how the Board of Supervisors could raise taxes limitlessly if needed to fund the stadium in the future.

The propaganda also explained that the portion set aside for youth and sports programs only had to go to the Recreation and Parks Department and could be used to fund a new limousine for park commissioners if that was their choice.

"Nothing is guaranteed except death and taxes, especially taxes," was one of their slogans on the anti-stadium fliers that went out. Billy also organized rallies against the measure, including one in the parking lot of Candlestick Park itself.

The usual public debates also were held with Billy, Jimmy, and even Benny Min speaking out against the proposed stadium, while Devins, Bogart, and other business leaders heralded the pro-stadium side.

Even the supervisors, who had gone along with the stadium measure simply to take the easy political road, were getting into the act. Knowing that the only way they could reap a political victory from a stadium measure passage was to stay with the campaign through Election Day, each supervisor made the obligatory appearances and pro-stadium comments during board meetings, community gatherings, and campaign rallies.

Callahan, who had yet to publicly change his stance on the stadium, waited at Billy's direction to proclaim his new opposition. Billy wanted to time things right so that Callahan's changeover would make a dramatic splash, and give the pro-stadium folks little time to counter-attack.

But the mayor was having second thoughts.

Callahan was not wild about switching his viewpoint. He knew that politicians were often given grief for flip-flopping. He didn't need to oppose the stadium. Sure, his homeless plan had gone down to defeat, for the moment. But for him to oppose what seemed like a popular project in the stadium, and have it win without his support, could be worse than losing the homeless initiative in the first place.

"I don't want to go along with this," Callahan told Billy during one of their usual Friday afternoon meetings at City Hall. "I know you want to get back at the newspapers, but I don't need this. I can just lay low and not campaign either way. If you really want to knock this thing down, you don't need me."

But Billy wouldn't hear of it. The mayor owed his entire election to Billy, and for him to stand off when Billy wanted to take on a major challenge was not acceptable.

"Look," Billy said, pointing his finger close to Callahan's face. "I put you in and I can take you out. Just do what I say and it will all come out in the end."

Callahan was startled. He knew that Billy had a volatile temper and a competitiveness unmatched in San Francisco's political circles, but this was the first time he'd ever openly threatened the mayor with any kind of retribution. The two had worked side by side for nearly two years through an election and policy creation, and the mayor had seen how Billy could formulate a campaign for almost anything or anyone with a drive and craftiness unmatched in local, or even national politics.

But for Billy to even hint at opposing the mayor showed how bad his drive for revenge had become. Callahan rubbed his chin in wonder after Billy left his office in a huff. He knew that Billy was taking things too far, that an oversized attack against the stadium could be dangerous for the mayor's future if, indeed, it backfired and put Callahan on the wrong side of a popular election victory.

Pondering the situation, Callahan walked outside of his private office toward the balcony that overlooked Polk Street and the Civic Center Plaza park.

Stepping into the breezy, late-afternoon air that swarmed over the balcony, the mayor watched as the sun set on the lazy Friday afternoon. Grinning slightly at the birds that were washing themselves in the fountain below,

Callahan waved mildly to small children who played on the new playground equipment he had helped procure within the past year.

The mayor also saw the homeless people who had reappeared in the park right outside his window... the same ones who were being led away just a month earlier under his homeless plan. Sure, some were being arrested and driven out to find new shelter. But others were being given help—mental and physical—by social workers who had joined with the police to allow his homeless program to move forward.

Scanning the park below, where a slight breeze whisked through the air as the last drop of sunlight fell, Callahan watched as two men set up a large cardboard box for a home and brushed away leaves and litter with an old broom.

Although his homeless program had only been in existence for three months, the mayor knew that it had done some good. Parks and doorways had been cleared of street people, and not all of them had been forced to search for other homes. Yes, some had been arrested and driven out of town, but others had been given the health care and social aid that they needed.

He also knew that if the homeless program had been allowed to continue, he could have put the rest of it into place. He could have cut the welfare payments, transferred the savings into the new homeless shelters and assistance programs, and made sure that those who received checks were using them for housing, not booze or cigarettes.

Sure, when Callahan first ran for office he had taken up the homeless issue as an easy target to pick on in the wake of Carlson's inept homeless approaches of the past. But since becoming mayor, Callahan had taken the issue to heart and realized that with an effective, fair, but tough homeless approach, he could keep the poor off the street and give aid to those who needed it, but make those who could get up on their own feet make the most of their abilities.

Walking back to his office, Callahan became more determined than ever to get his homeless plan back on track after all this stadium madness had ended. He believed that, with or without Billy Dale, he could succeed in putting a fair, compassionate, yet hard-nosed program in place. And he decided that he would not let Billy Dale's revenge or anything else hurt his chances for making his program a success.

The mayor knew that he had to keep Billy on his good side or risk further assaults from the hot-tempered campaigner. So he decided to stall speaking out against the stadium plan as long as possible. Callahan knew that if he opposed the stadium, and it passed without him, his support would be down to almost nothing, making a future resurrection of his homeless plan nearly impossible.

As he sat down again at his desk and leaned the chair back toward the picture window that framed an expansive view of the city, Callahan set in his mind the things he needed to appease Billy Dale and keep his own political future. He decided that he could forestall an open opposition to the stadium as long as necessary, even if it affected Billy's attitude. Hopefully, neither side would need his support in the stadium campaign... a wishful thought in this city where the opinion of the mayor, whether right or wrong, was always sought.

Even if Callahan laid low during the final three weeks of the campaign, that would not stop reporters from asking the question again and again. What was his thought? Why was he backing off campaigning if he still supported the stadium? And, if he no longer supported it, why was he not out front stating his opposition?

Callahan knew it would not be easy, but he knew that he had to maneuver carefully.

*   *   *

The following Monday, both sides in the stadium battle dug in their heels and went to work. Billy organized a major anti-stadium rally smack dab on the front steps of City Hall. He had the heads of several anti-tax groups speak, along with Jimmy Min and Danny Dugan, both of whom were out against the initiative.

Billy had even gotten support from several homeless rights groups, who had climbed aboard with the view that if the stadium measure failed, the taxes that were to be paid for the bond measure could instead be utilized for social programs at some point down the line. Although no one at City Hall had been contemplating any kind of homeless aid tax since Alzeti's debacle a year earlier in the mayor's race, Billy had persuaded some of the homeless groups to climb aboard his anti-stadium venture under the guise that, perhaps down the line, a tax to help homeless causes could be achieved.

"If the stadium tax is approved, you can be assured that taxing people for homeless needs later on will be out of the question," Billy had said in a letter to ten homeless and social welfare agencies seeking their help in the stadium opposition campaign. "Help us to defeat this effort and we will join forces down the line to strengthen the aid to the homeless."

Billy's tactic was remarkable given the fact that he had been the one to mobilize the homeless crackdown with Callahan in the first place. But Billy's shrewd and cunning political approach made him one of the few who could pull off such a change in strategy. Part of his reputation had come from being a kind of mercenary soldier in the campaign wars. Billy was good at taking nearly any campaign and putting his full weight and strength into winning. He often didn't care what the issue or battle was for, just that he wanted to win it and put the notch in his list of achievements.

On this day, the rally went off smoothly, the crowds in Civic Center Park were overflowing and the press was there as well. During the rally, the mayor's absence was not as conspicuous as one might have thought. Until Jimmy Min made a point of mentioning that the mayor wasn't there.

Near the end of the noon event, which occurred on a cool, but unusually fog-free sunny day, Jimmy took to the microphone and made a direct attack on the mayor.

Billy had not discussed with Jimmy yet how they would prod the mayor into coming out publicly against the stadium, so the idea of focusing attention on Callahan had not come up. Billy had planned to give the mayor time to think it over and only pressure him into a public stance if it became necessary closer to the Election Day vote.

But Jimmy didn't care. He was getting caught up in the frenzy of the rally and wanted to put Callahan on the spot that very day.

"Mayor," he yelled out to the crowd, looking up at the mayor's office window. "Where are you? We know you have been a supporter of the stadium, but we haven't seen you comment on this in weeks. Are you still going to support a tax-hiking, over-budgeted plan for a wealthy baseball owner when the homeless are still out in the street?"

Billy was stunned, but a mild grin crossed his face as he looked at Jimmy. Billy began to clap his hands and started a chant of "Mayor, mayor where are you? Mayor, mayor, what's your view?"

Up in his office, Callahan had been watching the rally and was startled when the chanting started. He began to feel his anger boiling over at the thought that Billy and Jimmy would do this when he had not yet told Billy of his intentions.

"How dare they put me on the spot," he thought to himself. Billy knew that the mayor was still mulling over the idea of switching his support. Although Callahan had decided within himself not to go out on a limb for the anti-stadium forces, he still thought there would be time to broker some kind of deal with Billy.

But, with Jimmy Min's sudden attack on the mayor, the time for waiting was over. As Callahan ducked inside the window from view, all the chanting heads turned up to see him, and the camera crews, reporters, and photographers headed for City Hall to get his reaction. The press corps didn't even bother for the elevator to the second floor, choosing instead to bound up the marble staircase, sweep past Callahan's secretary, and practically knock the door down to get his opinion.

"What is your comment?" "Mr. Mayor, how do you feel about the stadium plan?" "Are you going to switch your support as has been rumored?" The questions came fast and furious.

Callahan smiled a phony grin as he tried to come up with a way to play the middle of the road. He didn't want to state anything publicly, but as the chanting outside grew louder, and Jimmy and Billy egged on the crowd, Callahan knew that his time was up.

As questions continued to fly, the mayor peered out the window and could see Jimmy and Billy sneer their grins. That turned the mayor's frustration and uncertainty to anger. That was it, he thought to himself. If these guys want to play hard, he'll play hard. Screw them.

The mayor knew that supporting the stadium was the right thing no matter what Billy Dale wanted in revenge. He didn't care about getting back at the newspapers, he wanted to push forward with an administration that could do something. And if that meant supporting this stadium plan and letting the newspapers win a little bit first, who cared?

Besides, Billy was getting a little bit out of hand. He was forgetting the cool calculations of politics that had brought both him and the mayor to their current fame and power. With that, he took his stand.

"Yes, I continue to support the stadium plan and I will put my full political, personal, and complete support behind its passage," the mayor said.

As the reporters scribbled in their notebooks and the cameras shot his image for what would be a significant story in the stadium ballot battle, Callahan couldn't help but grin out the window at the two men below who would seek to battle him most. After working side by side for the past year, they now found themselves on opposite sides. Callahan knew that this split would change the future of all three, but how was yet to be known. ■

Chapter Nine

Deadly Night in the Village

Billy Dale had always been a man of hard work but even harder temper. From his days as a youngster on the streets of New York, his overweight appearance and attraction to other men at an early age had set him apart from other teens. When the boys in his class were ogling Playboy photos, Billy quietly ignored them and pursued his passion for other men.

During his childhood on the Lower East Side, Billy knew that he was gay. But as the child of a construction worker and a grade school teacher, the idea of a homosexual even living in the same neighborhood was unheard of. Let alone being in the family.

As he entered his teen years, Billy took more and more interest in the Greenwich Village gay scene. Although the rise of gay rights and influence was increasing in the mid-1960s, it still hadn't reached the level of acceptance that it would in the 1990's San Francisco, a situation that forced Billy to remain hesitant about his sexual feelings.

In school, Billy had few friends and his only interests were in political science and history, with no ability in sports and no social encounters with girls of his own age. He didn't even connect with the handful of gay boys that populated Fisher High School. Most of them were the well-built, body-building types who either played football or basketball or took an interest in dramatic arts.

Often, when he walked home from school, other, bigger boys would pick on him, call him names like "gay boy" and "faggot," and knock him down. The abuse became so bad that he would stay late and read in the library to avoid the attacks.

Once, two of the tougher teens who ran with a local street gang pulled a knife on him and robbed him. He could have brushed it off to simple street crime that permeated the area, but when one yelled "queero" as the two ran away, it was obvious that the attack was prejudicial.

The abuse made Billy cringe and attempt to hide his sexuality, but it also fueled his then-growing temper. He'd always been shy, but inside he boiled at the thought of his rights being violated and held on to the belief that gays had as much right to be outward with their feelings as any minority. With the emergence of black rights and women's rights evolving with the 60's movements, Billy knew that gay rights were not far behind.

For Billy, visits to the underworld community of gay clubs, bars, or cafes in the West Village piqued his interest more than school dances, Saturday afternoon football games, or social clubs on campus. After school, Billy often found himself touring the gay bookstores, which continued to hide under the cover of simply being used bookstores. One of his favorites, Barney's Used Books, actually had to keep its collection of gay and lesbian writings in the basement, which could only be accessed by those known to owner Terry Steele.

At the time, any hint of gay acceptance was tantamount to treason for some New Yorkers, and the police regularly peeked in to hassle the gay crowd if they saw that too many were gathering there.

"It makes me feel like someone in a Nazi-occupied country during World War II," Terry had once told Billy. "This has got to end."

On one particularly sunny day shortly after his 17th birthday, Billy found himself walking through the West Village when he passed the Starbanger Bar, a small watering hole that had been known as a place for gay socializing, but had always been hidden behind closed curtains and a locked door. Anyone who approached the establishment was carefully screened by the managers to maintain that no gay-bashers or law enforcement types looking to bother the clientele were let in.

Local cops occasionally hassled the management, but usually left the owners alone if they kept the socializing indoors and paid some cash to the cops to leave them alone. The most excitement that had occurred there in recent years was when a dead cat had been left on the front step as a prank.

But on this day, the place had changed. The previously closed curtains were spread wide and the windows were even pushed out to allow the gentle summer breeze in. The clientele, which remained sparse due to the early evening hour, was all men and, surprisingly, in no urgent need to hide their appearances.

In the 1960s, one of the keys to success for gay bars in New York, and elsewhere for that matter, was the fact that men could socialize without worrying about being seen in such a location. Police and those who opposed gay rights would generally leave the patrons alone because they "kept it indoors." Gay men, most of whom were reluctant to face the retribution of public scrutiny—especially if they were married and had families—were only willing to go to gay bars and clubs if they knew that they would be protected.

So for the Starbanger to open its curtains and windows and let the identities of patrons out was not only a major step for gay rights, but a risky one.

The club opened itself not only to scrutiny but to abuse by police and anti-gay attackers as well.

As Billy walked by, his curiosity about why the owners would let it all hang out overtook his reluctance. He entered the bar and, surprisingly, did not get asked for ID. Maybe the man at the front door didn't want to drive away a new young face, or maybe he just thought that Billy looked old enough.

Either way, Billy went in and immediately asked the bartender what had happened. "Aren't you guys taking a big chance?" Billy asked the bearded man who stood behind the long oak bar wiping out glasses. "What's going on?"

The bartender, who happened to be the owner, just kept working and smiled. "I've had it with this hiding," he said. "We need to take a stand and this is going to be it."

Billy smiled back with a grin that stretched his chubby young cheeks. After several years of hiding his feelings, it was refreshing to find someone with whom he could not only be open about his sexual preference but who was willing to fight for the right to be what he wanted to be.

"Well, I'm glad," Billy said. "I hope you can do it."

The bartender smiled. He stuck out a hand toward Billy and told him his name, Zack Ratner. He said he had just bought the bar a month earlier after working there as a bartender for five years and wanted to make the move to help the rights of gay people and gay businesses. He told Billy that he also knew Terry Steele and the two were trying to forge a new movement for gay rights, but had been moving slowly to forestall the backlash they knew would come.

Billy smiled and became excited himself. In just one day, he had crossed over into his first step of feeling good about being gay, and also in supporting his first worthwhile cause.

That night, Billy stayed for several hours, chatting with other men, talking to the owner, and feeling freer than he ever had. Although he had yet to take advantage of his gay feelings with another man, just being in this adult, open world was enough to make him feel proud and strong enough to withstand any outside pressure, be it from police, gay-bashers, or his own family.

As the evening wore on, Billy found himself attracted to several men in the place. As the youngest one there at 17, and surprisingly left alone despite being underage in a bar, Billy stuck out, but his overweight appearance and disheveled look made him less attractive than many of the other well-dressed, slimmer, and more physically appealing patrons.

At about 11:30 p.m., as the crowd hit its largest level yet and the patrons began spilling out onto the sidewalk, nerves began to fray as police strolled by and gave suspicious glances. Zack Ratner peered out the opened window to make sure that he could see any trouble that might be brewing as the police kept a close watch. No problems began, but both the police and Zack knew that the calm could not last.

For Billy, the possible trouble was an afterthought. He was enjoying the openness of the occasion and continued to meet and greet these men, most of whom were well over ten years his senior. Eventually, Billy found himself talking to a tall man who sported a rare handlebar mustache and a tank top with shorts. He was well-shaven and trim, but with a stringy head of hair. Billy and the stranger got to talking after Billy remarked that the man was smoking a cigarette with an unusual aroma.

"It's clove," said the man, as he drew in a strong puff and blew out the incense-like smoke. "Brought them from India. Want a drag?"

Billy gladly accepted. He'd not been much for smoking, but he was game for anything on this night. The man said he was a writer who was currently working in Terry Steele's bookstore. When Billy said that he had not seen him there before, the man said he usually worked late at night in the back and spent his days trying to write a novel.

"I'm Clyde Van Killen," the man said, taking Billy's hand in a friendly and somewhat sensual grip while grabbing the clove cigarette back. "What's a kid like you doing here?"

Billy shook his hand and became nervous at the thought that his identity was being revealed and his underage status found.

"Why? Are you going to turn me in?" Billy asked nervously. "I'm not doing anything wrong."

The man just smiled.

"Don't worry. If Zack doesn't care, I don't care," said Clyde. "It's just that we don't see too many kids your age in here. Nice to see you around."

After a while, the two began to chat more closely. Billy found himself strangely attracted to this man, a feeling he had suppressed for many years. But on this night, as his courage had brought him to a place where his sexual identity could not hide, he found his need to explore his feelings growing stronger than ever.

After about 15 minutes of talking, Clyde and Billy moved to a table inside and drank and talked until 1 a.m. Clyde told Billy how he had grown up as a gay teen who ignored the rants and abuse of others, including his minister father who openly preached against homosexuality in his church near the Long Island home where Clyde had grown up.

He told Billy that being gay had made his first aspiration to be a teacher impossible and explained how he had been driven out of his only teaching job by fellow instructors who pressured the school board in nearby Great Neck to fire him after finding gay material in his classroom. Although he had never given such material to students and had never been accused of taking inappropriate action with any children in his class, he had been forced out.

Billy listened intently as Clyde sipped margaritas and passed on his story of coming to the city without a job, finding a place to live and work at Barney's Used Books, and trying to piece his life together as an author and gay rights activist.

Feeling both admiration for Clyde's efforts and sympathy for his similar plight, Billy grew more and more attracted to Clyde's sense of identity and priority as the discussion went on.

"In my day, you would get more than just some name-calling and a little fight on the street," Clyde said. "When I was in high school, the teachers would stand right there while other kids picked on you, and even my own parents would not hold back. My father, a fucking minister, once kicked me out of the house and made me sleep in the park in the cold of winter for three nights after finding a gay novel in my room."

Billy was both stunned with surprise and warmed with compassion upon hearing about the tales of another man. After years of feeling isolated and helpless, here was someone who could share his troubles and see his view.

As the evening wore on and 1 a.m. became 3 a.m., both men became drunker and friendlier. Finally, at the end of the evening, Billy could hold back no more and put his arms around Clyde. His initial move was more out of a feeling of closeness for another man who shared his problems, his fears, and his beliefs than a simple sexual attraction. It could have just as easily been the feeling of a son hugging his father or a man comforting his dog.

But then his sexual impulses took over. Clyde pulled away from Billy and immediately leaned in to kiss him. Billy jumped back at first. He had never gone forward to express such feelings for another man. His fear, excitement, anger, and frustration all came out, but he could hold back no more. He wanted this and he knew the time was right.

After several minutes of feeling their desires in the back of the bar, the two left the Starbanger and went to Clyde's Fourth Street loft. Although Billy's fear of intimacy and embarrassment of his overweight, under-toned body remained, Clyde knew how to handle his worry and guided him through his first sexual experience with another man, and, in truth, his first sexual experience with anyone.

The two made love over and over for the next few hours, ending with a peaceful slumber together on Clyde's bed as the morning sun awoke overhead.

The next morning, Billy awakened and thanked Clyde for his first night of passion with anyone, let alone a man. He felt a bit less frightened, a bit less confused, but even more bewildered. He still knew that his feelings were for men, but he knew that life ahead would not be easy.

The past treatment had shown him that. While he was beginning to come to grips with his sexual preference and felt more at ease, the outside world would not.

When he got home, his parents were fuming.

"Where the hell were you?" his father yelled, with a slap of the hand on Billy's face that startled him before he could even speak. "Where the hell were you? Out screwing around? You are not to leave this house again without my permission. You got that?"

With that, his father slapped him again, shoved him on the ground, and sent him to his room. But Billy didn't even care. He had made his first move toward being who he wanted to be and that was all that mattered. He spent the rest of the day under his father's order, in his room. He spent time sleeping, but could not get Clyde or the revelations that he could be his own person out of his mind.

The next day, Billy walked slowly out of his room. It was Sunday, but his father had been working a long job downtown on a new building and had gotten some overtime offers to work the weekend. As Billy stepped into the kitchen, his mother saw him and hugged him. She asked where he had been, but Billy just said out with friends.

Mrs. Dale, a stern teacher but a lenient parent, did not pry. She knew that Billy had a tough time in school and in making friends, and had even wondered about his sexual orientation. But she had never asked and, perhaps, did not want to know.

That day, Billy went back to the area of the West Village where the Starbanger and Barney's were both located. When he crept into Barney's, he asked if Clyde was around, but Terry told him he would not be in until later.

As Billy went to leave, Terry surprised him by asking if he wanted a job.

"Doing what?" Billy asked. "I have never really worked in a book store, I don't know much about it."

Terry said that was okay with him. He just needed someone to take boxes in and out, help customers find things, and especially keep an eye out to make sure that troublemakers and the cops did not get "downstairs."

Since two months of summer were still ahead, Billy loved the idea of a job that would let him make some money, be in a friendly surrounding where he could get to know more about the gay scene, and be able to escape from the home life and neighborhood where his sexual persuasion was not appreciated.

He also didn't mind being around Clyde.

During the next week, Billy worked a regular 9 a.m. to 5 p.m. shift, bringing boxes in and out, getting books for others, and running errands for Terry and Clyde. At night, he often ended up inside the Starbanger, although Zack made him stay in the back tables or the basement lounge because of his age.

"I don't want to give the cops another reason to give me any trouble," Zack told Billy. "Just keep it low. You're a good kid and easy-going, but we have to be careful with this new, open approach."

Billy didn't mind. He was able to meet and talk with a slew of other men, no matter where he went. Older, younger, gay, straight, and "just-looking" types were in and out each night. Billy would talk with all of them and read his favorite books from Barney's until midnight. His parents eventually gave up trying to control how late Billy came home as long as he was making money and staying out of trouble. Since it was summer, they could not complain too much, although his mother still worried.

Clyde also liked having Billy around. The two would discuss their favorite books and movies at Barney's while they finished work and would enjoy time at the Starbanger or any number of other hangouts at night. They also explored different feelings of intimacy that Billy was growing to enjoy, while Clyde was finding a new birth of excitement with this younger, innocent man.

*　　*　　*

Several weeks passed as Billy came to indulge in his new world of interest, both sexually and intellectually. He knew that these men were leagues beyond not only his classmates at school but also his family at home. Through a litany of new books, Clyde introduced him to authors from Norman Mailer to Jack Kerouac, while also allowing Billy to teach Clyde about the music of the era that kids Billy's age were listening to. Billy had recently gotten into Bob Dylan and the psychedelic world of the Beatles.

The two men eventually found an interest in local independent films as well, and were often seen at any one of the Village movie houses. Billy was finally feeling like he could be himself and believed that a future of hope and independence could be his. After years of feeling isolated and afraid to be his true person, he now had the courage and excitement to move forward, not only as a gay man but as an independent man capable of striking out on his own.

At the same time, however, things at the Starbanger were growing more and more tedious. Each of the summer nights grew hotter in 1968, and more and more men were coming to the bar to be able to meet and drink in a place that opened up for cool breezes and did not force gay patrons to hide indoors where hot, stuffy rooms made life miserable.

Despite its open appearance and susceptibility to gay-bashers, more men wanted to be at the Starbanger because it was relaxing, enjoyable, and gave them the courage to be open about their feelings.

That openness, however, did not sit well with the local cops or Zack Ratner.

Although he had gladly opened up the doors—both literally and figuratively—to make a point and draw business, Zack knew that the police were getting edgy.

Even though there had been no major problems in recent weeks with the more open policy, some businesses in the area and older residents had complained that they "just didn't like that kind of situation." Police were being pressured to keep outward displays of gay affection toned down and were finding it hard to hold back.

That edginess was about to take over and create what would go down in local gay history as The July 4th Blowout.

July 4, 1968, was an unusually hot, humid night. With Zack Ratner's efforts to promote no limits of expression and a literal "open door" policy, the Starbanger had become the hot spot for gay men that summer.

At 11 p.m. that night, just as the regular crowd was getting into a late-night groove and a large group of people was arriving after viewing the East River fireworks, the cops made their move.

Billy and Clyde were sitting at a table just inside one of the open windows, sipping Summer Stingers—the bar's newly created rum and pineapple-orange juice concoction—as the first signs of trouble were occurring.

Both looked up as a single uniformed cop came into the place, walked straight to the bartender, and asked for the owner. The bartender asked him to show identification, then directed him to the basement where he knew Zack would be. The officer headed downstairs.

A few minutes later, Zack came running up with the officer yelling behind him and attempted to dash out the front door just as the cop reached the top of the stairs, a few feet behind him. As Zack grabbed the bar's front door, the cop slammed him into the doorway, forced his arms behind his back, and pulled out handcuffs, cuffing him tightly.

While he brought Zack to his feet, everyone in the bar began to boo and hiss. Several men quickly left, realizing that this was not a time to be at this kind of place. But for most of the patrons, who had known some kind of trouble might occur this summer, the first move was to stay put and fight.

Zack swore at the officer and attempted to shake loose, but the cop just pulled out a baton and whacked him on the arms several times, then on the knees. Zack dropped like a bag of bricks, wincing in pain. That's when half the bar got up and went into action.

Billy and Clyde were among about a dozen men who jumped the cop, grabbing the baton away, and tried to help Zack get to his feet to make sure he was okay. The officer, momentarily shaken, did not stay down long. He jumped to his feet and grabbed the first person he saw—Clyde—whacked him hard across the back and sent him reeling in pain as well. When Billy tried to help, he got a whack across the mouth with the cop's stick, which knocked out two teeth and sent blood streaming from Billy's lips.

Falling to the ground, Billy grabbed for his blood-soaked mouth as whistles began to blow and sirens wailed. Then about a dozen cops rushed in amid flashing lights and shouting people. All of the 65 or so men in the bar went to either run out the front door, shoot down to the basement, or try to fight the officers. Batons were banging, whistles were blaring, and at least one gunshot was fired.

Billy got up and immediately went toward the bar to escape the melee that was erupting. He looked around toward the street outside the bar just in time to see Zack being placed in a police car and swung his eyes around the bar looking for Clyde.

Punches flew, drinks splashed, and drops of blood splattered across the room as Billy made his way out, tripping over two cops who held down a leather-clad patron. Outside, Billy hobbled to the sidewalk where the night humidity struck him like a blast of heat from an oven.

All around, people were running, yelling, and punching. As Billy reached toward the edge of the sidewalk and stumbled to the corner he could see Clyde on the ground several feet away wincing in pain. Crawling over to find his friend, as blood continued to drip from his mouth and his vision slightly blurred, Billy drew closer and closer until he reached Clyde's near-motionless body.

Leaning over to touch him with a shaking hand, Billy could see the clear, clean bullet wound in Clyde's chest. An ambulance screeched to a halt at the curb. Billy pulled Clyde toward him to cradle his body. Blood oozed from the wound down Clyde's shirt and onto Billy's lap as he held him close and felt hot tears down his cheek.

Paramedics made it to the wounded man. Billy tried to block the wound from bleeding and attempted to put pressure on the area, but the blood continued to flow.

While Billy urged the paramedics to help, Clyde grabbed Billy's shirt, made one final tug, and went limp. Two bursts of blood spurted out of his mouth just as the paramedics reached him. Billy stepped back to let them in, but it was too late. After one of the ambulance workers tried to take his pulse and the other went to stop the bleeding, it took only a few seconds for them to discover Clyde was dead.

*　*　*

Several days passed before Billy could fully comprehend what had happened. In the span of about a month, he'd struck out on his own for his sexual feelings and his personal rights, and met a man who helped him achieve both.

In the end, he also saw that man killed right before his eyes. But instead of crawling back into his cave of fear and hiding, Billy took what Clyde had shown him and put it to work.

Just one week after the police shut down the Starbanger with that deadly raid, Billy helped Zack and some of the others stage a protest to force its re-opening. Eventually, the protest and several sit-ins at other area bars helped start one of New York's greatest gay-rights revolutions ever.

That led Billy to continue with more protests and speak-outs when he attended NYU after his senior year of high school. Those experiences grew into his involvement in student elections at the private university, where he helped lead two candidates to victory and even got a taste of city politics as an aide to several New York City council members while in college.

Along the way, however, as Billy learned to work the campaign trail and push the right political buttons, he never learned to put the deadly past behind him. Every campaign, it seemed, was personal and every member of the opposition seemed to be after Billy. He took too many campaigns as a direct challenge rather than an open, democratic contest.

Instead of allowing some defeats to teach him lessons, Billy let them contribute to his anger, an anger that began that day outside the Starbanger and continued right up to his latest battle with San Francisco's newspapers, and now with the mayor he had put in office.

That night at the Starbanger also prompted Billy to begin carrying a gun. Nothing huge, just a small pistol strapped to his left ankle. He would always have it ready just in case the police, or anyone else, got too close.

Today, as Billy found himself on opposite sides of the mayor he had put in power and the newspapers who had double-crossed him, he couldn't help but think back to that summer when a stranger led him to find his courage and his will to take on the opposition no matter what the challenge.

Unfortunately, Billy seemed to forget that what had killed Clyde was the same kind of anger that was mounting inside him. Instead of letting his cool, calm political abilities move him forward, Billy was slowly being overtaken by revenge and fury. What those two destructive emotions might do was yet to be seen. ■

Chapter Ten

Billy and Jimmy's Ace

Billy Dale leaped off the couch in his spacious Castro Street townhouse when he saw the news of the day about Mayor Jack Callahan's support of the stadium measure. Billy had already heard about the mayor's stance after the same herd of reporters who had cornered Callahan in his office earlier in the day had sought his comments shortly after. But this was the first time Billy had seen the mayor make the statement for himself.

"That son of a bitch, what a wimp," Billy said as he shook his head and laughed. "That fuckin' guy can't take on anyone."

With that, Billy turned around to look at Jimmy, who sat on the same couch trying to watch the television report but having his view blocked by the rotund Billy.

"Do you believe this bastard?" Billy asked his friend as he wiped pizza cheese off of his chin. "Doesn't he know he looks like a wimp if he does this?"

Jimmy was not paying attention. He was still trying to see what the television report said. With Callahan taking a pro-stadium stance while Billy, Jimmy, and the *Advocate* continued to push against the ballot measure, things were changing a bit. It was a lot easier for Jimmy when the mayor was sticking by the *Advocate*'s position on the stadium, not to mention with Billy.

The three had been a strong force from the first day he ran Mike McLean's column urging Callahan to run for mayor. From that moment on, each had a separate job to do to keep their agenda and power going, and had done it.

Billy had organized the efforts to raise public awareness of the issues, Callahan had brought them to the top of the government priority list, and Jimmy and McLean had pushed with columns and stories urging the issue to go a certain way.

Although the daily papers had usually taken the opposite stance and made a mark with their own power, the triple threat of Callahan, Billy, and Jimmy had risen to a serious political position in San Francisco.

"People are genuinely scared of these three," one political consultant had told a radio reporter several months earlier when the homeless program first received approval. "Together, they can mount an offensive on anything, and anyone."

Together was the key. Without Callahan in the same camp as Billy and the *Advocate*, Jimmy became slightly worried. No, he wasn't ready to back down on his opposition to the stadium issue, and he wasn't ready to break his own ties with Billy. But he was worried.

"Get out of the way, Billy," Jimmy said as he waved his hand to the side urging his friend to move. "I want to find out exactly where we stand."

Billy jumped out of the way as the reporter on the screen continued to ask questions. With each answer, Callahan made it clear that he was sticking behind the stadium proposal and believed it was good for the city.

"I know that others who previously supported the measure have found reasons to go back on their words," the mayor said, looking snidely into the camera, almost directly at Billy and Jimmy. "But the true political support of any issue is that support which is willing to stand the test of opposition and tough campaigning."

As Callahan smiled after his comments, both Billy and Jimmy couldn't help but laugh. "If it's tough campaigning he wants, that's what he'll get," Billy said. Jimmy just smiled another of his ear-to-ear grins and the two men set to work.

The next day, Tuesday, marked exactly two weeks before voters would cast ballots on the stadium measure. Jimmy and Billy were up early and organized a 7 a.m. meeting in the anti-stadium campaign headquarters. It included Billy, Jimmy, Benny Min, and several of Billy's longtime campaign staff.

For three hours, as they munched on bagels and donuts and downed black coffee, the group brainstormed ideas. The key was to debunk the arguments that the stadium campaign was making about how the project would boost the economy and raise money for athletic and school projects.

Although the measure had been changed to tighten control over where the school and athletic fund money would go, there was still the loophole that allowed the supervisors to raise the tax higher in the future if the stadium plan went over budget.

"That is what we need to key on," Billy said, after biting into a cream cheese-smeared onion bagel. "We have to drive that message home."

The ballot measure also included a provision that allowed the portion set aside for school and athletic programs to be used for any Recreation Department need, which, in theory, could include vacations for Recreation Commissioners and other abuses. While the commission would likely not allocate the money for such lavish items, the fact that it could occur had to be pointed out to make effective attacks on the ballot measure.

"We need to use it all," Billy said.

At the same time, Carl Devins, Vernon Bogart, and a handful of strategists sat around a conference table in a downtown office building. Devins had used the location for more than ten years, since he first started in campaign management as a small-time pro bono organizer of two school board races that propelled virtual underdogs onto the board.

Devins, who sported a trimmed beard, ponytail, and John Lennon-style round glasses, carried a calmer demeanor than Billy. Unlike his outspoken, overweight, and hot-tempered counterpart, Devins presented a more casual, mellow approach.

A graduate of Humboldt State University in the pro-marijuana area north of San Francisco, and of San Francisco's Hastings School of Law, Devins had had a successful ten-year career as a public defender in San Francisco. Six years before the stadium measure occurred, he had left the courtroom to become a campaign consultant.

His entry into politics had been somewhat of a surprise, considering that he'd always despised sleazy campaigns and wanted to work to defend those too poor to pay for their legal defense.

After running unsuccessfully for Public Defender in 1982, Devins swore off any association with campaigns again. But, when two friends from Humboldt State—Denny Jackson and Cheryl Abrams—asked him to help their underdog races for the school board, Devins reluctantly agreed. He didn't think he could help the two former teachers. But in the end, his straightforward, common-sense approach helped them win their seats as voters chose to try their direct approach over the other politically-competitive candidates.

"If you truly believe you can make a difference and just show voters how you will do it, don't promise what you can't deliver, and don't try to fool them. Victory can be achieved," Devins had told a television reporter the night of Jackson and Abrams' victories. "And never, ever campaign negatively. That is the first step toward losing voter trust."

With that in mind, Devins stepped forward with his plan to win the stadium ballot measure. As he explained to the group of strategists gathered around the office table on that Tuesday morning, he truly believed the stadium measure could win if voters realized exactly what it would cost and how it would help.

"If we lay it out in easy form and don't look like we're trying to hide anything, it's money in the bank," Devins said, glancing easily at each face. "Just tell it like it is."

After the meeting, the Devins forces went to work. With only two weeks left, they had their plan assembled. He'd already been producing three television spots that focused on how much each person would have to pay in taxes; exactly how the taxes would be repaid and where it would go; and the amounts that would be set aside for athletic and school programs.

Each spot also used charts to explain how much revenue was expected to be brought in from higher attendance at a new, comfortable ballpark and how much more the overall economy in the city would benefit if the Giants remained, and how much it would be hurt if the Giants left.

Those facts were the centerpiece of Devins's approach. He made sure to weave each of them into the spots, which began running constantly on local television stations.

Then, to drive the point home, Devins organized a number of neighborhood meetings, where he brought economic experts and city finance officials to explain the tax approach. While they admitted that the supervisors could increase the tax if needed and that the school and athletic program money was set aside only for the Recreation Department, they drove home the idea that both the supervisors and the recreation commissioners were beholden to taxpayers.

"The law requires that we have that flexibility in there," Devins told a crowd at a Mission District meeting one night. "But you, the voters, always have the control to tell these bureaucrats what you want. You are ultimately in charge because you can keep them in line."

Like Billy, Devins knew that voters liked being told they were in charge. And, of course, he made sure that local reporters from newspapers, television, radio, and even small cable outfits and weekly neighborhood rags were invited to every neighborhood meeting and given a copy of every television and radio spot.

The newspapers did a major job of covering the meetings and the pro-stadium campaign—especially, of course, the *Bulletin* and the *Journal*, which continued to seek passage of their necessary measure.

Callahan, meanwhile, appeared at almost every neighborhood meeting during the final two weeks, stressing that he'd backed the stadium plan from the beginning and was willing to break with Billy Dale to pursue it. Their split had received major coverage separate from the campaign itself.

Both the *Bulletin* and the *Journal* had written about the division between the campaign manager and the mayor he had brought to power, while Mike McLean had also written about it in several columns attacking the stadium proposal and accusing Callahan of supporting the project out of fear.

"Mayor Callahan has turned his back on the city that elected him," McLean wrote in a piece that ran one week before Election Day. "The mayor suffered a defeat on his homeless plan, so instead of sticking to his guns and opposing an unfair tax to support a millionaire baseball team owner, he sides with big business and the city's daily newspaper power structure, leaving the people to suffer the consequences."

Billy Dale also pulled out all the stops in efforts to debunk the progress that

Devins and the stadium forces were making. His television and radio spots offered opposing viewpoints from economists, city officials, and neighborhood and anti-tax groups that questioned the validity of the economic improvement arguments, especially the idea that the stadium tax would not be increased and the athletic and social program money could not, somehow, be diverted.

One of Billy's television commercials received strong attention and criticism when it showed dramatizations of Recreation Commissioners flying to foreign countries and the Caribbean with tax money. The spots were clear to say that none of the funds could be used for any purpose without a commission vote during a public meeting, at which time public comment could be heard. They also stressed that no one on the commission had indicated the money would be used for anything but the athletic and social programs.

Still, the commercials drove home the theme that the money was not restricted to only the programs for which it was targeted.

"Don't give away the city's hard-earned money to those who could abuse it," the commercial tagline indicated. "The stadium plan is a plan without thinking."

Billy ran the spots aggressively along with neighborhood meetings and rallies similar to those organized by Devins. As the campaign headed into its final week, both sides were neck-and-neck. Polls showed that the ballot measure was favored by voters, but only by a slim 49% to 51%.

Billy Dale knew that things could go his way with a more aggressive push of the negative factors, but he also knew time was running out. He needed an ace to spring on voters at the last minute. He had run his career on the aggressive tactics of hard-edged politicking, but also on finding out every piece of dirt on the opposition that was possible.

"We're in good shape, but we need more," Billy told Jimmy Min during a late-night planning session on the Wednesday before Election Day. With less than one week to go, the race was too close to take for granted, but also too close to assume no shot at winning.

Jimmy heard Billy's concern, but did not completely lose hope. For weeks he'd had his reporters out scouting for dirt on any part of the pro-stadium campaign. He knew that they couldn't really go after Callahan because all of the mayor's dirty baggage had been revealed in his mayoral race.

Besides, going after the mayor would not be enough in this campaign. He was only a well-known supporter. Attacking him on any grounds would not spell defeat for the stadium plan, only for Callahan's political future.

Instead, Jimmy directed reporters, and even Mike McLean, to dig into the Giants, Vernon Bogart, and everyone else involved with the stadium measure. Although they continued to seek dirt on both the *Bulletin* and *Journal* hierarchies, Jimmy knew that attacks on the two dailies also carried minimal gain.

The opposition forces had to target the stadium plan itself. And, while the information was good about the flaws in the ballot measure and the possibility that it could cost taxpayers more than they thought, it was obvious that it was not doing the trick.

Investigations into the Giants held few valuable nuggets of information as well. From tax records to criminal reports at Candlestick Park, the reporters dug up few useable items to throw out to voters. Even investigations into Bogart were proving fruitless. The Giants' owner, while an obviously arrogant money-grubber, had not been in trouble with the law and had not had so much as a parking ticket or a jaywalking citation in years.

Still, Jimmy's forces continued to search old newspapers, city records... everything they could find. They ran Bogart's name through every legal and illegal government check possible.

The efforts seemed impossible.

Then, late Thursday afternoon, McLean found something. While the outspoken columnist had not done deep reporting for several years, he'd given his all on this search.

Knowing that the key to stopping the stadium proposal lay in finding something to make Bogart look bad, McLean had gone to every end. He searched newspaper and legal archives throughout California, and outside of the state as well. That's where he uncovered what held the fate of the anti-stadium coalition.

During a check of names in the archives of the St. Louis Herald-News, the city's biggest daily paper, McLean found a 10-year-old story that could bring what the anti-stadium folks needed. A short item written before Bogart ever became the Giants owner described a simple incident that could hold Billy and Jimmy's ace.

The article described a traffic accident in which Bogart, in St. Louis on business at the time, had struck and injured a 15-year-old girl. The accident occurred at night and, although Bogart was not legally drunk, he had tested positive for alcohol in his bloodstream. Because of a legal technicality that allowed the results to be nullified if he had not been adequately informed of his rights, they were not used in court. Therefore, he was not found liable for the accident, which had left the young girl paralyzed.

The article was not long, but had made it into the newspaper because the girl was a star gymnast in the area. The story stated that Bogart had slammed into the girl as she rode her bicycle home from a friend's house. Initially, the article targeted her injuries and pain and the fact that her dreams of becoming a great gymnast would not be fulfilled.

Then, when word of the drunk driving test technicality arose, one follow-up story occurred mentioning Bogart. Since he was from out of town, he was allowed to go free and not worry about future legal hassles. No appeals were ever made because the law was clear. He had not been properly informed of his rights before the test and, therefore, he was gone and could not be shown to have acted improperly, even though he was legally drunk.

"This is a tragedy, but what can we do," said a prosecutor who had wanted to charge Bogart, but had to allow the case to be dismissed. "This is the way it is."

Parents of the girl, Laurie Jones, contacted a lawyer and attempted to take Bogart to court on a civil complaint seeking damages. But because there were no witnesses to the incident, they could not prove that Bogart had done anything wrong. All they had was a drunk driving test that was inadmissible and his word against the girl's. The entire matter ended within weeks. Since Bogart was a virtual unknown in San Francisco at the time, nothing was ever written about it in the Bay Area.

But now, things were different. The moment McLean found the story he immediately got on the phone to the St. Louis paper and found the reporter who'd written the original article. He had since moved up to editor, but had always recalled the quirky nature of the case. He did not remember Bogart's name and had to be reminded that he had since made himself famous as the owner of the Giants.

Through the reporter, McLean also tracked down Laurie Jones herself. She was still paralyzed, but had made a career out of teaching gymnastics and running a physical therapy clinic in a St. Louis suburb. The next day, Friday, McLean and Billy Dale flew to St. Louis and met her.

When they landed in the Missouri city, they found their way to Laurie's clinic and immediately set out to interview her. She had long gotten over the pain and frustration of what had happened, and even looked upon it as a message from God that she was put on earth to help other gymnasts and aid injured people in getting over their injuries, she explained.

"I am no longer angry," she told the two men during a brief discussion in her office. "I had a long struggle with this and with my career, but it's been over ten years and I don't want to go back. What good would it do?"

As the woman with sparkling blue eyes, deep dark hair, and a baby-faced smile spoke kindly, Billy and McLean listened as their enthusiasm dimmed. They knew that it would be difficult to get her to help them if she had put the case behind her. But they knew they had to do everything they could.

"I love my life, my husband, and my children. I love being able to help these kids do what I could not and bring others back from pain to try again," she said, smiling.

As Jones spoke politely to the two visitors, Billy glanced around her office. It contained the usual medical diplomas and association memberships of any health-related business. But, in one corner, he glanced at a sea of awards, framed photos, and magazine headlines from Laurie's days as a gymnast.

Those mementos, trophies, and medals were not out in obvious display, but the fact that they remained in view meant that they remained in Laurie's mind. She might have gotten over her pain, but it was clear she still remembered the joys and desires of being a competitive athlete.

"Well, how about if we let you show that you have overcome your pain," Billy asked as Laurie listened quietly and leaned back in her chair. "We only need you to tell people what happened. If you don't want to express anger or depression over it, that's fine. Tell them how you feel, no matter what. Maybe the fact that you overcame this tragedy could help others in San Francisco who might be going through the same thing."

McLean glanced at Billy as he waited for Laurie's response. He knew what Billy was trying to do and thought it just might work.

Laurie brushed her short hair back and put her head in her hands to think. As Billy and McLean waited for some sign of decisiveness, she lifted her head and wheeled herself out from behind the desk, toward the main rehab room of the clinic.

Looking through the doorway at three youngsters being put through daily therapeutic routines, she pondered the idea. After a minute, she came to a decision and spun her chair around quickly.

"Okay," she said, with an unemotional look on her face. "I'll let you tell my story and even let you take a photo, but I am not going to San Francisco. I don't want to turn this into a rehash of my life. But if it can help someone over there who needs to know that life goes on, I'll do it."

Billy flashed a grin at McLean, who smiled back.

Then, Laurie began to speak, McLean to write, and Billy to plan how best to make this work. After two hours interviewing her, both men got back on a plane and headed west. They went from the airport straight to the *Advocate* offices.

Billy had immediately called Jimmy once the woman gave the okay for the story to let him know what was happening and to allow him to create the front page of a special Saturday *Advocate*. Billy also borrowed a photographer from the Herald-News, who was glad to take some photos.

The Herald-News editors, once they got wind of what the *Advocate* was doing, also decided to run a story based on McLean's work and offered to trade photos for a copy of McLean's final story, which the St. Louis paper planned to run the following week as an update on Laurie Jones.

When Billy and McLean reached the *Advocate*, McLean was nearly finished with his story. He had begun to write it on the plane and needed only some final touches upon landing. He waited until just an hour before deadline to call Bogart's office and ask for his comment.

He didn't want anything to be leaked too soon, but he also knew that Bogart would not likely reveal this damaging information to competing papers.

Bogart was stunned. The Giants owner, who had already been planning a victory party for Tuesday night, responded with both shock and fierce anger at the *Advocate*. He had not at all forgotten about the incident, but he had rarely thought about it since a court had okayed him to leave St. Louis ten years earlier.

"What can I say?" Bogart asked McLean. "You know what happened. I was never proven to be at fault and I never broke any law. This has nothing to do with my baseball team or this stadium proposal."

But that didn't matter. Both Bogart and Billy knew that this could hurt the prospects for passage. Although the story of Bogart causing the crippling injury of a promising young gymnast in St. Louis more than a decade earlier had nothing to do with the validity of a stadium ballot measure 2,000 miles away, both men knew that anything showing the Giants owner in a negative light would mean a serious blow to the Election Day proposal.

The key lay in the fact that the ballot measure asked voters to pay for Bogart's new stadium so that his team could stay in San Francisco and, in essence, make more money. If Bogart was portrayed in any way as someone who is greedy or heartless, voters would find little reason to support anything he wanted. Especially if there is a hint that it could raise voter taxes, something Billy had already pointed out in earlier ads.

Billy and Jimmy Min knew that they were on to something. They quickly assembled the special issue late into the night Friday. McLean wrote the main story, along with a column that slammed Bogart for not only ending the promising career of a young, athletic girl because of a drunk driving mistake, but also for being allowed to walk away from it.

Although the story quoted Laurie as saying she'd moved on in life and truly found satisfaction in her career, it showed enough ambivalence in her mind about what she might have done had the accident not occurred.

"Sure, I will always want to know how far I could have gone," Laurie was quoted as saying in the main story. "But I will never know and I have come to terms with that fact."

That quote and the overall story held enough disappointment about a promising gymnast star being cut down to give nearly every voter in San Francisco reason to pause. Sure, most knew that Bogart's conduct years earlier was no indication of the stadium measure's positive attributes, but for those on the fence in such a tight race, it could be enough to make a difference.

McLean also pushed the point home with power in his column, which ran right next to the main story. In it, he slammed Bogart for not even visiting

Laurie in the hospital and for allowing the incident to be put behind him, while she "still lives with it every day of her life."

"The idea that a man such as Vernon Bogart, who took the dreams of a young girl away through his negligence and carelessness, would ask voters to trust him with their money is absurd," McLean wrote. "If Laurie Jones cannot trust Bogart to let her ride her bicycle safely, how can San Francisco trust him to handle our money or the future of one of the city's most important, and costly, public projects?"

The story and column were classic Billy Dale and Mike McLean. And the *Advocate* played both to the hilt. Using one of its largest headlines ever, the newspaper played it straight, labeling the story, "Bogart's Giant Skeleton."

The lead in the story said plainly: "Giants owner Vernon Bogart has a skeleton in his closet. Her name is Laurie Jones." The story went on to tell the tale of what had happened, with clear indications of how Bogart had been found not to have broken the law, but also specific information about the drunk driving test and the appeals efforts, along with Laurie's comments in a sidebar story on how she had put her life together but still wondered about her lost career.

Late Friday night, as the presses rolled, the *Advocate* also sent out press releases to each of the newspapers—especially the *Bulletin* and *Journal*—along with faxes and phone calls to each television and radio station. Some broke into their 11 p.m. newscasts with late word of the story, crediting the *Advocate* each time.

Channel 6 had even read the fax word for word right on the air as its anchorman used the item to close the show, given no time to even rewrite the press release or get a comment from Bogart. Several radio stations used the story, with only one having any word from Bogart, who offered a simple "I have nothing to add, this is behind me."

The special Saturday edition of the *Advocate* arrived at homes and newsstands about an hour late, but the damage had already been done. Since Jimmy had given advance word of the story to broadcast outlets, it was buzzing on the street about the incident before the paper was even finished delivering.

Should it affect the stadium vote? Should voters care if Bogart was involved in a crippling accident if the stadium plan is solid? And should voters give their tax dollars to this project if the Giants owner has had a mixed past?

All of those questions were being asked by residents, city officials, and the press.

At the pro-stadium campaign headquarters Saturday morning, Carl Devins pondered the entire situation. He was not surprised that Billy and the *Advocate* would pull this kind of stunt, but he was concerned about how it would play. The *Bulletin* and the *Journal* had not run a story on Laurie Jones in their Saturday issues, but he knew they would have to put something in the Sunday paper.

Ironically, the later story would help Billy and the anti-stadium cause more because it would give the story a second-day play and put it in the most popular edition of the week. Both Emily Ingle and Donald Grossman were immediately contacted about the issue by their editors and asked how to report it.

All the *Bulletin* or the *Journal* could do was play it straight, not look as though they were hiding anything, but also not give it too much major attention. The television and radio news, along with the *Advocate*, had already made sure that the word had gotten out, so there was no way to hide it. But both Ingle and Grossman knew that they could cushion the blow if they made it appear that Bogart was sorry and that Laurie Jones held no ill will.

For their Sunday papers, both publishers decided that a Page One story was needed, but at the bottom of the page. They also made sure that each showed Laurie only from the neck up, so that her wheelchair could not be seen.

The stories included comments from Laurie, who was contacted by phone and was willing to talk to the reporters who interviewed her. They provided mostly upbeat comments about how she did not harbor anger at Bogart and had actually been able to find "a new purpose in life."

Bogart was quoted as saying he'd spoken to Laurie on Saturday and understood that she'd gotten beyond the accident. He also said he had been truly sorry about it and would do anything to make it up to her, including financial assistance.

In addition, Carl Devins had been quoted as saying that, while the entire city is saddened for Laurie's tragedy, it should not affect the stadium measure, "which is a vital, civic need for the city."

The stories ran on Sunday with a string of new follow-up stories on each local broadcast medium about them, and several editorials on the television and radio stations offered mixed views of how the story should be taken by voters.

Some, such as KBKK Radio, slammed Bogart and told voters not to "let this criminal make off with your money," while others, like KKSF-TV, offered pleading requests for voters not to give in to "smear tactics from the anti-stadium forces who simply want to block progress."

Bogart even spoke at a press conference where he talked about how he wanted to do everything to help Laurie Jones, but also wanted to make sure that the stadium plan gave San Francisco "its best new project in decades."

On Monday, just 24 hours before the final vote, the *Advocate* came out with another special edition that included a poll showing a dead heat. 49.6% of voters were still in favor of the proposal, while 50.4% were against it. The poll was not even an *Advocate*-skewed survey, either. It had been conducted by one of the top independent polling groups from Los Angeles, well out of the Bay Area's influence range.

Billy Dale, who had commissioned the poll, said he wanted clear numbers showing exactly how the Laurie Jones story had played and what his chances were going into the last day.

Then, by about noon on Monday, Billy unleashed his final assault.

Since returning on Friday, he had been in touch with an outdoor advertising firm linked to the Min family and had them working on an all-out blitz of billboards and bus signs with a final slam against Bogart's drunk driving incident. The last-minute ad, which hit ten major billboards in town and more than half of the bus stop shelter signs, showed an expressionless Laurie Jones sitting in her wheelchair, in front of her medals and trophies, with a simple message below her: "This is what Vernon Bogart did to me, don't let him do the same thing to San Francisco—Vote No on the Stadium Plan."

The billboards and signs went up Monday afternoon, too late for any kind of real response from Bogart and just in time to put the message into voters' minds as they went to the polls Tuesday. Bogart saw the first one when he walked out of his downtown office for lunch. It was smack in the middle of Market Street, one of the city's busiest roadways, and faced nearly every car that traveled down the massive main corridor.

The minute Bogart saw it, he got in a cab and raced to Devins's office. He didn't find his campaign manager there but saw him walking up the street as he was leaving. "Did you see this bullshit they're pulling?" Bogart asked. "What can we do about it?"

Devins, who was not used to the hardball tactics and had long-ago refused to be roped into them, didn't tell his client what he wanted to hear. "I know it's a low blow, but we can't do much about it except keep putting our side out there," Devins said as he scratched his beard. "It's up to the voters."

That was not what Bogart wanted to hear. He grabbed another cab and raced across town to Billy Dale's office. When he got there, he ran past the secretary and broke into a meeting Billy was having with a pollster and several campaign workers.

"You son of a bitch, this bullshit is your doing and it's a rotten, fucking trick," Bogart said, throwing his briefcase against the wall. "I knew that you played dirty, but this is out of bounds. It's bad enough you come after me, but to drag some kid into it who's been through enough is pointless." Billy got up from his chair as Bogart ranted.

"I'm not the one who hit her and got away with it when the cops in St. Louis fucked up," Billy said calmly. "You did it to yourself. If you didn't want to play rough, you should have found another way to build your fucking ballpark. Now get the hell out of here before I call the cops. I happen to know a few of them pretty well."

As Bogart moved toward Billy, two of Billy's larger, taller campaign workers grabbed him and shoved him out of the office, sending him to the outer lobby, and out on to Van Ness Avenue. Turning away from the door, Bogart couldn't help but see another one of the billboards at the corner of Van Ness and Geary.

"I'll get you for this, Billy Dale," he yelled up to Billy's office, where he could just barely see him standing through the window. "You'll finally get what's coming to you."

The angry team owner didn't even think about where he was headed. All he could imagine was the manipulation that Billy Dale could wield. Sure, Bogart knew that he had made a mistake years ago, but never thought it would come back to haunt him. All he wanted was some reward for years of building up the wine business his father had dumped on him from his deathbed with a pile of tax bills and labor problems.

Bogart had jumped into the winery just days after graduating from Sacramento State University with a business degree 30 years earlier, but had no use for the wine business when he was 22. He always had an eye on the stock market and had dreamed of making his fortune in downtown San Francisco's Pacific Stock Exchange, then possibly on Wall Street. He knew that he could parlay any winnings into a successful political career.

While most lawyers thought they had a shoo-in to politics, Bogart knew even in the '60s that businessmen would be the next generation's political leaders. Not only because they had always been able to buy their way in, but because the state of politics was demanding that people with a head for fiscal common-sense replace those whose only ability had been to shake hands and utilize polling data.

Ironically, when Bogart first met Billy Dale a few years earlier at a cocktail party for the Giants, he immediately hit it off with Billy's savvy political sense. Billy had talked about the need to go all out in campaigns and put the other guy on the defensive. Bogart liked that approach.

"Politics will get easier for businessmen because it is already too difficult for people whose only attribute is a phony smile," Billy had told Bogart that night. "The money has always been the key, but now it will be politicians having to make money for the people rather than the other way around."

But after being dragged into taking over the family business after his father, Dylan Bogart, died of a surprise heart attack at the age of 49, Vernon Bogart's only claim to political success lay in the stadium ballot measure. Although he'd grown to love the wine business, he still longed for a taste of the political and business worlds that he craved as a college graduate.

Running the Giants from a distance had fulfilled some of that dream, although their fortunes on the field were often better than those in the ledger sheets. Bogart's desire to taste the fruit of politics remained unquenched. If Billy Dale were to take that second passion away, especially with such a last-minute smear campaign, Bogart would be livid.

Billy just smiled as he watched Bogart walking down to the corner to grab another cab. He didn't pay any attention to the threats; he was more concerned with making sure every phone bank was ready for Tuesday and that all of the campaign signs and billboards remained up and unobstructed.

"Have our people keep an eye on everything at all times," he told his workers. "We don't want any problems at the last minute."

*   *   *

On Tuesday morning, both campaigns were out in full force. Billy's people were on the phone reminding voters to vote and urging that they knock down the stadium plan, while Devins and the Giants pushed phone banks in favor of the stadium. Several Giants players from the current and past teams also walked precincts with workers, handed out literature, and even gave rides to elderly and poor voters.

As the polls closed, no predictions could be made beyond a high voter turn-out. Rain had been forecast but had not materialized and cool breezes moved with sun to make it one of the most beautiful Election Days ever. At City Hall, the Elections Director's office ran smoothly but predicted that results might come slowly due to the high turnout that was hitting 70% of registered voters, a huge ballot total.

As evening turned to nighttime, more people crowded into the Elections Director's office for the annual ritual of waiting for results. Reporters, politicians, campaign consultants, and even some homeless people milled about.

At about 9:30 p.m., the first votes came in and showed a continued dead heat. Out of about 250,000 votes cast, 127,000 were against the stadium, while 123,000 were in favor. But that was less than half of the total votes expected.

Neither Devins, Billy Dale, Bogart, or the mayor for that matter, had shown up by 10 p.m., when another 100,000 votes had been counted and the same close margin continued.

Radio and television reporters on the scene fed stories of the tight ballot count as all the broadcast stations cut in with updates. Reporters also interviewed everyone from sports bar patrons to homeless residents on what they thought of the stadium issue and the Laurie Jones story.

As expected, feelings were mixed. But either way, everyone knew that this vote was going to mean change for the city. The Giants would either stay for the next 50 years or so with a new ballpark, or likely move out with an angry

Vernon Bogart leading the way.

Most regular voters, however, didn't surmise the impact the situation had on Jack Callahan. The outcome of the stadium vote would be a key element in his political future, at least for the next year. Although Callahan still had three years to go in his first term, the failed homeless plan, coupled with a stadium measure that lost with his support, would be a big hole to dig out of when the following year rolled around.

If the stadium plan failed to win voter approval, Callahan would have two strikes against him and might face the prospect of supporters jumping ship and starting to look for someone else to support in the next election.

Still, as the night went on, most people were simply curious about where this vote would go. They didn't worry about the impact on Callahan's career, Billy Dale's scorecard, or even the *Advocate*'s political sway in the future. They wanted to know if the Giants would stay in town, and if they would have their taxes raised for a new ballpark to do it.

Results kept rolling in through midnight without a final determination when the clock struck 12, while the lead margin remained at 5 percent or less.

Then, finally, at 1:30 a.m., the final totals were in, when the voter turn-out topped 550,256. That breakdown with all absentee and late votes counted included 275,100 in favor of the stadium and 275,136 against.

The stadium plan had lost by only 36 votes. That meant Vernon Bogart had lost, Mayor Callahan had lost, and Billy Dale had won… again.

After the Elections Director read off the final numbers at City Hall, the small crowd of about 25 people, mostly reporters and camera crews, gave a mixed, emotional reaction. Some cheered, others booed, but most marveled at the close final vote.

At a downtown hotel where bunting, decorations and music were ready to celebrate the victory, the pro-stadium campaign sulked in defeat. Mayor Callahan gave reporters his mix of sadness and resentment, but with a vow to keep trying to help San Francisco do its best. Carl Devins said he would seek a recount and pointed out that he had maintained his record of positive campaigns.

But Vernon Bogart was nowhere to be found.

After hearing word of the final vote, he'd jumped in the limousine he'd hired for the evening and ordered the driver to take him to the anti-stadium campaign headquarters at the Longshoreman's Union Hall near Fisherman's Wharf. When he got there, he could hear Billy Dale giving a victory speech, with Jimmy Min at his side.

After entering the loud, celebratory room, which featured a band playing "Happy Days Are Here Again," Bogart looked around for his nemesis. He sneered when he saw the baseball hats that campaign workers were wearing.

They sported Giants team colors, but instead of the SF insignia, the hats proclaimed, "Stop the Stadium."

Bogart grew red-hot angry as he looked around to see the campaigners celebrating his defeat. Although it was almost 2 a.m., the place was still mobbed with people toasting champagne and eating everything from hot dogs to caviar. Finally, his eye caught Billy Dale as he proclaimed the election to be "a victory for voter rights and taxpayer truth."

As Billy began to leave the stage that held the podium, Bogart darted toward him. Shoving aside campaign workers on each side, the Giants owner became angrier with every step. Billy was busy hugging well-wishers and high-fiving campaign workers when he noticed Bogart coming forward. His first reaction was to prepare for a victorious, snide comment to fling at his rival.

But before he could put together his usual in-your-face tirade, Billy saw Bogart reach into his pocket for something and almost stopped in mid-step. As the man approached Billy, he walked faster and faster, nearly running when he reached the middle of the union hall floor and gritting his teeth as he got closer.

Billy didn't think to run, he was more curious at exactly what was happening than wondering whether to be afraid. Billy couldn't tell if Bogart was about to hit him or throw something at him.

Then he saw it.

Just as Bogart reached the bottom of the steps leading from the stage and podium to the floor, he pulled out a knife. The flash of bright, shiny metal glinted off the bright overhead lamps that flooded the room with light and momentarily struck Billy's vision with a flash.

Before Billy could duck, Bogart reared back and threw the sharpened object at him, using the same careful quick motion as a knife-thrower at a circus.

At the same time, Billy reached to his ankle for the small pistol he'd carried with him regularly since the Starbanger incident more than 20 years earlier and pulled it up to eye level.

Raising the weapon to its upright position, and squinting one eye quickly as he aimed, Billy squeezed the trigger with a loose, shaky grasp, firing two rounds just as the knife came at him.

The short blade caught Billy in the neck just as he tried to duck, causing him to drop the gun and grab for his throat with a squeal that pierced most ears in the room. When the gun went off, Bogart grabbed at his chest. The first shot struck him square in the heart, while the other darted into his forehead. Both men slumped to the ground, blood spurting from their bodies.

After only a moment it was clear. Billy Dale was wounded, but Bogart was dead. ■

Chapter Eleven

An Almost Impossible Situation

Steve Brown had not investigated a homicide in nearly ten years when word of Vernon Bogart's death reached him early Wednesday morning. Brown had climbed the police ladder during the previous decade, as he battled for department power, played the political games that were required of aspiring cops, and supported politicians such as Callahan who needed his help.

That time in the hand-shaking, back-slapping world had paid off handsomely just ten months earlier when Callahan chose Brown as his new chief. He had no reason to look into a shooting death

But this would likely be the biggest police case of the year in San Francisco on that late Election Night. This murder combined the death of the city's most well-known sports mogul with its most outspoken political campaigner.

On top of that, it held a good argument for self-defense, but also a likely charge of carrying a concealed weapon. To add to the insanity, police had at least 100 witnesses, including a handful of television crews that caught the incident on tape.

Brown entered the Longshoreman's Hall Wednesday morning just after 2:30 a.m. and let out an angry, loud yawn, scratched his head, and ordered the first officer he saw to fetch him a cup of coffee. Surveying the scene, which consisted of ripped down bunting, food wrappers blowing in the cool building, and campaign signs falling off walls, the rookie chief also caught a whiff of stale cigar smoke mixed with liquor and gourmet coffee.

Most of the crowd had left the scene, but a few campaign workers and Giants fans had stayed to find out what had happened, along with a string of reporters that had grown after the story of the night changed from a stadium ballot measure loss to the death of the Giants' owner.

The moment they saw Brown, every camera crew, reporter, and radio correspondent lunged forward with mechanical devices in Brown's face, and a mountain of questions to toss at him.

"What happened?"

"Is Billy Dale under arrest?"

"Did he act in self-defense?"

"What charges will be filed?"

Brown put his hands up to quiet the crowd like a teacher hushing a misbehaving kindergarten class, cleared his throat, and tried to say something authoritative.

"All right, all right. All I know is what you know. I just got here," Brown said as the camera lights shot on and reporters began writing. "We have the area secured and every piece of information is being gathered. I will let you know as soon as I know."

With that, two officers roped off the scene with yellow crime scene tape as Brown walked into the area where the shooting had occurred. Billy Dale had been moved to San Francisco General Hospital, where Brown had already heard by police radio that he was in stable condition with a serious neck wound.

But, of course, Bogart's fate was not as positive. The dead body of the Giants' owner lay crumpled under a white sheet at Brown's feet, with a pool of blood drying up around him.

Brown had not been forced to endure that sight since his last homicide investigation nine-and-a-half years earlier when he looked into the death of a Tenderloin prostitute who was shot to death by her drug-dealing pimp. Although not an unusual occurrence, the murder had received wide acclaim because the pimp had been a wanted man for allegedly killing a string of hookers in previous years.

Brown's efforts to catch and convict that killer had been one of the key reasons he was later promoted to commander, and then deputy chief before becoming chief. Brown had been recognized for his ability to profile a killer's motive and intent, along with personality traits. His college education in both psychology and sociology had aided him during most of his police career.

But the likely outcome of this case would require someone deft at the art of political science and public opinion more than criminology. As Brown guided the search for clues, fingerprints, and witnesses, his mind looked ahead to how the police would handle the unusual murder, and what, if anything, they could charge against Billy Dale.

Sure, there could be arguments made for Billy acting in self-defense. But carrying a concealed weapon was a felony right away, punishable by one to four years in jail. Since Bogart had likely struck first, the public could probably see clear to allowing Billy to serve a lesser sentence or none at all.

But anti-gun types, of which San Francisco had more than its fair share, might not take kindly to a political operative being allowed to slide past the state's tough gun control laws, especially when he is at least a former friend of the mayor's.

Brown took all of this into consideration when the coroner's hearse pulled up to the Longshoreman's Hall, placed Bogart's bloody body in the rear, and drove off to the medical examiner's office located just downstairs from Brown's office at the Hall of Justice.

For the next hour, Brown consulted with the police who had been on the scene for crowd control, while both D.A. Haynes and Callahan made their way to the crime scene.

Haynes, too, had been asleep when the early morning shooting took place. But Callahan, still hoping for a victory at the pro-stadium campaign head-quarters, was among the first outside the crime scene to hear the news. After the shooting, several reporters called over to the other campaign party to tell fellow reporters about the incident. Some had spread word around the head-quarters, prompting many—including Callahan—to race to the union hall.

For the mayor, the death of Bogart raised myriad thoughts and concerns. He felt anger at his old partner in political crime, Billy Dale, but also frustra-tion, guilt, and helplessness.

The mayor had been dragged into running for office. Sure, he enjoyed it. Hell, he had come to love the power of the mayoralty, which had given him both new prominence and control to do things he wanted to do.

Even though he had not had the idea to run, he knew that he could truly do some good now that he held the post. But during the past year and a half, he also discovered the down-and-dirty world of politics. A world that had made him fall into the traps of Billy Dale's strategies—be them backhandedness, deceit, or downright lying. Now, here in front of him, he had also seen death.

Sure, maybe Bogart deserved it for attacking Billy. He had always been an egomaniac who probably couldn't stand the thought of losing, and further couldn't handle it based on something in his past. That slam at Bogart's reputa-tion was probably the last straw that drove him to attack Billy rather than the loss of the ballot measure itself.

For Bogart, Callahan realized, having the fame and power that his own-ership title held was even more attractive than having a new stadium for his team to play in. But the mayor also realized that Billy's tactics had come home to haunt him.

Billy always played the hardest hardball there was, mostly because that was what worked and was the easier way out. But now Callahan saw that Billy's tactics were hurting the true needs of San Francisco, both on the City Hall front and on the daily lives of its residents.

After more than an hour, Brown, Callahan, and Haynes held a quick, im-promptu press conference before the reporters at just after 4:00 a.m. The news was not much different from Brown's first words to the press. Bogart was dead,

Billy was in the hospital in serious but stable condition, both weapons were in police possession, and no one else was hurt.

"We are still investigating," Haynes said, giving the standard law enforcement line. "We are not sure what, if any, charges will be filed and we still have a lot of police work to do."

The only other thing everyone wanted to know was what Callahan thought of this. Here was the owner of the Giants, a man whose stadium plan Callahan supported, killed by Callahan's former campaign manager—the man who put him into office, but had also just turned against him.

The mayor, knowing that whatever he said would be scrutinized for days, gave a simple, vague response.

"I have no comment on the legality of what Billy Dale did, but of course the loss of any human life is tragic," the mayor said. "Beyond that, I will wait along with you to find out what the investigation reveals."

Callahan, Brown, and Haynes spent another hour going over the details of what had happened among themselves and, more importantly, the different scenarios that could occur with the prosecution of Billy Dale, and the likely outcome of each.

Back in the offices of the *Bulletin* and the *Journal*, reporters were scrambling to put stories together, while photographers, all of whom had gotten some piece of the shooting on film, raced to develop their evidence and get it into the pages as soon as possible.

For the *Journal*, which did not produce its first edition until 11 a.m., and ran four editions up to 3 p.m., getting the shooting on the front page would not be difficult. Although the usual 3 a.m. deadline for the first edition had passed, Editor Tim Cross was confident that the delay would not hurt coverage. The paper devoted the top half of the front page to the shooting, with the bottom used for coverage of the defeated stadium proposal.

The stadium story in both papers also included a question about what would happen to the Giants now that Vernon Bogart was dead. Although the stadium deal had been defeated, the man who'd pushed for it and threatened to move without it was now deceased, leaving the future of the team up to the next owners—whoever they might be.

At the *Bulletin*, which had missed its deadline hours earlier, editor J.C. Townsend had been given direct orders from publisher Sam Allen to put out a special edition as quickly as possible. It featured a similar breakup of the front page between the shooting and the stadium defeat, but also sported a sidebar on the future of the Giants. Without Bogart there to direct its next move, the team remained in limbo, at least until a successor was chosen.

The frantic newsroom hum of any busy election night had increased tenfold with the shooting story. All of the election night results had to be shoved into the back and replaced with highlights of both Billy Dale and Vernon Bogart's lives and careers, as well as some explanation of the self-defense laws and the gun control legislation that had only recently been approved in Sacramento.

Finally, at about 11:30 a.m., both papers put out their first issues with coverage of the shooting. The *Bulletin* took the more business-like approach with its headline stating: "Giants Owner Shot Dead after Pulling Knife on Anti-stadium Campaign Chief."

For the *Journal*, which usually sported quicker, snappier heads, the top column read simply "Giants' Bogart Dead, Billy Dale Wounded."

As the newspapers hit the stands and hawkers roamed city streets pushing copies of the big story that late morning, Billy Dale woke for the first time since he had come to the hospital. Looking out of the sixth-floor window that gave him a scenic view of the Mission District, Billy choked as he tried to swallow and rubbed the bandages covering the puncture wound that Bogart's knife had made in his neck.

Watching the city buses go by on 23rd Street, Billy mulled over the night before. A nurse had brought up copies of both newspapers, which made Billy smile for the publicity but also sigh in frustration about what they meant.

Here had been one of his greatest comeback triumphs yet, along with one of his best backdoor slams of any opponent since Carlson's hotel room caper, and Billy knew he had scored big.

But he also knew that things had gotten out of hand. This killing could not only hurt his future efforts politically, but could also land him in jail for breaking the state's concealed weapon law, or even for murder.

As the sun tried to tap through the foggy clouds outside, Billy remembered writing a letter of protest against the concealed handgun law only months earlier. He had not gone out of his way to oppose it, knowing that such a move would put Callahan on the spot at the time. But he had used some of his influence in Sacramento to try to stop it. Knowing that he would not have been able to protect himself as he had for the past 20 years, Billy wanted his and other gun owners' rights served.

After a nurse brought him a change of bandage and some pills, and checked on his IV, Billy also thought back one year ago to the day after the last Election Day he had endured. That morning was a far cry from this one. Then, Billy had made his greatest move yet with a new mayor, new prestige, and also a boost to Jimmy Min and the *Advocate* just 365 days before.

But today he didn't know if he would be able to see any of that again. And, after nearly losing his life, he didn't know if he wanted to take the chance.

As Billy stretched and tried to rest, the pills did their best to make him drowsy and his mind soon wandered off to sleep.

About two hours later, a familiar voice filled the room as Billy remained groggy and tried to rest. Although he was barely awake, he could tell that high-spirited tone right away, but also noticed a familiar angry ring to it. Just as he opened his eyes, his voice took over before he could even make out the face.

"Hi Jimmy," Billy said, with a raspy gargle in his healing throat that sounded like a backed-up sink. "What are you doing? What time is it? What's the latest?"

Jimmy Min, still sporting the tailored suit he had worn the night before in anticipation of victory for the anti-stadium contingent, just spread his well-known smile across his mouth and leaned over to give Billy a hug. When he pulled back, careful not to knock the tubes coming out of his friend, Jimmy's eyes went from smile to serious concern.

"All we know is that Bogart died and they don't know what to do with you," Jimmy said, looking down at the bed and surveying the way Billy's hands were crossed on his lap. "I've been trying to call Callahan and see if we can work a deal with him, but Haynes is another matter."

Billy knew what Jimmy was talking about. Callahan could be swayed if he thought it was in the best interest of his career and the city to go easy on Billy. If Billy could convince him that holding off on a trial, any kind of trial, was the best for all involved—especially after such a deadly election debacle—it might keep Billy out of court.

But Haynes was a trickier matter.

Even when they'd cornered him into letting Benny Min off the hook, the move was hard to pull off. And Haynes had come away from that caper more an enemy of the administration and the *Advocate* then a friend. Besides, this incident was not like an alleged rape from ten years earlier. This was something that everyone saw and that ended with the death of a local celebrity.

Not since former mayor Kit Lange had been gunned down in his office had the city braced for such an important trial. But even laid up in the hospital with a cut throat, tubes sticking out of him, and a bottle of saline in his arm, Billy's mind continued to work.

"Callahan will have to come and see me at some point, and when he does, I will find a way to bring him around," Billy said with a mild grin. "After that, we can find a way to get Haynes to let go."

Jimmy didn't share Billy's optimism, but he smiled just the same and gave his friend's hand a gentle squeeze. The two men had an interesting relationship. Both were gay, both had found a powerful position in San Francisco, but had fallen into careers not of their choosing. Instead of ending up as lovers, they formed a strong bond as friends, a bond that kept them going in times of trouble, but also united their vast, driven energies to claim a major place in city power.

The truth was that Billy had a tougher time ahead of him than he wanted to admit. Haynes would be difficult to coax. After taking so many hits for letting Benny Min off, the D.A. had already put himself through the wringer with the press and the public. What did he owe to Billy? For Haynes, putting Billy away, even for a year, would be a great weight off his shoulders.

In a sense, Callahan could claim the same prize. Now that he and Billy had split over the stadium issue, the mayor also owed no debt to Billy. Callahan could use Billy's help, but if he had to choose between putting Billy away and working with him toward another political firestorm over gun control and self-defense, the best move for Callahan would be to prosecute Billy and get him out.

All of the possibilities gave Billy a bit of a headache. After a few minutes, Jimmy could see that he was in no mood to talk about it.

"Just hang in there, pal," Jimmy said, his smile turning to a serious look. "We will do whatever we have to and like always, you'll come out on top."

After giving his friend another brotherly squeeze on the arm, Jimmy headed out. Watching him leave, Billy wondered if he could pull off any kind of battle against this latest dilemma. This was not another campaign against some spineless politician put up by the other side; this was severe punishment and troubling situations involving life and death.

Billy had killed another person.

Although he had wanted to kill a lot of political enemies, figuratively, he never would have purposefully taken a human life. Sure, he liked taking down his opponents, especially someone like Bogart who stood for everything Billy hated—greed, abuse of the public, and living off of other's work. But to openly take another life, that was not his way.

Listening to the public address system announce that visiting hours were over, Billy hoped that he could pull off what seemed to be his biggest challenge since he came to San Francisco.

First Billy had to prove he had acted in self-defense, and then he had to prove he didn't break one of the strongest—and most popular—gun laws in the country. That thought made him close his eyes and go to sleep. While he tried to find his way into rest, just the hum of the many medical machines down the hall sifted into his ears.

*　*　*

Five days passed before anyone in the District Attorney's office or the police department even hinted at what kind of legal action would be taken against Billy.

Billy had grown stronger and doctors revealed that he would likely have no permanent neck or throat damage. His vocal cords and most major blood veins had not suffered serious injury and the tendons torn by the slashing would be brought back through therapy, doctors hoped.

On the Sunday following the incident, Billy was allowed to leave the hospital. Jimmy and Benny Min both came to take him home and noticed that, although he seemed subdued from medication, his spirits were up. Despite the problems that lay ahead, Billy took the tough, direct approach that he always fell back on when challenges approached.

Since the deadly episode, all of the city's papers provided middle-of-the-road coverage. Danny Dugan didn't take advantage of the bizarre situation in any way. The *Reader* reported both the shooting and stabbing with little bias, other than to say that heated political battles were to blame for such actions, and that local politicos should take a lesson and not let any future campaign upset them to the point of attack.

"For those who would view a political race with more passion than they view their own life's needs, the death of Vernon Bogart should be a reminder," the *Reader* editorial had preached. "For all men and women, the treasure of life is worth more than the expected prize on the victor's side of politics."

At the *Bulletin* and the *Journal*, a similar approach went into effect. Both editors, Townsend and Cross, made sure that they handled this deadly occurrence with careful thought, but also made sure to get all sides.

In the days that followed, both dailies speculated on what the strange turn of events would mean to the Giants, Billy's career and legal standing, and the city's economic health. According to the pro-stadium folks, the city was likely to lose millions if the Giants departed.

As for the Giants, only one newspaper—the *Journal*—bothered to check into who would control the team now that its principal owner was dead. Sure enough, it would be Bogart's son, Teddy, a junior executive in the Bogart wine business and not a man known for his love of baseball. But, because of all of the bizarre and tragic events surrounding his father's death, Teddy made no comments about the future of the team.

"This time is for the city of San Francisco to mourn the passing of a great man, my father," Teddy had told a *Journal* reporter. "It's also a time of healing for factions of the bitter fight over this ballot measure and for the legal system to do what is necessary to punish the man who killed my father. I'm not a vindictive person, but I do want to see justice done."

Although he had not gone out of his way to plead for Billy's head on a stick, that simple comment made it known that Teddy did not want Billy let off with a self-defense plea.

On Monday, nearly a week after Election Day, Steve Brown and Dennis

Haynes met for the first time to seriously discuss how to handle Billy's case. The mayor had wanted to be involved in the discussion, but agreed to step aside so that the two law enforcement leaders could air their feelings together privately without fear of his political input.

Billy, in his usual pushy, man-in-the-know way, wanted to meet with the two. But he also knew that it would not happen given the sensitivity of the case and his reputation for trying to change minds. So both Callahan and Billy waited, in their own homes, as the most important meeting in the Hall of Justice in ten years occurred.

Brown knocked on Haynes's private office just after 10 a.m. The District Attorney answered it personally, holding out a friendly hand to shake as he opened the door. While each tried to put on a momentary air of friendliness, both knew what they had to do.

This was an almost impossible situation.

They couldn't just let Billy off the hook if it appeared that some kind of political deal was going on. But they also couldn't make it look like someone acting in self-defense was being unfairly punished.

For a jury and the public to buy any kind of prosecution, it had to sound fair, with a touch of common sense and enough political censorship to be worth pursuing.

But both men also had their personal feelings to contend with, whether they liked it or not. Each had reason to want Billy put away. No one in the law enforcement community of San Francisco cared much for Billy's outlandish style, especially since he recently turned on the mayor.

After reviewing the evidence, which included transcripts of interviews from witnesses, police reports, and even one television station's video of the incident, both men concluded that they could not prosecute Billy for murder or even manslaughter.

"This would not hold up in court," Haynes told Brown as he watched the end of the television footage, which clearly showed Billy pulling his gun just seconds before the knife pierced his neck. "Worse, anyone who sees this footage, and we know they will, would not vote to convict."

That remark amounted to Haynes's first comment in the three-hour meeting about the prospect of public opinion. The three television stations that had footage of the shooting had agreed to hold off running it—under orders from Haynes and Brown—so as not to offend the families or hurt the investigation.

In truth, both men knew that showing the footage would not affect the investigation, but anything they could do to show control over the situation would help keep the press in line.

But once the investigation ended and a trial got going, Haynes knew the television stations would have the right to show the video. And, just as the Rodney King beating was given a public relations ride in Los Angeles because of tape of the beating, this case would, too.

"We can't do it," Haynes said. "But there is something we will do. Billy Dale broke the law by carrying a concealed weapon. If we go after him for that, you know that we can get a fair conviction and get him out of our hair for at least a year."

Brown smiled. He liked Billy in the beginning when he helped Callahan take office. Shit, he wouldn't be chief, indirectly, if it weren't for Billy helping Callahan win. But since the rift between them, and the trouble caused by Benny Min, Steve Brown had taken a decidedly different view of Billy Dale.

"It'll be a tough call," the police chief said, as he leaned back in the leather chair seated directly across from Haynes's oak desk. "We're going to get it from both sides."

Haynes nodded, but realized it was the best approach.

"We can always quote the law," he said, remembering the advice he'd received from a mentor as a first-year prosecutor. "Remember that the law always works, even if it's wrong."

After finalizing some details of the charges, and planning a timeline to prepare the case, Haynes had the difficulty of telling Billy about the situation.

He knew that to just announce charges would look unfair and might even give Billy a chance to run away, although he didn't expect that to happen.

Billy's style was a lot different.

Late Monday, after an early dinner in the coffee shop across from the Hall of Justice, Haynes and Brown both went to see Billy at his Noe Valley house. As they rapped on the door, the sounds of classical music wafted out a window. Billy had always been a fan of Beethoven and Mozart, but usually reserved their music for moments of unhappiness or doubt.

Billy lowered the sound just seconds after Brown knocked on the door, and then approached it wearing nothing but a robe and slippers, with a bulging bandage still sticking out from his neck. Grabbing the doorknob with one hand and straightening his bandage with the other, Billy closed his eyes with a quick wince of pain as he swung the door open and saw the two men.

Billy's first remark to them was, "I'm surprised it took you so long." He stood still, not even bothering to invite them into the house, and waited for their message with no visible emotion.

"Are you okay, Billy?" the chief said nervously as the two men stood still. "Do you need anything?"

"Yeah, I could use a new neck and some aspirin, but other than that, things are fine," Billy said sarcastically. "Life is just a party these days."

"Look, Billy," Haynes said. "We've reviewed the case thoroughly and we've decided we have to charge you with violation of the state's concealed gun law. We didn't want you to hear it from some reporter calling you up for reaction." the D.A. explained, as the chief stood still and tried not to look nervous. "We wanted to give you the courtesy of preparing for the fallout."

Billy wasn't surprised and was thankful for the notice. but deep inside his mind he was already figuring out how to not only beat this rap, but make these two—and the mayor—pay for trying to knock him out.

"Well, thanks for the visit, but I got things to do," Billy said as he shut the door. "See you in court."

*   *   *

The next day, Haynes, Brown, and Callahan held a press conference to announce the charges. Callahan did not speak at the press event, however, until reporters asked for his opinion. The mayor then spoke about the need to be fair to his former campaign manager, but not let anyone get away with breaking the law, then stepped back and let Haynes and Brown continue.

He and Carl Devins, who had become his ad hoc political advisor since the Election Night events, had talked at length about how the mayor would be presented in the aftermath.

Devins suggested that the mayor take a low profile, but remain concerned about the need to run a fair and just investigation.

The D.A. and police chief told reporters that they'd spoken to Billy Dale and his attorney, and agreed for Billy to surrender later that day in Haynes's office. They expected his bail to be below $50,000, since the charge was not for murder but for the weapons violation.

"We believe that no one is above the law," Haynes told the packed crowd of reporters who'd gathered in front of the Hall of Justice for the event. "Although we realize that Mr. Dale has suffered personal harm, that does not mitigate the fact that he broke a serious state regulation for which a jury must decide his fate."

Reporters shot question after question at the men, most dealing more with their opinion of Billy and his past campaign actions than the merits of the case. One person from a local radio station even asked both men if they had voted for the stadium plan, a comment that evoked a round of laughs.

"Look, this is not some kind of game," Brown barked after the stadium question. "I know you are all savoring the political fallout from this, but that has nothing to do with it. A man is dead, another has been wounded, and the law has been broken."

After about 40 minutes of questions and follow-ups, the press conference ended and Haynes and Brown went back to work. Both men met with their subordinates who would have to handle the day-to-day workings of the case, and especially the speculation of the media.

This trial, although not a murder case anymore, would still be covered heavily by the press because of Billy's reputation and his unusual propensity for making enemies. The *Journal* and the *Bulletin*, which had been so obviously against Billy during the recent stadium battle, would also be sure to point out every element of his character that had caused him past problems.

A few hours after the press conference, Haynes and Brown gathered in Haynes's office again, this time to wait for Billy. Precisely at 5 p.m., the man of the hour arrived, wearing a clean, faded sweatshirt, jeans, and one of his many baseball hats. Yes, it was a Giants cap.

Everyone in the room couldn't help but laugh at the irony of the situation.

"I thought this might help me get off," Billy said with a smile that quickly faded when he realized his joke was not wholly appreciated. "Well, it was worth a shot."

With that, Billy was led downstairs to Central Booking, where his photo was taken, his fingerprints recorded, and a statement signed formalizing his arrest. He was charged with violation of California Penal Code Section 234.66—carrying a deadly weapon in a concealed state.

After the formalities, Billy was placed in his own cell in the Hall of Justice jail. The moment he stepped inside the gray, dirty, six-foot-by-four foot structure with peeling paint and noisy steel bars, Billy was hit with the realization of just what was happening.

When he was in the hospital, most of the situation came over him as a foggy mix of events. All that he was worried about then was surviving the ordeal with his health and voice intact.

But Billy only imagined the effects of going to jail as he waited to return to good health. Now that he found himself actually inside a cell, this formerly powerful king of political maneuvers realized that this was a true-life situation, and if he didn't work to fight it, he could be here for a while.

After making his one phone call, he was released about two hours later when his attorney, Wayne Foote, appeared with a bond for the $50,000. Foote, who had made his name as a major criminal defense attorney in nearby Oakland, had known Billy only casually in recent years.

The two men ran into each other during one of the few East Bay campaigns that had drawn Billy's attention. The fast run-in occurred just three years earlier when Billy was working on the campaign of Oakland mayor Jerry Oakes, a hardball politico who had held office for more than 15 years, but who had needed Billy's talents to get out from under a messy cable television scandal.

Oakes, a former union boss, had been accused of taking bribes from a cable company competing to serve Oakland and was on his way to re-election when reporters for the Oakland News came across letters sent between Oakes and the cable company's president. The letters were clear proof that Oakes had wanted $100,000 and 5% of all cable revenues through the term of the ten-year contract.

Since the revelations came out three weeks before the general election, Oakes had been in the worst spot to fight back. He knew of Billy's talent for reversing scandals and creating new ones. Using private detectives and several handwriting analysts, Billy concocted a defense that claimed the letters were simply not written by Oakes, even though they carried his signature.

Using the handwriting experts, who were paid well for their trouble, Billy managed to have the charges dropped and ease Oakes to re-election. If Billy could survive his latest legal hassle, he would probably be asked to run Oakes's next campaign.

Wayne and Billy had conspired only briefly at a planning meeting where they discussed both Oakes's defense and a way to clean up his political image.

After the election victory gave Oakes another four-year term, Billy and Foote had no reason to see each other.

Until now.

The minute Billy was well enough in the hospital to speak and stay awake for more than an hour, he had been on the phone to Foote. He never forgot the way the attorney worked so well with Billy's calculating and often-underhanded approach to both politics and the law.

Billy liked that Foote held no reservations about manufacturing the truth if needed to get a client off, or more creatively, finding just the small, necessary element of doubt or blame on others to keep his client in the clear.

Fifty-three, thin, and tall, Foote was one of the few black men that Billy had gotten to know well in the area during his time in San Francisco. He did not consider himself prejudiced at all, after the prejudice he had faced himself. He just had not had much chance to work or associate with many blacks.

But Billy liked the way Foote came up through the poorer neighborhoods of Oakland as the son of a train conductor and a cosmetic saleswoman. After running with a local street gang, Foote had turned away from youth violence following a street fight where he caught a bullet that remained lodged in his leg.

During court appearances when he had to defend someone accused of shooting or violently harming a victim, Foote would often roll up his pant leg to show jurors that he understood how it felt to be victimized. But then he would always go on to explain why his client was innocent. The approach seemed to make jurors believe that if Foote, a past victim himself, could find the defendant innocent, they could too.

"The key to defense cases is not to allow yourself to be forced into making one," Foote had told Billy on the phone. "Make them swing at you. It's the same in a street fight. If the other guy swings and misses, the best trick is not to swing back, but let him hit something else."

Billy smiled as the guards led him from his cell to the entrance of the jail, where he saw Foote signing some release documents and handing over the bond. Scribbling quickly with the fountain pen he kept as a souvenir from his days clerking in the state Supreme Court, Foote did not even look up when Billy entered the room. He just commented to him calmly.

"Looks like you've gotten into a little spot," Foote said, shoving the papers to the clerk and grabbing Billy's release form. The attorney added, with a wink, "Let's see what we can do to get you out of it."

After Billy collected his things, the two men headed out toward the front of the Hall of Justice onto busy Bryant Street, and into the back of a waiting town car. Even in jail, Billy could see that Foote wanted him to feel at home, with the transportation methods to which he had become accustomed.

In the back of the town car, Foote flipped open a file that contained Billy's arrest sheet, clippings from all newspapers on the case, and a photo still of one of the shooting videotapes that clearly showed Billy fired only after the knife had been thrown by Bogart.

"This works in our favor" Foote said. "But this other shot also shows you took the gun out from your ankle-holster. That is pure concealment and that is what they can get us on."

Like a doctor examining a nervous patient, Foote went methodically through the evidence and potential defenses and gave Billy some tough news.

"It doesn't look good," Foote said, gazing out the car window at three kids running through a sprinkler on the unusually warm November morning. "We have to find something to hit them with. But I don't know what."

As the car rolled through the city and back to Billy's house, both men stayed silent, contemplating what to do. ∎

Chapter Twelve

The Verdict

During the next two months, Billy went through the rigors of the court system as a preliminary hearing found him fit to stand trial and pretrial motions bounced back and forth between Haynes, Foote, and several judges who were forced to share the pretrial hearing load due to the overcrowded courts.

Finally, on January 25, the trial date had been set. It would take place one month later.

Haynes, facing his own re-election soon, decided to prosecute the case himself. Although he knew that going after Billy could be both politically and technically difficult, he also knew that too much rode on this case. Haynes decided that he would feel worse if Billy got off and Haynes had not at least tried to prosecute the case.

The final decision came after a meeting between Haynes, two of his deputies, and Callahan. The mayor, although champing at the bit for a chance to watch the case unfold, decided to lay low during the trial so as not to attract speculation that he was "smacking his lips in anticipation of Billy going to jail," as one columnist had put it in the *Reader*. The mayor was relegated to reports from television and newspapers, plus those spies he sent in every day.

Haynes decided that a simple collection of witness testimony, photo stills from the videotape showing Billy grabbing the gun from his ankle, and a clear definition of the concealed weapon statute would be enough to convince most juries. But he also realized he had to make sure Billy's stabbing did not influence some of the jury to feel compassion or sympathy for him.

On the Friday before the trial date, however, Haynes got a boost like no other he could have hoped for. Due to some scheduling problems, the name of the judge who would oversee Billy's trial had been held up. But that afternoon, the presiding magistrate ruled that judge would be none other than Harold Weeds.

This was the same Harold Weeds who had butted heads with Billy four years earlier when Billy ran the campaign of Weeds's opponent, John Gilbert. And it was the same Harold Weeds who had won when William Carlson had found a way to knock Gilbert out of the race.

Not everyone in San Francisco knew about that underhanded ploy, but having been in the local court system for years, Haynes had picked up every piece of backroom fighting he could, and Billy's battle with Weeds was legendary.

Haynes knew that with Weeds on their side, they had an even better chance of nailing Billy. Sure, a judge did not decide guilt or innocence in this case, but his rulings on evidence and motions could steer the prosecution's way if he allowed his memory of what Billy had tried to do come back to bother him.

"We're as good as in," Haynes told another prosecutor he'd appointed to help with the case. "Going in with two strikes against this guy."

When Foote heard who the judge would be, he had a momentary letdown, but let it pass knowing that Weeds had a reputation for fairness in the court, despite his proclivity for passing out favors to friends. If he had to preside over a case involving something as serious as gun control, Foote believed that Weeds would temper his judgment with fairness, at least to a degree.

It was that degree that Foote and Billy had to keep an eye on.

*   *   *

On the following Monday, February 1, jury selection began and, surprisingly, a jury was chosen in less than one day. Although many people had seen the footage of Billy being stabbed, most had convinced both Haynes and Foote that they could objectively judge the case based on evidence and law.

"It's not hard to see who broke the law here," one young woman said during jury selection. "Almost anyone could want to carry a gun, but the law is the law."

During opening statements, Foote and Haynes each gave their direct, simple assertions of why Billy should be jailed or not jailed. Haynes, who knew how to speak to both a jury and a pack of voters at a rally, made sure not to come off like some kind of angry prosecutor wanting to put an innocent person away. Instead, he opened by explaining exactly what the law said about carrying concealed weapons and why such a law must be followed.

"The law does not judge who should obey based on their wealth, stature, or fame," Haynes told the crowd. "And it should not be applied only to those who suffer no wounds in the act of breaking the law. We do not seek to imprison Billy Dale because he has been wounded. We seek to imprison him because he has wounded the law-abiding fabric of this city by ignoring the law and brazenly carrying a deadly weapon that could be used on anyone without the ability to fight back."

Once Haynes finished his 20-minute presentation, which included a blown-up copy of the concealed weapon law and photos of Billy pulling the gun out, he sat down, gave a deep, nervous sigh, and folded his hands on his chest. Billy did not know what to think, and instead of wishing for help from above or from his attorney, he studied the faces of the jury to see what their reaction might be to the prosecutor's argument and oratory.

The mix of seven men and five women, including three black and two Latino jurors, was supposed to be the ideal jury, according to Foote's analysis. He believed that black people and men would understand more why Billy carried a gun.

After a moment, Foote got up and walked slowly to the front of the jury box, sprouted a wide-mouthed smile, and introduced himself. Many in the jury had already known Foote's name from the Oakes incident years earlier, as well as Foote's handling of other prominent criminal defenses.

As he began to speak, Foote chose not to dwell on the law, knowing that would not work. Instead, he painted a picture of Billy as a man who had come up from being a down-trodden, spit upon, confused young teen to a self-made, hard-working member of the community who was not afraid to take on the establishment, and who had earned every cent he'd made.

"This man has been through enough to give him good reason to want to carry a gun," Foote said, his voice rising as he described the scene of death Billy had witnessed first-hand outside the Starbanger decades earlier. "He was nearly killed thirty years ago when anti-gay cops tore apart one of New York's few establishments willing to serve homosexuals. He does not ask for pity because of who he is, he only asks for fair treatment."

Foote, who often wore shiny gold necklaces when he spoke, let them bounce off of his silk tie as he gestured wildly with his hands while explaining some of the examples of the abuse Billy had taken over the years. He also reminded the jurors of threats his client had received in previous campaigns, and even in the stadium vote.

"The truth is, ladies and gentlemen, if Billy Dale had not been carrying that gun, he might be dead and you might be here listening to someone defend Vernon Bogart."

Several people in the crowd openly gasped at the scenario drawn by Foote's opening comments. The truth was, he was right. Billy had to do what he did or face possible death or a worse wounding.

Billy sat back as Foote dropped down in his chair following his arguments and mussed Billy's hair like a father showing pride in his son. The jury offered some raised eyebrows and shaken heads, but little in the way of emotion that could indicate whether or not they had bought Foote's stance.

For the next two weeks, the trial continued with testimony from witnesses, gun law experts, and even past employees of both Bogart and Billy who shared the stage to testify that each man had been either a compassionate, kind boss or a tyrannical, foul-mouthed slave-driver.

At one point, Billy got up and called one of his former workers—a 25-year-old girl whom he had fired after she came on to one of his married male clients—a "fuckin' weasely liar" after she claimed that Billy had tried to drug her boyfriend to have sex with him.

The courtroom exploded into shouting and yelling when that incident occurred. It was the only time that Judge Weeds had threatened to clear the courtroom to maintain order.

The incident gave the daily newspapers, which were following the trial with several reporters each, a chance to breathe some life into coverage. Both papers slapped the photo of Billy jumping up and darting his finger in the air on the front page with headlines such as "You Liar!" and "Dale Objects."

During the remaining days of the trial, both the *Bulletin* and the *Journal* found small ways to pile on the pressure for a Dale conviction. The day the trial opened, each paper printed harsh editorials urging that the law be followed. While the daily publications were careful not to convict Billy before he had his day in court, each hinted that they would not accept anything that appeared to be a reduction in the rule of law.

"It is clear that Billy Dale has broken the law," the *Bulletin* argued. "Simply by virtue of the fact that he carried a deadly weapon with him, in a concealed state, is a violation enough to require conviction and the strongest penalty allowed. While we urge a fair and impartial judgment of the situation, we also urge that those deciding his fate not let sympathy or personal feelings stop them from doing their job."

For the *Journal*, the tone was similar. "Billy Dale stands before the law to take his punishment or vindication like anyone," the editorial stated. "We feel the pain that he has endured as a victim of a serious wounding, but we also feel the need to carry out the justice of law to the maximum degree possible. We will wait and watch like those in the courtroom."

At the *Advocate*, however, Jimmy Min's influence was as strong as ever. Although Billy was facing time in prison and Jimmy could easily have turned his back on his friend to side with Callahan, Steve Brown, or Dennis Haynes, he knew that that was not what friends did. He also knew that even if Billy had to go away for a year or more, his ability to plan, wait for the right move, and fight his way back would not diminish.

In a strong Page One editorial—a first for his family publication—Jimmy outwardly demanded that Billy not only be found innocent but be paid money from the estate of Vernon Bogart for the pain that he had suffered.

"Why is everyone looking beyond the facts in an effort to find someone to punish for this tragedy?" asked the statement printed the day the trial began. "Billy Dale is the victim here. He did not go seeking Vernon Bogart in a rage to inflict harm on him. Bogart had gone looking for Billy, hunting to take out some revenge because he could not handle a defeat that he deserved."

"We are, of course, sorry for the tragedy that has befallen Vernon Bogart's family. But we do not feel that it should be used to punish Billy Dale, a man who has given his career to help make San Francisco a better place, and a man who deserves to be treated better than this."

To top it off, Mike McLean bolstered Jimmy's argument with a few choice comments that were part of a column placed inside the same issue. McLean's argument, as usual, centered on what he thought was the absurdity of the charge against Billy. Everyone had seen Billy shoot Bogart in self-defense.

"If everyone who carried a gun in this town were to face a year in jail, we would have many more overcrowded cells than we do now," McLean wrote. "In a city where it has been shown police will pull their guns more often than the man on the street, it is incredible to argue that a man acting in obvious self-defense should not be allowed to use his weapon to protect himself. Billy Dale was not shooting target practice, he was trying to keep from becoming a target."

Meanwhile, the trial became the buzzword around town. In coffeehouses, bars, and even health clubs, questions over whether Billy Dale should be convicted or not were thrown back in nearly every conversation.

Arguments broke out in friendly card games, fights erupted in bars, and even gay-bashings increased slightly as gay men were preyed upon by those who opposed Billy's ability to use a self-defense argument. In one instance, a young gay couple was jumped after midnight during a walk through Alamo Square Park. When the two teens who grabbed and roughed them up left, they both shouted, "That goes for Billy Dale, too, you fuckin' faggots."

For the jurors, who were not sequestered but were told not to read or hear news reports of the case, life became almost hibernation. Some simply stopped talking to friends, while others had to switch conversations back and forth. At the same time, they were ironically forced to stop following news reports when one of the city's most interesting news stories was unfolding right before their eyes.

Still, most of the jurors seemed willing to sacrifice news viewing and open discussions with friends to be part of this amazing and historic situation. Even during jury breaks—when the jurors were ordered not to discuss the case— they would often trade comments about "how exciting it is to be involved" or "I hope we don't do the wrong thing."

That was also the feeling of both Haynes and Foote. As the end of the trial approached, both men began to have doubts. Haynes wondered if he should have the responsibility of such a major case just to feed his ego and showed concerns about possible failure, while Foote hoped that this simple defense and sympathy-begging approach would work. Foote knew that Billy was not well-liked in many circles, despite the support gun owners received from a cross-section of this jury.

Foote decided that he needed to make one bold and dramatic move to help push support for Billy as a man acting in self-defense and believing he needed to carry his gun. In a last-minute move, Foote decided to call a special witness. Although he had placed this person on his list of witnesses, that list had not been made available to the public, only to the judge and Haynes.

That witness was Jack Callahan.

"Your honor, I choose for my last witness, Mayor Jack Callahan," Haynes said.

The courtroom reacted with low whispers and mumbles. Even Haynes was surprised. Both attorneys had placed Callahan on their lists of possible witnesses at the trial's beginning, but since the lone charge of carrying a concealed weapon hinged more on Billy's reaction to Bogart, and to his obvious breaking of the law itself, neither had thought Callahan would be needed to be called.

Haynes, who looked through the periscope of political impact on most things in this case, had judged that calling Callahan to testify would place both of them in a murky position and decided he would only do it as a last resort.

But Foote believed that a stroke of chance was necessary. He had recalled Billy telling him at one point in the pretrial discussions that he'd been threatened several times in recent months during the stadium campaign, but Foote had only mentioned those in a general sense during his opening statement.

Since Billy had not taken the stand and was not likely to, no specific instances of any threats were being discussed, but Foote remembered Billy telling him about one incident in particular that had occurred while Billy was at Callahan's home. Foote surmised that if he could get the mayor to discuss the incident, and possibly his own fears for Billy, that could play into the sympathy for Billy that Foote sought.

All of those hopes and uncertainties raced through Wayne Foote's mind as the judge sent a messenger to contact Callahan and tell him he was due in court that afternoon to testify.

"I suspect that our fine mayor would not refuse the order to testify and spark a subpoena," said Judge Weeds, who had been unusually quiet during the proceedings. "I suspect he will be here in good order."

With that, Weeds ordered the lunch recess and everyone filed out. Reporters quickly ran to phone in the latest news that Callahan would be testifying that afternoon. Standing outside the Hall of Justice, which housed the courts on its lower floors, television crews went live for noon updates with the word that the sitting mayor and former client of suspect Billy Dale would be speaking on the witness stand later that day.

Callahan, who had been monitoring the case, received a phone call directly from the bailiff ordering him to appear as a witness. The mayor's first reaction was nonchalant, but surprised.

"So, maybe Haynes wants me to bolster his argument that Billy was a back-stabbing, cunning political operative," the mayor thought to himself. Haynes had discussed the possibility with the mayor that he might be needed as a sort of anti-character reference on Billy, but Callahan still hoped he would not have to be called.

With the initial reports of the trial offering a strong case for Billy's conviction, the mayor wondered why Haynes would have to call him in. But when the bailiff said the request for Callahan to testify had come from the defense, the mayor became concerned.

"What the hell would they want with me?" Callahan thought. "I can't help them. I was at war with the guy."

That's when the mayor realized why they wanted him. If Foote could get one of Billy's political enemies—especially a former police chief—to support the need for someone in danger to carry a gun, it could help sway the jury.

The mayor also had a reputation in town, despite his dealings with Billy, as a straightforward, honest person. Even with the run-ins with Benny Min and his well-known break with Billy, Callahan continued his honest, law enforcement demeanor. He hoped that wouldn't come back to haunt him as he was forced to speak for Billy Dale.

After grabbing a quick lunch in his office, despite a reduced appetite due to worry, Callahan went downstairs to take his town car to the Hall of Justice. Several camera crews were in front as he got in the car, firing questions that he waved off. Still more were parked outside when he arrived at court.

The mayor gave them little comment as he hurried in the building, followed closely by a clutch of aides.

Once inside, Callahan took a special private elevator reserved only for the police chief and other police officials. It went straight to the fourth floor, where the trial was being held. As the mayor stepped out of the elevator, he glanced around the hallways that he used to walk daily as chief but had seen only rarely during his time in retirement.

The marble floors and walls, with dark brown wooden trim, reminded him of what it was like to have been in charge of police instead of city bureaucracies. He remembered fondly how he felt when he could report that crime was dropping and morale was up during his days as both deputy chief and top cop.

He had wished at that moment that he had never met Billy Dale, Mike McLean, or Vernon Bogart. If he'd stayed out of public view, he thought, and enjoyed the relaxed life of retirement, he would not have had to face this.

Still, while pushing open the swinging door to the packed courtroom, the mayor also knew that he could not back down. During his police days, he'd always been taught, and always taught others, that you truly fail only when you do not go forth and take a chance. Or as his father would say, "Take your best shot, hang in there, and let things fall where they may."

Just as Callahan took a seat in the last row, Judge Weeds called the court back in session and asked Foote again if he had any other witnesses. The defense attorney, hiding his obvious nervousness with a confident outward image that had helped him gain his fame, said proudly, "I call the honorable Jack Callahan to the stand."

Small murmurs and whispers greeted the announcement as Callahan walked to the witness stand, took the oath, and waited quietly for Foote to question him. In the audience, he could see familiar faces of political enemies and friends, as well as reporters and columnists whom he'd know through the years.

Callahan's eyes also scanned to look at Haynes, who gave him a shrugged "I-don't-know-what-this-is-all-about" reaction, and his deputy prosecutor, who gave a similar response.

The mayor looked directly into the eyes of Billy Dale. This was the first time he'd seen him since the shooting and Billy's eyes shot back his famous penetrating glare, with just a hint of a smile. That knocked Callahan back a bit and told him just what Billy was thinking, that there was nothing Billy would rather do than see Callahan save him.

Foote started in with simple questions that revealed Callahan had known Billy Dale for several years, had hired him to be his campaign manager, and had won his present job with Billy's help.

"Would you say that Billy Dale is a good campaign manager who works hard for his clients and gives them his all?" Foote asked.

"Well...yes," a nervous Callahan responded.

"Would you say that he was a major part of your being elected a year and a half ago?" Foote asked.

"Yes," the mayor replied again.

"And you would say that you probably owe your political career to him," Foote shot back.

At that, Haynes objected. "This is not only immaterial, but a bit of blackmail," Haynes told the judge. "The defense is outwardly telling the witness that, in so many words, he should help his client because he helped him get elected."

Weeds thought quickly, then sustained the objection. Weeds was not about to let a question go through that made Billy look good, or at the least get him to look sympathetic.

Foote brushed it aside and went right into what he had planned all along.

"Mayor, before your obvious break with the defendant over the stadium issue, isn't it true that you two worked together rather closely in planning sessions to help the measure pass?" Foote asked.

"Yes, when he was the campaign manager of the measure in September, we met often to seek approval and plan strategy," Callahan said.

"Do you recall a meeting on September 8 at your home in which the defendant received a phone call?" Foote asked.

Callahan thought about it and did not answer immediately.

Foote continued. "A phone call in which the caller told the defendant that if the stadium measure passed, he would pay for the political victory with his life?"

The mayor hesitated as all eyes drew closer on him. Callahan remembered numerous calls coming in during that hectic period when both the stadium plan and the homeless program where being pushed. As his mind scanned the events of the past six months, it dawned on him what Foote was doing.

During a late-night planning meeting, someone had called Billy at Callahan's home, which was unusual because he had an unpublished number that only a few people knew, and because whoever called Billy at Callahan's would have to had known he was there.

"Yes, I remember the call," the mayor admitted.

Foote continued his assault. "And do you recall what the person had said?"

Callahan nodded his head and recounted the entire event. He told how he had answered the phone at the late hour because no one else was home, including Glenda, and said he was a bit groggy.

When the caller asked for Billy by name, the mayor had simply handed the phone to him, assuming it was one of his campaign workers who would likely have the mayor's number and know to reach Billy there.

But when Billy took the call, the man on the other end simply told him that he would "have to pay" if the stadium measure passed. When the person hung up, Billy handed the phone back to the mayor and continued working.

When Callahan had asked him who it was, Billy just said, "Oh, just another threat. I get them a lot."

"Well, do you do anything about it?" the mayor asked, growing curious. "We could get you some police protection or even a bodyguard if you think you need it."

"Nope," Billy said. "I got my bodyguard right here."

With that, Billy had raised his pants leg and revealed the gun that had been his sidearm for the past 20 years. When Callahan saw it, he was somewhat surprised but told Billy that he was glad he had protection.

"In other words," Foote barked. "Billy Dale showed you at that time that he was carrying a concealed weapon and you did nothing to discourage him? You, a former police chief and now mayor of this city, discovered that a citizen was carrying a concealed weapon, yet you not only chose to ignore it, you supported it? Is that the case, mayor?"

Several court viewers gasped at this revelation. Here was the former top law enforcement leader of the city, and its current mayor, openly admitting that he not only had known about the law at issue being broken, but had told the man accused of breaking it that it was okay.

Callahan moved uneasily in his chair, sweat forming on his brow and lip, and his hands churning together. He looked over to Haynes for support, at Steve Brown, even at the judge. But it was no use.

"Yes," Callahan said, his voice hoarse. "I guess I did."

With that answer, Foote's questioning was over. Those in the crowd whispered among themselves, while Billy patted Foote on the back when he rejoined him at the defense table. Billy also gave Callahan another twisted grin, making sure to hide it from the jury.

Jurors responded with as much surprise as anyone in the courtroom. But how this testimony would affect their decision was yet to be known. Although Callahan had supported what Billy was doing, that did not make it right. The law was still broken.

That was how Haynes sought to direct things when he rose to cross-examine Callahan. The mayor, who did not want to go near the witness stand when the trial began, now welcomed Haynes's questioning, which he hoped could ease the impact of what he had just admitted.

Haynes's tactic was to change the focus away from Billy Dale as fearful victim to Billy Dale as cunning, conniving operative.

"Mayor, in your previous testimony, you said that you believed Billy Dale was a good campaign consultant who gave his all to others and went into each campaign with a goal to win." Haynes said. The mayor nodded his head.

"Did that goal to win come at any cost? Such as dirty tactics?" Haynes asked. Callahan slowly responded. "Well, yes," he said, wondering where Haynes was going with this line of questioning.

"Didn't the defendant once tell you during your mayoral race that you should do everything to defeat the enemy, even if it broke the law?" Haynes asked.

Callahan thought quietly, remembering a discussion he and Billy had had during the mayoral race when they first mapped out this strategy and recalled such a statement.

"Yes," Callahan said.

Before Haynes could get out another question, Billy jumped up again, yelling. "That is a fucking lie. You never heard me say that, I never broke one goddamn law."

Before the court officers had to restrain him, Foote pulled Billy down to his seat and told him to remain calm. The outburst shook everyone in the courtroom, especially Callahan, who became more nervous with each response.

Haynes then continued with questions that painted Billy as a bitter, revengeful person. The D.A. asked Callahan to recall several instances in which Billy had made comments about how he had "gotten" certain political enemies through negative campaigns, mudslinging ads, and even blackmail that ranged from set-ups with prostitutes caught on film to drugs planted on people by paid-off cops.

"Yes, he told me about a lot of them," the mayor recalled.

Billy just stood still, seething with anger. He twisted in his chair, barely able to hold back, but he forced himself to remain calm.

Then Haynes went for the final blow.

"And mayor, do you remember at one point during your campaign for mayor that Billy Dale planned out the murder of William Carlson?" Haynes asked, drawing a collective gasp from the crowd. "Do you recall this piece of paper?"

Haynes then reached into his briefcase and pulled out the document that Callahan had given him weeks earlier as possible evidence. The paper was a memo in Billy Dale's handwriting that laid out elaborate plans to have Carlson killed through the use of a hired gun who would set up the murder to look like the act of an enraged, crazed person who wanted to take out the mayor as a protest against political power.

The document showed how the campaign could hire someone from one of the religious sects in Oakland that were popping up, pay them to kill Carlson in an ambush that Billy's friends on the police department would help set up, then have the assassin killed in a Jack Ruby-style slaying.

Billy had never had to actually use the plan, and had only really written it up as a partial joke to show Callahan his willingness to "go all out." Callahan knew that it was more a piece of show by Billy than a real plan, but in the light of day at Billy's trial, it was damning.

The jury ate it up.

"I do remember when he handed me that," Callahan explained, taking the memo from Haynes and re-reading it slowly. "He never said anything about it, but he made sure that I would see it."

"And what did you think when you saw his plan to kill your opponent?" Haynes asked.

"I was shocked."

Those were the last words of testimony in the entire trial. After brief closing arguments, in which both attorneys repeated their strategies for guilt or innocence, the jury began deliberations.

For several hours, as the jury discussed, debated, and argued the points, all parties waited in the courtroom, with silence stemming from most of the observers. All those involved wondered which argument—Foote's revelation that Callahan had supported Billy's concealment or Haynes's discovery that Billy was capable of at least thinking murder—would take over.

The jury reviewed the evidence for eight hours, finally coming in with a verdict at 8 p.m. on Feb. 14, ironically, Valentine's Day. A day that usually brings joy to many would be the day at least some in the courtroom would be defeated.

Once the bailiff got word of a verdict, he announced that it would be read within the hour. Although the court usually closed by 4 p.m., Weeds allowed the jury to continue working into the night when they told him they were close to a decision.

As soon as both attorneys were assembled, and Billy was back in his chair, the jury filed in. Showing little outward emotion, they looked neither at Billy nor Callahan and simply kept their eyes on the judge.

Once seated, Weeds asked the foreman to stand up. A short black man in his 50's slowly rose and the bailiff took the sealed verdict from him. Weeds then asked the question he had asked of hundreds of jury foremen before.

"Have you reached a verdict?" the judge asked.

"Yes, we have," the man answered. "We find the defendant, William, Billy, Dale, guilty of the charge of carrying a concealed weapon."

As soon as the words came out of the foreman's mouth, chaos erupted in the courtroom. Haynes and Callahan hugged, as the D.A. also high-fived all those in the prosecution table area. Several in the crowd cheered while others who'd supported Billy booed a low, direct moan.

Jimmy Min began yelling, "Bullshit! Bullshit!" and several in the crowd began to chant along.

At first, Billy did nothing; he just recoiled as he often did when faced with an opposition that had won. He knew his best move would not be to do anything now but to seek his revenge later.

As the bailiff handcuffed Billy to lead him out, he passed right by Callahan, who was taking congratulations from all and spreading his own kudos on the prosecution team.

Leaning over so that only Callahan's left ear could hear him, Billy whispered simply, "I'll get you for this." Then he was led out the back door and on to jail. ∎

Chapter Thirteen

St. Patrick's Day

St. Patrick's Day had always been a special holiday for Jack Callahan. Not only was his Irish heritage in full bloom on that day of green celebration, but it also sparked a day of festivities for most police and citywide community groups. As with many older cities, San Francisco sported a true Irish mix with both old-time American-born Irish and many younger natives of the Emerald Isle who found that the City by the Bay was often the best place to turn when they came to America. As the stretch barreled through the showers that were drowning O'Farrell Street on the hazy, wet Election Night, Billy glanced out the window just as the car passed the SwingTop Bar at O'Farrell and Polk.

Sure, many Irish went to New York, where they could blend in well with a strong group of Irish community folks. But in San Francisco, with its smaller, tighter community feel, the Irish—young and old—could feel the pull of community and a kinship not often found in New York, or even Chicago, which also boasted a powerful Gaelic presence.

For Callahan, whose grandparents had been strong Irish immigrants, the exploits of the family struggling to work when they first set foot on the peninsula of San Francisco in those Barbary Coast days were legendary. Many nights around his family dinners in the Mission District were filled with his grandfather, Charles John Callahan, telling about the fights that broke out in bars where Irish were not allowed in the first days of their immigration. Before the Kellys and Donohues started their own watering holes in San Francisco—which continued to this day—they would have to battle their way in for a simple shot of Bushmill or a pint of Harp or Guinness.

"If you knew how hard it was to even get allowed into a bar or restaurant, or a factory to work the overnight shift for that matter, you'd be grateful for the right to go to school," Callahan remembered his grandfather saying when Jack was only seven years old. "Don't ever forget how well you have it compared to when we first came here."

Furthermore, Callahan's grandfather would always make sure his grandson would never allow himself to treat others with the prejudice or lack of compassion with which he'd often been treated. Charles John would not hesitate to spank young Jack with a belt or a stick if he even thought that he was mistreating another child, especially if the behavior involved prejudice against a black or other minority.

Even though Jack's father, Michael, was the true disciplinarian, Charles John did not feel the least bit out of place in handing out punishment when he felt it was due.

Those memories of childhood and of St. Patrick's Days past wandered in and out of Jack Callahan's mind as he stepped aboard a Lincoln Continental convertible to lead the procession down Market Street in the annual St. Patrick's Day parade.

As usual, a light mist filled the air on that March 17th as crowds lined up and down the widest street in town, and the open-air car moved through the city. Police walked alongside the vehicle to keep an eye out for trouble, although most did not worry about violence and just made sure that drinking revelers did not get out of hand.

Callahan, who still felt some scars from the wild autumn that had preceded this day, was beginning to get over the strange death of Vernon Bogart, the changes and upheavals in his own political position, and the wild trial of Billy Dale. One month had passed since Billy's conviction, and two weeks had gone by since Billy was sentenced to one year in prison. Callahan had not gone to the sentencing, but news reports showed that Billy had stood up, expressionless, and taken his punishment without reaction.

When Judge Weeds had asked him if he had anything to say. Billy, in his typical aggressive fashion, said simply, "You haven't seen the last of me."

Weeds, who could not pass up the opportunity to make his own observations, responded by adding, "That I believe."

Since the concealed weapon law was a felony crime, Weeds had little choice but to sentence Billy to one year in jail. The state mandate allowed him to tack on additional years if he chose, but did not give leeway for the judge to give him less than a year. Billy had also been ordered to pay a $5,000 fine and perform 150 hours of community service when he got out of prison.

Just minutes after the sentencing, Billy had been whisked off to San Quentin, the waterfront state prison just north of San Francisco in Marin County. There he was given a cell, his prison garb, and ordered "to behave or be punished" by the warden who directed him when he entered.

"I know you are supposed to be this hotshot political hack," the warden said to Billy during a personal visit rarely granted to new inmates. "But in here, you are under my thumb."

For Callahan, Billy's situation was not something he would have to deal with until at least the following year. As the convertible steered slowly down Market Street, Callahan couldn't help but jump up on the back part of the car that allowed him a higher, broader view of the parade.

Buttoning up the collar of the long black overcoat he'd put on to stave off the misty chill wafting through the cold March day, Callahan braved a smile and waved his hands to one and all who welcomed him through the parade route.

The mayor couldn't help but smile as he thought about the calm future that seemed to lay ahead. Billy Dale was away for a while, and although the Giants stadium issue had failed, Vernon Bogart's son, Teddy, had announced just a day earlier that the team would not leave the city. Although he said a new stadium would be needed, and the city had to work with the Giants to create one, he vowed not to move the team until "all roads leading to a new home in San Francisco had been explored."

As the mayor sat upon the car's open-air back seats, Glenda, who had maintained a low profile in recent weeks, carefully inched herself next to her husband.

Glenda did not want to be caught in the backstabbing that had been going on in recent months and kept herself available for a few public functions to bolster her husband's campaign needs. But for the most part, she kept out of sight to spend time with Missy King. For the past year, since Callahan had taken office, Glenda and Missy had maintained their secret relationship.

But Missy had been getting considerably frustrated with the arrangement. While Glenda spent more time in Missy's bed than her husband's, the outward appearance continued to be that Glenda was Callahan's wife and, presumably, happily married to the mayor of San Francisco.

In the beginning, when Missy and Glenda had first gotten together, the much younger and wilder Missy had been a free spirit, not in a hurry for a shotgun commitment of any kind. She certainly would not have dared to approach Glenda with the idea that she was to leave Jack Callahan.

Missy liked being able to jump in bed with Glenda whenever the two could steal a moment, and follow it with playful, loving mornings of love-making, good food, and bedroom pillow talk.

"I don't need more than this," Missy would often say. "I will take you where I can get you."

But in the past few months, as Glenda and Missy spent more time together while Jack maneuvered his political games, Missy had grown more attached to her older partner, and more angered by her unwillingness to commit.

The night before the St. Patrick's Day event, Missy and Glenda shared an intimate dinner at Missy's apartment, which ended with a fight and a threat by Missy to go public.

"If you are supposed to love me, then you will come out and let the world know," Missy had shrieked during their late-night argument. "I am sick of being your whore, your closeted lover. Someone you can fuck with and leave, and then play like you are really this man's true partner when you are mine."

Glenda, who'd made no secret of the fact that she wanted to ride the political wagon that Jack Callahan had brought her, was in no mood for Missy or anyone else to take away her place.

"I worked too hard to get where I am and I'm not going to have you screw it up," she remembered telling Missy the night before. "If you want love, go get a puppy."

Those had been the last words from Glenda to Missy the previous night. She had not even bothered to call her on the morning of the parade to attempt an apology or make-up moment. Glenda's mind was only fixed on making sure she looked her best for this most public appearance, and that Jack also appeared well-dressed and confident. Glenda did not want any problems.

In the first twelve months of Callahan's administration, Glenda had joined the boards of directors of four local charities and three major corporations, including West Coast Life, a multimillion-dollar insurance company that was raking in the money.

At the same time, Glenda had carefully avoided the political battles that the mayor caught, while creating a high-profile social life for herself. She became a regular visitor to most of the posh parties and social gatherings in the city. With or without the mayor, she was at every opening of the opera, ballet, symphony, and most any major public project, such as the new library and the launching of a major waterfront shopping center.

Also, San Francisco's first lady was a frequent guest on local TV talk shows, such as the number-one-rated Morning Chat, and local radio programs. She had even filled in on one top-rated morning talk show during a holiday respite for its host.

As the procession moved closer to the water's edge near the foot of Market Street, Glenda recalled the previous night. Although she was sitting next to her husband, Glenda's thoughts were all about Missy.

Glenda had always told Missy that her bisexual ways had been prompted by knowing that a man could not give a woman what she truly needed in the area of physical desire. Namely, because he was a man. Glenda's urges could only be fulfilled by someone like Missy, and her body began to tingle at just the thought of Missy's young, toned muscles wrapped around her skin.

To the parade watchers, however, Glenda and Jack Callahan continued to smile and wave at the crowd, appearing to be the celebrated, loving first couple of San Francisco.

Inside, the mayor knew that his wife was not true to him, while she knew that she was able to have it all. At least for the moment.

*   *   *

About 50 miles north of the city, in a recreation room at San Quentin, Billy Dale sat with other inmates watching the parade on a community room television. The prison allowed its minimum-risk inmates to enjoy two hours of television a day. For some reason, Billy had an urge to see the parade and see what it was that Callahan would do on this most favorite of his days.

Billy remembered just one year ago when he, the mayor, and Jimmy Min had gone to the Green Bean, one of Callahan's favorite Irish bars, for a lunch that turned into dinner and then turned into a late-night drinking fest. That was one of the first days into the new administration that the mayor had been able to relax. He'd not yet been hit with the Benny Min controversy and his honeymoon period was still going.

As Billy watched the parade on the small, gray, somewhat fuzzy black and white television, he could clearly see when the mayor went by, waving his phony wave and smiling like a man who had a secret to hide. Billy knew that secret and he knew Glenda's as well.

In fact, it was during the mayoral campaign that Billy had a long talk with Glenda and Missy King about what Callahan needed from them in order to win. Just days after Callahan announced he was running for mayor, Billy made sure to convince Missy and Glenda to keep their relationship secret.

"We can all get a lot out of this if Jack wins," Billy remembered telling them over a drink in a dimly-lit corner of one of Castro Street's quietest bars. "You two can do whatever you want, and Glenda can ride her celebrity to the highest heights if she wants. But if you let on about your relationship, Jack could be history."

The mayor had not even known about Billy's meeting with his wife and her lover, but Glenda knew going in that she had to keep things hush-hush. Missy, a wild-eyed youngster, gave her agreement on the spur of the moment. Two years later, however, she wasn't willing to keep quiet.

While Billy watched the parade roll along, he had no idea that Missy had given Glenda such an ultimatum just twelve hours earlier. Hell, he had not talked to either Glenda or Missy since the summer before when they all attended a benefit dance to aid the firefighter's children's fund.

If Billy had said two words to either one at the event, it would have been a lot. And since Missy went to the dance under the guise of being a supporter of the children's fund, there was no way to connect her to Glenda anyway. The two women had made no obvious overtures to each other and even left separately, although they met up later in the evening for a drunken sex encounter that ended with a 4 a.m. pillow fight in the nude on Missy's balcony.

Billy just took a swig from the soda he'd been sipping when the parade started and shook his head. Watching Callahan at the top of the political game still gave Billy a small sense of pride knowing that he was the man who put him there. But, as Billy glanced around the room that reminded him of where he was, that pride turned to anger and festering revenge that continued to build.

At nearly the same moment, Missy King also kept a watchful eye on the parade route. Since it was St. Patrick's Day, Missy found herself in what passed for an Irish gay bar in the Castro District, a tavern known simply as Leprechauns. But for most of these patrons, the name held a slightly different meaning, as an analogy for bisexuals.

Nursing a Whiskey Sour, one of the things Missy had picked up from Glenda, the young, nubile woman held her feelings inside as the television showed the first couple passing by at the head of the parade. During one brief moment, as Glenda and the mayor kissed to show their outward happiness, Missy just licked her lips in mixed anticipation of kissing Glenda herself, and of seeking her revenge on the woman who had repeatedly sought to hide their relationship.

After what had happened the night before, Missy had decided that either she could have Glenda or the mayor could, but this charade would go on no longer. Missy had never considered herself a militant feminist lesbian. Sure, she marched in the protests if she felt her rights were in danger, and she would frequent the local gay bars out of a need for calm surroundings that many straight bars lacked. But having Glenda keep Missy on this leash, while she hid her own lesbian tendencies and reaped the benefits of being the dutiful, loving first wife to the rest of the city, was more than Missy could stand.

Just the sight of Glenda and Callahan being welcomed down the street as the Mr. and Mrs. of San Francisco was enough to make Missy want to shoot the television screen.

Missy knew that violence and ultimatums would stop nothing. She had to bring it to Glenda face-to-face. If the mayor's wife liked romping in the sack with a sexy, athletic young woman who jumped at her every sexual desire, she would have to own up to it and not just come by when the mood hit.

Licking the edge of the straw that held her drink, Missy thought about what she could do to bring her lover out and give her some true recognition. She knew that if she pushed too hard, Glenda would drop their relationship as quickly as possible. But she also knew that Glenda enjoyed their passionate moments as much as she did, if not more.

Missy reaped some benefits of her own due to this. Much of her rent was paid by Glenda, her car and many clothes and jewelry had come through her lover, not to mention trips to faraway places—the farther the better for Glenda, who never wanted to risk being seen with her female companion.

Missy did not want the kind of social attention Glenda was receiving. Being involved in the upper crust, back-stabbing world of politics was not Missy's way. But having a lover who was afraid to be seen in public with her was no longer acceptable.

As Missy slurped the rest of her drink and handed the glass back for yet another refill, she began plotting exactly how to handle this situation.

Back on the parade route, Callahan's convertible came to the end of the parade line just after 1 p.m. Well-wishers gathered around him and Glenda with flowers, drinks at the ready, and hands stuck out for a shake as the couple stepped off and headed toward a large tent that had been erected near the waterfront for the traditional mayor's party.

Both husband and wife greeted visitors proudly, hugging and kissing those they knew and shaking the hands of all others. As the foggy mist faded for sunshine to strike through, the sound of Irish music rang ahead from the marching band that was continuing to play while the rest of the parade moved closer.

The couple immediately split up at the tent, with Callahan moving toward a handful of corned beef sandwiches and a lemonade and Glenda grabbing a Whiskey Sour and an Irish roll to chew on while working the crowd.

With such a large Irish community in San Francisco, the annual parade brought visitors from nearly every political persuasion. Irish political club leaders, union bosses, employee groups, and even several gay Irish organizations sent their leaders to the mayor's annual event, each tugging at Callahan for a word about the issue or issues that were haunting them most.

As Callahan shook hands and bent to listen to concerns, Carl Devins—who'd become closer with the mayor since Billy Dale's jail sentence—stood next to him ready to help him answer or, more likely, deflect questions with something that sounded at least like an attempt to help.

"The mayor will be addressing that soon" or "We have a committee studying that right now" were among the comments that Devins delivered on Callahan's behalf. Although he did not have the direct, tough-minded political astuteness of Billy Dale, Devins had found a way to keep Callahan on track during the past few weeks as questions about his next three years in office continued to rise.

Callahan and Devins both knew that things would get tough again if the mayor did not come up with some new proposals, and soon. Just as Billy Dale had foreseen several months earlier when he created and pushed through the homeless program, the mayor's need to build a resume of achievements before his next election was crucial.

Sure, voters realized that Callahan and the city had been through some difficult times with the death of Vernon Bogart and the jailing of Billy Dale. Hell, Callahan had bought a good couple of months' leeway after seeing his former campaign manager injured and put away.

But soon things would get back to normal and if the mayor did not come up with some programs or ideas to push soon, opponents would be sounding the alarm for change quickly enough.

With that in mind, Callahan asked Devins to stay on with him and help to formulate at least a program of ideas for the rest of his first term. He knew that homelessness was hot, but also that the sting of the 11-0 supervisors' vote against his plan remained. Although the vote had been a setup, it still stuck in voters' minds and made it difficult for the supervisors to change their actions without appearing political.

"Politics can be very flexible if you give it time," Devins had said recently. "Keep your eye on the ball, but don't miss the other shots you have."

Callahan could go back to the homeless program later in the year, perhaps. But through Devins's political lens, it remained too hot an issue to go after right now. Right now, the two men were busy feeding sandwiches to supporters and sharing toasts of whiskey.

On the other side of the party, Glenda Callahan did her best to schmooze with the highest socialites, richest investors, and, of course, the most in-the-know gossip columnists. Glenda quickly put Missy King and her tantrum in the back of her mind while pouring champagne and spreading caviar on a piece of bread. With one hand on a Waterford champagne glass and the other shaking hands, the city's first lady was at her best as the politicking, poised social leader, with an adrenaline rush to rise even higher.

"We are on our way," Glenda thought to herself as the celebration grew more crowded and the comments by those in attendance showed that they clearly believed the mayor was headed toward positive things.

"Glenda, you look beautiful and I love Jack's suit," one prominent banker's wife commented. "You must come to our tea next Saturday. I know there are some people there who would love to meet you."

Glenda's smile grew larger, as did the expectations her mind was working on as it became more apparent that Callahan was coming out more popular than ever with the death of Vernon Bogart and the fall of Billy Dale. By sticking to his guns to support the stadium proposal, the mayor had shown that he would stay with an issue no matter what the political pressures held.

In reality, it had been the other way around. Billy had wanted Callahan to stick with him when the furor over the homeless program vote had struck, but Callahan chose to take the path of least resistance by supporting the stadium to ensure future support from the newspapers and the public that favored the stadium plan, too.

But to the voters, Callahan's decision to take on his own campaign manager in a quest for what he believed was good for the city paid off handsomely with a renewed image of a man who would stick to his guns and support what he thought was right, despite the opposition.

As they worked the crowd—on different sides of the party tent—both Glenda and Jack couldn't help but think about what a bright future they had ahead.

In two other places, on other sides of the Bay Area, Billy Dale and Missy King had something different in mind. Both were busy calculating their own plans that could eventually bring Jack and Glenda's bright futures down. ∎

Chapter Fourteen

A Hot Sensation

The lights came down with a startling quickness for patrons of the Blue Knight Grill, the lone blues bar in the Castro District that had packed its lineup with an unusual extended set of entertainment for the St. Patrick's Day festivities. The crowd-pleasing string of entertainers ranged from an old-time B.B. King-type trio to a newer, more synthesized brand of R&B.

For the packed house of drinkers, many of whom had been guzzling beer and other alcoholic treats since noon, the promise of more entertainment than usual made the quick darkness a welcome sign that the show was about to begin.

The crowd ranged from firefighters and cops, who frequented the bar named for police, to older gay couples to straight blues fans who had heard that the Blue Knight delivered a power-packed show. Today's celebration also brought a string of older Irish fans, many of whom had already tested the offerings at more mainstream Celtic taverns that day and wanted to see what this alternative venue had to offer.

Just as the house lights went down, a tinge of guitar could be heard offstage, sparking wild applause from the crowd. Along with the guitar riff, a steady drumbeat punched in and the multi-colored lights began to flicker.

Looking out from the backstage, the singer waiting to go on peered through the makeshift curtain to see what awaited her entrance. A misty, thick smoke breathed over the room, while beads of sweat could be seen rolling down the faces of those who made up the crowd in a mix of leather suits, tie-dye shirts, and at least one kilt.

With the drumbeat growing louder and the guitar strumming faster, the audience began to clap, hoot, and holler for their entertainment. One by one, the band members took to the stage, each joining in the beat and rhythm that had begun with a single guitar strum. As soon as all those except the singer were in front of the crowd, the lights dimmed further, leaving only a halo of a single light stream over the waiting microphone stand in stage front. "Yaaaah-hhooooooo!," someone in the back hollered in a tone that brought other, similar expressions of excitement. "OOOOWWWEEEEE!"

Such a startling welcome brought the singer forth, in her trademark denim skirt, white T-shirt and a multi-colored string of beads, the catcalls and screams growing with her every move. The stage began to shake as she strutted to the microphone, stuck her head out to the crowd and grabbed the mike with one hand, like a thief stealing a bottle of booze from a wino.

"How's everyone doing?" the singer yelled, raising the level of celebration even higher. "Did you all have a happy St. Paddy's Day?" The crowd just cheered as her question hit their ears. "I think you're still having it," she added with a laugh. "We'll let's get the party going."

With that, the crowd hit its most boisterous, the band wailed, and the woman began to sing.

Missy King was in the place she loved the most.

Despite her argument with Glenda and her anger at seeing her lover presented as some noble example of mainstream living, Missy would not let herself be down. From the first time she listened to a Janis Joplin record at 12 years old—one of the ways she had run away from sadness caused by her mother's abandonment—Missy had loved the blues. Singing along to Janis, she'd learned every line of "Cry Baby," "Move Over," and what became a standard cover at each of her shows, "A Woman Left Lonely."

It was the support she'd received from friends in the early days of her singing, and the way she identified with Janis Joplin, Billie Holiday, and other blues singers in pain, that had given Missy the ability to find her way out of a broken home in Bloomington, Illinois. After playing local bars and parties around the central Illinois town for several years in high school, Missy had taken her act on the road, literally, during the summer following her high school graduation.

Armed with two pairs of jeans, several old T-shirts, and a guitar that could barely hold six chords, Missy headed west with one eye forward and one thumb out on the first day of August five years earlier. Once in San Francisco, Missy had gone straight to the Castro District, where she'd heard the gay scene was centered.

Missy had never been with another woman, but she had always shunned boys during high school. At first, it wasn't a lack of attraction to the opposite sex, it was more like apathy. With a mother who had run off with another woman and a father who showed few signs of any kind of fatherly instinct, Missy found neither men nor women very trusting, loyal, or attractive.

"I can't see why anyone would want to spend a whole life devoted to someone else," she had once told a friend in high school. "You have to have fun, but you have to be free, too."

With that attitude, Missy had concentrated mostly on music during high school years and those that followed. After arriving in San Francisco and spending a few nights singing on Castro Street sidewalks, Missy was directed to other areas in the Haight-Ashbury and North Beach where the blues bars were. Several nights in front of the stage at The Grant and Green Bar gave Missy enough courage to ask for a chance to take the stage.

For the older, grumpy musicians who were playing that night, the chance to let a young, sexy woman dance and sing in front of them was not something to be rejected. But, once Missy let out her voice and whipped the crowd up in a mix of sexual energy and explosive voice, the band members knew she had more than a tight body to offer.

"Hey, lady, if you can do that every night, you can do that here," the club's manager had told her after her rookie performance. "You do something to the crowd."

After that, Missy had become a regular among the blues circles in San Francisco, with several gigs along the entire West Coast in recent years. Although national fame had eluded her, as it often does for true blues musicians who don't always know the art of self-promotion, Missy found a place in San Francisco to show her style and substance, including writing her own songs in recent years.

By the time St. Patrick's Day of 1993 rolled around, Missy was a legend in both the blues world and the gay club scene in San Francisco, splitting her time between both, and reaping the attention in the gay press and the blues tabloids.

In between, Missy had finally stumbled into the world of lesbian love as well, finding her first experience with a female drummer in the same band with which she'd made her first stage appearance. Since then, others had come and gone, but none had had the staying power of Glenda.

The first lady of San Francisco created a secret lesbian life for herself in recent years. Although rising to the top of the city's business scales in the past decade, Glenda had been able to hide her sexual passions by always finding men to escort her to the formal functions, then later grabbing young women to toy with for the rest of the night.

Glenda never socialized with lesbians in public and would frequent few public places with her chosen woman of the moment. Most of those on her arm did not mind the secrecy. Many preferred it since they, too, were not in a hurry to commit to anyone and wanted only a physical relationship that allowed them to experiment with others and walk away without problems.

But when Missy met Glenda three years earlier during one of her regular sets at the Blue Knight, she immediately tossed her old feelings out the window. Glenda, who had come to the bar with a male friend following an investment banker's party in nearby Noe Valley, took one look at Missy and felt a rush of desire and lust. After Missy's first set that night, Glenda quickly struck up a conversation with the young, gorgeous singer.

As her "date" approached her in the bar that night, Glenda quickly handed Missy her card and made up an excuse for Missy to call her to "talk more about that idea." The idea was a night of passion that would continue for three years.

During that time, both women had made it clear that their dalliances were just lust for the moment and that no true feelings could come in. Glenda had stuck to that agreement, but young Missy found herself growing closer and closer to Glenda's mystique.

Even when Glenda married Jack Callahan about a year after she had hooked up with Missy, the young woman still believed they would be together somehow. But since the day that Callahan took office, Missy had seen her lover grow more and more distant, and show fewer and fewer signs of giving Missy any kind of commitment.

Missy felt herself sinking deeper and deeper into an obsession for her partner. Seeing her with her husband on television earlier in the day had only made it clearer to Missy that she would not let Glenda go that easily.

As the crowd shook and yelled for encores that St. Patrick's Day evening, Missy felt the rush of excitement and adrenaline that always accompanied her performances. But, at the same time, she also felt a bit empty, wanting to share the moment with the woman to whom she felt closest.

Even as she came out for encores after more than an hour of playing, Missy continued to scan the audience in the vain hope that Glenda had come to watch her special show. Although she had not been to one of her performances for more than nine months, Missy's heart and soul reached for a chance that Glenda would be there to say she had changed her mind, that she had given in, and that she truly wanted to come out into the open and tell the world of her true feelings for Missy.

But it didn't happen. After the final encore, Missy shook hands and hugged and kissed the band, waved kisses and peace signs to the crowd, and went backstage to put her guitar and microphone away. As the next act took the stage and began setting up, Missy sipped the rum and orange juice the bartender had left for her and pondered what to do next.

Clamping the guitar case shut and swinging it over her shoulder, Missy realized that the only way Glenda would come around was by force. Her husband had learned from Billy Dale that arm-twisting is the best way to get anything, so now Missy knew it too.

Glancing at the clock in the back of the tiny dressing room shared by all performers, Missy saw that it was 10 p.m., which meant that Glenda was likely coming home from one of several St. Patrick's Day parties she'd been dragged to by the mayor. Unlike Jack Callahan, who regularly went to every party he could on this most Irish of days, Glenda often went home after the first few appearances, which Jack could explain to others by saying she had to get up early or had a headache.

That meant that Glenda would be home alone and in a position to hear Missy's latest ultimatum. Running through her mind exactly what she would say, Missy rushed out of the bar, not even noticing the table she bumped into or the drink spilled on a customer. She just headed up the street to her house and darted to the bedroom. Throwing herself on the unmade bed, Missy still noticed the aroma of Glenda's body, the smell of her perfume, and the sweat of their lust the previous evening.

She kicked her feet up in the air and waved them back and forth like an ant stuck on its back grasping to get up. Her thoughts mixed excitement at the memory of the previous night with frustration at her current situation. Finally, she went into action.

Carefully picking up the phone, she dialed Glenda's number. If the mayor answered, she would hang up. But when the first lady took the phone, Missy's face smiled brightly.

"Hello there," Missy whispered in a sensual tone that always drew Glenda's interest. "Coming over?"

On the other end, Glenda did not share Missy's interest in chatting. "Home so soon?" the first lady said, surprised that Missy had not stayed to see others perform.

"I couldn't stop thinking about you," Missy whispered back as she twisted her legs together. "I know some things I think we'd enjoy."

"I don't think I can make it," Glenda said, her mind still glued to the array of people she'd met earlier in the day and already planning who to follow up with for the highest social-ladder payoff. "I'll talk to you tomorrow."

With that, Glenda hung up and Missy's face went from hopeful excitement to sadness to growing anger. She slammed down the phone so hard it bounced off the cradle and dangled to the floor.

"Can't make it, eh?" Missy thought to herself, pounding her fist against the wall. "Okay, if that's the way you want it, that's the way I'll make it."

Missy then darted over to her nightstand and pulled out the bottom drawer. Under a mass of combs, scarves, pens, and handkerchiefs, she grabbed a worn, faded envelope of photos. Jumping up on her bed, she opened the envelope with a snide smile, carefully lifting out the contents.

Brushing her hair back as she squatted up higher on the bed, Missy began leafing through the pictures, smiling to herself while she glanced at each one and remembered the moments they were taken.

The photos, which Missy hadn't seen in more than a year, showed her and Glenda in some of the most erotic and sexual positions they'd ever engaged in. One by one, Missy's hand lifted the snapshots that showed her and the mayor's wife in everything from kinky, unusual positions with vibrators to tightly-locked sexual sessions to naked dances on her balcony.

The secretive photos were the result of a one-time use of a motorized camera that Missy had procured from a photographer friend for one of her birthdays. Although Glenda had agreed to engage in the unusual photoshoot after a few margaritas, she later made Missy promise to never have them developed.

Missy gave her word, but eventually had the prints made as a souvenir of that special night. Today, however, the young blues singer had other plans in mind for the forbidden photos. They would act as her revenge. If Glenda would not reveal their relationship to the outside world, and not even make time to come over that night to patch things up, Missy would take matters into her own hands and show the first lady for what she really was.

After a mix of laughter and anger at the thought of what Glenda was forcing her to do, Missy hit a few shots of Tequila and fell asleep on her bed, not even bothering to change out of her performance clothes. As she slid off to sleep, the photos fell from her hand on to the floor.

*　　*　　*

"I've got no time to talk to some second-rate blues singer," Tim Cross yelled through the phone to the receptionist who had stopped Missy King as she went looking for the *Journal* editor. "What the hell does she want?"

Missy was startled at the loud response from the editor. When she walked up to the floor that held the *Journal* newsroom, she'd simply asked to see Cross. But that was not good enough for the receptionist, who deflected dozens of people a day who wanted to complain to the editor or pitch some outrageous story.

When asked why she wanted to see the top man, Missy was reluctant to give away her whole story to some desk clerk, so she simply told her that she was a blues singer, thinking that might hold some weight.

Not quite.

Missy didn't wait for the receptionist to politely dismiss her. She went into her final reasoning. "I have something he might find very interesting," Missy said coyly.

"Like what?" asked the receptionist, who'd heard every person seeking a meeting with Cross claim to have some Watergate-like information. "Let's see."

"No," Missy responded, as she tightened her grip on the bag that held her precious photos. "Only the editor."

By that point, Cross's ears had perked up and heard Missy's reasons for coming to his office. Aside from being attracted to her young, slender looks, Cross also could not help his curiosity at what this nightclub entertainer would have that a daily newspaper might want.

"Well, then, come in, but I haven't got all day," Cross said as he led Missy to his office. "This'd better be good."

"Oh it is," she answered.

As Cross headed toward his corner office, with Missy close behind, the young woman who'd never been inside a newspaper glanced around the busy, noisy, messy room. From the framed front pages of past major news stories spread across the walls to the overflowing ashtrays on most desks, Missy was both disgusted and intrigued.

Missy sat down as Cross flopped in his chair and immediately grabbed the newspaper he'd been reading. Without even looking up at Missy, he asked what she wanted.

Missy said nothing, but simply placed the photos of her and Glenda in front of the editor, causing him to drop his newspaper slowly as he picked up the pictures.

"Who is this?" he said, both perplexed and excited. "I know that's you, but who is... NO! Not her."

As Cross looked up, his mouth formed a smile almost as quickly as Missy's grin took shape.

"That's her, literally in the flesh," she said.

Then Missy went into the entire story of the lesbian couple's long affair, their initial meeting, and the latest fight. With some tears rolling down her face, Missy explained how Glenda had led her on and then recently pulled back with a refusal to come out about their relationship.

As Missy presented the situation, Cross carefully reviewed each photo, holding some of the seedier positions up to the light for a better view. Soon, his smile turned to frustration and then despair. After another minute, the editor began to shake his head.

"I'm sorry," Cross explained, "I can't use these for anything. I don't know where they came from or if they were doctored or what."

Missy's smile also began to fade and she trembled slightly.

"But...but, I took them and I know what happened," she said. "I can verify all of it and stand by it."

But Cross just shook his head.

"Can't do it. Besides, our publisher has just struck up a new, tight relation-ship with the mayor," Cross added. "Ever since he backed the stadium plan, we've been in his corner. We don't need to pull something like this and ruin the chance of getting something down the line for the Giants or some other project they want."

"Does that mean you won't report anything wrong that he or she does ever again?" Missy asked.

"No," Cross answered, with a stammer. "We would never be that stupid. But we don't need to go out of our way to attack the guy, especially when the proof is so flimsy. Now if we had taken these shots or could tell for sure that they were real, you might have something. I'm sorry."

Missy rose slowly and stuffed the photos in her bag before running out the door, past the receptionist, and down to the street. She thought briefly about approaching the *Bulletin*, but figured they would be even more reluctant to engage in such a strange, lewd publication.

Missy also knew enough about the *Advocate* from her talks with Glenda to decide that they could not always be trusted, either.

That left one possibility.

Missy ran to the corner just in time to grab the Polk Street bus and climbed aboard. After about five minutes traveling north, the bus dumped her at the precise spot to which she had ventured: the front door of the SF Reader.

Once there, Missy went through the same game with their receptionist. But once she threatened to take her "information" elsewhere, the receptionist called Danny Dugan directly and he appeared moments later.

Inside Dugan's office, he carefully inspected the photos in almost the same manner that Cross had scrutinized them. But this time, Missy heard what she wanted to hear.

Flashing a rare smile, and looking up directly into Missy's eyes after reviewing each shot, Danny Dugan let out a cheer that could almost be heard at City Hall.

"Where the hell did you get these?" Dugan said, laughing and hooting at the same time at the prospect of holding evidence of such embarrassing activity by the first lady in his hand. "What made her do this?"

Again, Missy went through the same story of their meeting, love affair, and continued hidden relationship. This time, however, Missy shed no tears and, instead, made it clear to Dugan how the photos had come about, and why they needed to be published.

"This woman goes around acting as though she is the prim and proper first lady when the truth is she is unfaithful to her husband and carrying on a charade," Missy said, her voice rising. "On top of that, she is engaged in a major lie that should be known to the gay voters who put her and her husband where they are today."

That was the right thing to say to Danny Dugan.

Although Dugan would gladly go forward with anything that would make Jack Callahan look bad, playing on his sense of honesty in politics and public life—as well as his crusade to allow minorities to be treated equally—worked even more so.

Before Missy could even finish talking, Dugan called one of his top reporters in to begin working on a story about the entire affair between Missy and Glenda. After explaining to the reporter what was happening, and taking several of the photos to the photo department, Dugan asked Missy if she had any more proof of their relationship.

"Any letters, other photos, cards she gave you?" Dugan asked. "Anything that shows that this relationship exists?"

Missy promised to look.

Then Dugan hit her with two things she had not entirely thought about.

"Okay, here it is. If we write this, the gay community may come down on you for exploiting your lesbianism for notoriety," Dugan said. "Even if that is not your intent, you will get some backlash, you know that?"

Missy nodded, although she had not thought of such an effect. Then, Dugan hit her with another point, too.

"You will also be flooded with other media who may look into your life and may find things you don't want them to know," Dugan stressed. "You have to be able to handle that, too. It could also affect your singing career, and it may make it harder to go on stage."

Again, Missy leaned forward with an assuring, agreeable nod.

"And your relationship with Glenda will likely be over forever," Dugan said. "Is that something you can live with?"

Missy thought long and hard, putting her head into her hands and taking in a big breath. As she lifted her chin after a minute and let the breath out, she simply nodded her head. Although she said nothing, a small tear ran down her face at the thought of losing her longtime lover.

But she also knew that she had to do this or risk being at Glenda's beck and call for good. She had already decided she needed to have her self-respect and get on with life.

"Fine," Dugan said with a grunt. "Let's do it!"

At that moment, Missy and the reporter, a young, shy recent college graduate named Penny Atkins, went to the newspaper's conference room and began to talk. For the next three hours, Missy detailed how she and Glenda had met that fateful evening at the Blue Knight, how they'd been sneaking around for several years, and how Missy had come to feel something strong for her.

"I don't know if it's love," she explained as the young reporter scribbled in her notebook and kept the tape recorder going on the table in front of them.

"But it was something strong. Something I had never felt with any other person, man or woman."

Missy found herself wiping away tears as she realized that this exposé would forever destroy her relationship with Glenda. But, at other times in the interview, while describing the empty, angry feeling of seeing her lover with another man—or hearing her say over the phone on several occasions that she "couldn't make it tonight"—Missy's face turned bright red and her voice would rise.

"I was like a dog or cat to her," Missy shrieked at one point. "Someone who was supposed to be there just for her when she wanted me, and stay out of the way when it was inconvenient."

As Atkins wrote down each word, with one eye on her note pad and the other on the subject of her questions, she marveled at the flow of events. Thinking about how such a story could help boost her own career, she also felt a tug of sympathy for Missy. Especially when the singer described the way she had traveled to San Francisco to find herself and, after building a career and a fond relationship, had seen it fall apart.

"I can see why you feel this way," Atkins said at one moment during the interview. "This must really hurt."

Wiping away more tears, Missy couldn't tell if Atkins was just using the sympathetic B.S. that reporters often play to their subjects to gain trust, or whether she felt her point of view. Either way, it didn't matter to Missy. She was going to blow this thing open and, whether it sparked sadness, anger, or leftover lust for Glenda inside her, it would soon be done.

After the lengthy interview, Missy met again with Danny Dugan to ask how the story would be placed and when it would run. Since it was Friday, the issue containing the story would not be able to run until Wednesday, when the SF *Reader*'s next edition was out. That would give Dugan, Atkins, and the rest of the staff ample time to position the story correctly and decide which photos were best used.

"We're going to play it up big," Dugan told Missy as he escorted her out. "I will talk with Penny and see what she has and if we need anything else, we'll be in touch."

"Thanks, Mr. Dugan," Missy said, her mind still split over what was happening. "I appreciate it."

"No, thank YOU, young lady," Dugan said, his grin expanding to cover his entire face. "This is something that this town needs to do. It is the right thing."

As Dugan went back inside and set forth his plans, Missy took another bus home. She pondered her actions yet again. Should she have gone all out already? Maybe she could talk to Glenda and work something out. Maybe Glenda had realized that they should be together.

Her mind ran in a thousand places as the bus hit a bump and shook while crossing Noe Avenue on the way to Missy's home. This indecision was nothing new. Ever since her childhood, Missy had been unable to leave the past and big decisions behind once they were made. Her mother used to tease her when they went to the bakery for donuts or to the ice cream store for a cone.

"My little lady of indecision," her mother would say as Missy pondered each choice. "The little girl who can't make up her mind."

But as the bus rolled up to the curb and Missy departed, she decided to stay with her latest decision and see what came of it. As she got ready for that night's performance, Missy thought about calling Danny Dugan to put a stop to the story, but held back.

Then, just as she was dressed and ready to go to the club for her 9 p.m. performance, she picked up the phone and dialed Glenda's number. Pacing back and forth, Missy waved the phone around over her head and felt herself stammer. Just before someone could answer, she hesitated before hanging it up.

"Ah, shit!!" she yelped, feeling the pain and irritation of indecision. "What have I done? Oh, fuck it, fuck her, let it happen."

The singer then shut off the light and headed out, slamming the door behind her. As she bounded down the stairs and walked out into the breezy evening air, a wisp of fog settled over the night sky.

Trotting down the hill toward the Castro District for her night's work, Missy allowed herself to stop fearing the move she had made. Although she still worried about losing Glenda and facing her life alone again, she began to see the bright side of her actions.

Stopping at the corner of Market and Castro streets for a red light, Missy began to smile as the night's vehicles rolled by. Even the sight of other gay couples roaming romantically about that night did not depress her. Missy began to realize that it was the best move.

"This will free me up to be who I want to be," Missy told herself as she approached the club and saw the small poster outside with that night's list of performers, which included her. "No more waiting around for some horny old broad who wouldn't give me the respect I deserve. No more watching her fake her way through life as the wife of the mayor, who she doesn't even give a fuck about. And no more secret encounters where I don't know where or when I am going to be able to meet her next."

While waiting in the wings of the club's stage for her time to go on, Missy thought more and more about what the change would mean to her. Although she continued to fear an unknown future, she realized that it was the right thing and, hopefully, would lead to a better relationship in the coming months or years with someone else.

As the strumming guitar and slow drumbeat of the band went into gear to signal Missy's entrance, the young singer began to smile and feel a positive sensation about her future. When the rhythm grew louder and stronger, and the audience clapped to lure her out, Missy found herself more excited, alive, and ready to feel the adventure of life than she ever had.

In an unusual move, she ignored her usual entrance routine and ran out to the stage center, to the surprise of both band members and the crowd, and leaped right into a friendly greeting for the fans.

"Hi everyone, isn't it a great night?" she yelled, drawing screams and hoots from the fans. "Let's get alive and kick it."

With that, the band broke into one of Missy's favorite Stevie Ray Vaughn tunes and the show was on. As Missy sang, growing louder, crazier, and more explosive with each tune, her mind began to clear and her worries to fade.

Maybe it was the burst of the crowd. Maybe it was the ease of her mind knowing that her past was behind. Or maybe it was just the buzz of the Whiskey Sour she'd been nursing backstage. But either way, Missy was ready to take her life back by the horns and ride it for all it's worth.

That night's show was among her best ever. The crowd roared from start to finish, even dragging Missy out for three encores. Afterward, a small crowd jammed the backstage area grabbing for autographs. The excitement did not end until after midnight, delaying Missy's departure.

But she didn't mind. She knew that her relationship with Glenda would be over by the following week and she relished being able to stay out after her gig to mingle, drink, and chat with fellow musicians. On most Fridays, Missy had exited the place quickly to attempt to meet Glenda, often waiting at home for hours for the city's first lady, or finding herself stood up when Glenda failed to appear at all.

But tonight it didn't matter. She didn't care where Glenda was and, once the clock passed midnight, she didn't want to know.

At about 12:30 a.m., as the final night's performers ended their set, Missy got her things together and started her trek up the hill toward home. The next day was Saturday. She would have some time to work on some songs and get some things done before returning to the club for what was usually the wildest show of the week—Saturday night.

As she hoofed her feet up the hill toward her house, passing two men engaged in some kind of sexual act in a parked car on one side and an obviously drunk older woman on the other, Missy felt her sleep deprivation of the past two days catching up with her, but it didn't mar her spirits. Once up the hill, Missy fumbled in her pocket for the key, careful not to drop the bag that held her outfit and some song lyric books.

As she jammed the key into the lock and turned it quickly, Missy found herself laughing at the thought of all that had happened. Still buzzing from the mix of booze, music, and night excitement, she tripped twice on the way up the stairs but managed not to hit her head or arms.

Once at the top, she noticed something odd. The door to her apartment, which she religiously locked, was ajar. It wasn't wide open, and it had not been forced that way, but it was odd.

At first, the singer thought someone had broken in. Then she thought of who might have a key and needed a place to sleep on this wild Friday night. Missy was not above giving friends a key if they needed a place to crash, and decided that any one of a number of people she knew might have taken advantage on this "non-school night."

Still, she carefully pushed the door open so as not to let anyone know she was coming in. If the person who had wandered in was a burglar, Missy wanted to catch them before they caught her.

If the visitor was a friend, she, of course, did not want to wake them.

As the door creaked open and Missy peered in, her jaw dropped at the site of the unwelcome guest sitting on the couch, with a deep stillness that could be felt all the way across the room, Missy did not know whether to laugh, cry, or faint.

It was Glenda.

Glenda did not speak, but just tapped her cigarette on her knee and let its gray, brittle ash fall to the floor. She drew in a strong breath with a noisy gasp, pulled the cigarette out quickly with a yank, and blew the smoke above her hair as she slowly shook her head from side to side.

Missy calmly closed the door behind her and dropped her jacket with a lurch. She then walked carefully toward her surprise visitor, not knowing if she had come in war or peace.

"Uh...Hi," Missy said, attempting to gauge Glenda's purpose and mood. "This is a surprise." That was the best Missy could do as she attempted to navigate Glenda's approach and intent.

"I should think so," Glenda said, taking another cool, slow draw on her cigarette. "I suppose you hadn't planned on seeing me after that stunt you just tried."

That clinched it. She knew right away that Glenda had gotten wind of her photo exposé. She quickly surmised that Atkins had probably attempted to get some kind of response from Glenda about the photos for her story. That made sense. Missy had hoped, though, that the reporter would have at least waited several days for a comment so as not to give the first lady a chance to stop or delay the story.

But Missy's trepidation quickly changed to defense and, in a way, excitement. She had planned her caper and now, it seemed, it was being carried out.

Missy knew that Glenda would hit the roof after the story and photos ran, but had hoped it would not occur until the publication took place.

Either way, she had to face the fallout. Now was as good a time as any, she thought.

"That was no stunt," the young blues singer responded. "I got sick of your bullshit and after you decided not to give me the respect I deserved, I wanted to show you how it felt. If I can't be with you because you are so worried about your damn image, then screw that image. Let the whole world know what you really are."

Just as the words came out, Missy felt a hot sensation in her face and a lump building in her throat. Small, barely noticeable tears began to fill her eyes as the impact of the entire incident hit her.

"I didn't want to hurt you, but, dammit Glenda, you treated me like shit," Missy said with a whimper that slowly changed to anger with her next comments. "And I don't want that anymore. I won't fucking stand for it."

At that, Missy turned away from Glenda and headed into her bedroom to change. She had just reached the outside of the room when she heard Glenda's voice trailing behind her. Missy stopped short as she entered, noticing the bed where the two women had held their passion and lust for several years.

But, although that might have concerned Missy just days ago, she now felt a fierce pride in her actions and threw her clothes on the bed without a second thought. As Missy began to change into more casual jeans and a T-shirt, Glenda stormed into the room and demanded a confrontation.

"Well, my dear, it isn't over just like that," Glenda said, holding up a manila envelope that she'd brought with her. "You didn't think you could just waltz in and try to defame MY reputation after all I've done in this town. No way, sweetheart!"

Missy turned around quickly and glanced immediately at the envelope Glenda carried.

"What is that?" she said with curiosity and a returning worry. "What are you up to?"

Glenda just sat quietly on the bed and grinned. Crossing her legs, a move she knew had always excited young Missy, she carefully opened the envelope and pulled out her prize objects.

Before Glenda even finished, Missy could tell what she had done. There, lying on her ex-lover's lap were the exact photos that Missy had so carefully and diligently delivered to Danny Dugan hours earlier. Each one had been marked up on the back for expected publication, but it was obvious they were in the wrong hands.

"Hey," Missy said like a schoolgirl grabbing at a playground classmate for a stolen ball. "Where did you get those?"

As she spoke, Missy stuck her hand toward Glenda's lap to retrieve her property. But the first lady just whipped them away and placed them back in the envelope, gripping them tightly with one hand as the other rested softly on the bed.

"You had a lotta balls to think you could pull this one over on me," Glenda proclaimed. "When that ditzy reporter called me today to find out what I thought about all of this, I told her I would have to get back to her."

"Then I called my attorney and had a court order within the hour forcing the *Reader* to give me the photos and barring the newspaper from printing them," Glenda explained. "The only thing I still need is the negatives, which you're going to hand over right now."

As she spouted her order to Missy, Glenda stood up and grabbed her former lover by the arm.

"You better hand them over right now or there is going to be trouble," Glenda said. "Don't think I am through with you, either. Anyone who fucks with me pays."

Missy seemed startled by the entire story. She'd thought that Danny Dugan was in her corner, that he could print anything as long as it was true, and the fact that Glenda wanted the photos so bad showed it was true.

Glenda shook Missy's arm harder and harder as she demanded the negatives. At one point, Missy pulled away and darted to the other side of the bed.

"No," the young girl barked at Glenda. "You are not getting anything. This is my story and I will get it out somewhere. If not the *Reader*, then someone else."

The truth was that Missy had no idea where the negatives were. She had developed those photos more than a year ago and, like most people who take snapshots, had probably thrown them away.

But if Glenda thought that she still had them and might use them to expose her through another publication, that would be enough to keep the first lady on edge, something Missy was beginning to like.

Sure, she could have told her she didn't have them, which might have been believable. But that would have ended it and Glenda would have won out and been allowed to keep her phony image as the prim and proper first lady going.

This way, Missy was able to turn the knife deeper and deeper into Glenda's psyche, making her believe that she could lose her precious image at any time under Missy's control. It might even cause her to come back to Missy and give her the attention she felt she deserved.

But that was not on Missy's mind. She'd made her break and only intended to keep the idea of outing Glenda alive as long as possible.

"You are not getting them, you will never get them, and if you don't do what

I want, they will get out some other way," Missy shouted as she ran out of the bedroom and toward the kitchen.

Glenda quickly chased her out of the room and into the kitchen. Within seconds, Missy found herself backed up against a window that looked out into the backyard that she shared with four other tenants. Keeping one eye on Glenda, Missy quickly glanced out to see who was there but found only a neighbor's dog resting on the lawn.

As she looked toward Glenda, Missy saw that she would have to get away from her before admitting the truth of the negatives. But Glenda was not ready to let her out. She slowly moved toward Missy like a wolf closing in on its prey.

Bits of moonlight seeped through the open window, reflecting off both women's bright faces as they moved slowly in a circular motion. A few tears again rolled down Missy's face as Glenda's stare turned harder and redder.

"Look you little bitch, you are going to give me that fucking film and that's it," Glenda said, as she looked around the room for a weapon, keeping one eye on the subject of her anger. "You know I will get it, so just make things easy."

As the words left Glenda's lips, Missy took a chance and jumped to Glenda's right, knocking her arm aside and reaching out to get past. As she stretched her arm to make way around Glenda's body, Missy knocked over a bowl of fruit that had been on her small kitchen table, causing a crash when the porcelain shattered on the ground.

The sound caused both women to stop for a split second. Missy began to step forward again to attempt an escape, but Glenda grabbed her around the waist and flung her toward the side of the room.

The quick grab and throw pushed both women up against Missy's vintage 1940's gas stove, causing them to fall and slamming Glenda's head on the hard steel stovetop of the old-fashioned appliance that Missy had bought just weeks earlier.

Missy, too, was knocked in the head as the force of Glenda's action threw her across the stove and headfirst into the wall, right where the gas line into the stove was connected. As Missy struck the connection, part of the coil pipe that brought gas into the stove broke off, sending a low, wispy sound out, and allowing gas to escape into the room as the two women fell into unconsciousness.

The nearly inaudible sound of the seeping gas filled the room with noxious fumes as the two women lay there unaware and unable to move.

Moments later, Glenda's body dropped to the floor, banging her head again on the hard tile surface, while Missy's body stayed draped across the top of the stove, blood trickling from her head.

The cool night air continued to blow outside as both women remained still, and the deadly gas aroma filled the room, soon spreading to the living room and hallway while the injured occupants remained, unaware of what was building around them.

After several moments, Missy found herself awakened by the cool breezes and immediately began to choke on the gas cloud that had built up around her during her brief collapse. Tasting the blood that had dripped down from her head, she immediately touched her scalp where she had banged it and jumped back startled at the red liquid on her finger.

Coughing as she struggled to get up, and still dizzy from the impact of her head injury, Missy looked around the room, her eyes tearing from the effects of the gas and her lungs sucking for fresh air.

Her first reaction was to walk toward the door. But after only a few steps, she was forced to crawl her way around. Once headed in the right direction, Missy remembered what had happened and turned her head back to see that Glenda remained unconscious and still while the room's oxygen disappeared, replaced by the ever-growing fumes. Still coughing and wheezing from the odor, Missy crawled toward Glenda, hoping to reach her and drag her to safety. Tears welled up in Missy's eyes again as she fought off the fumes and began to panic at the situation.

"Glenda," she yelled, as she reached for her one-time lover's hand and pulled on the sleeve. "Glenda! Wake up. Hurry, we've got to go." Panic overtook her and she screamed and cried. "Please help! Help!"

Tears rolled down Missy's face as the panic increased and she knew that she had to get out. But she did not want to leave her old friend. Even though only moments ago Glenda had shown a desire to inflict pain on Missy, she still felt a desire to save her as anyone would want to protect another person from the possibilities of death.

Pulling and tugging on Glenda's arm with one hand, and covering her mouth to block the gas with the other, Missy felt herself begin to get dizzier. As the fumes grew, Missy was about to pass out when she turned toward the door and began to crawl out again.

"No! No! Help!" she cried, her face turning red and voice shrieking "Nooooo!!!!"

Blood continued to trickle down her face and her eyes watered more as the room grew stuffier. A misty haze filled Missy's eyes and she felt the room begin to spin just before she closed her eyes and dropped to the ground. As Missy's body drooped to the floor, she reached her hand out to grab on to the wall as she fell.

Once the gas reached the edges of the room, it seeped and through the stove to the area of the pilot light. Just as Missy slid to the ground, the vapors connected with the pilot light's flame.

In less than a second, the flame ignited, an explosion occurred, and the entire house erupted into flames. Before the blaze even began, the force of the explosion had killed both Missy and Glenda, knocking them from the kitchen into the next room and leaving their bodies to burn. ∎

Chapter Fifteen

A Great Lie

The thunderous bang of the explosion rocked the Castro neighborhood with a jolt that resembled an earthquake. Although it was Friday night, a usual time for the nearby Castro District bars and clubs to be hopping, the street on which Missy lived was unusually vacant when the powerful blast ripped off part of the roof and sent flames shooting more than 50 feet high.

Neighbors next door to the east were out, while those on the west side of Missy's home felt the explosion as fiercely as if they'd been at the front door. Half of Missy's second-story apartment went up in flames that glowed over the entire neighborhood and sent thick, black smoke billowing to all sides of the house.

The apartment had taken up the second and third floors, so the only people immediately affected were Missy and Glenda. The first-floor tenant, who also owned the building, escaped uninjured and, thanks to the firefighters, saw only a small, back bathroom scorched by the fire.

Several area residents immediately called the fire department to respond to the blaze that remained only in Missy's apartment but sparked fears of spreading, especially with winds whipping up on the cool, clear night.

Within minutes, flashing red lights filled the view of every corner of the neighborhood while piercing sirens wailed from one end of the street to the other. Soon, the street in front of the home was filled with a small crowd, some in their nightclothes; others in outfits worn for a night out on the town.

Within the crowd, some even began to speculate about who had been living in the home. A few locals knew that Missy had been there at some point recently as a tenant, but were unsure if she still resided in the Victorian. Those who knew her as a neighborhood singer also hoped for the best but braced for the worst.

None of the gossiping crowd, however, even hinted that Glenda might be there. That was due to the couple's imperative secrecy.

That secret would soon be revealed.

Once the gas company had shut off a main valve, within 20 minutes the fire department had doused most of the blaze. After about an hour of wetting down the area and containing the smoldering spots, several fire inspectors walked through the home and tried to determine if anyone was still there.

Attempts to get in and look for people as the blaze burned had been stopped because of the danger of further explosions from the gas. Firefighters had not heard cries for help, which would have prompted a rescue no matter what.

But now that the flames were out, Fire Inspector Wayman Keller hiked up the damaged front steps and entered to begin the arduous task of looking through the debris and determining what was left. Stepping carefully up the partially burned out stairs, Keller climbed over the blackened sections of steps and made his way up to the second-floor apartment that had been home to Missy, and now held her and Glenda's lifeless bodies.

Shining a flashlight through the front doorway, Keller squinted to see over the narrow light beam. The front living room area had remained partially intact, but the kitchen and back bedroom were destroyed. The veteran firefighter could see that much of the ceiling had blown off and cleared a hole up to the third floor. A look around the room showed shattered glass, burned furniture, and a kitchen that was completely blackened by the explosion and fire.

The signs of fire damage were nothing new to Keller, a 21-year veteran of the fire department who'd petitioned to join the inspectors ranks ten years earlier to help crack a string of school arsons.

Keller had been promoted after helping the department stop the seven-month series of school fires when he linked them all to a special flammable chemical that was made at a nearby lab. His investigative prowess determined that a high school senior with a reputation for pyromania who worked at the company had been using the chemicals to torch the schools for kicks.

Once the fire department cracked the case and Keller got his accolades, he became the man they turned to for any difficult case. Strangely, he had been on regular duty this night when the call came in for the fire at Missy's home. He went there thinking it was just any other case and, with the obvious cause of a gas leak, would take little effort to solve.

But he would soon discover that this case had more than a routine cause and effect, and would end up affecting his career, his outlook on fire investigation, and city politics for good.

Scoping the apartment with his hand-held light, Keller stopped suddenly once he reached the center of the living room when he saw the hideous sight. Just two feet in front of him lay the bodies of Glenda and Missy. The force of the explosion had thrown them from the kitchen into the area by Missy's couch. Because they had been knocked out of the kitchen before the flames engulfed it, their bodies were only partially burned.

Although he'd seen hundreds of dead bodies in hundreds of burned-out homes, the sight of them still caused grief. Keeping his flashlight pointed directly at the two women, Keller took just a moment to shake his head in sad anger.

"Fuckin' shame," he whispered to himself. "What a waste."

Taking in a deep breath and letting out a sigh, Keller was quick to check each woman for identification. Since Missy had been changing at the time of the couple's argument, she had only underwear and a shirt on, with no I.D. But Glenda was fully clothed, and lay on her stomach, her face out of Keller's view.

As the fire inspector leaned down to carefully turn the dead woman's body over, her head swung around revealing her face. Keller knew she seemed familiar. Her face was slightly burned, but not so that Keller did not have a vague recollection.

Then he realized who he had just found. Keller jumped back and grabbed his chest like a child frightened off by a dog's snapping bite. Rising slowly and putting his hand to his head, Keller just opened his mouth in disbelief.

"Son of a bitch," he said. "This can't be true."

He realized he had found Glenda Callahan, the first lady of San Francisco, dead. What's more, he had found her in the house of a younger, single woman, in her underwear. As Keller stood there wondering how to handle this one, his eyes caught another partially burned item in the home—a framed photo of Missy and Glenda that had been taken during one of their first dates at the Blue Knight following a Missy performance.

Looking around the room, Keller discovered two or three other snapshots of the couple in happier times, each showing more than a friendly embrace of the two. Although they were not as sexually explicit as the shots Missy had turned over to the SF *Reader*, they helped lay out exactly what the relationship between Missy and Glenda had been.

Not only did Keller have to deal with the death of the mayor's wife, which would draw enough media attention as it was, but to find her with a half-naked lesbian lover would not exactly help the mayor's image.

After ensuring that the fire had been put out in every part of the apartment, Keller immediately went outside and called Fire Chief George Moore at home. Moore, one of Callahan's inauguration day appointments along with Police Chief Steve Brown, and immediately got word to Brown, who agreed to phone the mayor.

As he called Callahan's number, Brown quickly realized that he would have to tell the man that his wife was not only dead, but had been found in a compromising position that could lead to Callahan's political downfall, or at least political wounding.

Callahan, who'd been out that same night with Glenda for a dinner with some friends, had gone to bed at about 11 p.m. and knew that Glenda would likely go to Missy's.

Since becoming mayor, Callahan reveled in the ability to make progress in the city and tackle public issues, leaving his anger or frustration about Glenda's sexual conduct in the back of his mind to be dealt with down the road.

When his phone rang in the early morning hours after the fire, the mayor had been sleeping soundly and did not pick up the call from the police chief until after five rings. Callahan lifted the receiver slowly, nearly dropping it as he leaned over the nightstand next to his bed.

Fumbling for the phone, Callahan knocked over a photo of him and Glenda that had been placed on the nightstand but made sure not to hit a glass of water that remained from his aspirin dosage hours earlier.

"Hello? Hello?" Callahan rasped into the phone. "Who is this?"

At the other end, Brown, still in his nightclothes, took a gulp before telling the mayor his tragic news. The police chief, who'd been the very man responding to the Billy Dale shooting months earlier, now had to tell his boss of a worse tragedy that would affect him both politically and personally.

"Jack, this isn't easy," Brown said, his voice cracking.

Callahan knew right away that something was different if his police chief would refer to him by his first name. Although Callahan was not one who demanded honorary titles and protocol, he knew that Brown always referred to any superior such as the mayor or state officials or supervisors by their proper title.

Even when the mayor had gone golfing with Brown and Moore and others, the chief constantly used "mayor". Callahan believed that Brown liked to remind himself that he was with such a powerful person.

"What is it, Steve?" Callahan said, still half asleep. "Come on, out with it."

"Well, I don't know how to say this, but…Glenda's… dead."

Brown just stopped after that as Callahan took in the news. It was strange. Even though the couple had been far apart romantically for more than a year, Callahan was the kind of man who took the idea of his marriage seriously, at least from a caring point of view.

Even when he realized that Glenda had been carrying on with Missy—and other women—he had accepted it and been able to find at least a close, caring relationship with Glenda. She stood up next to him during the campaign, and afterward as the friendly first mate. For Callahan, who didn't demand much from life beyond his calling to public service, Glenda was more than he had hoped for, especially after his first marriage had ended so badly.

When the police chief's words reached the mayor's ears, his first reaction was not the shocked crying and grief that many husbands would endure. After all, the deep romantic link to their marriage had been over for a while.

Still, Callahan found himself struck with sadness and a certain loss. When Brown told him she had been found with Missy, Callahan's first reaction was again not one of anger or jealousy, but further sadness that another person, a young, vital singer, also had perished.

But the fallout was not over, as Brown explained. Just as Callahan was trying to accept the death of his wife, he realized that the impact on himself could be tremendous. All of this was too much to bear as the mayor got up and prepared to head out and deal with the situation.

Running outside in the early morning hour, the mayor jumped in his chauffeured car—which was always on 24-hour duty—and headed to the scene. Callahan's feelings rocked back and forth from sadness over Glenda's death to slight anger over Missy's death to confusion over what to do about this secret of Glenda's that was about to be exposed.

Just as the town car approached the fire location, he saw the partially burned-out building and his heart sank. He knew that inside were the bodies of his wife and her lover.

Lifting himself out of the back seat of the vehicle, the mayor just stared at the scene. Mixed emotions of futility, anger, despair, and horror filled his mind and body. A sudden queasiness stuck in his stomach and he could feel the tears well up in his eyes. Leaning over with both hands on his stomach to hold back the ill feelings, the mayor held himself still right there on the street.

"Okay, okay, hold it in," Callahan told himself as he fought back the urge to explode and attempted to keep his mind and emotions straight. "Keep it together."

Then, bent over with his arms around his waist, Callahan forced himself to look up. He winced and felt his eyes and chest tighten as he worked through the initial shock. Like always, whenever he had come across a crime scene or tragedy in his police days that overwhelmed him, he would push all that aside and deal with emotions after the fact.

Somehow, he had trained his feelings to stop or be put on hold in situations like this and hoped he could do it again. Once he believed that was the case, the mayor unclasped his arms, stood up, and headed over to Brown and Moore, who had been talking together.

As they watched the mayor approach, both chiefs walked toward him and held out their hands to steady Callahan's walk and console him.

"Thanks for coming, mayor," Brown said, as he put his arm around his friend. "I know this is hard for you."

Callahan just nodded and whispered a quiet thank you, trying all the time to keep his eyes from looking at the building. He noticed, however, that the coroner's vehicles that had responded remained empty, with their doors open.

Before Callahan could ask about that, Moore extended his hand of condolence as well. When the mayor had appointed him chief, he had not known Moore as well as Brown, because the two had not worked in the same department, but had been told of Moore's reputation as a good administrator and, because of that, had made him chief.

"You have my sympathies, too," the fire chief said as Callahan nodded. "If there is anything we can do to make all of this easier, we can just take care of everything."

The mayor thanked him, but said, "I knew I had to be here and want to do what I have to."

At that moment, both chiefs looked at each other and walked Callahan over to the large mobile communications center that had been brought in. Ordinarily, the trailer-size facility would not have been set up outside a routine house fire, but once Brown realized that this involved Glenda, he wanted to have the most control over the situation that he could.

Inside, the three men sat down, each took cups of coffee and remained silent for about 30 seconds. Then Moore spoke.

"Mayor, we know this is a difficult situation for you and would not dream of making it worse," Brown said. "But we did not want to do anything until we checked with you about how to...handle it."

Callahan's raised his eyebrows in response, letting out a slight yawn at the same time due to the lateness of the hour.

"What do you mean?" the mayor said, although he had a clue.

"Well," Moore added. "We know that this...revelation about your wife could look, well, bad and we didn't want to do anything without seeing how you wanted to take care of it."

As Moore spoke, Brown offered an awkward nod to the mayor.

Callahan pushed his chair back from the table in anger and jumped up. "What the hell are you talking about?" the mayor said. "What do you mean, 'Take care of it'? This is a tragedy and we will do what is right. Carry out the bodies, do an investigation, and give them the proper burials that they deserve."

Brown, who knew a little better how to talk to the mayor and massage his right-from-wrong attitude, attempted to calm Callahan down.

"Look, mayor, we don't want to do anything improper, either," the police chief said, taking the mayor's arm and easing him back to his seat. "But, it has had to have crossed your mind during all of this that information about Glenda's involvement with this woman could... well... hurt you. Right?"

Still steamed, Callahan kept a stern grimace on his face. "That doesn't matter," he said. "This goes beyond my damn position. Two women are dead. One was my wife and one was a young girl. Sure, I am not happy about how it looks, but that doesn't mean we should go hiding the truth. That never works in these situations and it's not how I want to conduct my office."

At that moment, the mayor jumped up and shoved the chair back under the table with a bang. "You will run this case like any other and let me handle how to let out any 'embarrassing information.' You got that?" Callahan said, pointing his finger at Brown. "And I don't want to hear any more talk about handling things. There are enough things to 'handle,' like giving respect to the dead."

But that was not going to stop Brown and Moore. They owed their jobs to Callahan, but they also knew that if his mayoralty were damaged by the revelation that the Callahans portrayed their marriage as something it was not, public support would go out the window, and the mayor could be voted out in three years.

Worse yet, if the fallout were bad enough to spark real public dissension, a recall vote could be orchestrated and Callahan could be gone in less than a year. In that case, Moore and Brown would eventually have to either leave their jobs or be demoted to make way for newly-appointed chiefs by the new mayor, something neither wanted.

Both Brown and Moore had only three more years before reaching the top retirement level for their pensions, which would allow them to retire at the top chief's salaries and with the full amount of pension due.

Although it seemed morbid to discuss these things with two dead women just 100 feet away, Moore and Brown could not ignore the facts. They knew that Callahan had likely thought about it, but his honest, straightforward approach to police work and politics would not allow him to confront it as an option.

Just as Callahan was preparing to leave the command post and try to see what he could do to ease the impact of the first lady's death on the city, and the revelation of her gay lover, Brown took Callahan by the arm again.

The mayor gave a kind of helpless, tired sigh as he sat down at Brown's direction. Brown brushed his hand through his hair, while Moore tapped his nails on the table nervously. Callahan sat waiting for some kind of comment, rubbing his eyes in exhaustion.

"Okay, mayor, if we have to get like this, we will," the police chief said. "This is how it is. We cannot let this get out if at all possible because we know what it could do to all of us. So, we will find a way to separate the two women's deaths and no one will ever know."

Callahan began to react again, this time with an angrier tirade. But Brown cut him off.

"Look, dammit, we all worked too hard to get where we are, and not for you to throw it away," Brown said. "I will not let you jeopardize my career and future, or your own, by doing this."

Callahan's eyes widened in surprise.

"And just what are you going to do about it?" the mayor asked with disgust and curiosity. "I'm still the mayor, you know. I can kick you out of your jobs in the next five minutes without any reason if I want."

"Yes, you can," Brown said, coolly lighting a cigarette. "But then I can tell everyone, including those newspapers you've become so friendly with lately, about your little caper at the Mount Davidson Cross not too long ago. I was there and, remember, I know all about it."

Callahan grabbed at Brown's tie and pulled him close to his face. "You know damn well I had nothing to do with that set-up."

"Yes, I know that. But everyone else will see the evidence that you played right along. You think they will believe otherwise? Especially if your friend Billy Dale has something to add to the conversation?"

Both men just stared at each other while Callahan eased back into his seat and put his arms down. The mayor could see that more than a year in Billy Dale's hands had shown both of these men how to best put his dirty tools of the trade to work.

Brown had not wanted to pull this last-minute plan out of his back pocket. In fact, he was somewhat surprised that the mayor had not brought up the need to separate Glenda and Missy's deaths to save his administration himself.

But now that it had come to this, both men were holding their positions. Like two poker players waiting for the other to blink, they sat there. The flashing lights of fire and police vehicles continued to light up the night outside, while trickles of water ran down from the house where Missy and Glenda's bodies remained as the three men sat and waited.

"Well, if I go down, you will go with me and people will find out that you had as much to do with it as me, even more," the mayor argued.

But Brown was ready to shoot back. He told the mayor, rightly so, that the chief's involvement would not be as much at issue as the mayor's. He could prove that he knew nothing about it, but Callahan's link would do more harm.

"If you think so, go ahead and test it," Brown said, a nervous smile on his face. "See what happens."

The mayor put his chin on his hands nervously, panning his eyes back and forth between both men before closing them in a tired thought. He bit his lip as he processed all the scenarios, all the while ignoring the inner pain he felt about the death of the two women who lay just yards away from the conversation.

Finally, Callahan gave in, realizing that this revelation would only destroy everything. He held back tears at the thought of committing more dishonest moves in office, and raged at the way his police chief had him over a barrel. He also wanted to get over this and just get on with life, a life that at least had a chance of doing some political good if he kept his administration going.

He didn't even know at this point, with the death of Vernon Bogart, the jailing of Billy, and now this double tragedy, if his administration could even refocus on good government. But he realized he had to do whatever he could to see if it at least had the chance to carry on.

"Okay, you son of a bitch, let's do it," Callahan said, getting up and walking out in disgust. "But don't think I'll forget this."

Callahan shook his head in disgust and stepped out. Slamming the door to the portable building, the mayor was hit by a blast of raindrops that had begun to fall outside. The mayor closed up his coat and put up the collar to fend off the rain.

As the sirens diminished around him and the firefighters continued to wet down the area, Callahan walked toward Inspector Keller. The inspector, as Moore had told the mayor, was the one who had found Glenda and Missy and was the only other person who knew they were there. After Keller informed both chiefs about the situation, Moore had ordered Keller to keep other inspectors out of the building and do nothing with the bodies.

Keller told the mayor what his orders had been, and Callahan advised him that the chiefs had another plan. Keller nodded as he kept one eye on Callahan and another on the building, which had been sealed off to keep out firefighters, neighbors, and, most of all, nosey reporters.

Moore and Brown came out of the command post and presented their plan to Callahan. Brown's plan was simple. They would remove Glenda's body and place it in another location where a fire would be determined to have caused her death.

Moore suggested placing her body inside her car and letting it run into a tree along one of the shaded roads of St. Francis Wood, the exclusive mansion neighborhood in the Sunset District area. Glenda knew plenty of people in that area that she could have gone to visit on a quiet Friday evening; that could easily account for her being there rather than in the Castro District.

Since Glenda had taken a cab and not her car to see Missy, it was not obviously in sight at Missy's house, either. The first move was to get her car from the mayor's house in Pacific Heights to an area along St. Francis Wood Boulevard. Because of the late hour, few people would see the relocation of the car in such a quiet, residential street.

Moore would move the car and allow Brown to steer it into the accident. Moore would then return to the fire scene and take care of the investigation into Missy's death and the fire there.

Missy's death could be easily solved as being the result of her falling into the stove and knocking the gas line loose. The only change would be that Glenda was not there.

Callahan grew angrier and worried with each passing comment about the plan, gritting his teeth and wiping his brow as the details were presented to him.

"This is not going to work," Callahan said softly so as not to let the other firefighters and cops in the area hear. "How can we do this?"

"It's easy," Brown said. "None of the other firefighters have been in the home other than to douse the flames and no one has seen either body other than Keller. He will go along with us and we will make sure to have those who find Glenda's body be among our most loyal folks. We'll even sweeten the pot for them with some cash and a promotion."

Although Callahan disagreed, he let the two chiefs and the fire inspector put the moves in play. Moore went with Callahan back to their home and took Glenda's car—a 1990 Lexus—to one of the quietest, most hidden sections of St. Francis Wood Blvd. They also left the keys in the car for Brown and his people to find.

Back at the fire scene, Keller and Brown re-entered the house and carefully placed Glenda in a body bag. To disguise it, they covered the body bag with tarp sheets, so that it looked like a piece of burned-up rug that had been rolled up for disposal. They carefully loaded it, tarp and all, into a nondescript city pick-up truck that Brown's assistant had brought over.

By then, Moore had returned with the mayor. With Moore overseeing the fire scene, Brown could leave without attracting too much attention, especially since the fire was out.

Brown and Keller headed off to relocate Glenda's body in the car, while Moore directed other fire officials to begin the investigation into the cause of Missy's death. Since she had died of a head injury and other internal injuries caused by the explosion, and she was the only known tenant of the apartment, her death was ruled an accident and her body taken to the coroner for an autopsy.

Meanwhile, as Brown and Keller approached the parked car located on the other side of town with Glenda's corpse wrapped in back, they made sure to see that no one was watching as they pulled up. Callahan and Moore had parked the vehicle on a hidden curve of the quiet street, with about half of it behind ivy from the tall walls that ran along the roadway.

With one eye out for witnesses, Brown and Keller carefully placed Glenda at the steering wheel, positioned her body to have one foot on the gas pedal, and started the car up. Adjusting the steering wheel so that it would maneuver the car into the nearest tree, and avoid hitting other cars or homes, Brown started the ignition, placed her foot squarely on the gas, and let the car go.

At first, the vehicle just traveled along for about 50 feet. But then, as it hit a hill, it picked up speed, weaved back and forth, and smashed directly into an old oak tree, causing half the branches to fall and the horn to go off. The two men had also made sure it would hit head-on, allowing the best chance for an explosion.

To help their chances further, they also had punched some holes in the gas tank. Although this might make investigators who found the car suspicious of a setup, they believed that if the fire were bad enough, it would cover up the obvious arson aspects. They also knew that they could correct any fire investigation down the line that looked to hurt their plan

Just moments after the car struck the tree, with a loud bang, a small fire erupted in the gas tank. Less than 20 seconds later, the car exploded, sending flames up the tree and engulfing both the tree and the car in the blaze.

To make sure the fire didn't spread, Brown and Keller waited as several lights in area homes went on. Moore knew that someone would call the fire department. And sure enough, within five minutes fire trucks were on the scene to put the blaze out and make the grisly discovery.

*   *   *

Back at the fire scene in the Castro District, other inspectors had already pulled out Missy's body and sent it to the morgue for an autopsy. Several Castro residents gathered around the fire scene could easily see that it was the body of Missy King.

Some in the crowd even remarked that they were wondering if Glenda had been there, too. Although their relationship had been secret, they'd been seen together enough to make tongues wag about a possible affair in the close-knit lesbian community, even if it never traveled to the rest of the city's political gossip mill.

Once fire investigators in St. Francis Wood realized who had died in the car, they called in police to investigate. The ranking officers at the scene at St. Francis Wood—who knew nothing about the Castro District fire other than it had been a fatality—quickly put out the word to higher police ranks that the mayor's wife had died in a car accident.

When Brown received official word from police on the scene, he tried his best to play along with a surprise reaction.

Then he called the mayor.

Since Callahan had gone home after Brown and Moore pulled their double-cross on him, he was in the perfect place to receive yet another phone call informing him of his wife's death. Later, when reporters would grill him about where he was when word came, he could honestly tell them he was at home.

For the second time that night, Callahan jumped into his town car but drove himself to avoid suspicion. He steered directly to the scene where his wife's body had been found.

Even before the mayor showed up just after 3:30 a.m., several reporters and photographers and news crews were already on the scene. As he stepped out of the car, flashbulbs began popping, microphones were shoved in his face, and scribbling reporters jockeyed for position.

Shoving some of them aside in a fit of partially-manufactured anger and partially-genuine sorrow, Callahan headed toward the bank of microphones that the press groups had set up. As he passed the car, he could just barely see the remains of Glenda's body, which looked completely burned, except for part of her face.

That image sent shivers up Callahan's spine and caused him to stop for a second to wipe his face. No tears, but an obvious emotional reaction that the press caught with quick camera shutter clicks and videotaping.

Once he reached the microphones, Callahan held up his hand as if to say, "Please, give me a moment" and took several deep breaths. Just as he attempted to speak, he felt tears well up in his eyes.

To those in the press, the tears seemed to be genuine displays of sadness and grief at the sudden loss of his wife. To the mayor, they were a mix of some grief over her death, but mostly inner humiliation for taking part in such a despicable, cowardly stunt.

As words were about to come out of his mouth with some kind of statement in the early-morning hour, Callahan felt himself lose control and begin to sob uncontrollably. He grabbed onto the small mike stand to keep balance and wiped away the tears.

The scene was slightly surreal. The mayor was crying as he had never before in public, the burned-up car carrying his dead wife's body stood just a few feet away, and the misty fog that always permeated this area of San Francisco drifted across thicker and darker than ever.

Through it all, the camera shutters clicked, the video cameras ran, and the reporters jotted down every last description of it all. They knew they had a great story.

The mayor knew they had a great lie. And he knew that he was right in the middle of it. ∎

Chapter Sixteen

An Immediate Connection

Since it was past 4 a.m. when the bodies of Glenda and Missy were officially found in their separate locations, news of the grisly deaths could not make the morning editions of the *Journal* and the *Bulletin*, but the information slowly seeped out on Saturday morning through television, radio, and word of mouth.

The explosion and fire that occurred at just after 1:30 a.m. at Missy's apartment had been noted by police through their scanners and would have made news anyway. It had been a fatal incident and had occurred on a rather slow weekend. Both local news radio stations had mentioned the fire with just mild interest, reporting that it had blocked traffic on Missy's street.

But no more real reporting of the fire occurred until the next morning when police revealed that the dead body of a woman had been found. Only one of the news radio stations even bothered to mention Missy by name, adding that she had been "a little-known blues singer in the city's local music scene."

The *Bulletin* and the *Journal* also gave passing mention to the death of Missy in the fire. Each paper planned to include a photo of the damaged building, but only because a freelancer in the area had happened to shoot a picture as the house burned.

For editors, fires mean nothing unless many lives are lost, some exciting rescue of an old lady or cats occurs, or, most importantly, there are good photos. By Saturday morning, the *Bulletin* had already been printed and delivered, and the *Journal*, although distributed later, still had given only a photo to the fire.

As the Saturday morning staffs trickled in at about 9 a.m., each paper still planned to give the fire just a few paragraphs and a photo, likely on a deep inside page.

What everyone was frantic about that morning was the surprising, tragic death of Glenda Callahan, still believing it occurred in her car in another part of town.

When police responded to the calls of neighbors in St. Francis Wood at about 4:30 a.m., Glenda's car was still on fire. The front end of the vehicle had gone up in a blaze just moments after it hit the tree, but the back half remained untouched.

Almost as if they had steered it by remote control, Brown and Keller managed to position Glenda behind the driver's wheel and place the car at a proper distance from the tree so that the impact would not only make it seem as though Glenda's head injury had been caused by the crash but also miraculously leaked enough gasoline to spark an explosion shortly after the car struck the tree.

Once police and firefighters responded, they quickly doused the flames and watered down the car to make sure no additional fire or explosion could occur. Then, carefully, two firefighters looked inside to see if anyone needed to be pulled with injuries. The first thing they saw was Glenda's body, hunched over the steering wheel, her lower torso and hands burned black, but her head remaining somewhat recognizable, with a head injury that had swollen considerably.

After checking her I.D. and running the license plates, the investigators determined that this was, in fact, the mayor's wife. It was at exactly 4:41 a.m., according to police logs, that the confirmation came over the police radio system.

"Attention, headquarters, we have a female Caucasian dead behind the wheel at 3305 St. Francis Boulevard," the message blared throughout the radio system and any scanners that were listening. "Identification is as follows: Mrs. Glenda Callahan. Yes, the mayor's wife is DOA."

Although few were on duty at that hour, those photographers and reporters in hearing range raced to the scene, just in time to catch some photos of the vehicle and get basic information from the police and fire officials at the scene. As far as those who had responded knew, Glenda had died as the result of a car accident. They would have to see if she was drunk or impaired, but initial investigations showed a simple car accident.

"Perhaps she had fallen asleep at the wheel," one responding cop conjectured to reporters.

By 10 a.m., when the complete weekend staffs had shown up at both newspapers, editors were firing off assignments like rounds of a machine gun. Both J.C. Townsend and Tim Cross came in later in the morning, despite the weekend day off, to coordinate coverage.

The basic story about Glenda's body being found had to be done, along with a lengthy story about her and her husband. Several reporters were dispatched to the Callahan home to get photos, personal insights from her house staff and neighbors, and anything else that would help shed light on who she was.

Next, of course, was finding out what had happened, where she was going at that late hour, and if the coroner had found anything. The initial report from the medical examiner's office was that no formal autopsy could be completed until at least Sunday.

Someone also had to talk to the mayor. Although he had made some tear-filled statements at the scene where Glenda's car was found, no real insight could be gathered from Callahan at that early hour because he had just found out about the tragedy, or so the reporters thought, and he also appeared exhausted.

"We have to get the mayor on this," Cross bellowed to one of his reporters who had been called in along with a dozen others that morning. "Find out everything you can—from what shoes she wore to why the hell she was driving around that late."

TV and radio reports beat the newspapers with coverage Saturday morning, but they gave only limited information on the car accident and basic background on Glenda.

Broadcast stories reported only that she had met the mayor years earlier, had worked her way up in business, and had been known as someone who craved the rising social ladder.

"I remember her always wanting to be seated next to the biggest dignitaries in the room," recalled a social planner for the Fairmont Hotel. "She really seemed to want the social spotlight."

But other than that, little speculation was given to anything involving her marriage or possible affairs. The truth was few people in the mainstream media had bothered to pay Glenda much attention since her husband had been garnering it all.

The efforts to get to Callahan Saturday proved useless. Several reporters, news crews, and photographers staked out the mayor's house in the hopes of finding him, while another smattering went to City Hall to see if he would appear there.

For most of the afternoon, however, Callahan mulled things over in the office of Carl Devins. Devins had headed up to Napa Valley for the weekend, but called Callahan earlier in the day the minute he heard about Glenda. Knowing that Callahan would need a place to figure things out, he offered the office without waiting for the mayor to ask.

Callahan felt that he could adequately figure things out, and avoid reporters, while holing up in Devins's office. Since his relationship with the campaign consultant had not been widely known, few reporters or other interested parties would go looking for him there.

Callahan told Brown and Moore that he would need to be alone there for at least a few hours. Although they had already double-crossed him once, the mayor decided he needed to work with the fire and police chiefs if he was going to pull off this charade.

Moore and Brown, meanwhile, had to fend off questions of their own from reporters, and decided to hold a brief press conference at 2 p.m. that afternoon. During the session with a sea of reporters, including some from as far away as Sacramento and Los Angeles, the chiefs recounted the obvious events. Glenda's car seemingly burst into flames after hitting the tree that morning at approximately 4:10 a.m.

No! They didn't know where she was going.

No! There were no signs of drugs or alcohol in her system, although tests were still being done.

No! There was no one else in the car.

No! The mayor was not with her.

"That is all we have for now. We will get autopsy results on Sunday, maybe Monday at the latest," Brown said, ending the press conference. "The mayor is in seclusion and cannot be reached for comment. He may have a statement later. What you got from him this morning should be enough. The man has been through a lot."

With that, the reporters went back to file their stories.

The next day's *Journal* and *Bulletin* each burst with news in big story packages of coverage. Neither hinted at any foul play or sneaky, underhanded police tricks to hide the real story. Each made the story the lead, but neither blanketed the front page with the coverage.

Both newspapers also reported on the fire at Missy's apartment, detailing the time it occurred and the name of the victim—Missy King. The *Bulletin* had no information on who Missy was, but the *Journal* tagged on the same line it had earlier, that she was a local blues singer.

Strangely, in all the commotion on Saturday about Glenda's death, Cross had not even seen the Missy King story until the next day's paper came out and he read it over as he always did. But even when he came across the story about the fatal fire, the name—Missy King—did not resonate in his memory, even though it had been Missy who had come to see him just days earlier.

When the word of Glenda's death started to come out, Cross remembered for a moment that a young girl had come into his office with proof of a lesbian affair, but decided it did not mean anything. Since the news account the *Journal* had run of the fire at Missy's included no photos of the young woman—with just a shot of the burning building—Cross had not put the two together.

But others did.

*   *   *

Danny Dugan had been hosting one of his infamous dinner parties on the Friday night that Missy and Glenda died, so word of the fatal explosion did not reach his ears until late Saturday morning.

The affair in Danny's house was somewhat of a belated St. Patrick's Day gathering, but his gatherings needed little in the way of a true calendar holiday to be successful. Since his early days as a newspaper publisher, Danny had always spent long hours in the newsroom and production rooms of the *Reader*.

By the same token, he also let off steam in a big way with his cocktail and dinner parties. Unlike his daily news counterparts who often threw away money on lavish affairs in ritzy hotels and big-money restaurants, Danny liked to keep things casual and relaxed, often picking up nothing more than deli sandwiches, beer and wine, and an occasional bottle of Scotch.

His guest lists also departed from the Who's Who crowds of San Francisco's elite, with liberal authors, his favorite local columnists and writers, and often a third-party politician of choice.

This affair was no different.

Among the group were some former members of the Board of Supervisors, local low-level political community group leaders, and at least one campaign consultant who shared Dugan's views, Carl Devins.

Although Devins had recently aided Callahan—a Dugan foe—with some minor political maneuvers, he remained Dugan's friend and an invitee. In part because Dugan and most of the city had no idea that he was on Callahan's bandwagon.

Little did either know that night that the evening would end with Callahan drawn into a web of deceit, tragedy, and manipulation that would eventually directly affect them both. But, as Friday evening turned into Friday night, neither man worried about the unknown future.

Another guest and perennial favorite at Dugan's soirees was Marie Alzeti. The outspoken politico and former *Reader*-supported mayoral candidate had kept a low profile—as had most supervisors—since the stadium vote and homeless program defeat.

Still, Alzeti remained upbeat during Dugan's party. At one point in the evening, she even smiled when she saw the joy in her publisher friend's face as he played host.

Throughout the evening, Dugan hoisted up the drinks behind his faded basement bar, along with servings of lasagna, Irish stew, and other homemade dishes he and his wife, Shelly, had cooked up during the past few days. The guests, most donning nothing fancier than jeans or corduroys, scarfed down the goodies as fast as possible.

Not even the journalistic defeat Dugan had suffered just hours earlier at the hands of Glenda could be seen in his demeanor that night. Despite his friendly facade, every now and then Dugan's temper was flaring inside at the thought that Glenda had succeeded in quashing his story about her extramarital affair.

Even as he scooped out Italian meatballs and fresh brochette onto guest's plates, Dugan still fumed internally over the way the first lady had waltzed past his receptionist and straight into Dugan's office that afternoon, waving a court order for the photos he had secured from Missy.

Several hours of work on the exclusive that would have brought down both this socialite bitch and her inept husband had gone to hell in a matter of minutes, Dugan thought to himself. He replayed the scene over in his mind several times during his social gathering. Each time it burned his nerves more and more.

After long talks with his attorney, who had suggested that he give in to the order to avoid a costly legal battle, Dugan decided to put the issue behind him for the weekend and focus on enjoying this social event.

Still, it remained in his mind all night, through the end of dinner, the replenishment of cocktail after cocktail, and even an early morning bull session with the hangers-on who always waited around for the end of Dugan's parties to engage in the true, in-depth, and gossipy discussions that he and Shelly would inevitably lead.

Dugan's efforts to put the Missy and Glenda affair on the shelf for the weekend were shattered late Saturday morning when, along with the rest of the city, he heard the news of Glenda's death.

At first, he was just as shocked as anyone at the first lady's tragic demise. He never contemplated any link to Missy initially, just feelings of sadness for the loss of another person, even if it was someone he had openly ridiculed.

It wasn't until later that afternoon when he caught a brief news report on the Castro District fire that he thought about a possible connection. When the name of the woman found dead in the explosion early that morning was released, Dugan—unlike Cross—immediately made the connection.

At first, he only found it odd that both women had died the same night of tragic, fiery causes. But after recalling everything that had happened that week involving Glenda, Missy, and those photos, it stuck in his craw that something was up.

As the TV and radio reports spouted only praise for Glenda and sadness for her loss, Dugan decided that more might have fit into this strange circumstance than would immediately meet the eye. At about 4 p.m., he called Penny Atkins—the reporter who'd been preparing the story to go with Missy's damaging photos—and revealed his suspicions to her.

"This eats at me," Dugan said as he caught Penny in the middle of a workout at home. "Something isn't right here and I doubt if the dailies would be inclined to pick up on it, even if they felt the same way. Do everything you can to check out both deaths."

Penny, who had run across some similar concerns when she saw news reports that day, nodded as she listened intently to her boss.

"I hear ya," she told Dugan as her mind began to plot out how she would track the possibilities and when. Penny had been at the *Reader* for just over a year, but Dugan and other editors had already marveled at her ability to grab onto a story idea, plan out the research, and hit the reporting like a racehorse at the starting gun.

"I'm all over it," Penny said.

Like any good reporter, Penny was glad to jump on the story, despite the weekend assignment. She knew that grabbing a good story, especially one involving a possible cover-up and lesbian affair related to the mayor's suddenly dead wife, was worth extra hours at any time.

The night before, during Dugan's party, Penny had commented to some of her cohorts about the disgust she had for some of the unionized daily newspaper reporters who complained about working more than eight hours a day and cried if they did not get overtime for every extra second.

"A bunch of whiners," Penny had said, as she sipped her favorite Guinness and leaned against the bar. "They should be glad they're not walking a fucking beat or sitting in an accounting office all day."

Just moments after hanging up with Dugan, Penny went to work. As she jumped in the shower and washed off her workout sweat, Penny's mind raced through all the facts and possibilities of the story. Letting the shower's water douse her face, Penny's brain worked through every element of the situation.

She knew that the key element of the story—Missy and Glenda's affair—was true, at least enough for the two to have posed naked for some revealing photos. But to what extent that relationship had gone, and how much she could write about from just Missy's side of things, was yet to be determined.

The reporter also had to find out if there was anything underhanded in the deaths of the two women occurring on the same night, from somewhat similar circumstances. The fact that they both died in fiery explosions within hours of each other would have left anyone who knew about their affair suspicious. What the key element of that link was Penny had yet to discover.

Toweling herself off as the radio in her bathroom blared more news of the first lady's sudden death, Penny made a mental checklist of how she would go about seeking clues to prove the affair.

"I just have to figure out what goes where, but what can I show?" Penny said to herself as she buttoned up a blouse and pulled on a pair of jeans. "There has to be a link. Something had to have happened. This is not right."

With thoughts still racing through her mind, Penny threw on a sweater, grabbed her pocketbook and reporter's note pad, and ran out of the house to see what she could find. ■

Chapter Seventeen

Real Leg Work

At the same time that Penny Atkins began her search for clues, someone else was shaking his head as the news reports of Glenda Callahan's death continued to broadcast just about every hour on the hour Saturday.

Billy Dale, who kept a close eye only on certain news stories, had not found out about the two women's deaths until he checked out the late morning news inside the prison recreation room television, which had become his key link to outside news developments.

When Billy sat down that morning to tune in what he thought would be a boring review of Friday's otherwise slow news day, he nearly choked on his gum when he heard the bizarre tale of Glenda's demise. His first thought was that either a political enemy of the mayor's or some link to Missy might have resulted in the tragic loss of the first lady.

As he sipped a ginger ale— a poor substitute for the vodka he usually enjoyed—Billy carefully put two and two together when the short report on Missy's apartment fire and explosion followed the lead story of Glenda later in the newscast. Billy did not even link the two until the end of the apartment fire report when the reporter identified the lone, fatal victim as Missy.

"Hmm, imagine that," Billy said it himself with a broadening smile that grew during a sip of his drink. "That is quite interesting... Quite!"

Once the news report ended, Billy walked over to the pay telephone that served as his only direct connection outside the prison. Each prisoner had unlimited phone privileges, but if the guards thought you were speaking too long or otherwise wanted to punish you, they could take them away at a moment's notice.

Billy's ability to schmooze most anyone in authority allowed him to keep good relations with the guards, maintaining a pretty open phone link. While some other prisoners cursed out guards at every chance and made trouble with fights or noise, all Billy did was spend time reading magazines and political history books, or monitoring the few TV news reports he had a chance to watch. He also had a stash of novels ranging from Jack Kerouac to Jack London that kept him busy.

Some he had held on to since his days at Barney's Books. He had told friends that re-reading old ones and brushing up on newer titles that he had missed helped him get through the long hours of prison life.

After only a few months in San Quentin, Billy adjusted to the time he would serve, but not without an eye toward the future. Keeping his brain active and his links to the real world helped him remain patient until the day he could return to regular life.

Those thoughts were also what caused him to make a special phone call that day after seeing the reports of Missy's and Glenda's strange deaths. Punching in the numbers on the keypad, Billy bit hard on the gum he was chewing while taking the last swallow of his ginger ale as the call connected.

When the person on the other end answered, Billy said simply, "Jimmy, we have to talk."

The man on the other end, who also had been watching news reports all day and delving into the reality of the mayor's wife's death, was, of course, Jimmy Min.

Jimmy had not known about Glenda's and Missy's relationship, or he likely would have used it to his advantage once Billy and he had broken ranks with Callahan.

Billy knew that keeping the affair private during the stadium battle made sense. Most of that fight was about the image of Vernon Bogart and the financial elements of the project, not the sexual escapades of the mayor's wife.

The veteran political strategist also knew that such an outing could backfire if voters saw it as anti-gay and an attempt to slander the mayor's name for political gain. As a gay man who had long fought for gay rights, Billy also did not want to use someone's lifestyle against them, even if it was someone he despised as much as Glenda.

Still, now that both women were dead, the odd circumstances of their deaths could reveal some kind of underhanded involvement somewhere. He was not so interested in revealing the two women's affair, but in seeing if something illegal or sinister was involved in their demise. Which, of course, it was.

Billy knew that even a hint of scandal in the death of either woman, both of whom had links to the mayor, could tarnish Callahan's image... something Billy had been salivating over since the day the mayor had turned on him. His appetite for revenge had grown to almost obsessive levels while he had been locked behind bars.

Even though Billy was smart and patient enough to bide his time until his release, he remained fiercely competitive and angry with those who had helped put him there.

At the moment he heard Billy's voice, Jimmy Min smiled. He'd been keeping a close eye on the reports of the first lady's death—and had already dispatched Mike McLean and two reporters to begin seeking out details that Saturday morning. Once he heard Billy's voice, Jimmy relaxed and enjoyed just chatting with an old friend.

"Hey, how the hell are ya?" Jimmy asked, as if the two were talking over drinks at a neighborhood bar instead of through prison walls. "What the hell is going on?"

Billy got right to the point.

"This shit is crazy," Billy said, leaning against the rec room wall with one eye on the TV and the other on his watch. "What the hell happened with Glenda? Do you guys know anything? What's the word?"

Jimmy just responded with the same facts that had been reported on newscasts all day long. He didn't mention the Missy King fire, since he had no idea about its connection.

"That's it," Jimmy said. "My people are out looking for something more, but nothing has come up yet."

Billy felt his energy turn up and his adrenalin kick in.

"Well, you better keep them looking because there is something more to this," Billy said.

Then he began to tell Jimmy all he knew about Glenda and Missy, why he had kept it quiet, and why it likely showed something more than just a simple car fire death. He explained who Missy was and why their deaths were no coincidence.

"Understand?" Billy said with a harsh, direct tone. "We can get this fucker if we come up with something. It may not be there, but I have a hunch there is something to hit him with."

After saying goodbye to Billy, Jimmy Min threw on a coat and headed out toward the *Advocate* office. As he drove his convertible across town to the newspaper, he kept an ear on the news radio stations, which offered more news and retrospective on Glenda and the mayor.

Turning a sharp corner at Army and Mission streets, Jimmy ran the same thoughts through his mind that Penny Atkins had pondered that day.

"This is too good to be true," Jimmy thought as he blared the car horn at an intersection, swerving to miss a box in the road. "This guy has been a pain in our ass for months. Fuckin' traitor. Would love to nail him to the wall. Show everyone who the hell he is."

With that, Jimmy picked up the car phone that he always kept charged by the stick shift and dialed Mike McLean's number. Maneuvering through the city with one hand on the wheel, and holding the phone close to his ear with the other, Jimmy waited until his star columnist and dirt-digger picked up.

When McLean answered on the other end, still groggy from some partying the night before not far from the Castro District, Jimmy didn't even say hello but went right to work.

"McLean! Come down to the office right away, we need to get organized," Jimmy barked as the wind whipped by his head. "We got some real leg work to do and you are the man."

Even before McLean could offer a helpless comment, Jimmy slammed the receiver down and hit the gas pedal harder. As he pressed his foot, he grinned another of his well-known smirks and raced forward.

"I do love to hunt them down," he whispered to himself as the car vroomed toward his office. "Hunt'em like deer, skewer'em, and roast'em up."

Although Jimmy was not one for eating a lot of meat, he loved to compare the investigative nature of journalism to a hunter on the prowl. He liked the comparison for its animalistic nature.

Having grown up as the son of someone forced to defend himself to make a business run in a new world—and eventually losing his life in such a battle—Jimmy looked upon the work of his newspaper as that similar to a hunt. Sometimes a valid hunt for truth, but often an overzealous search to seek and destroy just for the sake of the contest.

Jimmy never felt bad for his approach. He had seen from his father that it was the way it had to be, at least from his vantage point. He had also seen how Billy's similar approach in the political world had served him well, and had more recently seen how someone like Billy could be harmed if he didn't do all he could to fight against his enemies.

The car screeched to a stop as Jimmy pulled into the *Advocate* parking lot. On a Saturday afternoon, the place was bare. All that remained were some shreds of loading materials and a few stray copies of that week's issue blowing in the breeze.

Without even opening the door on the convertible, Jimmy leaped out and grabbed his briefcase-shoulder bag as he hurried into the office. After unlocking the back door, Jimmy hit the light, ran up to his office, and immediately turned on his computer. Tossing his jacket on the couch, he wiped his eyes and sat down.

The hazy day outside continued to loom toward darkness as the computer on Jimmy's desk hummed to life, squawked a few electronic sounds, then beamed ready for use. Right away, Jimmy tried to find any information he could get on Glenda and Missy.

Glancing at his wall clock, he could see it was just after 4 p.m. Little by little his search provided bits and pieces of Missy's life, but nothing more than some scraps about singing appearances and a rare comment or two on a local gay chat room.

"Damn," Jimmy said to himself, slapping the computer like an owner hitting a disobedient dog. "Nothing? Fuck! Shit!"

Just as Jimmy voiced his anger, he heard a familiar voice.

"Now, now, that's no way to treat such fine machinery," said McLean, as he walked into Jimmy's office, still wearing shorts and a T-shirt. "You must be gentle."

Not one to waste time with pleasantries, Jimmy got right to the point, again.

"McLean, glad you're here," Jimmy snapped, not even bothering to look away from the computer screen. "Here is what we have."

The *Advocate* publisher then went on to tell McLean exactly what Billy had told him less than an hour earlier. He recited the story about the couple's affair, and also Billy's direct comments to them just two years earlier about hiding their relationship.

As Jimmy rambled on, McLean offered none of the surprise or astonishment that Jimmy had shown when he first got word of the nuggets of information.

The columnist, who learned as a young reporter never to reveal his excitement about a scoop for fear of losing the prime sources, just kept nodding his attention with all of the boredom of a high school student in biology class.

When Jimmy finished, broadening his grin to its widest ever, McLean remained quiet. Jimmy's smile began to recede when he saw that McLean did not share his enthusiasm over the news. He nearly became insulted.

"So, what gives?" Jimmy asked, almost annoyed. "Didn't you hear a word I said?"

"Sure, great stuff," McLean said. "But I've known about this for years. What? You think something like this just happens without word getting out?"

Jimmy shook his head, ready to unleash an angry tirade at McLean. But, just as he was about to begin a yelling fit, he smiled again.

"You bastard," the publisher said softly, almost affectionately. "You almost had me ready to lay into you. I know, I know ... always remember what's important. Well, so, what does this mean?"

"The thing is, this is not something new to the gay community or some select few people in the mayor's circle," McLean said as Jimmy listened with a rare quiet demeanor. "But it is not known by most people. So it could be a real bombshell."

Jimmy rolled his eyes.

"I know, you prick," Jimmy said. "But how do we prove it? Do you have anything that can set him up? Pictures, letters, some people who saw them somewhere? How about a fucking shot of them doing each other right in the middle of Golden Gate Park?"

With that, Jimmy laughed at himself as McLean shook his head.

"The point is, it isn't enough," McLean said as he took a seat. "Even if we nailed him with this stuff, it isn't a smoking gun. The most it could do is show that his wife was cheating on him. That could help him, get him some sympathy as the abused husband."

Jimmy was so busy being excited over how the information could embarrass the mayor that he didn't realize it could help him, too.

"And to target him now, just days after his wife was found dead and burned up, that could also backfire on us," McLean said. "You don't need that, especially from the gay community."

"So why didn't Billy think of that?" Jimmy asked his friend and employee. "He's usually ahead of the curve."

"Because Billy knows that it will hurt the mayor, and at this point—with his ass behind bars—that is all he wants to do," McLean said, getting up from his chair and yawning. "He's not far off. I mean, it would knock him down a few notches, and it would implicate him as someone engaged in an act of deception since, after all, he pretended to be in a good marriage with her. But, for us, it's not enough."

Jimmy could always count on McLean to take the broader view of newspaper stories. Even though he hit the bottle too much, smoked more than anyone he knew, and slept way past most deadlines, McLean had an eye for what would appeal to readers ... and voters.

Jimmy also remembered that McLean was the one who carefully orchestrated getting Callahan into office in the first place. And if anyone was going to help get him out, it was Mike McLean.

"So what do we do?" Jimmy asked, growing more frustrated. "We have to cover this one way or another. And we have to use it to our advantage to get that guy out."

"Sit tight," McLean said, using one of his father's favorite expressions. "You get one of your reporters to write a main news story as though it was just a simple death, and I'll start scouring for anything else I can find."

At that moment, McLean left, walked downstairs, got back in his car, and drove off. Jimmy got on the phone, called one of his best reporters, and sent him after the story. Then he tried to do whatever he could by phone or computer to dig up something useful.

During the next few hours, as Saturday became Saturday night, then Sunday, and finally slowed into Sunday evening, all four of the city's major newspapers were on the story of the death of Glenda Callahan.

Although the *Bulletin* and the *Journal* continued to play it up as the tragedy of a mayor's wife dying in a fiery car explosion before her time, with no link to Missy King or her death, the *Reader* and the *Advocate* were on the hunt for something else. Both of the weekly papers knew that Glenda and Missy had had an affair, but something specific had to be found to prove it.

And as far as Mike McLean was concerned, the affair wasn't enough. He didn't know about the mayor's dirty deal with his two chiefs, but he had an idea, an instinct. Or maybe just the common-sense cynicism that went with 20 years in journalism.

"Sometimes you just have to trust your gut," McLean would tell younger reporters. "You just know."

Editors who had often heard McLean refer to his "gut instinct" had recalled being irritated by it, but eventually seeing success in most cases.

"You piss me off, but you usually deliver," J.C. Townsend once told McLean when he worked at the *Bulletin* ten years earlier. "But, damn, why do you always have to hang us out on a limb to do it?"

McLean would just laugh and return to his desk to punch out yet another last-minute scoop. On this weekend, though, the *Advocate* columnist had disappeared. After leaving Jimmy's office Saturday afternoon, he laid low and was not in contact with anyone from the paper, or even Billy Dale, through the end of the weekend.

Penny Atkins, meanwhile, spent every minute seeking any possible link to Glenda and Missy's affair. Although McLean brushed off the lesbian relationship as a needless embarrassment, Penny and Danny Dugan saw it as a way to show the true side of the mayor and his wife.

*   *   *

On Saturday night, Penny started her efforts by perusing the fire scene. The flames had been put out the night before, but clean-up of the apartment had not begun. Although yellow tape covered the entrance, Penny carefully crawled under it and entered.

Walking up the same steps that Missy King had traveled just a day earlier after her uplifting blues set just blocks away, Penny pushed open the door slowly to make sure no one was there—no one who could get her in trouble for trespassing or kick her out.

Ashes floated up as Penny stepped across the doorway and creaked open the charred front door to the apartment. No lights were useable, obviously, but the setting sun outside still showed a beam through the windows to give the reporter a momentary view of the area.

Most of the scene remained the same, except for Missy and Glenda's bodies. When Glenda's body had been removed, Moore and Keller had made sure that no sign of her would remain. They didn't need anyone to notice that another body besides Missy's had been removed.

At first, Penny grimaced at the sight of the burned-out interior. Black streaks covered the walls, while burnt timber hung overhead and a smell of smoke and ash permeated the building. Carefully stepping across the floor of the living room, Penny coughed several times and rubbed her eyes that stung inside the stuffy, blackened room.

Taking out her notebook, Penny panned across the room looking for any sign of a link between Missy and the first lady. She saw plenty of pictures of Missy singing, some paintings that leaned toward modern art, and at least two concert posters—one of Missy's first headline performance, the other of Janis Joplin at Monterey.

The sun slowly faded outside the window while Penny crept through the rest of the house. In the kitchen, she could see where the stove had come away from the gas line, which had since been turned off. The bedroom also offered few clues, with most of the photos and other links between the two women having been carefully removed by Moore and Keller. For the next hour, the reporter went through the apartment inch-by-inch, piece-by-piece, seeking any kind of clue she could get. But nothing worthwhile was found.

Finally, as she reached the back window of the bedroom, which looked out into the small backyard that Missy had shared with a neighbor, Penny was ready to give up. If any proof of a relationship had been here, it was gone now.

Standing in the window as the sunset far away, Penny leafed through her notebook that, ironically, carried the notes of her conversation with Missy from just a day earlier. She knew she had a story, and still had Missy's words to back it up. But without her there to stand by the allegations, Penny knew she needed more.

Ready to drop it all and seek answers elsewhere, Penny was just about to turn and find her way out of the apartment when her eye caught something outside the window. Peering out of the burned-up frame that looked down from the second floor, Penny spotted what looked like a framed photo in the tall grass behind the house.

Although most of the grass had been blackened and sheared by the flames, a patch far from the house remained untouched and uncut, since neither Missy nor the landlord bothered to take a mower to the place.

Carefully finding her way out of the building, Penny headed toward the backyard area, making sure that no one would see her, and picked up the item on the ground. As she looked it over, Penny smiled. The photo was not as lewd or X-rated as those Missy had shown her, but it was a clear, close shot of Glenda and Missy in an obviously romantic embrace.

It appeared to have been taken on a waterfront somewhere in the Bay Area and showed Missy on Glenda's lap, with both women wearing tight-fitting summer dresses. Perhaps the photo had been thrown out by Keller or Moore, perhaps Missy herself had flung it some night during an angry outburst against Glenda, or, perhaps, it had been accidentally knocked off the windowsill by someone who had not even noticed.

Either way, Penny realized she had what she needed.

"Yes!!" Penny said to herself as she stuck the photo in her bag and hurried out of there. "It's coming together now."

Penny then got back in her car and drove off, all the time figuring out how to utilize this new evidence and determine what else would be needed. Without Missy or Glenda to comment on the situation, Penny would require testimony from those who knew both women. It would be difficult since the few who had likely seen Glenda and Missy together were probably close friends who would not want her secret revealed.

Once she reached her apartment and carefully placed the photo in her home where she knew it would be safe, Penny headed out toward the Castro Street bars to see if she could do a little digging.

Carefully chatting nonchalantly with women at several bars, Penny tried to get someone whom she could be sure knew Glenda and Missy to confirm their relationship.

As Saturday night wore on into Sunday morning, Penny's efforts proved futile. She was able to talk with many women, and gay men, in several spots. But she could not confirm any link between the two dead women.

Anyone who said they'd seen the women together could not specify any exact places or circumstances, while others who acted like they might know something were reluctant to say anything to a reporter.

By Monday, Penny's attempts had gone nowhere again. She still had the photo of the two women stashed in her apartment, but little else to back it up other than Missy's interview.

On this day, however, most reporters were paying attention to the funeral for Glenda that was to be held at St. Mary's Cathedral, the grand, expansive Archdiocese of San Francisco central church that was always the site of major funerals, weddings, and baptisms.

As the mayor's wife, Glenda would get the royal treatment set aside for most people of power. With Callahan's strong Irish Catholic background, he didn't even have to make any arrangements. Once word of Glenda's death had gotten out, the archbishop himself had begun to organize the funeral and only sought Callahan's approval after it was ready.

"I hope you don't mind, mayor," the church leader had said. "I didn't want to trouble you with any extra effort on your part."

Callahan had only kind thanks for the archbishop when he received his call. During most of the weekend, Callahan remained in seclusion at Carl Devins's house. After hiding out in the political campaigner's office for most of Saturday, Callahan took refuge in his friend's Telegraph Hill home on Sunday and Monday.

Of course, the mayor ventured out to attend his wife's funeral. He had returned to life during the past few days, but still felt a touch of anger, sadness, and inner humiliation. Devins, who'd been out of town during most of the weekend, returned early Monday to pick up Callahan and take him to the funeral.

An unusually sunny day greeted those who went to St. Mary's for this sad occasion. One mourner even remarked that Glenda would have felt special to have had so many politicians, well-known names, and power brokers at her funeral.

As the mayor and his campaign advisor approached the church, hundreds of mourners and friends, along with a large group of reporters from all media, were waiting. The mayor smiled as best he could as he exited the vehicle, hugged friends, and shook hands of supporters. He waved off the press upon entering the church.

Inside, the place was a virtual who's who of San Francisco politics, society, and press. Several *Journal* and *Bulletin* reporters were there, along with TV and radio crews. In the far back, almost unnoticeable, was Mike McLean, who had not been seen for two days by his colleagues and would jump back into hiding immediately after the service.

Danny Dugan and Jimmy Min also showed up, more out of curiosity than any kind of respect for Glenda.

The service was quick and somber, but with a stretch of choral songs not often found at funerals.

The mayor had said such a musical send-off would have been Glenda's request. The church also was adorned in a spray of Glenda's favorite flowers along with a row of candles, a tradition at Callahan family funerals that represented everlasting life.

Afterward, the press—barred from shooting photos inside the church—clamored for a comment as Callahan walked out. But he again waved them off, got back in the car with Devins, and left. At that point, most reporters went after visitors and mourners, seeking to get whatever comments they could about Glenda.

All except Penny Atkins.

She had a particular interview subject in mind: someone who might have shown up at the funeral to pay respects, not to the city's first lady, but to a fellow member of the gay community.

Sure, several gay leaders were on hand, but their presence was purely political. What Penny looked for as she roamed the large concrete plaza outside the church was someone who would be, well, out of place in the power structure of City Hall. But perhaps at home inside the social hours of Castro Street or the blues scene of the Blue Knight.

Trying to maneuver through the crowd and make sure to avoid those who just wanted press attention, Penny glanced among the hundreds of faces that roamed the church's entrance. Slowly wandering as the crowd filed back toward cars or to grab shared rides and buses, Penny's hopes for any kind of help faded with every person who left and every moment that passed.

Wondering how she could go about getting some real, human confirmation of her story, Penny began walking up Geary Boulevard toward her car as her mind puzzled out her next course of action.

As the cars barreled by, with occasional honks and skids on the busy thoroughfare that remained the only street stretched across the entire width of San Francisco, Penny couldn't help but notice the different array of people who attended Glenda's mournful goodbye. As with anywhere in San Francisco, the chances of seeing a three-piece suit next to a hippie tie-dye outfit next to a T-shirt and blue jeans was not unusual.

Just as the reporter was about to cross the street at the end of the enormous block that contained St. Mary's large building and landscape, she noticed a woman standing next to a tree, far removed from the crowd outside the church, but close enough to keep an eye on the proceedings.

The short-haired blonde woman, who wore just a tank-top shirt, blue jeans, and sunglasses—somewhat unusual in the cool March air—seemed to have been standing under the tree for a long time, but did not look as though she wanted to move. Penny stopped just a few feet from her and tried to see what she was looking at, but the woman's eyes just seemed fixed on St. Mary's.

After standing for a moment, Penny walked further away since the woman seemed annoyed at the reporter's staring. But, after just a few steps, Penny couldn't help but look back at the woman, still curious. As she did, Penny's eyes caught a small tattoo on the upper part of the woman's back.

Stepping closer quietly, so as not to be noticed, Penny looked more carefully at the tattoo and saw that it was the symbol for the blues bar, the Blue Knight. Penny knew that that was the home away from home for Missy King and decided that this was someone who might be worth talking with.

Walking behind the stranger, Penny used her well-worn direct reporter approach and tapped the woman on the shoulder. Slightly startled, the woman looked up and, before she could say anything, was confronted with Penny's question.

"Excuse me," Penny said, with a bit of a stammer. "I'm sorry, but, I couldn't help but notice that you were standing here watching the funeral procession. Did you know Glenda Callahan?"

Still annoyed by Penny's interruption of her thoughts, the woman slowly pulled her sunglasses off and gave the reporter an irritated glare.

"Why do you care?" she said, then quickly placed the sunglasses back on her nose. "Who are you?"

Quickly, Penny hesitated over whether to reveal her occupation and risk driving this person away scared, or make up something that might allow a more open response.

"I'm just a curious person who happened to know her," Penny said, with some truth. "I saw you standing here and was just wondering what brought you."

Still annoyed, the woman looked away, refocused her eyes on the church, and slowly responded. "Well, let's just say she knew a friend of mine," the woman said. "I just wanted to come and see."

Barely able to hold back her curiosity, Penny just blurted out, "Missy King?"

The woman's mouth opened in astonishment, and she pulled her glasses off again, this time with a quick grab.

"Why would you ask me that?"

"Well, I couldn't help but notice that tattoo on your back and I knew that Missy worked at the Blue Knight," Penny said matter-of-factly. "It was just a guess."

"Bullshit," the woman said, placing the glasses back on her head. "You know something more and I don't think I want to talk about it."

At that moment, seeing that most of the crowd from the funeral had left, the woman turned toward the west side of town and began to walk away. Knowing that this could be some kind of important lead, Penny walked after her.

"Wait," she said. "You need to tell me how you know Missy and what you know."

"Look, lady," the woman said, turning around to face Penny. "I don't know you and I don't want to tell you anything. What the fuck are you, a reporter?"

Penny stopped short. "Well, actually I am," she said. "And I am trying to let people know what happened. What really happened."

"What happened was that Missy died and that chick died and they ain't coming back," the stranger said, stomping one foot. "What do you need to know? It's over with."

"Yes, but people don't know the whole truth," Penny argued as she chased after the woman. "I'm trying to tell them. How are you involved?"

"Let's just say I knew them both pretty well and I didn't like the way it ended," the woman said as she kept walking, but slowed her pace. "But it's too late. I just came here to see what was happening and now I'm leaving."

With that, the woman began walking faster and ignored Penny's calls for her to stop.

"Please, just talk to me, it could mean a lot," Penny said. "People should know that Glenda was not who she said she was."

But the woman walked on, ignoring Penny's reasoning.

"They should know that not every lesbian wants to hide."

With that, the woman stopped short. Taking a deep breath, she slowly turned around with a curious glare and a suspicious snarl. Penny ran a few steps to catch up and pulled out her notebook.

"I just want to be able to make the truth known," Penny said, flipping the book open. "You know who they were, why not let other people know?"

The woman shifted her shoulders and rubbed her face with both hands as she thought about Penny's words. Fidgeting about, she was weighing what she wanted to do.

"Look, I knew them from the club and I liked Missy a lot. I would love to let everyone know how that fucking bitch treated her. Making her wait around and acting like Miss Perfect God-Damn Wife," the woman said. "But it's too late, it won't mean anything and I don't want to get in the middle of it."

As the woman walked away, Penny just grabbed her hand and slapped her card into it.

"Look, if you change your mind, call me," Penny advised. "We can do something about this. We are not some big paper. You know the *Reader*, we want to take on the big types, not play their game. Just think about it."

The woman shoved the card in her pocket without even looking at Penny and ran off.

Penny didn't know whether to feel hope or more despair at losing another potential source. Too many times in the past, she'd offered up a card in the hopes that a reluctant source would talk later, only to have them never call back.

But, like most reporters, she had seen enough occasions when would-be sources called back after getting a card and offered up information, or leads to a better source somewhere else. Walking back to her car, Penny realized that she needed to go after other possible pieces of proof of an affair, and quickly. Here it was, Monday morning, and she would need a story finished by Tuesday night if it were to make the Wednesday edition this week.

Although she had enough information for a basic story on Glenda's death and some attempts at linking it loosely to Missy's, it was not enough. While heading back to the *Reader* office, Penny tried one last attempt to seek some help in the Castro District and visited a few more lesbian bars. But, unfortunately, the noon hour on a Monday offered little in the way of customers.

When she headed back to the office at about 2:30 p.m., Penny was ready to give in when she checked her messages. Several were routine callbacks or story tips, but one stood out:

"Uh, hi, this is Kathleen Marcus," the person said with a pause. "I, um, I was the one you talked to outside the funeral and, well, I might be able to tell you something."

Penny's hopes rose with the message as she listened further.

"I, uh, I don't know what I can give you, and I don't want my name in the paper, but I think you might be able to do some good for Missy. You can meet me tonight at the club."

A smile crossed Penny's face as the message ended. Before she even had a chance to take off her coat, she was out the door and headed toward the Blue Knight. ∎

Chapter Eighteen

Hit 'Em Hard

Although Kathleen Marcus's message had said to meet her that night at the blues club, Penny knew that she had to track her down as soon as possible. With a deadline only a day away, any information would have to be obtained quickly. Even if this woman was giving her something of real substance, Penny would have to go over it with Dugan, piece it together with Missy's interview comments, and work in some kind of defense about writing about Glenda after her death.

Parking her car on 16th Street, just two blocks from the Castro Street blues bar that was the object of her mission, Penny hustled to the club that remained open during the day, but only for drinks and food. Penny had been to the place a number of times for both nighttime gatherings and interviews. But she had never gotten to know any of the owners.

Inside, concert posters covered the walls, along with colored, beaded lights, faded wood paneling, and a mist of smoke, even though no one was smoking at that moment. Penny scanned the room for someone, anyone, who looked to be in charge, and found a man on stage changing light bulbs who looked he could help.

The reporter walked straight toward him, reached up, and tugged on his pant cuff. Without looking down from his work, the man responded.

"Yeah, what do ya want?" he asked in a gravelly voice. "I'm busy."

Penny, never one to be shy, piped up. "I'm looking for someone who comes in here a lot, her name is Kathleen Marcus. Do you know where she might be?"

The man, still working with his tools and light fixtures, shook his head, but said nothing.

"Are you sure?" Penny asked. "It's kind of important. She's my height, short blonde hair, kind of thin."

"No," the man barked before Penny started to walk away. "Wait, I know who you mean. Yeah, she comes in here a lot, but I haven't seen her today."

"Do you know where she lives?" Penny said.

"Nope, can't help ya," he answered.

As Penny began to leave, voice from the backstage area called her back.

"What do you want with Kathy?" a question rang into Penny's ears from a very male-sounding voice. "She in some kind of trouble?"

Turning around to see who was talking to her, Penny looked to find the person, but could not see through the dimly lit backstage area. As she walked closer, the figure seemed to be sporting a very stylish woman's dress and hat, but with a man's voice. Yet another of the city's many wonders—a transvestite.

After five years covering politics and other stories in San Francisco, she had seen enough strangely dressed people to keep surprises to a minimum. Besides, she was more interested in how this person knew Kathleen Marcus than what he/she was wearing.

"No, she's not in trouble," Penny said as she walked within a few feet of the person. "I just want to talk to her."

The man carried himself with all the movement and poise of a woman. His skin seemed so closely shaven that no stubble or other male features could be seen. Even his legs were slender like a woman's. Other than his voice, you could not tell he was a man.

With slicked-back hair in a ponytail, heavy eye makeup, and a dark red dress wrapped around him, the man smiled nervously but held out a hand to take Penny's grip as he introduced himself.

"Well, I can find her for you, but what do you want with her?" the man said. "Are you some kind of cop or something?"

"No," Penny snapped, "I'm a reporter. I talked to her today at Glenda Callahan's funeral and she said she would be willing to talk about Glenda and...uh..."

"And Missy," the man finished for her. "Yeah, I know all about them. You see, Kathy and I are roommates. We both knew Missy really well, but didn't like that Glenda. She seemed like the phony type, but man could she give a good screw ... according to Missy, that is."

Penny's eyes widened as she expanded her interest and realized she might have yet another source for her story. "Did YOU ever fool around with the mayor's wife?" she asked directly.

"No, honey," he said, with a laugh. "I only dress like 'em., I don't do 'em. I'm strictly men, baby."

After a laugh, the man showed a serious face and introduced himself. "I'm Phyllis, Phyllis Bee. Bee as in Bee-have yourself, sweetie." The man laughed again.

"I'll take you to where Kathy is," Phyllis said. "She works at night usually, sometimes here, sometimes other places, so she might be home. C'mon."

After that, Penny's new acquaintance took her outside, up Castro Street several blocks, and into a first-floor apartment on nearby 24th Street. The building was just a three-story house, but each floor spread out with several bedrooms.

Along the way, Phyllis explained that he and Kathleen had met while working at the Blue Knight, where they did everything from tending bar to putting makeup on performers. He said he even did a drag show on slow nights when the manager allowed it.

As they entered the roommates' home, Penny could see that the place was no palace, but hardly a dump. Some scattered used furniture, a few cheap antiques and plenty of reprinted Georgia O'Keefes and Van Goghs on the walls.

Phyllis told Penny to wait while she checked the bedroom for Kathleen. She could hear the women talking in the other room, and after what seemed like an eternity—but actually amounted to about five minutes—a groggy, but smiling Kathleen emerged.

"Hi," Penny said. "Sorry if we woke you, but I got your message and wanted to see if we could talk before tonight, since I have a deadline and all."

Kathleen, sporting a T-shirt and sweatpants, yawned and nodded to indicate the intrusion was not a problem. After resting her head on her crossed arms across the kitchen table for a minute, the woman looked up as Phyllis took a seat and Penny pulled out her notebook and pen.

"Okay," Penny said. "Just tell me as much as you can about Missy, Glenda, and you two."

For the next hour and a half, Kathleen spoke about how she and Phyllis had become friends with Missy shortly after she began to sing at the club, and liked her friendly demeanor. They said they'd been bothered by the way Glenda had come and gone all the time and not shown any signs of supporting Missy emotionally.

"She treated her like shit and she took it," Kathleen said as she sipped coffee and munched on a bran muffin. "It really bugged me because she was a hot little number and could have had a lot of women. I think she liked the mystery of it all at first. You know, banging the mayor's wife and getting someone of power in bed. But, after a while, it became more than just a fling, she really fell for her."

Kathleen went on to tell about how the couple had become known to regulars at the club, but that none of them ever wanted to make it public because no one saw the harm in it.

"There are a lot of women around here who screw around on other people. Dykes cheating on their girlfriends, women married to men who come down for a good time, and men who have hidden gay affairs from their wives for years," Kathleen said. "So who cares if Missy is screwing the mayor's wife?"

"So why are you willing to talk about it now?" Penny asked.

"Well," Kathleen said as she stuck a lollipop in her mouth to kill the coffee taste. "It was something you said to me outside the funeral. Getting the truth out. It just bothers me that this woman will be remembered as some great first lady when she treated Missy like shit and..." Kathleen wiped away a tear. "She had to die this way."

Kathleen then rubbed her eyes and leaned back in her chair.

"Sorry, I think that is all I want to say," she said with a catch in her voice.

But that was enough for Penny.

Between Kathleen's long commentary and some helpful words from Phyllis, all on the record, Penny thought she had her story. After some more pleasant comments, Penny thanked her new sources, packed up her notebook, and headed out. It was about 5 p.m. when she reached the *Reader* office.

The place was frantic on this day before deadline, with people editing stories, working the phones for information, and fact-checking last-minute changes. Penny went right into Dugan's office when she arrived and told him what she had.

The editor was almost euphoric. "How do you know their stories are real?" a skeptical, but hopeful Dugan asked.

Penny recalled the tale for Dugan, saying that both women had brought up their relationship before she did and, at the roommates' home, they showed her a photo of Missy, Phyllis, and Kathleen together. So at least it was obvious they knew her.

"Okay, write it up, but be careful," Dugan said with a smile.

For the next two hours, Penny slowly constructed the story that said, plainly, that Glenda and Missy had had an affair, which Missy had revealed just a day before her death. The story also indicated that the *Reader* had Missy's comments on tape. That, along with the photo Penny had found, made the story complete.

Dugan decided to make no bones about the piece and placed the very same photo of Glenda and Missy on the cover, with the headline, "The First Lady's First Lady."

"If we're going to hit 'em, let's hit 'em hard," Dugan said.

*   *   *

The next day, as the papers hit the newsstands and news racks around town, the *Reader* also sent a press release to every news organization in town—including the *Advocate*, the *Bulletin* and the *Journal*. It was a simple, four-paragraph announcement promoting the story.

"The S.F. *Reader* offers an exclusive look inside the secret life of Glenda Callahan," the statement said. "Just hours before their deaths, the first lady's lesbian lover revealed the couple's stormy relationship, and her need to expose the mayor's wife."

Dugan faxed the press release to all recipients by 9 a.m. Wednesday, just five days after Glenda and Missy were killed and the regular publication day for the *Reader*. The reaction was mixed.

At first, only one of the city's two all-news radio stations mentioned the story in the morning, and none of the three noon TV newscasts said anything about it. After lunchtime, however, as word-of-mouth spread the salacious tale around town, all six local TV stations were on the story.

Reporters flocked to Callahan's office, home, and the Castro Street area as well to get comments and reactions from all those involved. That night, the story was broadcast on each television station newscast and both news radio stations.

Several broadcast reports also included live and taped comments from Kathleen Marcus and Phyllis Bee, who enjoyed the attention and gladly backed up their previous statements.

"This is about fairness for Missy," Kathleen told one reporter.

Most of the reports had comments from the gay community and some city officials, including several supervisors. Most said they were surprised that the *Reader* would run such a story just days after the women's deaths, while others outright challenged it.

"I don't believe our first lady would be involved in something like an affair," said Supervisor Mary Manning, who had been a friend of Glenda's. "I think it is shameful that this newspaper would stoop so low. Let her lie in peace."

But some gay politicians, such as Supervisor Ken Kragen, offered guarded support for the story. "I think the timing is a little off, but if it is true, the people should know and embrace yet another revelation for the gay community," he was quoted as saying.

Through all of the coverage, however, Callahan remained out of sight. Holed up in Carl Devins's apartment, the mayor was not in a mood to talk to anyone. Penny Atkins had called him continuously, at home and his office, on Tuesday for comment, but could not track him down.

When Penny had reached the mayor's press secretary, the spokesman had called the mayor to ask for comment and to let him know about the story, but the mayor was too upset and tired to do anything.

"Just tell them you can't find me," Callahan told the press aide. "I have to figure this out."

So when the *Reader* story appeared, it included the obligatory, "Mayor Callahan could not be reached for comment, and his office declined to comment on the story."

So, that night, barely one week after Glenda and the mayor were happily pressing the flesh at a St. Patrick's Day parade, Callahan found himself in the tragic position of losing his wife, and facing allegations that his marriage was a sham.

Switching from newscast to newscast that Wednesday evening as he watched television in Devins's home, Callahan couldn't help but find himself facing deeper problems than he had ever felt before in his life.

Even when he was forced to get on the witness stand at Billy Dale's trial and admit to advocating Billy's use of a concealed weapon, he didn't feel this bewildered.

One thing in the mayor's favor had emerged, however. Neither the *Journal* nor the *Bulletin* was planning to run anything on the story. Shortly after that week's *Reader* had been released, both Emily Ingle and Donald Grossman called their editors and ordered them not to follow the story, at least for the moment.

"This is not how we cover news," Ingle had told J.C. Townsend that afternoon, just as Townsend was ready to put someone on the story. "Just because some low-budget paper wants to spew rumors doesn't mean we do it."

Townsend knew from experience not to question Ingle, but he fumed within about passing up such an obvious story. Sure, maybe the *Bulletin* did not need to run the story as fact, but to ignore it outright was almost censorship. He knew, however, that Ingle had other motives.

"This mayor has been good to us in the past and we need him to remain," Ingle had said, reminding Townsend of her obvious ulterior motives. "If we lose him, it could be bad."

Townsend also knew that if Callahan was forced out—either by some legal maneuver or his own need to resign in the face of whatever scandal this might become—Board of Supervisors President Marie Alzeti would take the mayor's chair. With her in office, the *Bulletin* and the *Journal*, each of which had actively editorialized against her in the mayor's race, would be on her hit list.

And, if for some reason Callahan left office after just more than a year, that would give Alzeti almost three years to build up an incumbent's head start on the next mayoral race. Ingle didn't need to remind Townsend of that fact. He knew where she was coming from.

Over at the *Journal*, Grossman had almost the same discussion with Tim Cross.

"Hold off," he told the more hot-tempered Cross. "This is not our story, let them take it. We will stay away." Cross just responded with a limp "Yes," and went back to work, sneering the rest of the day.

The most volatile reaction to the *Reader* story came from Jimmy Min, who days earlier had heard Mike McLean say that he had this very story, but did not want to run it. Jimmy yelled loudly when the fax from Dugan announcing the story reached his hands.

"Son of a bitch!" Jimmy yelled so loud that employees two floors above his office could hear him. "That fucking idiot had it in the palm of his hand." ■

Chapter Nineteen

Revelations and Guilt

Of course, Jimmy was talking about Mike McLean, who had left his office four days earlier, vowed to dig up something more than just a lesbian affair between the two women, but had not been heard from since—except for a brief moment at the funeral.

Jimmy walked from his office into the newsroom and let everyone know his anger.

"Where the fuck is he?" Jimmy screamed to the small group of reporters and interns in the newsroom that afternoon, and who weren't sure who he was talking about.

Jimmy turned around and headed toward his office again with a scowl. Just as he entered the room, he saw a familiar figure sitting behind his desk.

Of course, it was Mike McLean.

"How ya doin', boss?" McLean said, as he put his feet up on Jimmy's desk and clasped his hands behind his head. "Why so tense?"

As McLean sparked a small laugh, Jimmy showed he was in no mood to joke.

"Get your feet off my desk, you pain in the ass," Jimmy said, knocking McLean's legs away as his chair bounced him upward. "Look what you've done. We had this fucking story and now the *Reader* breaks it, everyone else has it, and when our next issue comes out tomorrow, we'll be last."

McLean just smiled as he stood up with his face right in Jimmy's eyes. Putting his hand on Jimmy's shoulder, the columnist tried to ease his boss's irritation.

"Not a problem," McLean said. "We have something better. Come with me."

At that moment, McLean led Jimmy out of the office, down the stairs, and out of the *Advocate* building. As cars whizzed by on the usually desolate street that housed the newspaper's headquarters, McLean kept a sly smile on his face while walking Jimmy down the street to the nearby Sea Fair Bar.

Opening the front door to the saloon that McLean often frequented, but Jimmy rarely approached, McLean urged his boss to go in.

"I don't want a drink," Jimmy said with frustration. "We got work to do."

But McLean just shoved him inside. At just after noon on a Wednesday, the place held only a few lunchtime eaters. McLean waved a hello to several familiar faces as he ushered Jimmy to a back booth where a short man sat facing away from the two approaching men. When McLean reached the booth, the man stood up and shook his hand, then turned to see Jimmy.

Jimmy thought he recognized the middle-aged man, but wasn't sure. Before he could try to guess who the man was, McLean quickly introduced them.

"Jimmy Min, meet Wayman Keller," McLean said. "That's Fire Inspector Wayman Keller."

The man's name and title did not click in Jimmy's head. He looked at his columnist with a frustrated glance that seemed to say, "What the hell are you doing bringing me to meet this guy?'"

But Jimmy held his tongue as the three sat down. Wasting no time with his busy boss, McLean asked Keller to get to the reason they had come together. Jimmy was only marginally interested until Keller, his eyes panning around the bar to make sure no one was listening who shouldn't be, explained, "Ya see, I was there the night that Glenda and Missy died. I was the first one to find them."

"You mean you were at both locations where the bodies were found?" Jimmy asked.

"No," Keller said. "They were found at the same location, then they were moved."

Keller went on to explain what had happened... how the mayor and the two chiefs had orchestrated the rearrangement of Glenda's body, and the new car accident, to cover up her affair with Missy.

McLean just sat and smiled as Keller recounted the tale he had told McLean just hours earlier when the two met at McLean's Berkeley house.

Keller had gotten to know McLean during his early years as a firefighter union organizer. He had approached the columnist a day earlier after hearing through the grapevine that he was looking into the mysterious death of the mayor's wife.

"I wasn't going to say anything to anyone," Keller explained as he sipped a beer and stammered over his words. "But, well, I got a pain in my gut about it after seeing that funeral and all the coverage of the mayor's wife, but nothing on the girl who died in the fire. It didn't sit right."

Then Keller said he wanted to tell the story through McLean, but that he only had his word as proof. He said the only others involved were the two chiefs and the mayor. The inspector also said he believed the mayor did not want to be involved, but had been blackmailed into it, although he didn't know how because he had not been privy to the whole Mount Davidson Cross escapade.

"I don't know how much I can do to help, but I will," Keller said.

With that, the three men headed out of the bar and back to the *Advocate* office. It was just before 2 p.m., a good few hours before the 8 p.m. final deadline needed for another special edition to be printed. Jimmy did not often run special issues, but believed this story could call for one and didn't want to wait a week for his next regular publication date.

With just a single source, Jimmy and McLean would have to write the story from the angle that it was the account of a high-ranking official in the fire department. Although Keller's word was the only proof, his position as a major fire investigator with a good record and reputation for hunting down things like the school arson case would give the paper some credibility.

Jimmy knew that, coupled with the *Reader* story about the affair, Callahan would be put on the spot to make some kind of response. As McLean wrote up the story, like Penny Atkins, he tried to contact the mayor for comment. But, also like her, got nowhere as calls to the mayor's home and office went unanswered.

McLean also had to call Moore and Brown to get their reactions. Each acted as though he was crazy when asked about Keller's accusations.

Brown, who'd originally dreamed up the idea to relocate Glenda's body, told McLean that the story was "false and without any possible proof."

"This guy is full of shit," Brown told McLean that afternoon. "What the hell would he know? Why would we do something like that? It's crazy."

Moore, on the other hand, sounded much more concerned when McLean telephoned. "You're putting that in the paper?" he asked. "You can't do that. It's...it's not true. It's all a lie."

But the *Advocate* stuck to its guns.

While McLean was calling the right people for comments and putting the story together, Jimmy couldn't help but touch base with Billy Dale... not only to tell him what they had found, but also see if he knew anything about it.

"No fuckin' way, but it's great," Billy said as he pumped a fist in the air while talking to Jimmy from the prison's recreation room phone. "Are you sure about this? It would make a lot of sense. I never trusted either one of those bastards. Especially Brown. The guy looked like a conniver."

Jimmy agreed and hung up. Then he went to see McLean.

With the story finished, the editors put the special issue of the *Advocate* together and the next day, Thursday, it hit nearly every house with the front-page headline, "Callahan, Brown, Moore in First Lady Fire Cover-up."

The story took up the entire front page, except for an editorial at the bottom written by Min that called for an investigation into the Keller allegations.

"We implore the District Attorney to launch an immediate inquiry into these charges. If the mayor and the city's top law enforcement officials have stooped low enough to disturb a police scene and cover up details of a fatal fire, they should be held accountable," the editorial stated.

As with the *Reader* story, reaction to the *Advocate* allegations came slowly Thursday. But by the end of the day, they also had made it on both news radio stations and all of that night's local newscasts.

Each reporter had also gone to D.A. Dennis Haynes to see if he was planning to respond with any kind of investigation. Haynes's initial reaction, expectedly, was "No comment" or "I have to review the situation first."

In reality, the D.A. didn't know what to do. He knew that Keller had a stellar reputation and had no reason to lie about something like this. But he also knew, yet again, that politics had stuck him right in the middle of the local papers, Callahan, and Billy Dale.

"I can't get a break," Haynes told his wife Thursday night after the newscasts had ended. "This is ridiculous."

The only news organizations that continued to ignore the stories were the *Journal* and the *Bulletin*. After the *Advocate* story came out, Ingle and Grossman found themselves on the phone, once again, telling their editors—point blank—to hold off.

"Don't change anything," Ingle had told J.C. Townsend that afternoon. "This is not our fight."

As all the other news organizations scrambled to cover the breaking information and Haynes tried to figure out his best approach to avoid a political nightmare, Callahan remained hidden at Carl Devins's home.

But the mayor knew that he could not stay there for long, especially now that a criminal allegation had reared its head. He realized from experience that he'd either be found out in his seclusion, or his reputation would be destroyed forever without a response. One thing Billy Dale had taught him was the worst place to be in politics was on the defensive.

"Hit 'em before they hit you," Billy had often told the mayor.

So he began his counter-attack, hoping only that it wasn't too late.

*   *   *

Thursday night, after the local newscasts completed their rehashing of the week's scandalous events, Devins and Callahan met in Devins's living room to map out a strategy.

The mayor, still weary from a lack of sleep and slightly nervous and depressed, wore a pair of slacks and a polo shirt as he sipped a soda and tried to relax. Devins, who'd practically kept vigil with the mayor since his wife's funeral, tried to comfort his friend and asked what he wanted to do.

Callahan took a deep breath, slurped down his last sip of the soft drink, and shook his head to clear his mind. Within the past week, everything that could go wrong personally and politically had fallen in front of him. He had been placed in the position of facing true criminal and moral punishments, as well as again distracting himself from the issues that he most wanted to address as mayor.

It had only been a week since the St. Patrick's Day festivities when the mayor refocused his attention, and he believed the city's attention, on forging ahead with new programs—such as the homeless plan—which he still thought could begin to work, at least sometime in the near future.

But now, he had no idea which way to go. Callahan knew that if he tried to conceal his part in the cover-up of Glenda's death further, it could backfire if he were discovered.

On the other hand, of course, admitting what he did could put him in the position of being voted out of office in three years or, worse, being recalled if enough people sought to remove him for his part in the crime. And there were criminal punishments to think about, especially if Moore and Brown decided to testify against him as part of some plea bargain that either or both of them were low enough to chase after.

None of this computed well in Callahan's brain. As he pondered the different scenarios, Devins felt the need to speak up.

"I have to say that the best way may be to admit everything now," Devins said, having found out from the mayor just hours earlier about his part in the cover-up and the plot.

Devins, who of course espoused the honest, direct, non-negative campaign approach that was the antithesis of Billy Dale, believed that getting the truth out could only help Callahan in the court of public opinion. He told the mayor that the connection to his wife's death, and the related story of Glenda's affair, could help ease the impact of Callahan's admitted cover-up.

"People will have sympathy for you," Devins said. "If this is done correctly, you will be seen as the victim who was roped into doing this in the wake of a terrible tragedy."

Devins's advice, which made a lot of political sense, was to lay the blame on Moore and Brown and admit a mistake. He believed that by being forthright and admitting a mistaken action—especially one in the aftermath of such a personal tragedy—would be seen in a sympathetic way.

"People would be able to put themselves in your shoes," Devins said as Callahan bit his lip. "That would also make it difficult for the D.A. to take any action. It might make it easier to lay the blame on Brown and Moore."

Callahan saw Devins's side as he listened to the explanation while chewing on a pencil from a stack on Devins's desk. But he also thought about what Billy

Dale had once told him.

"Never admit anything you don't have to," Billy had said in the heat of the mayor's race more than a year earlier. "If they got you, act surprised. Don't lie, but don't admit you were wrong if the proof is not absolute."

Callahan believed that, although Keller was seen as a reliable, honest source for this story, Billy's approach still applied.

The mayor had found through his own career and those of others during the past few years that truth does not always win out, despite one's personal beliefs. He did not believe that he'd reached the point of no return simply because the *Advocate* had a story.

Callahan also knew that the *Journal* and the *Bulletin* could be persuaded to at least question the *Advocate* story and sources in their coverage and possibly help. They still owed him for his support of the stadium plan and he, like Emily Ingle and Donald Grossman, knew that having Marie Alzeti in office was not something either daily paper wanted.

"I don't know, Carl," the mayor said after listening to Devins's soliloquy. "I think we can still dance around this one."

After some more discussion, both men decided that the mayor would issue a simple statement carefully denying the accusations, but with no direct lie. Calling his press office, Callahan dictated his comments that would go out that afternoon to all media, including the *Advocate*.

The statement simply said, "Mayor Callahan finds the story alleging his involvement in a cover-up of Glenda Callahan's death to be improper and without a true basis. The mayor played no part in any cover-up of the first lady's death and takes umbrage at the *Advocate* or any other news agency's efforts to trivialize her passing with such baseless accusations."

The statement went on to say that the mayor would make no further comment on the issue and would not be available that weekend. The press release went out the next day, Friday, sharply at 9 a.m. so that it could make the early news reports, noon news, and be sure to be given fair coverage in the Saturday papers.

The *Advocate*, of course, built a story around the denial that included more counter comment from Keller and another editorial in which the *Advocate* stood by the story.

Once again, TV and radio newscasts covered the mayor's comments, but with little more than the simple statement from Callahan and some reaction from city officials.

The big change in coverage came from the *Journal* and the *Bulletin*, which decided that if the mayor was willing to respond to the *Advocate* story and, in a way, the *Reader* story, the daily papers had to cover it. This story was no longer just the weeklies making allegations, but the mayor responding, even if it was just a written response.

"We can cover it, but place it inside the local section, not on the front page," was Emily Ingle's directive to Townsend Friday afternoon. "Make sure to print all of the denials and have only enough of the accusations to be fair."

Townsend reluctantly agreed, as did Tim Cross when he received a similar directive straight from his publisher. While the *Bulletin* said very little about the rumored affair between Glenda and Missy, the feistier *Journal* re-ran the *Reader* photo of the two next to the story.

"Hey, fuck the publisher," Cross had told a reporter. "This is news and this photo is part of it."

In a rare act of cooperation, Danny Dugan made the photo available to any news source that wanted it. Several TV stations had shown it on newscasts the day the first *Reader* story appeared, but the *Journal* had been the only other newspaper to reprint it.

Each news report that day also sought further comment from the D.A., who again said he was still reviewing the case and all allegations.

In reality, Dennis Haynes was in yet another political conflict between his connections and the law. He knew that the charges would be serious if, in fact, the mayor and his chiefs conspired to block a criminal investigation.

But Haynes also wanted to make sure he didn't lean either way. As the weekend passed, and Haynes did a quick investigation on his own, he decided that the best political and legal move was to convene a grand jury to look into the deaths of Missy and Glenda.

On Monday morning, Haynes held a quick 9 a.m. press conference in which he simply stated what the grand jury would investigate and what its very basic directive would be.

"In order to avoid any appearance of a conflict of interest or political favoritism, this grand jury will review all evidence in the deaths of Glenda Callahan and Missy King to determine if any illegal or improper activity occurred on the part of any city employee or San Francisco resident," Haynes said during the press briefing in his office. "Then and only then will the D.A.'s office determine if criminal charges should be filed."

Leaving the decision up to a grand jury took some of the heat off Haynes, but it also threw open the public opinion door as well. With regular residents placed in charge of deciding the mayor's fate, efforts to sway, or even outright threaten, grand jurors could be heightened.

But Haynes believed that this was the way to keep his political protection in place and avoid a true political game from being played.

"There is enough speculation to warrant this action," Haynes told several reporters after his announcement. "Two newspapers have found cause to make some accusations and we just want to check them out as we would in any other case."

The grand jury, ironically enough, convened two days later on April 1—April Fool's Day. All parties in the case found that irony only slightly amusing and set forth to get their sides of the story to the grand jury and to the public.

After the grand jury convened, it spent the next two weeks going through witness testimony provided by police, Callahan, the chiefs' private attorneys, and the fire department. Depositions were taken from Callahan, Moore, Brown, and Keller, as well as several aides to all four men.

During the two-week period, the four newspapers took every approach possible to give counter information about each other's reports.

The *Journal* and the *Bulletin* weaved in background information about Callahan's troubled first marriage and his honest history as both police chief and mayor to try to sway opinions. Although the grand jurors were ordered to avoid reading newspapers or hearing news reports and discussions of the investigation, it was certain that some of the reports were going to be read or overheard.

That was the approach the *Journal* and *Bulletin* counted on. They also peppered the two weeks of coverage with carefully-placed columns and editorials painting a picture of Callahan as a tortured, tragically injured husband who not only lost his wife in a fire, but also found out the same day that she had had a lesbian mistress.

"Mayor Callahan may or may not be guilty of any crime involving the death of his wife," said one *Bulletin* editorial three days after the grand jury convened. "But he has already paid the highest penalty possible: the loss of his wife, his privacy, and his happiness. No matter what the outcome of this investigation is, we must be certain that a man's life is not further damaged."

The *Journal* joined in the supportive statements on several occasions, including a column by one writer that called Callahan's plight "...something that could only be seen in a Greek tragedy. He is our Hamlet, Romeo, and Macbeth all in one. Have mercy."

For the *Advocate* and the *Reader*, however, a stark contrast emerged in their coverage of the grand jury review. For one thing, while the dailies did little to try to dig up internal evidence or information about what the grand jury had, the two non-dailies each found moles in the investigation who would turn over evidence and testimony to reporters.

First, the *Reader* managed to come across a copy of Callahan's deposition in which he stated, "I did not oversee any illegal actions, and did not participate in any cover-up." But, the same deposition also quoted the mayor as saying, "One might understand why I would want to hide this relationship since it was destroying my personal life. One could understand why it would destroy my public life if it were revealed."

That statement, published on the front page of the *Reader* one week after the grand jury convened, offered some telling information. The *Reader* also quoted sources as saying the grand jury evidence linked Moore and Brown to a cover-up more than Callahan.

The key element was that Keller targeted the two chiefs as the ones who hatched the cover-up plan, while saying the mayor had only gone along with it after being coaxed. Keller did not know that Brown and Moore were blackmailing the mayor, only that they seemed to be leading the charge.

"I recall Chief Brown having to push the mayor into this effort, and the mayor resisting the temptation to hide everything," Keller said, according to deposition statements printed in the *Reader*. "I don't think his heart was in it."

At the *Advocate*, McLean and Jimmy Min focused on heavy editorials that urged the indictment of all three men for "the sake of San Francisco's honesty in government and settlement of this issue in the proper way." The *Advocate* also claimed that "Mayor Callahan's image as a leader has been tarnished too much for repair."

That was a subtle hint that a recall effort might have been in the works, no matter what the grand jury decided.

As usual, TV and radio news simply reported the findings of the newspapers, crediting each, but giving no new information of their own. The mayor had come out of hiding and continued to go through public events, trying to proceed with city policies. But it was not easy, as every reporter—and nearly every citizen—would approach him with questions about the investigation.

The *Advocate*, in a very unusual move, even printed a guest column by Billy Dale. Still in prison—but seeing possible parole just a few months away—Billy had persuaded Jimmy to run the column.

In the piece, Billy said Callahan "had obviously become too attached to his office and had become like other politicians who were willing to lie and deceive in order to keep it, even if that meant destroying the memory of his wife."

The chilling column added, "Even if the mayor did not lead the deception, any part he played in it deserves scrutiny and punishment."

The column drew a lot of attention among newspapers, including those that criticized the *Advocate* for publishing it. But Jimmy and Billy didn't care. They loved the attention and the ability to make news themselves.

*   *   *

During the weeks of investigation, police, and firefighters also took some matters into their own hands to help their bosses avoid problems. Several reporters from the *Advocate* and the *Reader* —including McLean and Penny Atkins—found themselves pulled over by police on several occasions.

In one instance, Jimmy Min was even stopped, allegedly for speeding, and ordered to submit to a drunk driving test and a thorough search of his car. He was not taken in, but the officer in charge of the stop made the snide comment that Jimmy "better watch which way you're going, if you know what I mean."

Publishers at the *Journal* and the *Bulletin* also kept the pressure on. At one point, Emily Ingle even wrote an editorial herself that propped up a defense of Callahan as a "mayor who was putting the city on the road to recovery."

When word spread through the newsroom that the publisher had written an editorial—unthinkable in some places—two reporters filed complaints, and one quit outright.

Finally, after two weeks, on April 15—another irony as income tax day—the grand jury made its decision. In a quick, direct statement, Haynes read the outcome of the investigation to a large band of reporters assembled in his office at 8 a.m. that morning.

"After an exhaustive and complete review of the case, the grand jury has found enough evidence to indict Police Chief Steve Brown and Fire Chief George Moore on one count each of conspiracy and one count each of interfering with a criminal investigation. Each charge is a felony, which carries a sentence of between five and 15 years."

Cameras clicked, videotape rolled, and reporters scribbled in their notebooks as Haynes spoke.

"The grand jury also has determined that insufficient evidence exists to bring any charges against Mayor Jack Callahan."

Haynes then said that Brown and Moore, who were not at the press conference, agreed to surrender later that morning and would have to post $50,000 bail to avoid any jail time before trial.

The newspapers rushed to get the story in, while most newscasts broke into regular programming with the news. The city's two major law enforcement officials were under indictment, while the mayor—who had been close to an indictment that could bring him down—was off the hook, at least for the moment.

The reaction at the *Journal* and *Bulletin* was ecstatic—so much that Emily Ingle called to congratulate the mayor and ordered her editors to play the story up big, with a special emphasis on the next step: a trial of the city's fire chief and police chief that was likely to be a news grabber for weeks.

"We have to keep this going, especially so it can help us out," Grossman had told Tim Cross.

Although Callahan had gotten off the hook, the *Advocate* and the *Reader* each had reason to celebrate, too, since their accusations were essentially correct. Even if Callahan was not linked enough to the cover-up to face charges, the grand jury had found the two chiefs culpable enough to indict, thus legitimizing both stories.

As it turned out, the mayor was also right that his position as a suffering victim had worked. But was it enough to repair his damaged reputation? Just because this grand jury of 20 people did not think there was enough evidence to convict him didn't mean that voters would agree.

Callahan also was unavailable for comment as the grand jury decision was released. Back in his own home, with Devins at his side, the mayor only authorized his office to issue another release that said he was "relieved at the decision, but still mending his feelings of the tragedy and pursuing great things for the city."

For Billy Dale and Jimmy Min, the outcome, although backing up their story about a cover-up, did not have the desired effect of taking Callahan out of office. It seemed from the public's reaction that he was as loved and pitied as ever. That meant that he would likely remain in office through the end of his term.

Even as both Moore and Brown were tried, and eventually convicted and sentenced to terms of four years each, Callahan seemed to slip through the proceedings unscathed. During the joint trial of the two chiefs, attorneys tried to link Callahan to their scheme, even insinuating at one point that he had dreamed up the idea.

But despite even Callahan's testimony that he had known about the plot, the jury would not allow the mayor to take the blame, once again giving in to the efforts to make Callahan a victim.

In the end, the rookie mayor came out of the legal proceedings a bit bruised and politically battered, but not down for the count by any stretch of the imagination. He could go on to fill out his term with little to stop him.

Unless, of course, something else could pull him out.

That something else was what Billy, Jimmy, and, to an extent, Callahan, had to keep an eye out for as April turned into May, then June when the chiefs' trial finally ended.

"We are not done yet," Billy told Jimmy during a prison phone call the day the chiefs' guilty verdicts came in and Callahan walked away with his political life intact. "We just gotta keep going after him." ■

Chapter Twenty

Building Blocks

Donald Grossman opened his copy of the San Francisco *Journal* with a bit of reserved hope and anxious relief on the afternoon of June 17. The *Journal* publisher, like most readers, went first to the front page breaking story about the guilty verdicts of Police Chief Steve Brown and Fire Chief George Moore, which screamed across the front page under the headline, "Chiefs Guilty."

Since the jury's verdicts were read just before noon that cool Friday morning, the *Journal* was able to get the story into its late afternoon edition, while the morning *Bulletin* was out of luck and forced to wait until the next day to publish the top story of the week, losing a major news advantage.

And since Saturday newspapers, as Grossman knew, were the least–read papers of the week, the *Bulletin* would likely see little circulation gains from the guilty story, which would certainly be old news a day later no matter which day of the week it occurred.

As Grossman scanned his newspaper's latest edition, he couldn't help but grin knowing that his publication had grabbed the first word of the major event. He knew as well as anyone that the timing of the verdicts was perfect for his afternoon deadlines, and the exact story to give the paper a newsstand sales boost.

"Love it, just love it," Grossman said to himself as he read the main story and glanced through the two sidebars during a late afternoon break in his office. One of the side stories focused on how Callahan had survived the trial of his chiefs without criminal or political damage. The other was on the process that would be used to choose two new chiefs, and some background on the two men who were about to serve at least two years in prison.

"Yes, it does pay to get the story first," Grossman whispered again as he turned the page and began perusing the inside for another, different story. Although the chiefs' double guilt was the obvious big news of the day, it was not the most important piece of news to Grossman.

Turning page after page in a scramble to find the exact article he was seeking, Grossman's anticipation grew. His fingertips continued to fill with newsprint with each turn of the page, as his eyes scanned every corner to make sure he did not miss the item that evaded his search.

Beginning on the upper left-hand corner of each page, Grossman scanned down the left side, then across the bottom, up the right side, and finally down the middle to see if the article appeared.

Just as the publisher was ready to yell out of aggravation, his eye caught the story. Stuck back in the business section, on an inside page, was the article for which he had been grasping.

He didn't even have to read it, since most of it had come from him. But, as with most subjects of news stories, Grossman simply wanted to see it. He even read the headline out loud to himself.

"Mack Corp. Launches Plan for Massive Hunter's Point Complex."

Grossman beamed as he leaned back in his chair, just enough so that it touched the glass of the giant picture window behind him that looked out from his 43rd-floor office in the Mack Corp. building over both busy Market Street and the expansive San Francisco Bay.

A grin crossed Grossman's face as he spun his chair around away from the desk and the newspaper to face the view of the city and its famous waterway. As chairman of the Mack Corp. for the past six years, Grossman had always been in a position to make a mark in the city and the development industry as a whole, but had always lacked the one great project that could put him over the top.

Since he reached the company's top post years earlier, the 53-year-old executive had been trying to launch a major project that could put his name out front as a successful builder, but also land his company the big deal it needed to get back on top after the real estate slides of the late '80s.

The 100-year-old Mack Corp. had made its money building and operating real estate developments, including some that dated back to the turn of the century. Started by Grossman's great-grandfather on his mother's side, Emil Mack, the company had gone from its start as a five-room boarding house along Fisherman's Wharf in the late 1890s to one of the Bay Area's largest development and real estate concerns.

Although the company continued to maintain a steady profit following the real estate dives of the 1980s, it was still under tremendous debt and had had no new projects in six years. Here it was, 1993, and the company was eager for a new plan.

Grossman, who had worked his way up from a junior architect 30 years earlier to a manager, public relations executive, and vice president, took over as chairman when his uncle Sidney Mack retired in 1988. Since then, he'd tried to come up with approaches to reduce debt and launch a successful new venture.

But with the fallout from the economy a constant hindrance, Grossman had been unable to move his efforts beyond preliminary planning. For five years, every idea he created was bogged down with a lack of financing, building code problems, or a sluggish market.

Just two years earlier, Grossman had approached a local bank with an idea to build San Francisco's tallest office building, hoping it would get a green light from the sheer novelty of being the largest skyscraper.

But the banker, who had worked well with Mack in the past, said the poor real estate market for office space at the time, coupled with the likely opposition from San Francisco's liberal and progressive communities who hated high-rises, offered little hope for success.

Grossman's time had also been eaten up by his double role as publisher of the *Journal*. Since his Uncle Sidney led the way for the company to buy the afternoon paper in the mid-1980s, it had become something of a pet project for the corporation.

Sidney Mack, who had always loved the power of the press and had tried to make his own way in journalism for years before joining the family business, made the newspaper purchase his final attempt at having an impact on the city's press establishment.

When Sidney retired in 1988, he nearly forced Grossman into becoming publisher, telling him that the newspaper "needs the family's direct input if it is to do its job well."

Although Grossman had strenuously objected to taking on the double–occupation, Uncle Sidney forced him, threatening to cut him out of the company completely if he did not assume the publisher's role along with the chairman's post.

Grudgingly, Grossman accepted. During the past six years, he'd been able to focus most of his attention on the development side of things, leaving the newspaper to run its day-to-day operations without him, except for mild input on major issues and stories.

After a disastrous break-up with his wife two years after he took over, when she ran off with a former *Journal* reporter, Grossman focused even more on the family businesses, but with an eye toward the building and construction end more than the newspaper.

Tim Cross liked Grossman's hands-off style and, frankly, became annoyed whenever he stuck his opinion or directive into things. Cross knew Grossman had no journalistic experience and even less interest.

Grossman's lack of concern for the newspaper showed when Emily Ingle was leading the effort to pay off the Board of Supervisors for votes on the stadium project, and even when the two papers banged the drum for Callahan's innocence following the deaths of Missy King and Glenda Callahan.

The *Journal* publisher tended to go along with whatever Ingle thought might help both papers, but his heart was never in it.

"I'm not the newspaperman in the family, I am the builder," Grossman had told Cross once. "Keep it going and stay out of too much trouble and I'll leave you alone."

Cross had smiled when Grossman made the comment during his second day as publisher. The editor, who thrived on the controversial and confrontational news story, knew that he could have his way, with Grossman offering only a half-hearted interest in things.

As Grossman looked out over the city on that news-filled Friday afternoon, he smiled even more broadly as the sunset on the Golden Gate Bridge and the light fog moved in over Telegraph Hill, which rested easily in the landscape beyond his window.

This project, Grossman thought, could be the one that got him attention for more than just half-running the city's afternoon newspaper. This could make him known as a prominent developer in his own right.

Standing up to get a full view of the city below, Grossman put his hands on his hips and peered out to see how far he could view the street. His eyes just made out a news hawker handing over a copy of the *Journal* to a customer in exchange for the 25-cent fee, which he placed in his pocket.

Grossman then quickly turned around, plopped down in his large leather chair and snatched the newspaper off his desk for another quick read of the article.

The story stated simply that the Mack Corporation, after years of financial struggle, was announcing plans for a new development project in the city's Hunter's Point area—the 600-acre site of the former naval shipyard that had closed two decades earlier as part of the federal government's massive military cutback.

The shipyard, which offered a prime real estate area because of its access to State Highway 101 and its location next to San Francisco Bay, had remained undeveloped for several years because of the 80s economic problems but was now ready for new life.

Mack Corp. had purchased the land from the Navy three years earlier and had been set to launch a project with the help of former Mayor William Carlson. But after Callahan won the election and knocked Carlson out of office, Mack Corp. officials decided the new mayor would not be receptive to their proposal since the *Journal* had just spent several months attacking his candidacy and supporting his opponents.

Grossman was ready to kill the plan completely after the election and try selling the property. But since the *Journal* and the *Bulletin* had both become allies of Callahan, virtually proclaiming his innocence during his recent brush with the law, the prospects for success with the project had changed.

Mack executives, especially Grossman, realized that Callahan owed them a favor following his successful dodge of criminal charges, and had begun laying out the development's key elements the day after Moore and Brown were indicted.

They knew then that Callahan would be most receptive to their idea after the newspaper all but led the way to his innocence.

Specifically, the proposal called for redevelopment of the entire Hunter's Point Shipyard area. The plan outlined construction of 4,000 residential units, a major mall and retail shopping center, a school, industrial and office parks, playgrounds, and a 13-screen movie theater.

If Grossman could ensure approval from the City Planning Commission, he had already secured promises from several banks and private investors for the $800 million the five–year project would likely need.

Mack financial planners estimated that the development, once completed, would generate about $150 million in annual profits for the company, with the first $50 million after just two years.

"It could be a gold mine," one of the company's analysts told Grossman. "And it's just a matter of making all the parts come together."

The *Journal* had purposely run the Friday afternoon story on the inside of the business section so that it would not draw too much attention from likely opponents, such as local neighborhood groups in Hunter's Point, environmentalists who always opposed big projects, or competing developers.

Grossman had told Cross to run a basic story, without graphics, after rumors at the newspaper surfaced that the *Bulletin* had gotten wind of the plan and was preparing a slightly more negative piece.

"I think we need to get a jump on this and tell it our way," Cross had told Grossman after hearing that the *Bulletin* was on to it. "We can keep it low-key, especially with the chiefs' verdicts coming down, but we need to run the spin."

Grossman had not wanted to announce anything until he had his plan completely in place, but reluctantly agreed with the *Journal* editor and told him to run the story.

Ironically, the *Bulletin* did not run anything on the proposed project, deciding to throw much of its reporting staff behind the guilty chiefs' story. Since the *Bulletin* had gotten a late jump on the story compared to the *Journal*, *Bulletin* editors wanted to give it extra attention for the Saturday paper, with more reaction, indepth coverage of the verdicts, and the overall impact on Callahan's future.

When the *Bulletin* finally got around to running a story on Sunday about the development plan, it was basically a brief, recounting what the *Journal* had written about its parent company. The *Bulletin* story offered no opposing viewpoint or original reporting. It might as well have been a weather report.

That didn't bother Grossman, who remained confident and positive as he read the *Bulletin*'s Sunday paper, which included the short development story. Reviewing the papers that Sunday morning in his Nob Hill condominium, the publisher/CEO chuckled a few times as he reviewed both newspapers over his favorite pancakes and sausage.

But, while he sipped a glass of orange juice and swallowed his last taste of coffee, he also realized that in the topsy-turvy world of San Francisco politics, business, and journalism, anything could happen.

In just the past few months, the *Journal* had made some new friends in Callahan and his supporters, but also some lively enemies in the *Advocate*, the *Reader*, and a handful of supervisors who had not taken kindly to threats and forced payoffs.

Grossman also wondered how the multitude of citizens' groups that often opposed any major construction or development, especially one that sat next to the San Francisco Bay, would react. He worried that the environmentalists would jump on his proposal before he could even break ground.

The first thing he had to do was get the political support lined up. That meant getting Callahan and his four appointees on the Planning Commission behind him.

Since becoming mayor, Callahan had been able to fill four of the seven planning commission seats with his own appointees. The others, chosen by Carlson two years earlier, still had two years to go in their terms. Because Callahan held the majority of votes with his commissioners, all Grossman and Mack Corp. had to do was gather their support. A goal that seemed within reach.

On Monday, Grossman held a quick meeting with his chief engineer, Greg Scott, and his top planner, Mark Wilson. They were the two men who helped bring the plan together during the past four years, with details worked out down to the last inch of concrete.

Wilson, who worked for the city for ten years before joining Mack Corp, was a wizard at city regulations, not to mention space-saving design. He knew exactly how to build to meet city codes and how to avoid them without getting caught.

Scott, who studied just south of the city at Stanford University, was known in the area as a crack designer in his own right, having lent his talents to several major earthquake retrofit projects and buildings. He made sure the proposal would withstand strenuous earthquake testing and open land requirements.

During the Monday meeting, the three men went over the basics of the proposal for two hours and ordered the first scale model of the project to be built. Grossman hoped to use it during a formal unveiling of the plan in two weeks. After the meeting, Grossman went into his office to make an important phone call—to the mayor.

Since the harrowing events of the past few months, and the trial of George Moore and Steve Brown that had ended only three days earlier, Callahan had decided to take a few days off that week, spending time with some friends in Napa Valley. His secretary told Grossman that he would not be available to meet until the following Monday. The publisher grew impatient, wanting to get things wrapped up as soon as possible, but agreed to meet a week later.

During the rest of the week, news reporting on the project was almost nonexistent. The *Bulletin* did not follow up at all, while the *Reader* and the *Advocate* each ran short stories with little new information or criticism.

The *Reader* published only a short editorial from Dugan that simply advised residents to "watch this project carefully," a warning the *Reader* would give to almost any major construction plan, but especially to one by a company that owned one of its bitterest rivals.

*   *   *

The following Monday, Grossman arrived at Callahan's office about ten minutes early for their meeting, sporting his best blue vested suit, and even a handkerchief. He decided to come alone in case some side deals with the mayor were necessary.

Although the *Journal* had provided its share of support for Callahan in recent months, Grossman had learned from Ingle that a little extra attention was often needed.

After waiting about 20 minutes, Grossman was led into the mayor's inner office, where he shook hands, sat down, and explained his situation to Callahan. The mayor, always ready with a gentle smile but still a bit upset and shaken by his legal entanglements, listened carefully.

"So you see, mayor, this could be a real boon for the city," Grossman said, with a slight nervous stutter as the mayor nodded. "We believe it will come under all environmental limits. It will create jobs and homes—including 20% for low-income families—and will come under all city requirements for minority contractors."

Callahan smiled with each element that Grossman described, knowing full well that each of those concerns would likely be raised by some community group or union that could cause the mayor trouble.

"And it will all be done without city money or a tax increase," Grossman added, smiling slightly himself. "We just want to see what we can do to make sure it meets your needs so we can count on your support and that of your commissioners."

Callahan nodded several times as Grossman finished his comments, then leaned back in his chair and clasped his hands behind his head.

The mayor knew he could readily support the plan, but also that he could use it to leverage the paper's help for him in the future, a trade-off that Billy Dale himself had taught Callahan less than a year earlier.

"Well, I see no problem with this, provided you do one thing," the mayor said as Grossman leaned forward to listen. "I am planning to bring my homeless program back for another attempt soon. I hope that I can expect your support for it again."

Grossman didn't even hesitate. He jumped up, stuck his hand out, and took the mayor's hand in a firm, up-and-down grip.

"You got it," Grossman said, believing that such a simple endorsement would be easy. "No problem."

With that, Grossman left the mayor's office, smiling even more as he realized that he had the first of his necessary pieces of the puzzle locked away. Inside the mayor's office, Callahan also grinned slightly, knowing that all of his recent problems and embarrassments might actually be fading, and his original plans to make some kind of mark on the city could be back on course.

*   *   *

Jack Callahan had not been to the Hunter's Point Shipyard site for more than 20 years when his town car drove past the recently reopened front gates on the sunny, breezy morning just days after Grossman had entered his office. The last time he happened to visit the former naval facility was during his patrolman days when he responded to a shooting at the military base.

Although military police had always patrolled the location well, the shooting—involving a navy engineer and a civilian thief who had sneaked onto the base—required outside police attention.

A beat cop in the Mission District at the time, Callahan had been called to help investigate the situation because most of the nearby Bayview District station cops were out at a chemical spill blocks away.

Callahan recalled that the shooting had been handled rather quickly and easily because the thief admitted trying to steal the engineer's wallet, and the engineer was let off with a simple self-defense argument and the use of a legal, licensed gun.

Although he'd only been at the base that one time, Callahan always recalled it as an unusual mix of waterfront beauty and calmness with industrial and military chaos and strength. He had never thought of it as a development spot.

But, here he was about to help launch the program that would be the biggest of its kind and could be a major notch to Callahan's reputation and political record.

Stepping out of the town car to a waiting bank of microphones, Callahan was quickly met by Grossman, who walked straight up from a crowd to shake his hand and lead him to the area where they would reveal the scale model, announce the five-year timeline, and begin the positive spin that would be needed to counter the objections—both real and political—that would likely occur.

Grossman had assembled Wilson and Scott at the mikes to field the press inquiries and help explain the stronger points of the project, while Callahan had corralled his four planning commissioners to at least appear supportive of the plan.

In reality, only two of the commissioners—Tony Deal and Susan Herman—were on board. The two others—Don Pullman and Betty Selleck—remained undecided, according to Callahan, who believed they could be won over.

"Why not?" Callahan had told Grossman on the phone a day earlier. "This is a great project. Some people just have to make a little noise, especially in this town where it all grabs headlines."

Grossman wasn't worried. He also believed that the project could sell itself. But he remained antsy, knowing from experience that anything could rock the boat.

During the press conference, Grossman called the project "Hunter's Point Plaza" and said it would be the "greatest 'people' development ever created."

Callahan also chimed in supportively, describing the mix of housing, retail, and industrial, as "a win-win-win for San Francisco," utilizing one of the most overused phrases in politics.

After the 20-minute formal presentation, which included the scale model and several artist's renderings, Grossman and the others braced for the obvious questions.

"How will it affect traffic?"

"Will there be enough parking?"

"Will you give enough jobs and business to minorities and women?"

And the most tricky one, "What is the impact on the environment?"

Wilson and Scott were quick to knock off each question with detailed plans for contracting work, reconstructing roads, and laying out parking plans that exceeded the city's minimum requirements.

Then Wilson added one for good measure, telling the assembled press and officials that the project also included an extensive toxic clean-up plan to make sure the shipyard's polluted areas—which had been dirtied from decades of chemicals used for the massive ship repairs and decay—would be complete.

"We will make this ground cleaner than it was when the Navy first got here," Wilson proclaimed. "We know exactly what to do and how to do it, and it won't cost the city a dime."

Although neither Grossman or Callahan had asked Wilson to mention the toxic clean–up elements—not wanting to bring it up unless they had to—Wilson believed that getting the issue out in the open was the best way to deal with it and put it to bed for good.

"Don't worry, this was bound to come up sooner or later," Wilson told Grossman after the CEO asked him why he had mentioned it. "You have to make it our non-issue before any opponents can make it their issue."

As the press conference went on, the engineer and planner handled most of the minor questions that often came up with big projects, such as timeliness, impact on the surrounding area, and costs.

Grossman, Wilson, and Scott answered each concern with confidence and directness, telling the reporters that the $800 million project would take five years and not involve public money.

Just 90 minutes after the press event had started, it was over, and Callahan, Grossman, and the others returned to City Hall.

At the same time, each of the reporters returned to their newsrooms. As usual, the television and radio crews would do the standard big development story that looked at some potential negatives of the plan, but mostly focused on the positives. At least two television stations also offered some old military footage of the shipyard to give a nostalgic reference that most old-time San Franciscans couldn't help but love.

For the *Journal*, the story about its parent company launching such a big undertaking was told with an obvious positive approach, including an editorial that bordered on the insulting as it raved about the plan. Grossman himself had directed the editorial that Tim Cross wrote with little enthusiasm.

"This project offers San Francisco its greatest hope for both economic boosts and housing expansion," the *Journal* editorial stated. "We urge all city residents to get behind the plan and city officials to see it through to a swift approval process at City Hall."

As for the other newspapers in town, coverage was hardly pro-development, but not exactly bitter attacks either.

Both the *Reader* and the *Advocate*, which would not publish for another day due to their regular Wednesday publication dates, presented a general overview of the plan, but with specific concerns about the toxic clean-up, the minority contracting for local small companies, and the inclusion of low-income housing.

"If this project is to be approved by the Planning Commission, it must be assured that all concerns about the environment, jobs, and housing for San Francisco's neediest be stipulated," the *Reader* editorial that week said. "We implore city officials to scrutinize this proposal thoroughly so that it does not only serve the big business and development elite, but also the community."

The *Reader* also included a side story with comments from three well-respected environmental engineers about the need for extensive toxic cleanup of such an old, polluted site. The story urged a thorough and specific toxic review to make the area safe, especially for homes.

"Toxic soil erosion is a tricky thing," one of the experts said in the *Reader* story. "It is just as important to know exactly how much clean-up is needed as it is to actually do the cleaning. If you only do a partial job, it can be as bad as doing no job at all."

The *Advocate* reflected the same views in its story that ran next to a front-page column by Mike McLean, in which he warned residents to "never trust a government bureaucrat who says things are clean enough. If they won't live there, no one else should."

As for the *Bulletin*, which usually took a calmer approach than its alternative sisters, concerns about the Mack Corp. project went beyond just the usual developmental issues. This one hit home since it clearly had links to a rival newspaper.

Although the *Bulletin* and the *Journal* had come together on several issues in recent months, forging some positive outcomes as well, business was still business.

That was exactly what Emily Ingle told J.C. Townsend when she called him the day of the Mack Corp. announcement. She stopped short of ordering Townsend to publish a slam against the development plan, but made it clear that she wanted every possible negative element of the project published and investigated.

"It is bad enough that they are getting attention from this proposal," Ingle had said. "But if it actually gets built, they will reap a huge windfall, which can only be used to beef up their paper and come on stronger against us."

Although the *Bulletin* topped the *Journal* in circulation and advertising revenue by leaps and bounds, Ingle knew that those measurements could change if her rivals had some money to play with.

And if the Hunter's Point project turned out to be a success as well as a plus for local minority workers, companies, and poor folks looking for homes, the *Journal*'s image would also rise, and likely sell more papers.

"If there is anything there, let's make sure we get it," Ingle had told her editor. "Don't give them one inch on this without making them fight for it."

For the rest of that week, readers and television viewers took in all corners of coverage on the Mack Corp. project, from the highly-favorable *Journal* stories to the warnings from the weeklies, to the *Bulletin*'s scrutiny. None of the stories had a major impact either way, but they clearly showed that the project was not going to be let off without attacks from all sides.

Finally, on Friday, the Planning Commission announced it would hold a hearing on the proposal in one month, setting a date of Sept. 5, the Friday after Labor Day.

Until then, commissioners and any interested residents would be invited to review the plan and file their opinions on it, as well as speak up during the hearing. The Planning Commission would be asked to approve the request for zoning changes to make certain areas of the shipyard residential, industrial, retail, and school zones.

In all, the commission would have to approve six different zoning changes, as well as the permits for the project to be built to its proposed specifications. The Mack Corp. planners also would have to provide environmental reports showing exactly how much cleanup would be needed, and how much time it would take to complete.

Grossman and his planners were not worried. Environmental reviews that had already begun three months earlier would soon be completed, and would likely indicate that only six months of cleanup—for an estimated $15 million— would be needed. All of the detoxification had been budgeted into the plan, with an extra $5 million added just in case more was required.

"This will flow like clockwork," Greg Scott told Grossman after the hearing date was set. "There is nothing that should stand in the way."

Grossman was confident. But after 30 years in construction and development, he knew that nothing was assured until it was done. His Uncle Billy had always told him, "Don't build the roof until you have four solid walls."

Grossman realized that and told all of his staff to take it one step at a time, do what needs to be done, and don't make mistakes. Aside from the obvious uncertainties about the commissioners, toxic tests, and costs, Grossman also had real concerns about the three other newspapers that were going to watch the project's every element. Especially the *Bulletin*, whom Grossman, as well as Ingle, knew would not give an inch. ■

Chapter Twenty-One

"Just As We Had Feared"

Larry Burger did not often venture out to the worksites of the projects his company constructed. The 49-year-old environmental consultant and planner—who'd built his business from a landscaping shop with one truck 25 years earlier to the Bay Area's most lucrative and respected environmental review company—preferred to work from the business and political angle, instead of getting down in the trenches.

Known as an avid art collector who filled his Sausalito office north of San Francisco with everything from Van Gogh originals to simple amateur charcoal etchings, Burger had seen enough of the down-and-dirty grunt work as an environmental engineer through the late 1970s and 80s to avoid viewing it again.

After earning his stripes in the environmental game as an investigator on projects ranging from the Embarcadero complex to experimental trash burning equipment—while building his business up to a prosperous concern along the way—Burger now placed more attention on bringing in business, especially high-profile projects that he knew could earn him public contracts and prominence in the area.

As Burger had learned, and had taught most of his staff, city-funded projects were among the most lucrative because, well, city officials don't care how much they spend. Since it's taxpayer money they are throwing away, few government bureaucrats give a damn how much things cost.

And, if it's spent in the name of environmental testing and caution, the payoff for cities is even greater, Burger had learned. For every citizen demanding some new project or program to increase transportation, housing, or business, there are ten ready to complain about the environmental impact—especially in a liberal city like San Francisco. Make residents think the money spent on an environmental study is good, and they will push for more.

"It's not like taking candy from a baby," Burger once told a member of the Board of Supervisors. "It's like having them hand you the candy and tell you they have more later if you want it."

So it was key for his company to get the big, costly, high-profile projects whenever possible. That would include the Hunter's Point development.

And, in the past few years, Burger had needed as many projects as he could get. Although he'd built up a successful franchise through the years that had business piling up, he'd seen a slight dip in the past eight months.

The dip was prompted by a lawsuit that had been filed, and won, against his firm after residents of an Oakland housing development began showing increased levels of mercury in their blood. The lawsuit revealed that Burger's testing of the project had been incomplete, and that a report he'd submitted claiming the area was safe for construction of 32 condominiums and a retail shopping center was wrong.

In the end, the plaintiffs could prove only neglect on Burger's part and not the direct culpability for their ailments they had sought. But the jury in the case had still given the 15 plaintiffs a cash award of $225,000 each, a move that had almost bankrupted Burger had it not been for some emergency loans that were still having to be paid off.

So when Mack Corp. began laying out definite plans for the shipyard development in late March, Burger—who had known Grossman slightly from some previous business dealings—got wind of the proposal from a construction friend and made a personal visit to Grossman. After promising the CEO a sweetheart deal for the environmental review and cleanup, knowing that he could easily raise the price later if needed, Burger put his best crews on the review and told Grossman it would likely be a simple job.

First estimates of the 600-acre area showed typical pollutants that would be removed under a basic six-month plan. Before any plan was released to the public, Burger indicated that he did not see a problem and urged the publisher to announce the project.

Now, two weeks after Grossman and Callahan made their plans public, Burger's estimates remained unchanged. So far, the testing had been completed on all but about 100 acres, with few surprises found.

When Burger received the two-week update on August 14, rather than call Grossman and the mayor and arrange for an update meeting over drinks at Stars or Moose's to celebrate the good word as he usually did, Burger drove himself down to the shipyard, past the security gate, and straight to the last area of testing. There he confronted his chief engineer, Ted Kenting.

Slowing his jeep to a halt just a few feet from the test area, Kenting, a tall, blond man in his 50's, waved to Burger and walked toward his boss with a smile.

"How's it doing?" Burger said in his directive tone. "Are we still on course?"

Kenting, nodding with assurance, provided what Burger wanted to hear. "Yes sir, we have some different elements of oil and solvents, but nothing that looks like a problem," Kenting said as he brushed the dirt off his fingers and flipped through a note pad. "We should have most of this testing down by next week, then get our report together."

Burger smiled as he nodded and yelled over the sound of the machinery rumbling several yards away.

"Great," he barked. "Keep it up."

With that, Burger drove off and headed straight for Grossman's office to give him a positive update. After a short meeting with the CEO, Burger headed back to his own office, then home.

It was a Friday and he was planning to head to Lake Tahoe for the weekend with his wife, Melba. He'd invited Grossman to come along, but the CEO wanted to stay close to the city in case any problems arose.

During Friday night and Saturday morning, Burger enjoyed the leisure, nightlife, and relaxation of Lake Tahoe, while Grossman kept his mind occupied with summer San Francisco outings, joining several of his senior editors for dinner Friday night and taking his boat out for a sail on Saturday.

For both men, the day was a chance to get away from development proposals, business worries, and stress. They each took it to its fullest.

Until Saturday afternoon, at precisely 2 p.m., when Burger's pager went off.

The minute he saw that the number was Kenting's, he knew it must be the Hunter's Point project. And for him to be paged on a weekend away, he knew it had to be serious.

"Boss, thanks for calling back," Kenting said when Burger phoned back on his cell phone from his picnic spot on the Lake's beach. "We found something in the tests that shows things are a lot worse than we thought. I can't be sure until we do some more testing, but it looks like this last 100 acres has a high level of lead and mercury. You know what that means."

Unfortunately, Burger did know. If the 100 acres was found to have high levels of lead or mercury over at least half of its area, which is how it sounded, the cleanup would likely take up to three years and cost Grossman another $20 million to $30 million.

After talking with Kenting for another five minutes, Burger slammed shut the phone, placed it in his briefcase, and told his wife they had to return to the city. As he drove the three hours back to San Francisco, he dreaded having to tell Grossman and the mayor what he'd heard.

Sure, it wasn't a surprise to find pockets of highly toxic chemicals on such a site. Hell, during the decades of military use, the shipyard had seen everything from howitzer cannons to nuclear missiles. But the impact this could have on the project was unnerving.

If Grossman decided the cost and cleanup was too much, he might just give up and sell the land to someone with less loftier plans. The publisher also might just keep it and find a cheaper environmentalist to clean it up, which means the $15 million Burger had expected from the original six-month cleaning job would vanish. All he would get is the $1.5 million for testing—nothing compared to what he had planned on.

Such scenarios played out over and over in Burger's mind while he drove across the Bay Bridge and headed onto Highway 101 toward Hunter's Point. He had called Grossman at home during the drive and asked him to meet at his office at 7 p.m.

Although Grossman had a dinner plan with some family members, he agreed to meet when Burger told him it was urgent and involved the Hunter's Point project.

"And don't bring anyone, especially the mayor," Burger requested. "This has to be between us."

That didn't sit well with Grossman, but there was little he could do besides wait and hope for positive results. It was 6:15 p.m. when Burger entered the city and steered toward the shipyard. Although the crew had left for the day at 5 p.m., Kenting had waited around to update his boss on the bad news.

Laying out some test results on the hood of Burger's jeep, Kenting detailed the situation. "The brunt of it is in this area," Kenting said, pointing to the shipyard section that, unfortunately, was slated for two major housing structures. "We found traces that show levels of lead that are 20 times what we thought, and the mercury is about five times as high. I would guess that that means the cost will be about $20 million to $30 million above the original $15 million estimate, and would likely take another three years."

Burger was clearly angered but just nodded in agreement. His business experience taught him that such results were usually on the money, and he was not a man to doubt Kenting.

After thanking the engineer for his time, Burger directed him to hold off writing up any kind of report until the testing was through, and to "keep this information confidential, tell no one."

Kenting agreed. He knew it was not unusual to keep such test results quiet until everything was done and a formal announcement could be made, especially on projects involving public land and big investments.

With that, Larry Burger climbed back into his jeep and headed out of the shipyard, back up Highway 101, and toward Grossman's Mack Corp. office. A cool summer breeze blew over the open-air vehicle as Burger steered it toward San Francisco's colorful sunset.

Burger could take such information; it was all business to him. In fact, he decided, it might help his image if people knew that his company was able to dig up potentially dangerous elements in such a major project and keep a possible health hazard from being opened to the public.

He also knew that there was an outside chance Grossman would be willing to delay the project for several years and allow the extra cleanup, since the development was such a lucrative idea and had already taken up so much time and money for Mack Corp.

But unfortunately, Donald Grossman didn't see it that way.

The CEO listened carefully as Burger laid out the situation in the early evening. Although he didn't launch into an angry response when he heard that the project would be delayed and the price for cleanup would be jacked up, he did grow irritated while Burger presented the options.

"The deal is you can either kill the plan, put it on the shelf indefinitely—which might ease the public reaction and make it possible for something down the line—or pay for the cleanup and put the timeline back a few years," Burger said, gesturing with his hands like a judge weighing both sides of a case. "It doesn't matter to us. We'd like to be able to keep going, and I think you could recoup the extra costs since the development will still be tremendously rich."

Grossman understood the situation and made no initial moves either way. He told Burger to have his crews finish with the study and provide a copy of their final report to him as soon as possible. He also thanked him for keeping the information away from the mayor and asked that the final copy be made available only to Grossman.

*   *   *

After a week, Burger's crew revealed the news they hoped would not occur, but expected. The last 100-acre section of land did indeed have 20 times the lead expected, and five times the mercury, and would require a cleanup period of approximately two years and 10 months, which would add at least $23 million to the project cleanup cost that had initially been set for $15 million.

On the Friday following Burger and Grossman's initial Saturday evening meeting—and one week before the planning commission was set to consider the project—Burger returned to Grossman's development office and sat in the same chair he'd occupied six days earlier.

This time, however, his bad news was final.

"It is just as we had feared," Burger said, believing that such information would mean immediate cancellation of the project and no cleanup contract for him. Little by little, Burger laid out exactly what had been found, where, and what would be needed to clean it up enough for the development.

Grossman nodded as he leaned back in the chair, his head tilting against the large picture window spanning San Francisco. His nods were not necessarily in response to Burger's comments, but more his own weighing of the options.

After several decades in the planning game, Grossman had learned to expect setbacks like this and gauge how and when to best go forward with a project, cut losses and end it, or put it on hold. Burger sat waiting like a patient child in the principal's office who'd been called in for punishment as Grossman stood up, turned toward the city view, and continued nodding.

Pushing the large pine chair back under his desk, Grossman walked around behind Burger and continued to review the situation. As he paced back and forth slowly, with a hand under his chin and another crossed under his arm, Grossman hummed slowly to himself.

His mind was working. Like a skilled doctor considering a diagnosis or a canny attorney summing up all sides of a case to plan his move, he put the pieces together, just as he'd always done when deciding how to go forward with a project or a plan.

Suddenly, as he reached the door to his office, with his back to Burger, Grossman spun around slowly and looked Burger straight in the eye. The environmental consultant jumped back when the publisher's stare pierced him.

"How about this?" Grossman said as Burger's hesitation grew. "Could you change the report a bit, if needed, to make it appear that all that was found was the same level of toxins as the rest of the shipyard? That all that was needed was the six-month cleanup and the $15 million cost that you originally expected?"

Grossman moved closer to Burger as he offered the alternative, stopping with his hands firmly on the back of Burger's chair, practically shaking the piece of furniture as he spoke.

"Is that something you could do?" Grossman said in the same soft, slow tone with which he'd been speaking.

Burger's first reaction was disgust. He'd never blatantly faked an environmental report, especially not one as damning as this. He knew that if the project were built with only a basic toxic cleanup on the last 100 acres, the area could and would be a health hazard. But he also knew that if he didn't agree, a potential $15 million to $30 million payday for his company was gone, and they would be stuck with just the $1.5 million for the initial study.

Burger let out a frustrated sigh as Grossman lifted his hands off the chair and went back around the desk to sit down. The environmental veteran was not surprised that such a request would be made. He knew Grossman's situation and Mack Corp.'s need for the project to be built.

But that didn't make it any easier for Burger to hear such a request. Sure, he could turn it down and probably do well with other projects and contracts. But he also knew the influence a man like Grossman had in the Bay Area. Who knew what he could pull to hurt Burger's future?

"Could I think about it?" Burger asked, vowing not to reveal this illegal proposition to anyone. "This is a lot to ask."

Knowing he had Burger hooked with the potential for a big payday and a major contract, Grossman told him to sleep on it, urging him to make his mind up as fast as possible so that the altered report could be available in time for the planning commission hearing.

Burger left Grossman's office in a haze and quickly drove home, hoping to spend some quiet time with his wife, making no mention of the offer. He knew she would never approve, but he also knew that such a cash flow would put him forever in the black financially.

After a mostly sleepless night in which Burger kept being hounded by the tug-of-war in which Grossman had placed him, Burger arose to find his mind had steered him to do what Donald Grossman asked. He would falsify the report and, he convinced himself, be doing it for the good of his family and his business.

The more Burger thought about it, the more he decided it was not his concern. Sure, the area had pollution in the ground, but what danger did it really possess so far beneath the surface? Little by little, the lure of money and security took over Burger's mind, knocking out everything he'd ever learned about the dangers and hazards of pollutants.

Burger had spent years fighting to learn more about how toxins would erode into the ground and seep into drinking water, lakes and streams, and even the ground under people's feet. It had been his passion to make sure that such pollutants were properly investigated and removed.

But he'd also made a great living on his work and never hid the fact that he did it for the money. The moral view of protecting citizens from harm and guarding environmental needs had been a side feature of his career.

Today, however, with more competition from other environmental firms, with younger, modern-educated investigators, Burger decided he had to watch out for himself and take this challenge.

Burger immediately phoned Grossman at his home. The two men talked quickly and quietly, and agreed that Burger would have an altered draft of the report by Monday morning. That would meet the deadline for background items that had to be submitted for the planning commission hearing on the following Friday.

"I know we are doing the right thing," Burger lied to Grossman as they hung up. "I know that this kind of development is good for the city."

But deep down, Burger knew it was only good for Grossman and himself, and just held on to the hope that nothing dangerous would befall those coming on to the project land in the future.

Late Saturday morning, after his wife went out to shop and meet a friend for coffee, Burger got dressed quickly and drove down to his office.

There he found the draft report his crew had written and simply reworked it. After only an hour of alterations, which had to include a change in testing data that did not look too obvious or contradict the rest of the shipyard's data too much, Burger had his final masterpiece.

After placing the report in the proper form, with letterhead cover, photos, and other visual aids that always accompanied such reports, Burger left the office and dropped the report—in a plain brown wrapper—at Grossman's Mack Corp. office.

While driving away, Burger felt another tinge of guilt, but quickly eschewed it.

"Why the hell should I feel guilty?" he said to himself. "It's not my plan. Besides, I have a right to this project. I haven't worked my whole life and built up a business to have it knocked down by some pint-sized newcomers who talk a little quicker and show off their work a little flashier."

Late that afternoon, Burger returned to his house to find his wife. He gave her a half hug, indicating his mind was on other things. But she did not notice, quickly suggesting that they eat out that night.

Wanting more than anything to get his mind off what he had done, Burger agreed and suggested some North Beach Italian food.

The couple headed out about an hour later, found a rare parking spot in front of their favorite restaurant, and went inside. Just as they sat down, the couple was recognized by none other than Supervisor Marie Alzeti, a strong environmental advocate who had come to know Burger through previous projects.

As they spoke, Alzeti asked how the review of the Hunter's Point shipyard plan was going, knowing full well that Burger had the contract.

"It's great," he said shyly. "The final report will be at the Planning Commission this week." Then Burger turned back to his wine and sipped it nervously.

Alzeti smiled. "That's great," she said. "We're all counting on you to make it right." ■

Chapter Twenty-Two

Deadly Overkill

On Monday, like clockwork, Grossman officially submitted the altered report from Burger as part of the formal request for approval of the plan. The report was presented to all city planners reviewing the proposal, as well as each of the seven planning commissioners.

On Wednesday, Sept. 13, the report was made public. And, of course, both daily papers did a story on its "good" findings.

As expected, the *Journal* offered a glowing, yet subdued, story indicating that the Hunter's Point Plaza was given the first green light on its road to completion.

"With an environmental thumbs up from one of the area's most well-known consultants, the city's largest-ever development project moved a step closer to reality yesterday with a report indicating only mild toxins at the shipyard, which should be properly cleaned within six months," the *Journal* article stated. "With such proof that the area and the proposal are safe, the planning commission should have little reason to vote against this project on Friday."

The *Bulletin*, however, took a more skeptical approach. Although it laid out the story fairly and accurately, there was a bit more negative outlook, as expected.

"While it seems the Hunter's Point Plaza plan is jumping a major hurdle with a positive environmental report, no dirt will be shoveled, cleanup conducted, or construction begun until the Planning Commission offers its approval," the *Bulletin* story stated. "That, as most San Francisco developers know from past experience, can be a tricky thing."

Since the *Advocate* and the *Reader* would not publish until the following Wednesday, they had no stories because the report had come out a day after their Tuesday deadlines, but they planned to put the greatest negative twist on the project, no matter what the Planning Commission decided.

"This thing goes down no matter what," Jimmy Min told Billy Dale, who was counting the days to his release. "We will make sure that every scrap of this plan is checked. No way we let the fucking *Journal* get this kind of cash cow."

When the two daily stories came out Thursday morning, announcing that the project had gotten a preliminary clean bill of health—with a likely smooth environmental cleanup—reaction was generally good. TV and radio stations, who had not bothered to jump on the story a day earlier, parroted the *Journal* and *Bulletin* reports all the way. After all, the TV and radio stations would also benefit from a project that brought thousands of residents and shoppers to the city. They also knew it would present future stories to cover as the project went forward.

One person who was not so pleased, however, was Ted Kenting, Burger's chief engineer. When Kenting got wind of Thursday's big environmental news about Hunter's Point Plaza, he nearly screamed.

Since he had to continue preparing for Friday's Planning Commission meeting, Kenting had rushed to get to Burger's office as early as possible Thursday morning and had not bothered to check the morning papers.

The story hit him the minute he got to his desk and saw the *Bulletin's* front-page headline: "Hunter's Point Development gets Initial Environmental Okay".

The story went on to tell the exact opposite of what Kenting's report had found. He had not spoken to Burger since finishing the final version last week, but had assumed it had been given to Grossman for submission to the city.

Kenting, who grew redder and redder as he scanned the story, had been surprised that Grossman continued to go forward with the approval process, given the lengthy delay and cost increase of the cleanup effort. But without word from Burger to the contrary, he just assumed that the project was still being pushed ahead.

Kenting jumped up, threw the newspaper across the room in disgust, and made a beeline straight for his boss.

Just as he got to the door, he could see Burger looking over the same news story, his eyes scanning furiously and his finger scratching his head. Although it was a bit early for Kenting to be in, at 7 a.m., it was the usual time for Burger, a man working deals from dawn to dusk and often beyond, to be in the middle of pitching a deal or reviewing a new project plan.

Kenting wasted no time and did not even bother to knock on Burger's private door. He burst in, almost breaking the lock, and slammed a fist down on Burger's desk.

"What the fuck is this bullshit?" the engineer asked in red-hot anger. "What the hell are you trying to pull?"

Burger knew that this kind of reaction would come from Kenting, but had avoided having to think about it. Still, there was no holding back and he simply told Kenting the truth.

"Look, this is what we have to deal with," Burger said calmly. "The real report was not enough for Grossman. He was ready to shut down and we would have lost at least $15 million and one of the biggest projects ever. This way, we keep it going and no one knows anything."

Kenting was livid. He turned around and slammed his fist sideways against a wall, then kicked a chair across the room. To Kenting, his job was not just business. He was an environmental hound who lived and breathed his work.

A former specialist for the EPA, Kenting had gone into the private sector after believing that federal and state government bureaucrats were too bogged down with regulations to do any good. When Burger approached him five years earlier to join his staff, Kenting believed he could simply do good work and make sure projects like Hunter's Point were handled properly and carefully.

He didn't care if the whole company went bankrupt and he had to work in a McDonald's somewhere down the line if that's what it took to run a fair and honest shop.

"Larry, you know this will never work," Kenting said, as sweat formed on his forehead. "You know what happened to you with that lawsuit. This will be ten times worse if something happens."

Burger shuffled his feet nervously and rubbed the back of his neck. This was something he had been going over in his mind for the past week.

"Look, you know how we've been sliding," Burger told his employee. "If we lose this job, it will take five more good-sized contracts to make it up, and they are not coming in. I am not going to lose my business over this. This plan will put us back on top."

Kenting wasn't buying any of it. And he wasn't sure if he was more overwhelmed by his anger at Burger or his surprise in the way his boss was handling the situation. Heading toward the door, still, at a full boil, Kenting knew he was going nowhere.

"You can do what you want, but I am off this project," Kenting barked as he stormed out. "You can do it all yourself."

Burger realized that there was no way Kenting would stand in front of the Planning Commission the next day and lie through his teeth.

Then it dawned on Burger that Kenting might do more harm than just refusing to help. A chill went up his back when he realized Kenting's righteous attitude could cause him to let the company's secret out.

With that fear in mind, Burger ran after Kenting and caught up with him down the hall, near Kenting's desk and work area.

Grabbing him by the upper arm, Burger turned Kenting around and lightly shoved him to the wall.

"Look, mister, it's one thing for you to stay out of this, it's another for you to ruin it for me," Burger said with a stern, lecturing voice. "I can understand your not wanting to be part of this, and I'll respect that. But don't even think of letting this information out anywhere."

At this point, Kenting didn't care about anything but getting away from that place. He headed straight out of the building and to the nearest bar. It was 8 a.m. and he needed a drink.

*   *   *

The next day, the Planning Commission met promptly at 10 a.m. Although the seven-member panel usually gathered on Monday afternoons, they had agreed to hold a special session on the Hunter's Point project on Friday, knowing that it would involve in-depth reviews of the impact on housing, traffic, utilities, jobs, construction, and, of course, the environment.

Each commissioner had been interviewed by several reporters a day earlier and seemed to maintain the stances they had taken just weeks before when the plan was announced. Tony Deal, Susan Hayward, Betty Selleck, and Don Pullman—all Callahan appointees—had said they remained in support of the plan, as long as it seemed like a good project.

The three other commissioners, appointed by former mayor William Carlson, were Lance Beltran, Jody Solomon, and Chris Tanner. Although they were in the minority, they had spent more time on the commission than the previous four, with two years left in their terms. The city charter did not allow the mayor to remove sitting commissioners, only to appoint new ones as terms expired.

Since Callahan's majority remained, he was confident the project would get through. Burger and Grossman hadn't told Callahan anything about the original report, so the mayor assumed all systems were "Go" when the commission started its proceedings.

"Let's come to order," Commissioner Deal, who served as chair, said as he pounded the gavel before the packed audience. "We have one issue today, but it is of major importance, so we must get to it quickly and get through it thoroughly."

With that, Deal asked Planning Director Marty Cole, also a Callahan appointee, to present the proposal and the formal request for numerous approvals. Cole, who'd worked his way up through the department from his days as a San Jose State University intern, was known as a straightforward director, with a fierce loyalty to the mayor.

He had helped the mayor's campaign just two years earlier by hanging signs, passing out flyers, and even making brownies for campaign workers. On one occasion, Cole had even taken Billy Dale home one night when the campaign strategist was beyond his usual vodka limit.

Today, he gave a direct account of the plan, offering both its obvious appeals and obvious problems. He laid out exactly what Mack Corp. offered in the way of traffic expansion, parking, and assurances of minority job requirements, as well as estimated tax revenue increases from the expected retail and business efforts.

Cole finished with the presentation of the environmental report, which he read verbatim and summed up with the words both Grossman and Burger wanted to hear.

"The environmental status is unsafe, but the recommended clean-up effort is considered minimal for a former military site and is expected to take only six months," Cole announced.

Once finished, Cole sat down. His presentation had taken about two hours, with several interruptions from the commission for questions.

Next, Cole called Grossman to the podium and asked him to formally present his plan. The CEO stepped up and gave a direct and concise pitch for the project, calling it everything from "a vision for the city's future" to a "testament to the progress of the post-cold war movement." An obvious reference to re-using military bases for better, peacetime purposes.

Grossman went on to repeat the same assurances that Cole had recited, but with more of a salesman's pitch. "Trust me, ladies and gentlemen," Grossman said. "If this is approved, it will help all of us, especially you sitting right there."

The last comment was a veiled reference to the *Journal's* ability to politically support, or damage, most anyone in town. He knew that several of these commissioners were eyeing higher office, including the Board of Supervisors, and could ideally use a break from the afternoon paper somewhere down the road.

While most in the audience would not pick up on the comment, Grossman knew that at least some of the commissioners took the message to heart.

Following the formal presentations, which took about four hours, the commission took a break. When they reconvened at 2:30 p.m., the public comment began. First, the pro-project groups such as the unions, who would reap hundreds of new jobs for local workers, and the Chamber of Commerce and other business groups—who would see their memberships and power grow with new retail, industrial and tech businesses—spoke for expanding at Hunter's Point.

Last, as always, were the neighborhood and other opposition groups. Many Hunter's Point area residents said they worried about more traffic, a drain on city resources, and the simple noise of construction hurting them as the project went forward.

Some minority groups also spoke out. Although they welcomed the project's new job potential, they also worried that they would somehow be left out. Lastly, three environmental organizations, including the powerful San Francisco Nature Support Alliance, weighed in and said any parcel of land that has pollutants should be required to undergo more than a six–month cleanup.

"This area should be pumped, scrubbed, and unearthed for several years before one patch of dirt is turned over for construction," said Alliance president Victor Miller. "Sure, I know what your report says, but I also know what they said at Love Canal."

Miller's last comment left many in the audience and the commission slightly shaken, but without knowledge of what Grossman and Burger had done, it did not last.

As the comments ended, the clock above Deal's head struck 7 p.m. After asking if any more comments were to be made, with no response, Deal said the commission would meet two weeks later to formally decided what to do about the requests.

"So as not to make a hasty decision, and to allow for further study of all that has been presented to us today, the commission will recess for two weeks, and take up this item again on Sept. 29," Deal said. "Until that date, this group is in recess."

The crowd filed out noisily. As usual in these types of hearings, both the opposition and support groups were claiming a lead advantage.

Callahan, who knew the project could be a boon for him, was confident, as was Grossman, who had all but given up worries about the environmental truth coming out.

But Burger was another case. He stayed in his seat, twitching with uncertainty and concern. That last comment comparing his work to Love Canal was haunting him. He knew that a similar situation in San Francisco could hurt his business, destroy his reputation, and even land him in jail. Not to mention the health problems it could cause for potentially hundreds of people.

Burger sat in his seat and grabbed himself around the waist, putting his head down between his legs and trying to calm his volatile stomach. As he closed his eyes and breathed in and out slowly, his nerves stilled. After a moment, he raised his head, sighed slowly, and stood up to leave the chambers.

While walking out, Burger convinced himself that this project could put him back on top for good and slowly put the potential negatives out of his mind as he caught up to join the mayor and Grossman.

"How about a drink, boys?" he said to them as they walked down the stairs and out City Hall. "I'm buying."

*　　*　　*

Two days after the Planning Commission meeting, both the *Journal* and the *Bulletin* offered in-depth stories on the Hunter's Point plan. Both were naturals for a Sunday paper, where editors liked to show off with expansive articles, lots of photos and graphics, and an attempt to at least appear to be giving the reader something new.

Although neither story said a whole lot about the project beyond the previous details, each used the chance to take decidedly biased views on the proposal.

In the *Journal*, the coverage included artists' renderings of the finished plan, but showed none of the broken down former shipyard's crumbling, polluted buildings as they currently looked.

Along with a main story that laid out the exact plan, with a graphic outline of where every building, store, condominium, and stoplight would go, the *Journal* also ran a story on the economic plight of the area—which had a 50% unemployment rate—and the sales tax revenue increases that would come from such a project.

Finally, to stroke Grossman's ego more, the paper ran a side story about the publisher, which painted him as a man willing to handle two executive jobs because he "loves the chance to both make news and cover it."

At the *Bulletin*, however, the approach was different. The main story offered a similar rundown of the plan, but with the use of current photos of the shipyard instead of the artist's rendering. A similar layout of the shipyard and the planned improvements also accompanied the main story.

A neighborhood-based side story also appeared in the *Bulletin*, but it highlighted residents' concerns about the project, which they feared would shove them out and make life worse with traffic, noise, and congestion.

Finally, the *Bulletin* hit home with a story it knew would cause grief: a look at the environmental concerns. The piece included some military scientific comment from a former Navy engineer who said toxins in the ground at the shipyard could be more dangerous than they thought.

"The various types of chemicals used in that shipyard for the past 60 years include some of the most lethal gases and fuels ever made," the veteran said. "Some are so dangerous that they are no longer used by the military, in any capacity. I hope that those conducting such tests take this into account before giving any approval to any development, especially for homes where children will play."

As usual, few radio or TV stations offered any follow-up on Sunday, although two newscasts Sunday night made passing reference to some of the negative *Bulletin* stories. The following week began with basically the same status as before for the project.

On Monday, both the *Advocate* and the *Reader* were putting the final touches on their stories for the next issues set to come out Wednesday.

As expected, Jimmy Min had dispatched Mike McLean to write the kind of hatchet job of which he was more than capable, not only to slam the Mack Corp. and the *Journal*, but also to take aim at Callahan. McLean, never one to hold back, wrote in a column that the entire review process and project were an organized sham.

"Here we have the city fathers, all of whom are in concert with each other to rush this expansive, frightening project through," McLean wrote. "We have a mayor who is helping a newspaper publisher get his massive money-maker built so that both can reap success. The only people who have any say in it are four people whom the mayor put in place to do his bidding.

"And all we have to tell us if it is safe or good for the community are the mayor's hand-picked community leaders, and an environmental consultant hired by the publisher who wants to build it," McLean went on. "This is the proverbial fox in charge of the hen house."

The *Advocate* also included a main story slanted against the project and a side story on the environmental worries of residents.

At the *Reader*, things were no different. As usual, Danny Dugan took an environmental view over a political one, with a front-page photo on his tabloid that showed Victor Miller holding a sign in front of the shipyard that said simply, "Love Canal 2."

Inside, the *Reader* offered a major piece only on the ecological concerns, skeptical of the Mack Corp. report, and a call for an independent review by the city, with oversight from the S.F. Nature Alliance.

Dugan also followed with an editorial that stated: "We cannot sit by and watch this project go forth without making sure all reviews are complete. If this proposal is indeed valid, as its promoters contend, then a true review of its impact will not hurt. And, if it is found to be a progressive, positive plan for the city, the S.F. *Reader* will be the first to endorse it."

As the *Advocate* and *Reader* editions were being put together, Grossman, Burger, and Callahan used the time to their advantage, appearing on talk shows, radio interviews, and any piece of positive press coverage they could get.

All three men made sure to push the positives—city tax revenue increases, more minority and labor jobs, and more low-income housing. The mainstream press ate it up and pushed the project as something that could rival even New York City's massive developments.

"This could put San Francisco on the map as a place for positive growth, not just a home to the weird," Callahan had said in an interview that drew at least a few opposing comments. "We are the most beautiful and most visited city in the country, but this could help us become an example of a true progressive opportunity for residents, and a place that others will look to not just for a vacation or a convention, but for a direction on how to take a city to the 21st Century."

During all of the spin, reporting, and coverage, Ted Kenting remained silent. He had not said a word to anyone and had not even gone into the Burger offices since his blow-up with Burger the previous Thursday. He chose, instead, to stay in his North Beach apartment and keep up with other projects by phone. He had not even spoken to Burger since their argument and Burger was smart enough not to push him, given the wealth of information Kenting had.

When Wednesday arrived, and the *Reader* and the *Advocate* stories hit the streets, Kenting read each with a careful inspection that morning, nodding his head in agreement almost the entire time, and knowing that the project should not continue.

Inside, his stomach churned and his nerves became ice as he thought more and more about what kind of havoc this project could cause. His mind kept seeing visions of small children playing in toxic land, pregnant mothers being told their unborn children were sick, and others discovering they had cancer— all of them wondering if it could have been avoided.

Just after noon, he could wait no longer. Grabbing his jacket and running downstairs to his car, Kenting jumped in, slammed the accelerator, and steered the Honda Accord to his office, nearly running three red lights and a stop sign on the way. Once he reached the building, he stopped with a skid, jumped out, and ran up to Burger's office.

When he got to the owner's door, he saw it was closed, but heard voices inside. Ignoring any semblance of manners, he barged in and found Burger talking with none other than Grossman himself.

"Ted, do you mind? I'm having a private meeting." Burger said angrily, surprised that Kenting would come in without knocking. "This is not a good time."

"I'm sorry sir, Don," Kenting said, nodding to Grossman. "But I have something to say in private."

With that, Grossman got up and shook Burger's hand. "So we are on target?" Grossman said to Burger. Burger nodded and Grossman left.

As the door shut behind the exiting CEO, Burger attacked. "What the hell are you doing barging into my office?"

"I can't sit by and watch this happen," Kenting said. "I won't let it happen. That true report will be made public, and you can't do anything to stop it."

Kenting turned to leave, but Burger grabbed his arm. Turning him around with one quick jerk, Burger pushed him down into a chair and pointed a finger directly at Kenting's face.

"Now you wait one fucking minute," Burger boomed. "Don't even think of fucking this one up boy, or you will be out on your ass. I'll also sue you and make you an accessory. Remember that the final report, altered or not, has your signature on it."

Kenting jerked back in the chair. "I didn't sign it."

"I know, I forged it," Burger said. "Looks pretty realistic, too. Doesn't it?"

Kenting was more disgusted than ever. He was determined to set this farce straight. Leaping up from the chair, he pushed Burger out of the way and headed out of his office, down the stairs, and back to his car.

As he turned the ignition, hit the gas and sped up the street, Kenting tried to figure out the best way to get the word out on what was happening.

Back in Burger's office, the environmental consultant pondered Kenting's actions and realized this could blow up bigger than he had thought. Sure, his threats of dragging Kenting down with him if any heat were to come might keep the engineer from spilling the inside dirt, but he had to be sure.

With that, Burger picked up the phone and dialed a number he had used only on one occasion. When the person on the other end picked up, Burger didn't even say hello, he just had a message.

"This is Larry Burger, I have a little job for you. Can you do something tonight?" Burger asked the person on the other end. "Here is the situation." He then proceeded to give the person Kenting's name, address, and phone number, and hung up.

By then, Kenting was miles away, headed toward his apartment, where he hoped to sort things out. But just as he was driving up California Street's mammoth hill that topped out at Nob Hill before heading down the other side toward North Beach, he passed one of his favorite coffee houses, Cup of Joe's, and pulled over to go inside.

Once in the coffee shop, he took his favorite Cafe Mocha and sat down. Being in this place, where he had worked off and on during college years, always relaxed him and let him think. On this day, he needed space to think more than ever.

As he sat down, Kenting thought back to the day that the "good" environmental report had come out and Kenting had had his blow-up with Burger. Afterward, almost out of habit, he'd gotten a copy of the real report from his files and made several copies, which he later kept at home.

When he went to see Burger, he had a copy of the true report with him but had not taken it out. Now, as he tried to calm down and figure his next move, Kenting pulled out the six-page report and leafed through it.

There it was, before his eyes, the words and data that would knock Donald Grossman and Larry Burger out, and make sure a toxic time bomb was not built.

But, how was he going to get the word out? The press, the media, obviously. But which one? He knew the *Journal* wouldn't touch it, and he didn't think the *Advocate* or the *Reader* had the full credibility to make the entire city and establishment sit up and notice.

Then he realized the *Bulletin* was the answer.

Kenting had always had a good-and-bad relationship with the press. From what Kenting could see, reporters either slammed a project that needed toxic cleanup as unhealthy, no matter what was involved, or thought people like him were hired stooges who would do anything a client wanted, even lie.

In this case, unfortunately, they were right, Kenting thought to himself while he sipped his mocha and scanned the quiet, sunny coffee house. As he looked out the window, he saw the California Street cable car cruise by with its usual load of tourists and a loud bell clanging. That sight made the native San Franciscan smile somewhat as he contemplated his problem.

Kenting drained the cup and walked out the door to his car and began driving again, his mind nervous but firm in its resolve. He would not go to his apartment. He had some errands to take care of first, then he would see who at the *Bulletin* could help him out. It was exactly Noon.

By 3 p.m., Kenting went to the *Bulletin* offices in search of someone who would listen to his story, but he began to feel a bit ill. Perhaps it was a cold, the flu, or just nerves and the overwhelming feeling of what was happening.

As he got to the front door of the newspaper, Kenting suddenly felt physically sick and decided to postpone his effort. He would start again Thursday and get a hold of someone in the morning when he could be sure to have time to sit down, provide the report, and document his claim that things were being falsified.

Slowly walking back to his car, he doubled over and began to vomit. As Kenting puked onto the sidewalk, his head began to weave and he slumped to the ground.

After a few minutes, he regained his composure, stood up slowly, and wobbled to the car. His mind was a little clearer, but he knew he was sick. Calmly opening the door, Kenting crawled inside, started up the vehicle with a weak turn of the key, and headed straight home. It was almost 4 p.m.

Walking up to the second-floor unit, his stomach still quivered but felt less nauseous than before. Kenting wanted only to lie down and rest, putting all thoughts of Burger, Hunter's Point, and this horrible day aside, at least for one night.

Opening the door slowly, the first thing Kenting noticed was that a pillow from his couch lay on the ground in front of him. Since he lived alone, Kenting knew that no one but him would have been able to move it. As he reached down to pick up the pillow, Kenting immediately saw that everything in the room was out of place.

The couch was disheveled, drawers in the kitchen and living room were opened and emptied, and even the living room furniture had been overturned.

The television, VCR, and computer were all gone and several pictures and wall hangings had been taken. As the door slammed shut behind him, Kenting turned and saw a black figure appear from behind the closing door.

The stranger wore black pants, a black t-shirt, and a black ski mask. He grabbed Kenting's arm and twisted it behind his back. Kenting felt a twinge of pain, then the hot breath of the man's voice as it said, calmly, "give it up or you will regret it."

At first, Kenting thought the man wanted his wallet. But, when Kenting reached for his pocket money and pulled it out, the man only gripped him harder and yelled.

"Not that, you son of a bitch, the plans, the report, the proof," he said.

As he struggled to loosen the grip of the mystery intruder, Kenting barked back, "No way you bastard, get the hell out of here."

Suddenly, the man pulled a knife and stuck it sharply in Kenting's back. As he felt his blood trickle out, the pain of his stomach that had been annoying him all day grew more and more potent. Blood began to flow more quickly from his back as Kenting's legs wobbled, forcing him to his knees.

By then, the intruder had let go of the knife, and watched Kenting fall forward, lying on his face and stomach, while the blood seeped out. The intruder pulled the knife out and began stabbing Kenting further. In the heart, in the neck, and in the stomach.

As he left, the man reached into the same pocket that Kenting had just groped and took his wallet and gold watch, kicking him in the head on the way out the door. While the man made his way down the back steps, Kenting's still body stayed slumped on his carpet, blood flowing into a pool as he weakly gave in to death. ∎

Chapter Twenty-Three

Digging up the Dirt

It was just past 7 p.m. Larry Burger was about to go home when his office phone rang. He immediately recognized the voice on the other end. Putting his feet up on his desk as he slowly listened to the person, his face began to redden and grow more wrinkled with worry on each word.

"You what!?" he said loudly into the receiver, then suddenly turned to a whisper. "What the hell happened? I didn't want that, I wanted him roughed up, not dead. I....."

But before he could say anything, the person on the other end broke in, explaining the situation. Burger listened calmly, the whole time biting his nails and slamming his fist on the desk.

"I don't care if you made it look like a robbery, this is not what was supposed to happen," Burger yelled, then stopped for a pause to listen. "Okay, but if this comes down, I have nothing to do with it."

Burger then felt a pain in his stomach and leaned over to collect his thoughts after hanging up.

The man on the other end was none other than Joey Kelly, an old-time local Irish club organizer who had made his name in gambling, prostitution, and, on occasion, murder for hire.

Kelly had not even roughed up anyone for pay in three years, but he knew Burger from their days in the Navy about 20 years earlier and had beaten up one of his employees 10 years ago when he threatened to blow the whistle on a project. That situation had not turned to murder. But this case was different, Kenting was dead and Kelly had done it.

Burger could rightly assume that Kelly had handled the job carefully enough so that it looked like a robbery gone bad. But that didn't ease Burger's mind. Instead of his environmental report fraud being discovered, Burger was now an accessory to murder—at least from a distance.

Reviewing the implications of what he had just heard, Burger began to quiver, rocking his chair back and forth and shaking slightly. He went over to the bar in his office and poured a glass of scotch. After a few sips, he calmed down and convinced himself that things would be okay.

Burger began to feel relieved, knowing that the threat of Kenting exposing him was gone forever. Kenting was dead and the original report showing the high traces of toxins in the shipyard was buried in Kenting's office.

At that thought, Burger quickly walked to Kenting's desk—his drink still clasped in his hand—and found the numerous copies of the real environmental report that Kenting had made.

Those copies showed Burger that Kenting had, indeed, been serious about exposing things. He quickly took the copies back to his own office and put them through a shredder, almost smiling as he watched the flakes of paper separate and spread around the garbage can.

*　　*　　*

The next day, Thursday, police arrived at Kenting's apartment after a neighbor reported hearing noises the night before. Sure enough, his body was found with the stab wounds in the disheveled, ransacked apartment.

Police would conduct a full investigation, since Kenting had no known enemies and had not told anyone about his plan to go to the *Bulletin*. The cops had no other reason to believe anything had occurred but a botched robbery.

Taking statements from neighbors, who only reported seeing someone in dark clothes leave the home at about 5 p.m., the police would likely chalk this up to a burglary gone bad, with no other reason for foul play.

Burger, still wracked with guilt over death and lies that had mounted in just a few weeks, managed to keep his feelings hidden and forge ahead with the plan.

On Friday morning, just one week before the final Planning Commission hearing, Burger met with Donald Grossman, Jack Callahan, and Planning Director Marty Cole to go over the situation. As the men mapped out a preliminary schedule of cleanup and reviews, each gave his opinion on the status of things.

When it came time for Burger to give his assessment of the situation, he just smiled nervously and made a simple statement. "Everything, from my end, is ready to go."

Pete Martin was busy Friday afternoon when the strange letter addressed to him arrived at his desk in the *Bulletin* newsroom. The veteran planning reporter, who had spent the past few weeks focused on the Hunter's Point Shipyard project, did not even bother to open the strange piece of mail until late in the afternoon, around 4:30 p.m., after spending most of the day catching up on other stories.

After two weeks of practically non-stop research into the backgrounds of Donald Grossman, Larry Burger, and the entire Hunter's Point Shipyard's history, Martin was glad to get up to date on some other projects and had spent the day putting together a follow-up story on plans to expand the main library—a project that would come before the Planning Commission the week after the shipyard development.

As he sat down with his usual late afternoon cup of coffee, Martin spied the letter that someone in the mailroom had placed on his chair. It had no return address, just a San Francisco postmark.

After wincing when he accidentally burned his tongue sipping the hot beverage, Martin put the cup down and ripped open the envelope with his thumb.

The rush of another approaching deadline had filled the busy newsroom with clattering keyboards, ringing phones, and the usual rush of a Friday afternoon. As Martin rubbed his burnt tongue against the roof of his mouth to ease the pain, he pulled out the contents of the envelope, which appeared to be an environmental report, similar to the one presented to the planning commission by Burger.

Martin had already received a copy of the report that Burger submitted with the request for approvals involving the shipyard project, as did most every reporter working the story. But this version was different. It clearly said, in essence, that the clean-up necessary for the project to go forward needed to be much more extensive and costly than the official report stated.

"What the fuck?" Martin whispered to himself as he perused the item carefully, downing coffee as he read and wincing when his tongue was hit with the hot beverage again.

Martin pulled out his expansive file on the Hunter's Point Project that contained the report he'd been given by the Planning Commission. Laying both side by side, he saw that they were nearly identical.

Both had been written on Burger Environmental company forms, both were signed by Ted Kenting, and both had been dated the same. The lone difference, however, was that the one given to the city offered a much cleaner picture of the land.

As Martin reviewed the two, his first thought was that, yes, someone had altered the data. His second question was, who had sent this version and how could he get in touch with that person?

Of course, that person was Ted Kenting. Having followed the *Bulletin* stories on the project for weeks, Kenting knew that Martin was the best person to whom the information should be leaked. Just two days earlier, when Kenting had decided to let the *Bulletin* know what had happened, he had not been sure how long it would take to get to the right person. On the day he was killed, Kenting dropped a copy of the original report in the mail to Martin, just in case something happened.

Kenting didn't think he'd be killed, but he was afraid he might lose his nerve about going public with the truth. This way, he could let Martin decide and, if he had to, he could confirm the story later off the record.

But now that Kenting was dead, he left Martin with just a copy of the report, no knowledge of who had provided it, and some uncertainty over how to proceed. Martin's first thought was to call Kenting, since his name was on the report, and try to see what he knew.

When Martin made the call, however, the secretary at Burger's office would only tell him that, unfortunately, Kenting had died. Although startled, Martin just thanked her and hung up the phone, becoming even more suspicious.

The strange turn of events led Martin to see J.C. Townsend. Although it was a busy Friday near deadline, Townsend let Martin into his office. Slowly, the reporter explained the change of events to his editor while Townsend listened with his own interest and bewilderment.

"So what does this mean?" Martin asked his boss after he finished. "Does this mean the project is not as clean as we had thought? And could it just be a coincidence that this guy is dead? And how can we handle it?"

Townsend, who always had a quick directive for reporters seeking guidance, was flabbergasted. He took the reports from Martin and, just as Martin had done, laid them side by side, studying each and growing unsure of what they meant.

"Hmmm. Well, if all we had to deal with was this report, it would be kind of difficult to get a story from it because we don't know which one is the fake," Townsend said in his best journalism professor explanation. "But when the guy who signed both of them winds up dead, who knows what to think?"

Townsend asked Martin everything he knew about the project, including what he might know about Kenting. Martin said he'd never talked to Kenting because Burger had done all of the official commenting for the company, and only his words were used. As far as Martin knew, Kenting was just an employee who did his job.

"I'm not sure where we can go with this, but we have to do something," Townsend said. "Call Burger and tell him what you know. Just say that you have two copies of this report, both signed by Kenting, and ask what he might say about it. Then ask him what he knows about Kenting being dead."

Martin nodded, left his boss's office, walked over to his desk, and dialed Burger's number. When the secretary answered, he asked for Burger. She told him to wait, then put the call through.

"Yes, this is Larry Burger, who is this?" he said.

"Hi, Pete Martin from the *Bulletin*, how are you?" Martin said.

"Pete, what can I do for you?" Burger said, having recognized the reporter's name from past interviews.

Martin proceeded to tell him about the reports. He did not say where they came from but said he'd obtained them and was planning to write a story that would question the authenticity of the one that had been submitted to the city.

"What do you know about this?" Martin said.

Burger suddenly went blank. His throat tightened and his stomach knotted. He couldn't figure out how Martin had gotten this report, since, he believed, Kenting had been killed before he could have gone to the press. But he had to say something.

"I don't know what you are talking about," Burger said, stalling in a calm voice. "Any other version of the report is obviously a fake. Someone is trying to pull your leg, I'm afraid."

Then Martin asked about Kenting, wondering if Burger found it strange that his chief engineer would be killed in an apparent burglary. Burger stumbled over his words again, but managed to get out a comment.

"Son, you have been a reporter for a long time, you know that strange coincidences happen," Burger said. "We're all deeply upset about Ted Kenting. He was a great worker for us, but these kinds of things happen in a big city. We are just trying to get through it and get on with this project. Ted would have wanted us to finish it."

Martin, running out of questions, said goodbye and hung up. But he was not convinced. Too much was going on that didn't add up. On the other end, Burger also hung up and found himself worrying again about all of the angles. But there was little he could do except keep going with the original plan.

Back in the *Bulletin* newsroom, as the afternoon rolled into evening, Pete Martin remained unsteady. He knew there was something wrong going on here, but he had to glue it together. Having two identical reports signed by the same environmental engineer, but with two different results, was not something to be ignored.

Sure, the report he received anonymously could be a fake, a decoy drawn up by someone with access to Burger's office and a good forger of Kenting's signature who wanted to kill the project and sucker the *Bulletin* into helping.

It also could have been something aimed at making the *Bulletin* look bad. If the *Bulletin* and Martin were to print the anonymous report as fact, and it turned out later to be false, the *Bulletin* would be wide open to a heavy libel suit, not to mention a loss of credibility.

Still, the report could very well be the real evidence of the Hunter's Point Shipyard project, showing that, indeed, the area was much more polluted than people had been led to believe and, in fact, the report submitted by Mack Corp. was the phony.

After about 15 minutes of reviewing all these possibilities, and glancing back and forth between the two reports, Martin was more confused than ever. He decided to go see J.C. Townsend again.

Townsend, as usual, was busy at the computer going over copy, but gladly stopped again to chat with Martin over this strange circumstance. The reporter told him about the call to Burger and his evasive but expected answers. The two conferred over every possible angle of the truth and decided they did not have enough evidence to link anything substantial.

"That is the bottom line," Townsend told his reporter. "All you have are two pieces of data. One you know was submitted as fact, and the other, for all you know, is a fake. But you also have reason to believe that the second one could very well be the real report.

"The only person who could tell you for sure which is which is dead, and the only other person with factual knowledge claims the second report is a fake," Townsend added. "Looks like you need a lot more."

Martin nodded, then paused. His mind was looking for a way out that could legitimize his theory.

"Well, it looks like the key is to find some other way to tell exactly how polluted that soil is," Martin said. "We need to somehow test it ourselves."

Townsend nodded, but raised his finger with caution. "The only way you can do that, though, is to get into the shipyard, get a soil sample, and get it tested," the editor said. "That means breaking and entering private property, which I cannot condone."

Martin understood his boss's situation, but still liked the idea and pleaded with his eyes. Townsend could feel the reporter's need to check this out thoroughly.

"I cannot condone such an act," Townsend repeated. "But, if some evidence from a soil sample were to be found and brought into this newsroom without anyone asking for it, that could provide the missing clue."

Martin's eyes lit up. He knew where his boss was going.

"But if it comes down, I never gave approval for any of this," Townsend said, in a serious tone. "You will have to be on your own."

Martin had heard enough. He went back to his desk to plan how he was going to get into this gated installation, find the area he needed to test, and then get out. After several years covering the planning beat—which included numerous environmental-related stories—he'd gotten to know a string of ecological firms, any one of which would likely test the stuff for him once he got it.

But getting it, and not getting caught, was another matter. Martin pulled out both reports and studied them carefully. Each stated that the entire 600-acre former shipyard contained various levels of toxins, but none above critical limits. Any polluted areas were expected to need only six months' worth of basic toxin removal.

The only difference was in the report he had received in the mail, which cited the 100-acre parcel in the northwest corner—which had been slated for numerous housing units—as being 10 times more polluted with lead and mercury than the rest of the parcels.

If Martin could show that the soil was, indeed, polluted to a level 10 times more than what was considered safe, he could at least prove that the land was not as clean as the city had been led to believe. The only way, he realized more and more, was to break in, get a sample, and have it tested.

But how? Martin pondered it as the evening wore on, knowing full well that whatever he had to do needed to be done quickly because the Planning Commission's final vote was only a week away. He decided to simply drive over to the shipyard and take a quick assessment of the area.

Martin left the newsroom, got into his car, and drove down to the desolated shipyard area. Since it was rush hour, traffic on Highway 101 was its usual bumper-to-bumper. Still, Martin made it before 6 p.m., just as the sun was starting to settle over the Bay and the wind was beginning to pick up.

Although the shipyard was an expansive piece of land with great bayfront access, it still was accessible from only one road, Evans Avenue, which began near Army Street and traveled south for several miles before hitting the shipyard gate. One of the reasons for such limited access was to better guard the site during its military days.

Even though the former naval base had once been heavily patrolled by military police in its heyday, it was now privately owned by Mack Corp., so security was minimal. Since the location remained a toxic area by definition, anyone caught trespassing would also be charged with the added penalty of entering onto a toxic site.

As Martin drove up toward the front gate, he pulled over quietly so as not to be seen, and surveyed the area. From what he could tell, the front gate would have 24-hour guards, with others posted at certain locations around the base.

But as he recalled from his visit to the shipyard for the initial press conference announcing the development, little security existed near the waterfront. That meant that someone approaching from the bay might have a chance to get on land, especially in darkness.

Martin continued to scan the area for another 10 minutes, then jumped in his car and headed home to his Richmond District apartment.

Once there, Martin got on the phone to his friend, Todd Zeeley, and asked if he could borrow the rowboat he kept at the Oakland Marina. Zeeley, an avid sailor, had rarely used the rower since he took up sailing and bought a true racing yacht, but he still kept it for occasional uses.

When Zeeley asked why he wanted it, Martin decided not to let him know, fearing the more people who knew about his scheme, the more chance for problems. He simply told him he wanted to practice his rowing, knowing that Zeeley was fully aware of his past crew competitions in college.

Getting ready to go out for the evening, Zeeley didn't give the request a second thought and told Martin where the boat was parked. Martin thanked him and hung up. It was 7:30 p.m.

Martin knew he could get to the rowboat until midnight because the marina kept its docks open later on weekend nights. He left his apartment just after sunset, at about 8:30 p.m., and drove to the Oakland Marina. The lively area was bustling with activity as diners came and went from the many restaurants on Jack London Square, while others dined, partied, and relaxed aboard boats both docked and stationed out on the waters.

As Martin searched for Zeeley's rowboat, he made sure not to attract attention, carrying only a small canvas bag with a hand shovel, a coffee can in which he would place the soil, and protective gloves to keep the polluted dirt from infecting him.

The chatter of parties, the flow of music, and the clang-clang of buoys just off the marina mixed in Martin's ears as he made his way along the gangplank to the rowboat, which sat next to Zeeley's yacht and was covered by a gray tarp. The boat was so well hidden behind the larger vessel that it was almost impossible to see.

Once he reached the boat, Martin set down the canvas bag, pulled off the tarp, and carefully climbed inside. He looked for the flashlight that Zeeley said would be aboard and clicked it on. Carefully situating himself between the oars and making sure not to rock the vessel, Martin started rowing. He had rowed for years in college but had not done any in the past five years.

Gripping the oars with all of his strength, Martin pulled them back with both hands, feeling the heaviness of the water as it pushed against his effort. The slight drift of the wave cascaded against the boat.

The wind grew heavier and the night darker as the reporter continued to stroke the oars and push ahead. He made sure not to venture toward any of the yachts or sailboats that were out enjoying the bay evening. But since he was headed to an area of the bay not known for its recreational prowess—Hunter's Point—the chances of hitting someone were minimal.

The chances of running into the coast guard or a police boat, however, were great for everyone on the bay. Still, Martin just cruised ahead, working the oars and navigating as best he could. The waves swished higher with each movement of the oars, while the wind whipped in Martin's grimacing face.

Little by little, he could see the large drydocks of the shipyard approaching him as he rowed onward. The large drydocks, which rose several stories, were easy to spot in the dark shipyard. Rowing continuously, Martin found himself just a few yards away from the port and then looked to find the docking area that he knew would be the right place to park the boat.

During his previous tour of the shipyard, Martin had recalled the small dock located on the southeast side, which had been used in the past for small boats like his that rarely, but on occasion, brought military personnel to the area under cover of a water entry.

Tonight, however, the small dock was empty and dark as Martin moved toward it, all the while keeping his boat quiet and his light down. When he finally reached the dock front, he eased the rowboat in, grabbed a portion of the dock to pull himself onto, and tied up the miniature ship.

The entire trip across the waterway had taken about 40 minutes. Martin stood up and looked into the shipyard's dark stillness. He now had to find a spot to get a soil sample, avoid the guards and security, and get back.

Slowly, he hoisted himself up from the small dock to the ground level of the shipyard, making sure to keep his head down and the bag strapped across his back. Keeping flat on his belly as he pulled his body forward, Martin scrambled across the dying grass that stretched from the water to the first empty field house that had once been used by lookouts.

The houses were now merely empty remains of their former military use and a good spot for Martin to hide his efforts, at least for the moment. Once safely reaching the first house, Martin got to his feet but remained in a low crouch as he looked toward the entrance to spot any movement. All he could find were two guards at the far entrance gate, with no noticeable moves other than a continued lookout.

Next, Martin peered across the other way toward the parcel of land that was his goal. The shipyard was broken up into six fairly-equal parcels of about 100 acres each, and the area of heavy pollution was in the most northwestern parcel.

After a last glance to make sure he wasn't spotted, Martin waited for the lone rotating spotlight to pass by, then started on a dead run toward the far corner. Making sure to avoid anything that would trip him up, and running as fast as possible with his bag dangling over his shoulder and the night's cool air whipping by his hair, Martin darted to the other side of the base.

A flash of spotlight suddenly appeared from nowhere behind him, causing Martin to dive for cover at a nearby supply shed and hide just as the light passed over the shed's roof. Peering around the shed to make sure he had not been spotted, Martin leaped up again and continued his run for the corner.

Less than one minute later, he was near the far northwest corner, which was as good as any place to find a sample of soil. Carefully crouching, with one eye on the guard post gate, and the other on his small shovel and coffee can, Martin carefully put on his gloves, took several shovels of dirt, and placed them in the metal container.

After filling the can with as much dirt as it could hold, Martin sealed it with the plastic top, removed the gloves, and placed the entire contents back in his bag. Keeping low, the reporter swung the bag back across his shoulder, took a deep breath, and darted out again for the water.

Panting with nervous energy, Martin kept a full gallop as he moved closer and closer to the rowboat, finally landing as the spotlight again passed overhead, just a few yards behind his final step. He stopped at the tip of the small dock, put the bag in the boat, and climbed in himself.

After untying the vessel, Martin just slumped down—partly to hide and partly to rest—as the boat drifted across the waterway. He did not even begin rowing until he was at least 150 feet from the shipyard, then made his way back to the marina, where he tied up the rowboat, covered the tarp, and quietly, carefully walked to the car.

His mission, for the most part, had been successful. Now all that remained was to make sure his findings were worth finding.

*   *   *

To help him with the next phase of his reporting, Martin called Buck Charles, a longtime soil researcher at the University of California, San Francisco's agriculture unit.

A botanist by profession, Charles liked to do side work on toxic soil and other environmental causes. Martin had gotten to know him through a series of articles he'd done five years earlier on soil contaminants under the Golden Gate Bridge. Charles had come to Martin with that story after conducting some tests of his own on the bridge soil. The series got the city to close off the area under the bridge after children became sick from playing there .

Charles was a bit apprehensive. He was not in a hurry to get involved with someone who had trespassed on a toxic, privately-owned shipyard.

But after Martin explained the differing reports and the possibility for some toxins to remain in the ground when development occurred, Charles agreed, but only under the condition that he remain anonymous. Martin was reluctant, but gave in knowing that if he could prove the soil was 10 times more polluted than Grossman and Burger claimed, that would be all that mattered.

Martin took the soil to Charles's lab Saturday afternoon and Charles said the testing would be completed by Monday. Martin went home to wait.

Late Monday morning, at about 11 a.m., Martin was still waiting impatiently in the newsroom. He had purposely avoided Townsend all morning so that he would not have to face his editor until he knew what he had. He just kept himself busy with updating other stories, but his mind remained on the Hunter's Point shipyard.

Finally, at 11:35 a.m., Martin's phone rang. He grabbed it before the first ring could end and said a quick, "Yeah?"

It was Charles and his message was simple. "You got it," he said. "Exactly what you thought, 10 times the limit and there is no doubt about it."

Sticking his fist in the air like a defiant rebel soldier, the reporter let out a "Hooray!" that startled everyone in the room. The boys in the composing room three floors below could have heard it.

Charles agreed to give Martin the report, but with no trace of where it came from. Martin knew that with the evidence, and the remaining samples of soil, he had the proof he needed. After hanging up the phone, Martin jumped up from his desk and went looking for Townsend. He was told the editor was at lunch with none other than Emily Ingle, and would not be back until at least 1:30 p.m.

That gave Martin enough time to get to Charles' office and pick up his proof. An hour later, he was back in the newsroom to plan the newspaper's next move with Townsend.

After another hour, Townsend finally returned and had barely sat down at his desk when Martin came running in with the reports, the coffee can of dirt, and a major desire to get on the story. After calming down enough to speak, Martin told his boss what had happened. How he had sneaked onto the base, gotten the sample, and had it tested by Charles. He also told him how Charles had agreed to conduct the test as an anonymous participant.

As Martin recited the story, Townsend's eyes widened and a smile appeared, although he remained skeptical and cautious about how best to handle the next move.

"Okay, Pete, settle down," Townsend said as he put his hands on the reporter's shoulder and led him to a seat. "We have to move carefully on this. The first thing I have to do is call our lawyer and see what he thinks."

Martin then left the office as Townsend phoned the newspaper's attorney, talking to him for about half an hour. Afterward, he brought Martin in again.

"At this point, anything we write cannot indicate that we did anything illegal, like trespassing on the shipyard land," Townsend said. "So we must make clear that we obtained the sample, but not state how. The fact that it is clearly contaminated at the level we say should be enough to prove our case. But any illegal involvement will hurt this paper. You got that?" Martin nodded, ready to run and begin typing his story.

"And another thing, like I said before, there is no way we will take respon-sibility for sending you on this illegal venture, either," Townsend said firmly. "You also have to be willing to go to jail if needed to hide any sources involved in this. Are you?"

Martin just nodded enthusiastically and began to twitch with impatience as Townsend talked. All this reporter wanted to do was run and write the story. After some more directives from Townsend, the editor sent Martin back to his desk to begin work.

It was 2 p.m., Martin had about four hours to get the story together. As he began to write, Townsend made a call to Emily Ingle to give her the good and bad word about the situation. Of course, the owner was thrilled to know that her newspaper was about to drop a bomb on Mack Corp. and, indirectly, the *Journal.*

Although she also understood the sticky nature of this latest development, she also reveled in the chance to get her rivals and bring them down.

"Tell him to give 'em hell," Ingle told Townsend. "Stick it to 'em good." ∎

Chapter Twenty-Four

The Mayor's Vote

For the next four hours, Martin carefully pored over his three documents—the original report from the city, the anonymous one sent in the mail from Kenting, and Martin's own report from Buck Charles.

He carefully laid out the story, but said only that the *Bulletin* "had obtained a sample of the soil and had it tested to determine its toxic level. The tests indicated that the true toxicity of the soil was 10 times higher than the acceptable level according to state EPA standards, not the safe levels that the report to the city had indicated."

Martin then went on to ask several local environmental consultants what the cost and timeline for a clean-up of toxic soil over a 100-acre parcel with such lead and mercury contaminations would be. Answers varied from two years and $20 million to three and a half years at a cost of $35 million.

The story went on to simply say that this differed sharply from the report submitted by Mack Corp. Along with it, Townsend himself wrote an editorial that urged the Planning Commission to look into these findings, and the district attorney's office to look into the possible illegality of a likely conspiracy between Grossman and Burger to hide the truth.

"If there is any evidence that anyone tried to hide the potential dangers of the Hunter's Point Shipyard at a time when it's being considered for a massive development project where thousands of people could be put at daily risk, this plan must be halted and those responsible held to pay the price," the editorial read.

Townsend also directed Martin to write a side story about Ted Kenting and his sudden death in an apparent botched burglary. He did not mention the report sent to him anonymously, because it still had no validity as far as Martin or Townsend knew.

The next day, Tuesday, the story appeared on Page One under the headline, "Hunter's Point Soil 10 Times More Toxic Than Estimated." The story included comments from both Burger and Grossman, who, of course, denied everything and grilled Martin to find out how he had gotten a soil sample.

Grossman accused the reporter outright on the phone of stealing it.

But Martin, a veteran of dodging such challenges, quickly turned all questions back on Grossman and hung up once his portion of the interview was through.

The *Bulletin* editorial, meanwhile, took up the entire space on the opinion pages. When that day's *Bulletin* hit the newsstands on Tuesday, just four days before the planning commission hearing, TV and radio jumped on it, along with reporters at the *Reader* and the *Advocate*, who, of course, had to plan their own spin for Wednesday when their next issues would be published.

Grossman and Burger did not expect them to be played up as heavily as they were, with full Page One treatment and extra-lengthy space.

Burger had not seen such treatment of any public project ever before. But then again, this was no ordinary project. This was the city's largest-ever single development, and it was being backed by the *Journal*'s parent company, a fact not completely lost on either Grossman or Burger.

"Doesn't surprise me at all, those fucking pricks," Grossman had told Burger just before 8 a.m. on Tuesday when he arrived at his office and saw the paper. "Those bastards will do anything to make us look bad."

For nearly an hour, Grossman and Burger talked on the phone about how best to approach this dilemma. The most important goal was to find some fault with the *Bulletin* story and make sure it did not affect the Planning Commission outcome.

The two men debated whether to push for a later vote, to have more time to counter the charge, or allow the vote to go forward with the hope that the story would be seen as lacking evidence and as a revenge piece by the *Bulletin* against its competitor.

"This ain't good," Grossman told Burger as he pondered the next course of action. "We have to figure out how to shoot back, but in the most careful way."

Burger didn't know what to do. He was still mad that he'd allowed Grossman to talk him into fabricating the report in the first place. But he now knew that the past was done and if they did not act quickly, they could lose a major money deal for both of them, and even face criminal charges.

"Okay, okay, I'll see what I can come up with," Grossman told Burger just before hanging up. "But make sure you don't talk to any reporters, keep it quiet. The last thing we need is someone taking something we say and using it to back up that fucking story."

With that, Grossman slammed down the phone and kicked his desk. He wasn't sure if he was angry because he had done something that could blow the deal, or just angry because he had not done more to cover it up. But before he could decide, the phone rang again.

In a split second, as he picked it up, Grossman had an eerie thought of who it was. When he pressed the receiver to his ear, he winced when he heard the voice of Jack Callahan.

"Grossman, I hope you have a good explanation for this kind of bonehead move," the mayor said, displaying a rare burst of temper. "What the hell happened?"

Grossman's brain raced for something, anything, to say that would stall Callahan. So far, all the mayor knew was what he'd read in the *Bulletin*, but it was obviously enough to anger him and possibly bring the entire project to a halt. Grossman knew that what worried Callahan was the political impact of this project if it was found to be dangerous. In San Francisco, environmental dangers—especially those that are perceived as cover-ups—were political death.

Any politician, or developer for that matter, who appeared to be hiding information about a health hazard was crucified. As Callahan waited for a response on the other end of the phone from Grossman, the publisher asked him to wait and quickly hit the hold button.

Like a nervous burglar about to be found by the owner of a home, Grossman began to pace around the room in a helpless effort to find something that could keep his project afloat. If the mayor even smelled a cover-up, he would halt the Planning Commission review and take his four votes with him.

Grossman thought hard, sat in his chair, and leaned back against the window as the hold light on his phone blinked quickly.

The key to this, Grossman went over in his mind, was proof that the development was unsafe. When the *Bulletin* story came out, that was the first thing most people saw, including Callahan and Grossman. But, as he pondered the situation further, Grossman realized that the answer was not changing the elements of the story, but changing the perception.

During his time as publisher, he'd learned several things about the newspaper business and journalism. One of the main lessons was that stories are often interpreted in a way that the newspaper wants them to be.

If the *Bulletin* could make the Hunter's Point Shipyard development an issue of toxic pollution and health, then Grossman could turn it back on the *Bulletin* and make it an issue of motives. Instead of having the public look at what the *Bulletin* was reporting, Grossman needed to twist the perception so that the public looked at why it was being reported.

His solution was clear: competition. If Grossman could turn the tables on the *Bulletin* and make it seem as though its report was biased and done solely to hurt its competitor's parent company, he might be able to throw enough doubt on it to let it die away.

So far, all the *Bulletin* had reported was that it had obtained a sample of the soil, tested it, and found it was more polluted than original tests indicated. But the *Bulletin* had not provided any documentation of testing—because its tester requested anonymity—and had no way of proving the soil had come from the shipyard site.

Grossman decided that, if he could make enough of an issue out of the *Bulletin's* potential motives, he could kill its credibility on this story.

Grossman knew it would be difficult, but he also knew that it was the only way to attempt to keep the project going, and the money flowing into his pocket. He quickly leaned forward, took the mayor off hold, and went into complete denial.

Pleading with the mayor for support, Grossman harshly and sincerely denied everything in the *Bulletin's* accounts and then accused the morning newspaper of making it up to hurt his project.

"Mayor, this is outrageous," Grossman said as he made his case. "They have nothing, I promise you. This is a pile of bullshit. That land is as toxic as we reported, and will be spotless in six months so that we can start to build.

"You know what is going on here, those bastards are trying to knock us down, but they can't find anything real so they are making it up," Grossman lied. "What do they have? Some sample of dirt that could have come from anywhere? And they claim it was tested and shown to be dirtier. By whom? Where? And in what way?"

After about five minutes, Grossman stopped. Callahan said nothing for about a minute, taking in Grossman's reasoning. It was true that the *Bulletin* could very well make such a move to hurt the *Journal* and Mack Corp. But Callahan also knew that the *Journal* could just as easily misrepresent the facts.

The mayor knew that both papers had done their best to twist the truth during his campaign for mayor two years ago, a fact that still stuck in his craw despite the friendly relationship he'd forged with both papers.

"I see what you're saying," Callahan said after thinking through the situation. "And if you are telling the truth, and it is a fake story, then you should be allowed to go ahead. But you also know that something like this puts a black cloud over everything."

"If a paper like the *Bulletin*, says we are covering up some real pollution, the public is not going to sit by," the mayor added. "We can't let this go forward without a response."

That's when Grossman launched into his answer. He said he would hold a press conference in his office later in the day to renounce the *Bulletin* story, question their proof, and take a direct shot at their motives. He vowed to Callahan that he could turn the tables and make it look like the *Bulletin* had been the dishonest ones.

"Trust me, mayor," Grossman said. "They have nothing and when we show that they are using their newspaper to falsely accuse their competitor of improper behavior, it will be all over."

Callahan stuttered a bit and hesitated. He knew that any sign of his covering up such pollution would kill him politically. But he also knew that he had to appease the *Journal* if he wanted support down the road.

At the same time, however, Callahan also did not want to do anything that made it look like he was opposing the *Bulletin*, whose support could be more important than the *Journal* because it held a larger circulation.

In the end, the mayor decided that he would let Grossman attempt to turn the issue around. He realized that if Grossman could call the *Bulletin*'s bluff and show that they had no proof—and a vendetta against him—the entire onus would be off Callahan and Grossman and on the *Bulletin*.

He also decided that the Planning Commission would be able to approve the project, and the clean-up plan, if Grossman could show that the *Bulletin* had no real proof. But only if nothing else came out.

"Okay, you do what you have to do and I will keep my mouth shut," the mayor said, reluctantly. "I won't go out on a limb, but I will hold back if nothing more comes out. If any reporter approaches me, I'll just say that there has been no hard evidence and the project appears to be as safe as before."

Grossman grinned when he heard the mayor's promise through the phone. But then Callahan added another warning. "But, if any hint of proof comes out that you hid anything, it is all over," the mayor said.

Grossman agreed and hung up. Then he went into action, drafting a harshly worded letter that slammed the *Bulletin*, Pete Martin, and even Emily Ingle for five pages.

In his most heated language, Grossman attacked the morning newspaper as a "self-serving sham rag that is misleading the public about a positive project in an attempt to hurt its rival. For a newspaper to do such a disservice is not only yellow journalism and unfair, but downright criminal."

"If the *Bulletin* must stoop to such levels to hurt its opponents, instead of engaging in an honest newspaper competition, then its credibility must be called into question," the letter continued. "I take umbrage at this cheap, low-level tactic and call for the *Bulletin* to immediately admit its lies or show its proof."

Then, to end the letter, Grossman laid it on the line.

"I challenge the *Bulletin* to produce one shred of evidence that indicates its report is at all accurate," the letter concluded. "From the story printed today, all that the *Bulletin* can claim is that it has some dirt. Well, from what we see, it has dirty news coverage as well."

When the letter was finished, at about 2 p.m., Grossman gave it to his secretary, along with a carefully worded press release that announced he would comment on the *Bulletin* story later that day, at 5 p.m., in his office. He directed his secretary to fax it to every media outlet in the city.

Since most of the radio stations and television news programs that day had reported on the *Bulletin* story, Grossman was confident that they would respond to his counter attack. Sure enough, at 5 p.m., his office was mobbed with reporters from every TV and radio station in town, as well as the *Advocate*, the *Reader*, and of course, the *Bulletin*, which had dispatched Pete Martin to hear Grossman's attack, and also be available to respond if needed.

Just after 5 p.m., Grossman launched into the second act of his defense, reading portions of the letter and taking a direct stand against the *Bulletin*. Staring straight at Martin, Grossman summed up his tirade after about 10 minutes with the simple line, "I challenge you to produce any other evidence."

Martin's face turned red and his temper boiled. He stared right back at Grossman and did everything he could to hold back his anger, but it wasn't enough.

"Hey, you know that we have all the evidence we need, you liar," Martin yelled from the front row of the press group. "Don't you try to turn this back on us. You're full of shit and you are not going to get away with this."

Just as he finished saying his piece, Martin stepped back and looked around, realizing that he was now the center of attention and wondering if he should have spoken up. Then he decided it was the right move. If they were going to play hardball, he had to keep shooting back.

A murmur began to flood through the press corps about what had just happened. Grossman was laying blame at the feet of the *Bulletin*, while Martin was defending his paper with a very unusual piece of commentary.

After Martin's outburst, no other reporters spoke up. Grossman saw that as his chance to step down. But, before he could get too far, a barrage of questions flew at both him and Martin. Some reporters wanted more comments from the *Journal* publisher about the project, while others—such as the *Advocate* and the *Reader*—went to Martin for more of his take.

All the *Bulletin* reporter could do was give a standard "I stand by the story" as he thought better of turning too much attention on himself at a time when all news reports should be focused on the project and the uncertainty of its safety.

When Grossman heard that Martin had turned to a "no comment" line of answering, he laughed. "You have nothing to stand by," he said to Martin. "And if your yellow journalism and lies hurt our project in any way, our lawyers will see to it that you will be sued until your head spins."

With that, Grossman ended the press conference and the reporters filed out, with some still trying to get more comments from Grossman and Martin.

Walking out, Grossman knew that he had done all he could, while Martin pondered what impact the publisher's attempt to turn the story back on him would have.

As he slowly left, Martin knew that his story had been correct, but he also knew that Grossman's tactic was working, at least initially.

Once Grossman launched his attack on the *Bulletin* and brought up the question of proof, many of the reporters in the room had turned toward Martin, seeking the additional proof that Grossman wanted. Although Martin knew he was right, he had nothing more to provide.

He could not reveal his testing source, and the only other proof he had was the remaining soil sample. The only way to prove that had come from the shipyard was for Martin to admit that he had stolen it and had trespassed, something else he could not do.

Martin knew he was stuck and Grossman knew he was off the hook, at least for the moment.

The question now was, what would it mean to the Planning Commission?

*   *   *

Tuesday night, nearly all the TV and radio stations reported on Grossman's strong denial of the *Bulletin* story, along with Martin's potshot back at him. And it seemed that Grossman's effort had at least a small impact, as most of the reports began to question the motives of the *Bulletin*.

Although each report stated that the *Bulletin*'s reputation was among the strongest in the city press corps, they couldn't help but insinuate that the paper would have a valid motive for wanting to see the Hunter's Point Shipyard project go down and hurt its competitor.

"Although no proof exists that the *Bulletin* story is not true, its use of unnamed sources and untraceable soil samples has drawn questions about how valid its reporting on this issue is," said one TV reporter.

Grossman watched the broadcast reports with great interest that night, smiling when he noticed some tips against his opponents, and grumbling when certain stations shoved his theory of bias by the *Bulletin* aside.

Either way, he knew the real test would come the next day when the city's four major papers would report on the events of Tuesday, and begin speculation about how it would affect Friday's scheduled Planning Commission meeting.

Sure enough, the story made front-page news in the *Journal*, the *Bulletin*, the *Reader*, and the *Advocate*. The *Journal* story, as Grossman directed, had been a top-heavy angle that highlighted Grossman's denial of any misrepresentation and a clear assessment of his theory that the *Bulletin* had fabricated.

For the *Bulletin*, Martin offered a straight story on Grossman's press conference that recounted his original story about the inaccurate report, along with Grossman's denials. The *Bulletin* also printed another story by a different reporter that explained Martin's comment to Grossman.

Danny Dugan wrote one of his strongest editorials ever to accompany the main story in the *Reader* that week, which was slanted against the development and called the project "a Trojan horse that has some likely hidden dangers."

The *Advocate*, known for its opposition to anything involving the dailies or Callahan, simply recounted the *Bulletin*'s allegations of fraud and described Grossman's accusations of biased reporting by the *Bulletin* as "weak."

Each story also reminded readers that none of the jockeyings for public opinion by Martin, Grossman, or Callahan—who remained conspicuously silent on the whole matter—would mean anything until the Planning Commission voted. Although each of the four newspapers presented a scenario for a commission vote, only the *Reader* had polled the seven-member panel to see what effect the *Bulletin* story and Grossman's denials had had on their thinking.

Surprisingly, the commissioners gave the recent events little credence. Three of those who'd been in favor of the project—Callahan appointees Susan Herman, Betty Selleck, and Don Pullman—said Grossman's defense that the *Bulletin* was using the issue to hurt its rival made sense, and they still planned to vote for the project, barring any new evidence to stop them.

"The *Bulletin* story uses unnamed sources, soil samples that have not been proven to have come from anywhere near Hunter's Point, and is published in a paper that hates the developers," Selleck told the *Reader*. "I see no reason to block this great proposal."

But for the Carlson appointees, Lance Beltran, Jody Solomon, and Chris Tanner—each of whom had been waiting for two years to stick it to Callahan—the *Bulletin* accusations were just the right thing to throw in the mayor's face. All three told the *Reader* that they wouldn't support the project until a new, independent study was done.

"This is asking potential tenants of the development to commit suicide," Beltran had said on a radio news report. "There is no way anyone should be able to step foot on that property until we know what is happening."

There they stood, three to three, just two days before the vote. The only commissioner who remained unsure was Chairman Tony Deal. A longtime supporter of Callahan, who'd hosted two fundraisers for him during the election, Deal also had a reputation for independent thinking and disgust for abuse of power or corruption.

He had made his name in San Francisco as a florist, who started delivering flowers as a teenager and worked his way up to the owner of 24 flower shops through the Bay Area. Deal had only supported Callahan because he believed he was an honest man with a clean record, which was true at the time.

Deal also had had some run-ins with Carlson over business tax increases, which Deal opposed and Carlson had implemented in an effort to reduce a city deficit. He liked the way Callahan thought and had supported the project based on Callahan's backing of it.

But with such new and frightening hints of toxic danger and cover-ups, Deal reconsidered, according to an interview he gave The *Advocate*. He said he'd not completely backed away from the project, but simply was not sure.

"I don't know why we can't do some more testing and run things through again," Deal said. "Why is everyone in such a hurry?"

When Grossman read that comment in Wednesday's *Advocate*, he became worried. It seemed that the other commissioners who'd backed the project were holding firm, most likely because each had received a phone call from Grossman that all but promised them future *Journal* endorsements for any political office they sought if they voted his way.

For the commissioners, such a promise was gold in the fiercely political city where even one of the daily newspapers' support was key.

But for Grossman, not having Deal on board was a thorn in his side. He quickly called Callahan on Wednesday morning to see what he suggested to be done about the dilemma. The mayor, still angry that he'd allowed himself to be talked into this farce, told Grossman that he had to figure it out himself.

Callahan wanted nothing to do with this vote. He had offered mild, low-key support and had promised not to call for a delay or retesting of the soil. But that was it. The mayor had no need to get more involved in this cover-up than he already had.

"It's your problem, Don," Callahan said during their conversation Wednesday afternoon. "I have nothing to do with it. I said I would support it, but once that commission convenes and votes, I'm out of it."

Grossman understood and hung up. He pondered the situation again.

Sure, Deal could come around and give him the fourth vote he needed, but he could also change his mind and vote no, a move that would at least delay the project, and most likely kill it completely. After such a vote, the only way Grossman would get approval in the future would be to get some outside consultant to test the soil, which would reveal not only that it was more polluted, but that Grossman and Mack Corp. had obviously lied.

Grossman thought further about what to do as the Wednesday evening TV newscasts recounted the situation in even stronger tones, taking a countdown-to-the-vote attitude with the story. After watching the newscasts, Grossman picked up the phone and called Deal.

The two men had a short but cordial conversation. Grossman knew Deal's reputation and realized that threats and bribes were of no use to him. The publisher simply laid out his case and pleaded with Deal to give the project a chance.

"I can only do what I think is right," Deal said. "At this point, I have yet to decide. But I promise you I will take everything into account."

After the two men hung up, Grossman became even more nervous. He knew time was running out and the outcome was as unknown as ever.

He realized that he would have to let things play out themselves, but that didn't stop him from letting ideas race through his mind that might make the vote turn out his way.

*   *   *

On Thursday morning, the two daily papers offered little in the way of stories about the pending vote, but the issue hardly dropped from public view.

Two environmental groups staged protests at the gate outside the Hunter's Point Shipyard at noon, while Grossman and Burger made it a point to call each planning commissioner during the day to ensure that none had changed their minds. Their check-in produced the same results: the 3-3 split remained, as did Deal's undecided stance.

"This tension is getting unbearable," Grossman told Burger that night. "I have a bad feeling about this. We need to do something, but this guy is unflappable."

Burger nodded as the two men shared a beer at a small, out-of-the-way tavern in The Sunset District, where they went specifically so they could strategize without fear of being spotted. But Burger had no answers either.

"Sometimes you have to just let it happen," Burger said.

Less than 18 hours later, it happened. Just as dawn rose over San Francisco on Friday, residents awoke to find that Tony Deal, the staunch supporter of Mayor Callahan and defender of honest government, had made up his mind.

He had decided to oppose the project and vowed only to support it if further testing was done to prove that the original soil tests were accurate. Deal, who had not called anyone with his decision that day, announced his vote publicly for the first time while appearing on San Francisco Morning, a top-rated local TV show where he was interviewed just after 8 a.m.

Deal had called the producer the night before asking to be on to comment on the Hunter's Point project but had not hinted that he'd reveal his decision. He told his wife, Jean, that he didn't want to give anyone a chance to talk him out of it before going public. On the show, he simply stated his position and said he was open to a future reconsideration of the project, but only if more testing was done.

"There is no reason to rush this along," Deal had said on the show. "Before we commit to such a major project, we must know that it is absolutely safe."

After the show ended, City Hall was buzzing with talk of the announcement. What would this mean? Would the project have to be delayed? Would it be killed outright? Would Mack Corp. be able to afford or agree to more testing? Would they sue the city? Would other commissioners change their minds?

All such questions began to fly as TV and radio reporters swarmed over City Hall to get a reaction from the commissioners, Grossman, Pete Martin, and of course, the mayor. By 1 p.m., when the commission planned to convene, the word was out that, strangely, none of the other commissioners who supported the plan had been affected by Deal's announcement.

Most still saw that *Journal* endorsement dangling in front of their faces like a carrot to a hungry rabbit and had no reason to change. Besides, if Deal was going to bring the project down with his vote, they could still vote for it, collect their endorsement prize, and not be blamed for rejecting the development.

"We all respect Tony Deal, but we still have to stand by our convictions," Betty Selleck told a reporter. "Each person must make up their own mind."

The Board of Supervisors' chambers, where the Planning Commission always met, began filling with interested parties at 12:30 p.m. As the clock struck 1 p.m., the place was packed. Extra police were brought in to maintain crowd control and speakers were set up outside so that those unable to enter the chambers could know what was happening.

One by one, each commissioner entered, shaking hands with supporters and waving to others in the same way that the supervisors had always done. By 1:20 p.m., the entire commission was sitting, except for Deal. The chairman had been running late but had called his City Hall office and asked an aide to tell the meeting that he was on his way.

Susan Herman, who served as vice-chair and could hold the meeting in Deal's absence, said the group would wait for the chairman for another 15 minutes. Still, no Deal arrived and his secretary did not know where he was.

Herman called for a break after the 15-minute wait as the crowd began to stir nervously and impatiently and said they would wait another 10 minutes.

Almost everyone in the room had a stake in the development, in one way or another, and did not want to wait any longer. But for City Hall veterans who'd either worked in the building or attended such hearings in the past, delays were nothing new.

Miles away, as Deal steered his Miata convertible down the winding hills of Twin Peaks—the upscale neighborhood in the south part of the city—he became impatient. His delay had been caused by his new two-door sports car's failure to start.

After a morning that included his television appearance and several hours of florist-related paperwork, Deal had gone home to catch a quick nap before heading to the meeting. But after waking and making himself presentable, the commission chairman had been unable to start his car.

Only with the help of a passing motorist was Deal able to get the vehicle going with what appeared to be a simple spark plug connection. He knew he was late but still hoped to get to the meeting in time to cast his crucial vote.

Although Deal did not believe the meeting would start without him just because of some tardiness, he realized that, if he did fail to appear and the 3-3 tie stood, it would be up to the mayor to cast the deciding vote. The city charter included a little-used provision that allowed the commission to ask for the mayor's vote in a tie-breaker.

The commission could also delay the vote or table the item, which is what usually occurred in ties. But, with such a hot issue on the table that had drawn a lot of increased attention, Deal knew that the commission—especially those favoring the development—would do everything to see that a vote was held.

Glancing at his watch, Deal also saw that it was 1:20 p.m. and hit the gas pedal harder as he swung around the curves of Portola Drive, which would carry him down from Twin Peaks toward the city's main drag on Market Street and, eventually, to City Hall.

Curving the vehicle around a sharp turn near the intersection with 23rd Street, Deal felt a quick jerk on the steering wheel, which would not follow his command to turn, and remained stuck. Pulling the wheel with all his strength in an attempt to bring the car through the turn, Deal suddenly realized the car was jammed and saw that it was headed straight for a utility pole.

Yelling in a helpless wail and ducking down just as the car jumped a curve, Deal covered his head and put it between his legs just at the moment the car slammed into the tree. The car horn let out a piercing wail as it hit, which continued while Deal's head wavered back and forth.

In a shocked haze, he unbuckled his seat belt and dragged his body out on to the front lawn of a small home, still blinded by double vision and pain to his head and chest.

As the car horn continued to blare, Deal stumbled a few feet away from the open door and opened his eyes momentarily before falling to the ground. Steam sifted out of the car's hood while gasoline, water, and oil dripped out from the undercarriage, collected in the gutter, and rolled down the street into a sewer.

As he lay on the ground, trying to call for help, Deal felt a quick tinge of pain and winced before closing his eyes.

Just three miles away at City Hall, as 1:20 p.m. turned to 1:30 p.m. and then 1:45 p.m., Herman realized that Deal was not coming and quickly moved for the commission to take the vote without him, knowing that the development stood a better chance of passage with the mayor's vote than with Deal's.

As expected, the same 3-3 vote occurred and all heads turned to Jack Callahan, who had sat quietly in the last row of the chambers, hoping to avoid exactly this situation. When the tie became official, Herman calmly stood up and made her move.

"In accordance with the rules of the City Charter, it is our duty to request that the mayor break this tie," Herman said to the gasps, cheers, and boos of the crowd. "Mr. Mayor, please come and do your duty."

Many in the audience were not familiar with the rarely used charter provision, so when Herman made the request, the greeting was a shock to some. But few were as shocked as Callahan himself.

Sure, the mayor knew that this situation could arise. He had been a student of the city charter since his days as a young police officer. But the last thing he wanted to do was take a public stand on this impossible issue.

Callahan had told all those involved that he wanted to stay out. He'd promised Grossman and Burger that he would hold back any efforts to stop the development if no further information about higher toxins came out, and had been able to stick to his vow.

But now, being put in the middle of the controversy could do nothing but hurt his image, disrupt his alliance with the newspapers, and worse, make him culpable if any future health problems arose from the Hunter's Point toxic problem.

Slowly, Callahan arose, looked at the myriad eyes fixed on him, and walked quietly toward the front of the room.

The mayor could feel the looks piercing his body as sweat formed on his brow, upper lip, and face. Wiping small perspiration beads from his eyes, Callahan tried to walk without showing fear or hesitation. But those who knew him knew it would be difficult. As he reached the podium and shook Heyward's hand, the mayor kept running every scenario through his mind.

If he approved the plan, he would face the revenge of the *Bulletin* and environmental groups, not to mention the chance of being in the middle of a toxic mess if further pollutants were found. But he also knew that voting against the plan would lose him serious business support, the *Journal*'s backing, and the favors of unions and minority groups.

As his heart beat faster and, it seemed to him, louder, Callahan stepped in front of the microphone that sat atop the podium and turned toward the crowd.

Most of the audience was on the edge of their seats, none quite sure what to expect.

The mayor cleared his throat and loosened his collar in nervousness, then felt a knot in his stomach as he tried to speak.

"Madam Chair," Callahan said, turning toward Heyward, "I vote yes."

As the crowd burst into a mix of applause, catcalls, and a shrill of boos, Callahan calmly walked down from the podium, across the chambers, and out to the hallway. While he made his way out, ignoring the thunderous response he had just invoked, he couldn't help but see Steve Burger at the end of the hall.

When the mayor approached the environmental consultant, Burger grabbed him and shook his hand. "Thank you, Jack. You have helped us move forward with the greatest development the city has ever seen."

Callahan, feeling a mix of uncertainty and guilt, shook his hand back, then leaned over and whispered in his ear.

"Sure," he said. "But I'll never go there." ■

Chapter Twenty-Five

Meet Walter Beard

Anyone who's ever been to San Francisco knows that Halloween is among the city's most celebrated days. For decades, the gay community—along with most other residents—have used the spirited time to take on other personas, frolic in the streets into the late hours, and revel in the diversity and acceptance of the city's liberal culture.

In a tradition that started in the Polk Street gay community of the early '70s, and later exploded in the latter-day Castro District that still defines the city's gay culture, Halloween nights have meant only one thing: wearing the most outlandish costume, joining friends out in the city streets, and being as wild as ever.

And no one knew that better than Billy Dale.

Even as the city's most powerful and dangerous political consultant, Billy had still made time for Halloween escapades in the Castro, often dressing up as one of his favorite movie stars—usually in drag—and carousing with friends and lovers into the early morning hours.

On one occasion, Billy had even climbed to the roof of a local bar at 18th and Castro streets and stripped naked, staying that way until police brought him down in handcuffs. He didn't care, he just kissed each one on both cheeks and waved to the crowd.

The cops were so surprised, they simply ordered Billy to put his clothes on and let him go, still laughing as they drove away.

But on this Halloween, Billy's mind was turned toward anything but celebrations and wild sexual encounters. Nearly a year had passed since he shot Vernon Bogart on Election Night, and eight months had come and gone since he first set foot in his jail cell.

Although he'd been able to serve his time fairly calmly, making calls to outsiders when needed and monitoring the city's political scene through television, Billy's patience was growing thin. After trying appeal after appeal to get out, with no results, Billy had set his mind on serving his time and waiting until his release in February, calmly counting the days until then.

But in recent months he was striving more and more for his freedom. Aside from the obvious mental toll the lockup was taking on such a free spirit, Billy also had grown more and more resentful of Jack Callahan.

Little by little, Billy's anger at Callahan's testimony against him at his trial was mounting. Coupled with the mayor's misdeeds that Billy had seen from afar—from the mayor's cover-up of his wife's lesbian affair to the latest secrets hidden in the Hunter's Point Shipyard project—Billy wanted to get out so he could get even.

But since his one-year sentence was mandatory—with no early release possible—Billy had simply been waiting.

That's all he could do.

Until now.

As Billy's thoughts of the Halloween he was missing circled more and more in his head, he racked his brains in search of a way to get out, or at least to get something to bring Callahan down.

He realized that the easiest way would be a recall election. If Billy could get 15% of registered voters, about 50,000 people, to sign a petition calling for a recall election, he believed he could persuade them to oust Callahan and put in someone else.

Recalls are a long-running California tradition, and a true abuse of power in many cases. State law is in place so that recalls, in which voters choose whether a public official should be removed from office before their term expires, be used in the event of true abuse of power or criminal activity. But in many cases they come down to political needs or revenge.

Billy's goal was no different.

With his keen sense of political winds and his ability to twist almost any issue in favor of his candidate and against an opponent, Billy knew that he could use the stigmas of Callahan's first two years in office against him.

But, he had two problems.

First, he was still in prison.

Second, he had no one to run against Callahan.

Although the mayor had taken a beating during the past year, his poll numbers were still somewhat high. He still retained sympathy for becoming a widower, no matter how questionable his wife's death had been. And he remained the leader of a city undergoing major economic growth and reduced crime.

Polls showed that none of the current supervisors or other known potential candidates would likely knock off Callahan, especially in a recall election, which took an extra punch of corruption to pull off.

While some voters might gladly oust Callahan after his term was up, most might not feel it was right to kick him out early without proof of wrongdoing.

Others might not want to replace him with the likely alternative candidates such as Marie Alzeti or William Carlson.

For weeks, since the Hunter's Point Shipyard development was approved, Billy had pondered the idea of recalling Callahan and had run several scenarios through his mind about who would be the best shot to unseat the mayor.

For some reason, the right name did not come to him until Halloween.

When his idea did surface, he wasted no time and went straight to the pay phone he shared with other inmates, placed a collect call, and waited.

When the woman on the other end answered, he told her his name and said he needed to speak to her boss. After a momentary pause, the call went through.

"Hi, it's Billy Dale. Ya got a minute?"

On the other end was none other than the most powerful man in the California Legislature: State Senate President Walter Beard.

Beard, the black son of a Kentucky coal miner, had hitchhiked his way to California 35 years earlier with $5 in his pocket and had risen to become one of the most powerful men in state history. Having held the Senate president's post for 20 years, Beard commanded more respect and power in many cases than the governor.

Using a mix of hardball politics, intelligent scrutiny, and dealmaking that rivaled the shrewdest used-car salesman, Beard had become a state senator at the age of 27, then rose to Senate president only eight years later. At the time of Billy's call, Beard had created a political power base that stretched all the way to Washington, D.C.

Although Billy had never headed one of Beard's campaigns, the two men got to know each other through other political circles. Beard had even visited the courthouse during Billy's trial but held back when asked to testify as a character witness.

"I don't think that would look good for any of us," Beard told Billy's attorney at the time. "But when you get out, I'll be glad to do any favor you need."

Beard liked Billy because he shared Beard's appetite for good parties and good political fights. Although Beard—a straight black man who kept himself fit and shunned alcohol and illegal drugs—was the complete opposite of Billy in every other way, their joint interest and taste for political battles had bonded them years earlier.

When Beard heard his secretary's call that Billy was on the line, the Senate president was surprised but pleased. Putting down the state insurance commission report on proposed new restrictions for the industry that had donated handsomely to Beard's many campaigns, he kicked his feet up on the 200-year-old antique desk that took up most of his office and leaned back in his mahogany, red-cushioned chair.

Removing the Cuban cigar from his mouth and blowing smoke out toward the chandelier that graced his office, Beard smiled with a mix of surprise and wonder.

"Billy! What the hell is going on?" Beard said into the receiver with a friendly greeting. "What are you up to? How's prison life?"

Laughing slightly at his jab to his friend, Beard listened as Billy responded in what seemed to be a rambling tone.

"Walt, how are ya?" Billy asked. "Listen, there is a lot going on in San Francisco and you should be damn worried about it. Jack Callahan has shit flying left and right and pretty soon that city you represent is going to be in the shitter."

Such comments were not a surprise coming from Billy. Beard, although not active in city politics beyond his own re-election every four years, had followed the strange twist of events that seemed to surround Callahan's administration. And he knew that Billy had become Callahan's worst enemy.

"Yeah, I know. So you hate the guy. What else is new?" Beard said, puffing his cigar again. "What does it mean to me?"

That's when Billy hit him with his idea. Billy knew that one of the thorns in Beard's side in the coming year would be the implementation of term limits. After California voters approved term limits two years earlier, all state elected officials were immediately faced with the prospect of losing their elected offices.

For Beard, who had built up 20 years of power and seniority, such a limit would not only kill his power but also lose him his job. Sure, he could go back to being an attorney—a post he held for years before taking office. But he wanted the limelight.

For months Beard had been trying to block the start of term limits with every kind of court injunction and legal loophole possible. But none had worked, and he was getting tense.

Billy knew Beard's dilemma, and that was the center of his plan.

Billy decided that Beard would be the perfect man to run against Callahan in a recall election. He also determined that, if anyone could get Billy out of prison early, it was also Beard.

"You have more pull on that parole board than anyone," Billy said, flattering Beard and speaking a well-known truth. "If anyone can use a few markers to get me out of here, it's you."

Beard couldn't help nodding as Billy recited the facts.

"But if I do get you out, what's in it for me?" Beard asked.

Billy then went on to explain that he would help launch the recall of Callahan and manage Beard's campaign to become mayor.

"If I have my calculations correct, I could get a special election called for June of next year if you can get me out of here by Thanksgiving," Billy said.

"The deadline for a recall petition to get to the Director of Elections would likely be late winter for a June or May election. That would give us several months to get a campaign going, then hit the petition in January and have two months to collect names."

Beard raised his eyebrows at the thought. He'd never considered running for mayor in San Francisco because of Callahan's popularity, not to mention the idea of having to wait two more years. But what Billy was saying made sense.

Callahan would be vulnerable with the right campaign against him. And no one could take advantage of a vulnerable candidate like Billy Dale.

"Let me think about it," Beard said. "Let me see what I can do."

As the two men hung up their respective phone lines, each pondered the thought of such a campaign. For Billy, it would not only mean getting out of prison a few months earlier but also would represent his best chance to stick it to Callahan.

Beard, a man seduced by power and as good at wielding it as anyone, saw it as a potential chance to keep his strength going after being forced from office. The Senate president spent the next several days reviewing the idea with his closest advisers, his estranged wife, and even his longtime girlfriend.

*   *   *

Two weeks after Billy had first called Beard, he received his wish. Without even a tipoff to Billy from the powerful politician, the warden himself visited Billy's cell just two weeks before Thanksgiving and gave him the welcome but surprising news.

"I don't know what happened," the warden, who had enjoyed talking politics with one of his most famous inmates, told Billy. "But you are out. Just some paperwork and you will be walking out of here tomorrow morning."

The warden didn't even notice when Billy reacted with little surprise, he just shook his hand and congratulated him.

The next day, Friday, Nov. 14, Billy Dale was a free man.

He didn't learn until he phoned Beard's office late Friday afternoon after returning to San Francisco how he'd been released. It was pure California power play.

Beard had placed several members of the state parole board in their seats through references, threats, and called-in debts. He had leaned on just enough of them to cause Billy's early release.

Officially, the board ruled that it had found Billy to be "a model prisoner and no longer a threat to society."

And while the state gun law that had sent Billy to prison in the first place stated a one-year minimum prison sentence, it had a small provision that gave the parole board broad powers to reduce the sentence if a majority of members found "special circumstance." Even though that circumstance was never defined.

Naturally, Billy's release made news among the San Francisco press, which did numerous stories on his early departure from prison. Television and radio only scratched the surface of his freedom, with a short quote from the man himself in which he said only, "I am grateful to the parole board and eager to get back to work."

What that work would be, Billy did not say. When talking to the four newspapers in town, Billy again kept his long-term plans a secret, saying only that he hoped to re-open his business and get back into campaigning.

After answering the reporters' questions outside of the prison, Billy was given a ride by one of the prison guards he had befriended and immediately jumped on his phone after entering his house.

"I'm out!" Billy triumphantly told Beard over the phone late Friday. "Now we get down to business."

It was a rare warm day in November at Stinson Beach, the exclusive retreat nestled in the seaside hills north of San Francisco. Although late autumn usually meant a foggy chill in the small, sand-covered oasis, this day brought a rare gleam of sunshine that locals used to their advantage. With the usual weekend crowds from the city staying away, only half as many people were lying about on the brown-colored sands as seagulls called overhead and the rush of waves echoed along the beachfront.

The hint of a radio playing Johnny Mathis could be heard just under the usual beach sounds as Billy Dale lay in the warm climate, stretched out on a towel that was much too small, and soaked up the rare sun rays.

With sunglasses guarding his eyes and a copy of the *Bulletin* draped over his stomach, Billy tuned out most of the noises and lulled in the newly found outdoor quiet, which had eluded him during his long stint in jail.

All he could feel was the heat of sunshine on his face as he wafted to a near-still sleep and let his body drain itself of the last month's worth of worries, pressure, and isolation.

Just as Billy was about to fall into his first completely restful sleep in more than six months, a shadow suddenly blocked the sun. The sudden intrusion startled Billy, causing him to brush the newspaper aside and lift his new sunglasses.

He didn't get up, but just barely opened his eyes to see the shadowy figure that loomed before him. The man seemed out of place in his dark brown suit, shined black shoes, and handmade silk tie as he stared down at Billy, who sported nothing more than a wrinkled swimsuit and a Hawaiian shirt.

But then again, this man didn't need to dress differently for anyone. As Billy saw who it was, he smiled and raised his hand. The dark figure reached out as well.

"Hiya, Billy," the voice of Walter Beard said. "Welcome back."

As the two men shook hands, Billy sat up and squinted after taking off his sunglasses. Beard, crouching down but remaining careful not to wrinkle one of his many prized $750 suits, met Billy halfway and smiled.

"So, why did you want to meet out here?" Beard asked as he looked around, picked up a handful of sand, and quickly brushed it away. "Isn't this a bit, well, outdoor?"

Billy laughed as he responded. "Well, ya know Walt, after the year I've had, I can take as much outdoor living as possible," he said. Beard smiled and carefully sat down on the towel, making sure that no sand touched him or his clothes.

"Besides," Billy said, turning to face the man. "I figured we would have little chance of being seen together, or overheard, out here. Especially in the middle of the week in November."

Beard understood as he looked around and winked at a young woman sitting a few yards away. "That makes sense, but still, a corner table at Star's or Frank Fat's might have suited me better," Beard added.

Then the two men got down to business. Beard had done his part and now wanted to see how Billy would go about getting a recall election started, and position Beard to win it.

"The most important thing to me is that it looks like I didn't start it," Beard cautioned in a low tone. "I don't want to be seen as the bad guy who is pushing Jack Callahan out just to get elected to a new office after my term limits start."

"What needs to happen," he continued, "is for you to spark the groundswell of support for a recall, get the petitions collected and approved, and get the election going. Then, and only then, can I come in after the calls for me to run begin."

Billy nodded with excitement and a clear understanding of what had to happen. Both men knew that any sign of a manipulated recall election could backfire and, possibly, propel Callahan into re-election two years later.

No. For this to work, the recall election had to happen without Beard's involvement, then a wave of support had to arise to draft him to run. Billy had no problem being the one to launch the petition drive for a recall and lead the effort to oust Callahan.

Everyone in San Francisco politics knew about the falling out between Billy and the mayor and, for many, it would seem odd if the feisty and vengeful Billy Dale did not take a whack at his former client. Billy knew that he could talk Jimmy Min and the *Advocate* into helping him launch the drive against Callahan, just as they had helped launch the drive to get him in.

Billy could almost read verbatim what a Mike McLean column might say.

He knew McLean and Jimmy could spin some powerful stuff against Callahan, especially given all of the problems the mayor had had. And once the ball got rolling, it would likely be easy to get enough public sympathy to collect the 50,000 signatures needed.

"And I will do everything behind the scenes I can to help, but I must be out of the picture," Beard stressed, as he looked to his right and left to make sure no one heard his comments. "You do what you have to get it started and I will be there when the time is right."

With that, Beard was gone, still brushing sand off his suit as he walked away. Billy, meanwhile, laid back down with his sunglasses on, his face warmed by the sun's rays. He couldn't help but laugh as he began to plan the next move.

Billy's first decision was to wait until after Thanksgiving to launch the petition drive in his usual way—with a big, splashy surprise. He decided that he could use the upcoming Christmas holidays as a theme.

After meeting with Jimmy Min and Mike McLean over the next two weeks, the three set a press conference and rally on Dec. 1, the Monday after Thanksgiving, with the theme of the recall as "A Christmas Present to San Franciscans."

Scheduling the recall drive announcement for Civic Center Park, right outside of Callahan's City Hall window, Billy, Jimmy, and Mike McLean constructed a large sign that listed a string of Callahan's most embarrassing moments. They included his failure to get his homeless plan approved, the near-loss of the Giants, his wife's "questionable" death—and efforts to cover it up—and, of course, the Hunter's Point Shipyard development approval.

"Callahan cast the deciding vote for what many believe is a toxic time bomb," the sign proclaimed about the development.

And of course, Billy and his supporters invited every media outlet in the city to cover the announcement. Since it was held the day after Thanksgiving weekend, it received major play because of a lack of other news.

Beginning exactly at noon, Billy opened the event with the playing of "Happy Days Are Here Again," then brought out a group of community leaders dressed in Santa Claus outfits.

It was pure theater. Pure San Francisco. And pure Billy Dale.

One flight up, in his City Hall office, Callahan watched with a mix of disgust and worry as the rally opened up. Although he had known that Billy would likely take some revenge at him upon his release from jail, he'd hoped it would not occur until February, when Billy's full one-year term was over.

But, Callahan also realized that Billy Dale had almost as many friends in state politics as he did, probably more. So when he suddenly received an early reprieve, the mayor was hardly surprised.

As the small crowd chanted and yelled louder and louder during the noon hour event, Callahan tried to eat lunch in his office and ignore the happenings. But his curiosity forced him to keep at least one eye on the activities, while the noise of the rally forced him to listen to at least some of it.

The mayor, still feeling a smattering of guilt over the Hunter's Point Shipyard project, was just beginning to plan his next big move—the return of his homeless plan—when Billy's prison release came through.

Callahan and political consultant Carl Devins—who had remained an advisor during the past chaotic year—met just a week earlier to map out the best way to reintroduce the homeless plan. They knew it would have to be done carefully and had hoped that the holiday season between Thanksgiving and Christmas might find people in a festive and open mood.

But now they would have to put the plan back on the shelf again and focus on knocking down the recall effort. Devins, who had done some preliminary polling weeks earlier on several issues, threw in a question about support for a recall just to see what it would show.

The results were heartening. They showed that only 20% of likely voters would sign a petition to recall, and only 25% would vote to remove Callahan if such a recall election took place.

"That's pretty good, considering all of the turmoil," Devins told Callahan when the results came out. "Most of the reason seems to be that there is no real challenger waiting in the wings."

And, at this point, there still wasn't as Walter Beard's planned candidacy remained hidden. Devins's advice to Callahan was to ignore the recall drive completely.

Sure, the political consultant knew that the press would question Callahan about the recall effort, especially since it would be coming from his former campaign manager. But Devins decided that, until polls showed more support, the mayor was better off just downplaying the entire event.

If he had to answer a reporter's probe on the matter, all he would have to do was say that anyone had the right to circulate a petition. That was all.

*   *   *

When Devins and Callahan met several hours after Billy Dale's rally, the mayor agreed to lay low on the issue and answer in the manner suggested. Sure enough, when Callahan left his office at the end of the day, a slew of press cameras, tape recorders, and reporters with pen and pad were waiting to ask him about the rally and petition drive.

Donning a half-phony smile of confidence, the mayor sat patiently through all of their questions, then gave a simple comment. "Anyone can circulate a petition if they choose, that is the democratic process," the mayor said quietly. "I am proud of my record and I believe San Franciscans are as well."

With that, Callahan left the building, got into his car, and was driven home. But, while he seemed unconcerned and all smiles in front of the media, his nerves remained rattled at the thought of facing a recall, having to go through all of the turmoil of the past year, and also battling Billy Dale.

The next day, the two daily papers led with the recall drive rally, especially the *Bulletin*, which still owed Callahan a few knocks for approving the Hunter's Point Shipyard project. The paper gave the story almost all of the top section on the front page, with the headline, "Mayor's 'Old Friend' Launches Recall Drive."

Inside, the paper also had a timeline of Billy and Callahan's on-and-off relationship, as well as a repeated listing of Callahan's problem moments that the rally sign had indicated. The editorial did not endorse a recall, but carefully hinted that Callahan was open to attack if he didn't move to counter this action.

"Mayor Callahan has seen a tumultuous year," the editorial stated. "One would not be surprised if a recall effort took shape and succeeded in placing his future on the ballot, especially with such a powerful and hardball foe as Billy Dale."

In the *Journal*, the story also made Page One news, but with a slightly softer headline and no related editorial. The *Reader* and the *Advocate* were also planning major anti-Callahan stories, with accompanying editorials.

"This is where we stick it to him," Jimmy Min told Billy on the phone the next morning as he directed his reporters, McLean, and his staff to make the most out of the rally. "We're on our way."

But so far, the recall petition drive was far from successful. After submitting the petition for approval by the Director of Elections, who okayed it three days later on Dec. 4, Billy, Jimmy, and company still had to gather the 50,000 signatures, and had only 60 days in which to do it.

That meant, in reality, they would more likely need at least 55,000 signatures to make sure that they had enough valid ones. Billy and Jimmy both knew from experience with ballot measure petitions that, on average, about 10% of signatures submitted were often found to be invalid.

To make certain that the petition was approved with enough signers, the 55,000 mark was an essential goal. And, despite having about 50 volunteers ready to hit the streets to get names, Billy and Jimmy remained unconvinced that any of this was a sure thing.

During a lunch meeting at Tiger's Diner on Friday, December 5th, the two discussed how to ensure that the signatures would be gathered over the next two months. Over a corned beef sandwich and a cheeseburger, they realized that they needed to deploy the volunteers in strategic areas to cover the entire city.

But Billy also realized that they would have better luck getting anti-Callahan support in the poorer, less-conservative areas such as Bayview, Tenderloin, and the numerous gay neighborhoods. But even that wasn't enough.

Billy decided to go to his old friend, Jerry Fields, who had created the full-time career of petition signature-gatherer. In recent years, as California had seen a ballot measure boom sparked by more citizens wanting to take their issues directly to voters, more petitions were being circulated and more propositions were landing on the ballot.

It had all started in the late 1970s with Proposition 13, the nationally known voter-driven ballot measure that cut property taxes in record numbers. Since then, voters statewide, especially in San Francisco, regularly took almost any issue they felt was worthwhile to the ballot.

Fields, who'd been a teacher for about eight years with a strong side interest in local grassroots issues, had turned signature collection into his own marketplace in only the past few years. Billy had hired him on several occasions to collect signatures for ballot measures on everything from an environmental restriction ordinance to a measure eliminating city dog license fees.

But he had never gone to Fields with such a major political challenge. He didn't even know if the man would be willing to sign on. His uncertainty did not last long, though. Just five minutes after Billy visited Fields in his rundown Mission District office, where he kept pets ranging from a snake to a baby crocodile, the political operative agreed to take the job.

"Why not?" Fields said as he petted his dog during the quick Friday afternoon meeting with Billy. "That son of a bitch has done enough. Besides, I can always use the money."

Fields agreed to collect the signatures for $1 each, his standard fee. Billy took the deal. But now Billy had to turn his attention toward raising money. If his volunteers got at least 30,000 signatures and Fields got the remaining 25,000 or so, that would run him at least $35,000 to Fields for his part.

The petition drive also had to figure on renting an office, providing food and transportation to the volunteers, and, eventually, spreading the campaign theme through local advertisements.

Billy knew that the *Advocate* would give the campaign a cut rate on ads, while also promoting the issue through news pages and McLean's column. He also figured the *Reader* would be willing to give some space for anti-Callahan views.

Still, money would be needed. Not just for the recall campaign, but also for Billy himself, who had only been out of jail for a few weeks and had done just some part-time consulting for some supervisor candidates and school district races.

Since Christmas was approaching, no one was thinking about campaign consultants for at least another six months. That meant Billy's business opportunities were slim.

"Don't worry about it," Jimmy Min told Billy Friday night during a dinner at Jimmy's house. "I'll help you out. After all, if we get rid of the mayor and get somebody good in, we will all benefit."

Billy gave Jimmy a rare hug between the two men. Billy always knew Jimmy as a loyal man, a trait to which even Jimmy's workers would attest.

Over the next month, the petitions went out, volunteers—as well as Fields and his few employees—combed the city to grab every signature they could get, while also making sure to check if the signers were valid residents.

Callahan continued to ignore the recall moves and refused to give more to the press than his basic comment of allowing anyone to participate in the democratic process. Privately, though, the mayor still wondered if the approach was correct. He knew how slick and conniving Billy Dale could be and argued with Carl Devins over whether such a strategy was working.

"I don't like this," the mayor told Devins the night of the official Christmas tree lighting in Civic Center Park outside City Hall. "I know this bastard, he does not hold back. We need to knock him down early."

But Devins did not budge. He truly believed that Callahan would do better if he ignored the recall until he was forced to defend himself in an election. "Hang in there, mayor, we can take it," he said. "This is nothing, yet."

And Devins knew what he was talking about. He had conducted another recent poll that continued to show only one in four voters would be willing to recall the mayor. As long as those numbers stuck, he believed any retaliation at this point was extreme.

On New Year's Eve, three weeks after the petition drive launched, Billy and Fields met to assess their progress. They had to have 55,000 signatures by February 4. Here it was, almost one month into this, and they had collected only 15,000.

Billy Dale was irritated.

"We need to do better," he told Fields, during an early dinner that preceded the annual New Year's Eve Ball that took place at the San Francisco Opera House, an event most of the city's elite would visit. "We need to get the word out that this mayor is the wrong man for the job."

Fields heard his worries, but he also knew that petition drives took time and that, often, most of the people come around late, after realizing that their signature was needed.

"Trust me, Billy," Fields said. "We are doing all we can. You have to be patient."

But patience was not in Billy Dale's arsenal. He had spent eight months being patient in a cellblock while Callahan ran around screwing up the city and getting away with bad decisions and near-criminal activity.

As the two parted ways—Fields to go to a friend's house for a small party and Billy to get ready for the ball—Billy realized more and more that he had to do something to attract attention to his campaign and make sure the most signatures possible would be collected.

The problem, he realized as he returned home, showered, and put on a tux, was that Callahan refused to respond. Although the mayor didn't believe it, his strategy of ignoring the recall petition was working. And Billy knew it because that was the same advice that he would have given the mayor if he were directing him.

"That fuckin' Carl Devins knows his stuff on this one," Billy said to himself as he combed his hair, sprayed on some cologne, and brushed his teeth. "We gotta get around him."

While Billy finished getting prepared, he heard the familiar knock on the door of Jimmy Min. Jimmy, always one for a good party, loved to whistle as he knocked. Billy let his friend in and offered a drink.

Jimmy, wanting to get to the ball as quickly as possible, declined and the two set out in Jimmy's car. Since neither was in any serious relationship, they decided to go to the ball together but did not promise to leave together if either found someone with whom to ring in the new year.

As Jimmy steered down the hill from Billy's house, Billy shared his frustration with his friend. "Jimmy, this guy is doing a good job of ignoring us and he is getting away with it," Billy lamented. "I don't know what else to do. We can't fake signatures. I mean, God knows I've tried in the past, but it doesn't work."

Jimmy nodded as he honked the horn to warn a group of teenagers crossing Van Ness Avenue in formal New Year's Eve attire. Making a left turn toward the Opera House, Jimmy offered the only advice he could.

"Well, Billy, you've got to get him to come out somehow," Jimmy said. "But, you know, it has to be done right. I wish I knew."

Billy wished he knew, too. He decided to put such thoughts out of his mind on this New Year's Eve as Jimmy pulled up to the valet parking and stepped out. Billy let himself out of the passenger side and the two went inside.

Just a few steps into the 100-year-old landmark building and visitors could see the remarkable decorations that had been placed for the end-of-the-year festivities. Two orchestras were set up on the first and third levels of the four-story building, with numerous food and bar locations scattered about.

Billy and Jimmy moved through the crowd greeting those they knew, from former mayors like Bela Williams to local business leaders and dignitaries, and even William Carlson, who gave his former nemesis a quick and biting smirk. The two men couldn't help but smile when they saw that, then continued through the crowd.

By about 10 p.m., the place was packed, the music was loud, and the booze was flowing freely. Billy, never one to turn down a drink, had been splitting his time between champagne and the vodka tonics that he often craved. He was as wild as ever on the dance floor, tripping the light fantastic with both men and women.

For Jimmy, such occasions were more for hobnobbing with the social and powerful set, although he did share a dance or two with Senator Williams, and even one with his reporter, Tammy Sharp.

By 11 p.m., many in the crowd were still waiting for Jack Callahan. While the mayor was an expected guest, tradition dictated that he did not arrive until 11 p.m. or so, having had time to visit other parties and gatherings before showing up at the main event of the evening.

Since the death of Glenda just eight months earlier, Callahan had still not found any new romantic interests, so he often asked friends or relatives to accompany him to such formal occasions.

On this night, he was with his cousin, Victoria, a local college professor who'd been a friend since childhood. The two entered at precisely 11:15 p.m. to the applause of most, and the hoots and catcalls of some detractors.

Billy, who was still whipping up the dance floor when the mayor arrived, felt his temper flare at the sight of Callahan. After the song ended, Billy made a beeline for the front part of the first-floor room where Callahan had entered and stood busily shaking hands.

By the time Billy came within about 50 feet of the mayor, he was at a full boil. In his state, he could barely walk, but he stood up without any problems. As he moved closer to the mayor, Billy ran through his mind all of the things he had seen Callahan do, including testify against him at the trial.

Billy was nearly arm's length away from the mayor when Jimmy, who had seen Callahan enter and noticed Billy heading toward him, ran up to his friend and held him back.

"Billy, don't be stupid," Jimmy whispered in a pleading tone. "This is not the time or the place. Let him go. You will accomplish nothing here."

But Billy just pushed Jimmy aside and walked right up to Callahan's back. The mayor, still shaking hands and waving to people, did not notice his former campaign manager until he spoke.

"Hey, mayor," Billy barked as he stood just a foot away from Callahan. "Hey, turn around, I'm talking to you, dammit."

With that, Callahan turned slowly and looked around the entire room. The music continued to blare as the chatter grew louder when the mayor faced Billy. He neither smiled nor sneered while Billy gave an sinister smirk back.

"I have nothing to say to you," Callahan said, trying hard to follow Devins's advice. "Excuse me." Then the mayor turned and walked across the dance floor as Billy followed.

"That's right you son of a bitch, walk away," Billy yelled, slightly slurring as he spoke. "You got no guts. We're going to kick your ass, you wait and see—you are going the fuck down."

As Billy laughed, the mayor kept walking. Jimmy, fearing just such an outburst from Billy, knew that this kind of negative approach would backfire badly. He could just see the next day's paper's proclaiming "Billy Dale's desperate attempt to revive the failing recall petition drive."

But Billy didn't care. He continued to shout profanity over the loud music as Callahan walked away and, eventually, reached the other side of the dance floor, his cousin still at his side.

That's when Billy lost it and charged across the dance floor to the surprise of everyone. The couples who were dancing stopped to look while several got out of the way to avoid his drunken run. At one point, Jimmy thought he was going to tackle the mayor right there.

But, Billy merely walked up in front of him and stuck his face right in Callahan's.

"Hey, Mr. Mayor., Mr. Hot Shot, you know you'd be nowhere without me," Billy yelled as Callahan pushed him aside and walked on. "C'mon, can't you take it? Go ahead and hide, we'll find you and we'll toss your ass out of office so fast you won't know what hit you.

"We'll kick your ass just the same way your wife died and you left her body in some car like a dead whore!" Billy said.

At that, Callahan stopped suddenly and turned around. Although his cousin tried to pull him back, she and many others knew that he had reached his limit.

Quietly and quickly, Callahan walked the few feet to where Billy had stopped, grabbed him by the front collar, and punched him square in the jaw. Billy dropped like a piece of dead wood as the music suddenly stopped and all eyes turned toward the two men.

Not satisfied with his first punch, the mayor picked Billy up again and landed another shot right on his nose, drawing blood and, most likely, breaking the bone. At this point the few press photographers at the event caught wind of the incident and began shooting. Flashbulbs popped and cameras whirred as the mayor landed the final blow.

Not sure what to do, and still angry from Billy's words, the mayor simply turned and walked out of the room. Billy lay on the dance floor, bleeding and moaning, but with a smile slowly curling his lips.

"Thanks a lot, mayor," Billy whispered to himself as a crowd gathered and he wiped blood from his face. "Well done." ■

Chapter Twenty-Six

The Fight Is On

As the New Year's Day sun rose over San Francisco, Jack Callahan dreaded turning on the morning news or reading the newspapers. He knew it would be all about him. All about the stupid stunt he had pulled, and all about new questions over his fitness for public office.

Getting himself out of bed and downstairs for a cup of coffee, Callahan replayed the moments of the night before again and again in his mind, every time yelling at himself for allowing Billy Dale to pick such a fight.

He realized that if he had just ignored him, it would be Billy who would likely have been written about in the papers as the one trying to start a fight and make Callahan look bad to help his recall campaign.

But instead, it was now Callahan who would be judged as the one acting improperly. Although Billy had provoked such a move, Callahan was the one who had struck him, and the one who was mayor. Sitting at his kitchen table, the same one where he and Billy had often met to plan campaign strategies nearly three years earlier, Callahan shook his head and tried to figure out how best to handle it. Pondering the situation, he opened his front door in somewhat of a haze and picked up the *Bulletin*.

Although the New Year's Eve fight was not the lead story, it was featured on the bottom of Page One, with a shot of Callahan landing the punch. As the city's most-read newspaper, the *Bulletin* had, of course, assigned someone to cover the ball, so a photographer from the paper was naturally there when the fur began to fly.

The story began by saying, "Mayor Jack Callahan, who is currently fighting a recall campaign launched by his former campaign manager, Billy Dale, twice punched Dale during last night's New Year's Eve ball after being provoked by Dale, witnesses said."

The story went on to state what happened, give witness comments, and a harsh statement from Billy. Callahan, who'd left shortly afterward, had not been interviewed.

As he read the story on his front stoop, lifting a cup of coffee to his lips twice and wincing with each hot touch of the cup, Callahan grumbled, then shut the door and went back to his breakfast. But that didn't end the problem.

Later, as he prepared to attend a New Year's Day party for a local children's center and meet with some friends for lunch and a little football watching, the mayor came across the afternoon copy of the *Journal* and numerous TV and radio newscasts.

Since it was a holiday—a slow news day—every TV and radio newscast was on top of the previous night's story. When Callahan reached the children's center party just after 10:30 a.m., a swarm of reporters found him and put the questions to him.

"Why did you do it?" "What provoked you?" "Do you think this will increase chances for the recall to succeed?"

Callahan just waved them away, went inside, and tended to his business for the day.

Elsewhere, Jimmy Min and Billy Dale also were meeting, with more joy than Callahan. Billy had not planned his tirade against the mayor, or so he said, but it still could hold a positive outcome for him with the petition drive.

Doing his best to allow the public sympathy to remain with him, and not with the mayor, Billy told reporters and the police that he did not want to press charges against Callahan. But he made sure his objections to the mayor's actions were known.

"I'm not the kind of person who will seek revenge," Billy told one television reporter that day. "I think our courts and police can be used for other things. But this should show the voters out there that Jack Callahan is not the man they thought he was and should be removed from office."

Late New Year's Day, a Thursday, Jimmy and Billy planned their next move. Billy fired up the petition volunteers for a major weekend push, while Jimmy and Mike McLean got to work on a slam issue of the *Advocate* for the following Wednesday.

Since the New Year's Eve fight had occurred on a Wednesday night, neither the *Reader* nor the *Advocate* had been able to cover it yet. But Jimmy made sure the following week's issue would slap Callahan but good.

Over the weekend, Billy's troops and those working for Fields were quick to hit the streets and found an avalanche of support for a recall. When asked why voters were quicker to sign up, many acknowledged that Callahan's New Year's Eve punches had changed their minds.

Some volunteers simply had to set up a table on a major street to get signers, while others used the old-fashioned door-to-door approach, also gaining more names.

When Monday morning rolled around, Billy was amazed to find that he'd collected 5,000 signatures through his volunteers in just three days.

"Kickin' ass," he told Jimmy on Monday morning. "This is going to keep going. We are on our way."

Jimmy, meanwhile, spent Monday writing a harsh editorial against Callahan, which he planned to run on the top of Page One, just above Tammy Sharp's story about the New Year's Eve fight. Sharp's piece would emphasize the negative reaction from political leaders citywide, and even in Sacramento.

Among those showing dissatisfaction with Callahan's behavior was none other than Walter Beard.

"I have known Jack Callahan a long time," Beard told Sharp. "And I am disturbed that he would act in such a manner."

Although Beard had wanted to stay out of the fray until a recall election was set, Billy believed that just a short comment in a story with dozens of political opinions might be a good way to get his feet slightly wet.

As for Jimmy Min, he held back nothing in his front-page swipe at the mayor.

"Once again, Mayor Callahan has shown his unfitness for public office," the *Advocate* editorial screamed. "Anyone who doesn't believe such actions—on top of his numerous questionable decisions during the past year—are grounds for removal must be living with their head in the sand."

The *Advocate* also carried a story updating the recall drive in its Tuesday edition, with the exclusive information from Billy Dale that 5,000 more signatures had been gathered over the weekend and that the campaign was picking up about 1,000 per day.

"We are doing better than even I expected," Billy was quoted as saying. "But we still need everyone's support."

As for the *Reader*, which had also been unable to cover the New Year's Eve fracas due to its Wednesday publishing date, coverage hit Callahan hard. Although not as biased as the *Advocate*, Danny Dugan still took the liberty of composing an editorial that called Callahan's mayoral administration "out of control."

The *Bulletin* and the *Journal* had not written much on the incident since their New Year's Day stories. Each had reported that Billy Dale would not press charges and that Callahan had little in the way of comment during the following days.

After the *Advocate* reported the rise in petition signatures, each daily paper published a small story on January 7th, but offered little in the way of expanded coverage.

As the petition drive went into high gear during the following weeks, with the February 4th deadline approaching, the *Advocate* continued to report the collection of more and more signatures, while the other papers also noted the reports, along with an ongoing silence by Callahan.

Finally, three weeks after New Year's Day, Callahan spoke up.

By then, reports showed that Billy Dale and company had amassed 45,000 signatures and were closing in on at least 50,000 by the following weekend

During a brief meeting in his office with Carl Devins, Callahan realized that he should say something about what happened on New Year's Eve and make some sort of apology. Still steamed from Billy's ability to draw him out, the mayor was hesitant.

But after several minutes of conversation with Devins in his private office, the mayor gave in.

"Jack, no one understands more than me how you feel, but you see where this is going," Devins said, as Callahan listened patiently with teeth clenched and his right hand in a fist. "If you apologize and seek some absolution, you might be able to stop this tidal wave of opposition."

Callahan rose out of his chair, walked over to the view of Civic Center Park that he had looked to for guidance so many times before, then turned around.

"Okay, Carl," the mayor said. "You and my press staff set up something for tomorrow morning and I'll do it."

The next day, Callahan met the throng of reporters on the steps of City Hall who had gathered for his comments. He walked out quietly and nervously, looked around with a weak smile, and began to read from small index cards.

"Thank you for coming here today. I wanted to say something about the incident that occurred on New Year's Eve," the mayor began, clearing his throat slightly between words. "As you know, I have been through a lot during the past year with the loss of my wife and the difficult battle over the Hunter's Point Shipyard development. While that is not an excuse for my behavior at the ball, it is, in fact, part of the cause."

As the television cameras rolled and reporters scribbled in their notebooks, Callahan stepped back, coughed again, and continued.

"In recent times, Billy Dale and I have parted company and come to disagree on the future of this city. As you know, he has been behind a campaign to remove me from office," the mayor said. "Such actions have further divided us in our views of the city's needs. However, such disagreements in no way excuse one from acting as I did. Therefore, I profoundly apologize to Billy Dale and to the City and County of San Francisco for my actions. I am deeply sorry and hope that you can forgive me and work with me to make this city as great as it can be."

With that, Callahan walked away as reporters called after him for more comment. He went into City Hall, up the stairs to his office, and past his secretary's desk without saying a word. Once inside his private office, the mayor went into his small personal bathroom, got on his knees over the toilet, and threw up.

One week after Callahan's apology, it seemed that his words were having some effect on the petition drive. The campaign, which had been at 45,000 signatures just a week earlier—with an average of 1,000 to 3,000 coming in daily—had stalled at 49,000.

With just one week to go, Billy Dale and the campaign were back in trouble again. They had just one week to get at least 11,000 more signatures if they hoped to have enough of a cushion to handle the likely number of invalid names.

Jimmy Min boosted efforts with yet another issue of the *Advocate* that blasted Callahan and his apology, complete with an editorial, story, and a column by Mike McLean. McLean had been writing columns against the mayor for weeks, but this one took an especially harsh tone, calling him "a liar who hates Billy Dale and did not mean a word of his apology."

But while the *Advocate* and the *Reader* continued to hit Callahan about his attack and his apology, the City Hall speech seeking forgiveness had actually gotten some positive feedback from the *Bulletin* and the *Journal*. Each wrote straightforward stories that included comments from voters who believed the mayor's sincerity.

The *Journal*, which still owed Callahan for his Hunter's Point vote, even editorialized that his apology showed "the strong side of a man big enough to admit mistakes."

As the last week of the petition drive shifted into overdrive, Billy's volunteers, Fields's workers, and even staff from the *Advocate* hit every possible place where a valid signature could be found. When the final day of collection appeared on February 3rd, the campaign counted 48,000 signatures.

None of the newspapers were able to print the campaign count because Billy would not reveal it, choosing not to give the mayor's forces any hint of where the petition drive stood. And, at Billy's request, the *Advocate* that week only stated: "The petition drive campaign is confident that it will have enough signatures to ensure approval."

While the 3,000-signature cushion was adequate, it was not what Billy had wanted to make things iron-clad. As Billy recounted the stacks of petition papers on the night of February 3rd, he shared his concern with Jimmy.

"This is okay, but is it enough?" he asked his friend. "We need something more. Some way to ensure this."

But neither man was sure what to do.

As the night wore on, Billy—as he had always done in the past—went over the options and drawbacks in his mind. As he and Jimmy worked into the late evening hours, they were hopeful that the 48,000 signatures would be adequate, but remained uncertain.

By 11 p.m., Jimmy left Billy's home as Billy got ready to sleep. He was planning to bring the petitions to the Director of Elections as late as possible on February 4th. He had until 5 p.m. when the office closed.

But Billy also held out hope that he could either delay the deadline somehow or scramble to get another 7,000 to 9,000 signatures. He knew things looked slim and, at most, he might be able to scrounge up another 500 to 700 signers during the next day's canvassing. Although it didn't look good.

With all of those scenarios running through his mind, Billy went to sleep and tried to forge a way to get over the top.

Across town, although just a few miles away, Jack Callahan was pondering a similar situation. He had no idea if his apology had done any good. In a late-night phone call to Carl Devins, the mayor received some calming of his fears. But he still knew that, in this city, anything was possible.

Pacing the kitchen floor of his home—which still seemed lonely without Glenda—Devins told Callahan he shouldn't worry about what he could not control, but that didn't help him.

"Carl, do you have any more speculation or reason why we might pull out of this okay?" the mayor asked his friend over the phone as he continued to pace with the receiver in one hand and a cigarette in the other. "I need something to hang hope on."

Devins, who always took the optimistic viewpoint—even when all evidence pointed the other way—merely told Callahan to keep his hopes up.

"Mayor, you can't miss the fact that you sparked a real drop in signatures with that apology," Devins advised. "Besides, people know what kind of a guy Billy Dale is—a real scum. They can see through him."

Devins's words calmed Callahan a bit, but they didn't make it any easier for the mayor to fall asleep. He tossed and turned for two hours before succumbing to exhaustion.

*   *   *

The next morning, the final decision time for the petition drive was at hand. Both Jack Callahan and Billy Dale awoke with a mix of hope and pessimism that the petition drive would turn out their way.

First, Billy called his volunteer organizers and Jerry Fields to make sure that they took complete advantage of every waking hour to gather more signatures. Fields and his workers staked out as many subway and bus stops as possible beginning at 5 a.m., while Billy's volunteers concentrated on continuing the door-to-door effort in neighborhoods that had not been approached.

"Hit every person possible," Billy had told his chief organizer that morning in a hurried phone call. "If they're breathing, sign them up."

All of the petition collectors were ordered to be at City Hall and in the Director of Elections office at 4:50 p.m. sharp. Billy did not want to take any chances that some might be late, but he also didn't want to end the search for signatures too soon and possibly miss some.

Throughout the day, the canvassers swarmed the city, not even taking time to count the signatures for fear that it could take time away from getting more names. Finally, at 4:30 p.m., all hands reported to City Hall, arriving just at 4:45 p.m.

A mob of press already staked out the small Director of Elections office as Billy Dale and Jerry Fields led the group of petition organizers in and officially submitted the stacks of papers bearing thousands of names.

Callahan did not attend Billy's grand submission of signatures, saying he did not want to give it more credibility for the press than it already received. Devins, however, showed up out of curiosity, but stayed in the back, almost unnoticed by the throng of political insiders who seemed to show up at every San Francisco event.

The event, such that it was, did not last long. It only took about two seconds for Elections Director Susan Rover to formally accept the petitions and give Billy a receipt for them. She would have 10 days to determine if enough valid signatures were among the final tally to meet the 45,000 requirement.

If the number of required signatures was reached, Rover would call the election and set a date for it, along with other dates for candidates to file and for Callahan to state if he would seek to remain in office. The city charter included a small provision that gave the mayor the option of dropping out and allowing others to run for the seat without him.

Billy had not even had a chance to count the additional signatures in his rush to get them in, but privately believed that he had garnered about 60,000. Although he told none of the reporters, fearing it would give Callahan too much confidence.

He wanted the mayor to sweat it out as much as he had.

For the next 10 days, the two sides would have to wait as the checking occurred. Of course, Rover and her staff would not seek to verify each signature, but rather do spot checks on about 1,000 of them. If too many were deemed invalid, she could rule the petitions insufficient.

The truth was that much of the checking was, in fact, at Rover's discretion, something that Billy had noted early on. Rover announced that she hoped to have the review done within a week, although she noted again that she had until February 14th 10 days away.

Then, just as Rover was about to kick everyone out, lock up the petitions, and shut down shop until the next day, another group of people barreled through the front door, actually knocking it open as one of Rover's aides was preparing to lock up.

The rumpled group, many who seemed out of breath from running, barged in the door with piles of their own petitions to submit. They were about 10 in all, including some homeless people and lower-level political volunteers.

Billy, Jimmy, and Devins thought that some of the faces looked familiar, but were not sure. Then, as all three continued to glance from face to face, the final member of the group came running in, breathless and panting, and dumped her own stack of petitions on the office counter.

This face everyone recognized. It was none other than Marie Alzeti.

"Am I too late?" Alzeti said to Rover as she began taking piles of paper from others in her group and adding them on top of those she had brought. "Are we too late?"

A startled Rover asked her, "too late for what?"

As she attempted to catch her breath and explain her situation, Alzeti said, "too late to submit these petitions for the recall?" she said.

No one spoke for about 60 seconds. If the Pope had walked in naked and stood on his head there couldn't have been a more surprised reaction among the political honchos. All eyes focused on Alzeti and her group as they laid out the petitions, which seemed to number in the thousands, and officially submitted them to Rover.

"Madam Director, I formally submit these petitions for the campaign to recall Mayor Callahan," Alzeti said, her breaths coming slower. "We request a receipt and a verification as soon as possible."

With that, Rover accepted the paperwork and most of the group who had come in with Alzeti applauded.

Jimmy and Billy had no idea what to think. Jimmy's first reaction was joy that someone else had been collecting signatures and had provided them to boost the overall count.

But Billy, who always thought two steps ahead, realized that if Alzeti was collecting signatures to help force a recall of the mayor, that meant only one thing: she was going to run for mayor against Callahan herself.

And, of course, against Walter Beard. Billy began to shake his head as the reality of this changing scenario took hold of him. He then let out a short whisper, "Dammit," he said. "All we fuckin' need."

After all of the official paperwork was in, Rover then told the crowd they had to leave so she could close up.

All sides departed, although slowly, from the office as the clock ran past 5 p.m. The press—newly invigorated by Alzeti's entrance into the campaign—pressed her for comments about why she had joined up, and if she would run for mayor in the event of a recall.

The Board of Supervisors' president, whose name recognition would do much to help her in a mayor's race, withheld any firm decision about running, saying only that she "wanted to help put the recall on the ballot so that San Franciscans could have a chance to review their stance on Jack Callahan.

"Mayor Callahan has been involved in a lot this past year," Alzeti continued. "A lot of questionable things have happened and voters should have a chance to say if they want him to remain. I am not usually in favor of recalls. But, in this case, I think it is warranted."

When asked what he thought about Alzeti getting into the act, adding what seemed to be at least 5,000 signatures to the recall drive, Billy Dale provided a kind comment. "We can use all the help we can get," Billy said with a puzzled look toward Alzeti. "We are glad to see others sharing our view."

But inside, Billy was fuming. He knew that such a move could only hamper his plan to get Beard in office. With a third candidate, all the anti-Callahan votes would be split, requiring an even greater margin of victory.

As Alzeti led her troops out of the office when Rover closed up, Billy couldn't help but feel the steam rising inside him. His ears turned hot, his face reddened, and he nearly let out a yell.

But with Jimmy's calming influence, he kept his thoughts to himself and joined Jimmy and Mike McLean for a casual dinner in North Beach that night.

Rover ended up needing only nine days to review the petition, announcing on Friday, February 13th, that enough valid signatures had been found and the election would be held three months later, on May 13th. Candidates would have 30 days to file for a spot on the ballot, with the deadline for filing on March 13th.

The moment the petitions were approved, Billy Dale began working out his plan to destroy Jack Callahan, knock out Marie Alzeti, and elect Walter Beard. Although this was not the race he had envisioned—with the last-minute entrance of Alzeti throwing some new hurdles on the track—he still knew he could adapt.

"It's not who you fight, but how," Billy would tell a reporter the day after the petitions were approved. "And no one knows how to fight like me." ∎

Chapter Twenty-Seven

Strike One

The strange timing of the recall election deadlines was not lost on anyone in the campaign, least of all Billy Dale. The fact that the recall petition signatures had been approved on Friday the 13th was seen by Billy as some kind of strange good luck sign. And, since Valentine's Day fell on the next day, Billy decided that that was some kind of signal as well.

Not one to waste time getting into action, or waste a chance to poke fun at the unusual timing, Billy decided to begin the recall campaign effort the very next day. To launch the anti-Callahan push as strongly as possible, Billy found an old San Francisco Police Department bus, covered it with Recall Callahan signs, and prepared it for a citywide tour on Saturday.

As his campaign operatives spread the word about the tour through the press on Saturday morning, one reporter also noted that February 14 happened to be the one-year anniversary of Billy Dale's conviction for illegal weapons possession. Billy claimed that he did not even remember such a date. But in reality, the irony also played into Billy's wanting to launch the recall campaign then.

When Saturday morning arrived, Billy personally drove the bus to the front of City Hall at 8 a.m. and joined the dozens of volunteers who were ready to board it for the tour. Billy also had gathered up about 25 police officers who were joining the recall campaign. Many had not liked Callahan as a chief or mayor, while others had backed off their support following the recent string of questionable moves involving Glenda's death and the Hunter's Point development.

Billy draped the bus with several banners he had prepared for the tour. Each targeted Callahan as a former police chief who had failed as mayor. Placing them on the sides of the vehicle, Billy explained the strategy to a TV reporter.

"People of San Francisco elected Jack Callahan two and a half years ago because they liked his record as police chief and wanted to put someone with law enforcement ability into office," he said, while taping up a corner of the sign over the dark blue bus. "But his actions have shown that he cannot be trusted to make the proper decisions or enforce the law."

The two banners were direct. The first said, "Callahan is not a Friend to Men in Blue." The other explained simply "Police for The Recall of Callahan."

Billy made it clear at the morning rally before the tour that the police union in no way had endorsed the recall, although Billy had already met with the union president and was working to obtain such support. He said this was simply meant to show that at least a few dozen cops were calling for the ouster of their former chief.

After Billy climbed aboard the bus with Jimmy Min, Mike McLean, and about 50 other volunteers, the driver started off and honked to supporters as the group toured the city. From City Hall to Chinatown, North Beach, Fisherman's Wharf, and even the outer Richmond and Sunset neighborhoods, the bus strolled along, blasting recorded anti-Callahan announcements and passing out flyers that called for the mayor's removal.

Each flyer and pamphlet also listed the same questionable incidents surrounding Callahan that the large sign at the rally to launch the petition drive months earlier had offered. They included: the death of Glenda, the near loss of the Giants, the "uncertainty" over the Hunter's Point Shipyard development, and the mayor's failure to get a homeless plan in place.

And, at the bottom of the pamphlet, was a picture of Billy Dale with a black eye—obviously the work of the mayor's New Year's Eve punches. Next to it, the simple phrase: "Jack Callahan gives San Francisco a Black Eye."

From stop to stop, the volunteers shouted for support, handed out flyers and pamphlets, and blasted recorded announcements calling for Callahan's removal.

"Throw out the mayor, we'll see him later," was among the chants that were heard as the bus barreled through the Mission, Castro, and even Pacific Heights, where it parked in front of Callahan's home for an entire half-hour.

But the mayor was not there at the time. Instead, he was in Carl Devins's office trying to plot some strategy of his own.

"Carl, I know we had to back off and not make any moves about this recall until it was a certainty," Callahan told Devins as the two men shared coffee and Danish on the hectic Saturday morning. "But now it's happening and I need to figure this out."

Devins nodded as he sipped the hot, black beverage. Setting the steaming paper cup on his desk and brushing away a stack of the day's newspapers that the two men had been reviewing for the past hour, Devins fixed his eyes on Callahan and gave one of the emptiest looks possible.

"Jack, I really don't know," Devins said with a blank, helpless face. "The most we can do is counter with some positive things. Talk about the money and jobs you have brought in and attack Billy's past as a revengeful political hack with a criminal record."

Although Devins had always preached against negative campaigning, he believed that, in this case, Callahan had to do whatever he could. After only two years in office, the mayor had a right to say that he'd not had a chance to achieve as much as someone in office for four or eight years.

Devins also had come to realize that, against Billy Dale, hardball politics was sometimes necessary. "You know I hate it more than you, mayor," Devins continued as he leaned back in his chair and took another sip. "But in this case, they are attacking you. You can shoot back if it is seen as self-defense, not overt offense."

The two men then spent the rest of the day planning how to use Billy Dale's negative past and the few Callahan accomplishments to their advantage. They knew it would take time, but they also wanted to get to work fast.

South of City Hall, another pair of campaign veterans also shared a breakfast on this Valentine's Day morning: Danny Dugan and Marie Alzeti. Although Dugan had not known about Alzeti's interest in the recall until she showed up to file her petitions, he was as happy for her move as anyone.

Just hours after she dropped off the paperwork, Alzeti phoned Dugan and told him what she'd done. While she gave a non-answer to reporters that night about her possible campaign plans, she told Dugan that, if the recall occurred, she would throw her hat into the ring.

As expected, Dugan was ready with all the firepower and support possible. Now that the petition had been approved and the recall was definitely on, Dugan and Alzeti wanted to forge their own plans for a campaign.

"The key here," Dugan said as he picked up a forkful of scrambled eggs from the Styrofoam tray of bacon and eggs he had brought in that morning, "is to charge up the negatives on Callahan, but also build up your qualifications as a replacement. We have one plus on that side, Billy Dale is already leading the charge to oust the mayor. So we can begin to build you up as the positive alternative."

Although both Alzeti and Dugan smiled at that notion, they also realized that this was only part of Billy Dale's plan. Each knew that Billy would not go to all the trouble of knocking out the mayor if he didn't have someone lined up to replace him.

"That will be the true fight," Alzeti said, continuing to bite into the bran muffin that stood as her breakfast. "We have to be ready to pounce on whoever is Billy's person. Knowing him, it could be anyone."

Dugan and Alzeti then talked about when Alzeti should formally get in.

She knew that she would be open to attacks earlier if she formally filed as a candidate. But, as Dugan noted, she also would have more time to gain support, money, and acceptance if she jumped in the race sooner. Dugan stressed that if Alzeti was the first candidate to enter, it would give her more clout and sincerity than whoever Billy Dale tossed in later.

"We have to time this just right," Alzeti said. "We have to be careful."

As all the players pondered the campaign that morning, each had to also factor in the unusual circumstances of the recall election. A recall was not like a straight race for office. Under the recall rules, voters would be asked two very separate questions.

First, they would be asked if Callahan should be recalled: Yes or No?

Then, they would be asked who among the challengers should replace him if he is recalled.

Right now, Alzeti was the only choice.

But when Billy unveiled his candidate—Walter Beard—the voters would be, technically, picking between Beard and Alzeti.

So, in essence, there were two campaigns: the fight to recall Callahan and the battle between the challengers to replace him.

"We do first things first," Billy told Jimmy while he steered the bus toward the Bayview district that afternoon at about 4:30 p.m. "Our goal now is to knock out Callahan. We need to focus on cutting down his credibility and pumping up his mistakes. Then, when we have his poll numbers sufficiently toppled, we can unleash Beard on them."

Since Walter Beard had until March 13th to file for the recall, that gave Billy and Jimmy a month to whittle away at Callahan. Billy said he would wait and see when Alzeti got into the race to go after her.

"I figure we can attack her more once Beard is in the race because we can stand him up as the better choice," Billy reasoned to Jimmy. "It is easier to get people to boo someone off stage when you have someone better waiting in the wings."

*　　*　　*

For the next week, the bus tours continued, along with rallies and more literature handed out to people at bus stops, bank lines, and even City Hall events. One day, Jimmy Min took a stack of "Recall Callahan" pamphlets and left them inside the mayor's office reception room.

When Callahan saw them the next day, he yelled at his staff and personally tore them up and threw them away. "This is still my damn office," he said as he stormed out of the room and into his private office. "I'm still the mayor."

By February 21st, polls showed Callahan had lost some support, but not nearly enough to ensure that a recall would occur. Billy and Jimmy's barrage of literature and attacks had helped some, but without any central issue to light a fire under the recall—or any definite candidates to put up against the mayor—

the likelihood of removing Callahan remained slim.

Billy knew he had to come up with something to throw in the mayor's face, or at least distract him, during the campaign. Sure, the screw-ups by Callahan over the past two years—especially the New Year's Eve attack on Billy—were useful, but not the kind of nail-in-the-coffin killer Billy liked.

On Sunday, February 22nd, Billy ended the police bus tours—at least for the moment—and spent the morning at a brunch inside Gabbiano's, a waterfront favorite of his, with Jimmy and Benny Min, Mike McLean, and several campaign volunteers. The gathering was a bit more social than the usual breakfast meetings Billy favored for strategy sessions.

As rotund as ever, Billy always believed he thought better and strategized more clearly when he ate. Bacon, eggs, and sausage were his favorite fuels, while Jimmy—although thin as a rail—favored the sloppy syrup of pancakes and waffles.

On this Sunday, the meeting had a touch more festive atmosphere than most. Still, the group focused on finding that ever-necessary slam that could knock Callahan down.

"Okay," Billy began as he stuffed sausage in his mouth and spoke between chews. "Here it is. We have three weeks before we can put a candidate in the race and Callahan remains too high up. Polls have him at a 66% approval rating, and that is not enough for a recall. What can we hit him with?"

All those at the table looked at each other, none able to act with anything specific.

"We've already slapped him with everything he fucked up on this year," one volunteer said. "And with the New Year's Eve thing, that should be enough."

"Well, you idiot, it isn't," an angry Billy shot back. "It's enough when his polls are down to 30% and our man is making his victory speech."

For the next hour, the men talked, traded ideas, and chowed down everything on the buffet table from croissants to hash browns. But nothing workable arose. After more than two hours in the restaurant, the group broke up and headed on their separate ways.

Billy went back to his house to go over the following week's plans and do some work on some other, smaller elections he was running in areas south of the city. Benny Min, who still worked at City Hall thanks to his contract with the city, stopped by his office for some weekend cleaning up, while Jimmy Min went to the *Advocate* office to go over some business and paperwork.

Once Jimmy reached his desk, the only room in the quiet building that was lit on Sunday, he began to peruse the Sunday edition of the *Bulletin*. The large paper carried the usual expanded mix of news, travel, business, features, and sports.

As Jimmy scanned the local section, he spotted a small item about the

Municipal Railway System, better known as the Muni. The short, four-paragraphed story said the Municipal Railway Workers Local 999 had reached an impasse in its talks for a new three-year contract.

With little other comment, the article stated that the union president, Sal Paulsey, had wanted a nine percent raise for his workers each year over the next three years, while Muni Director Eric Kleiger had offered only four percent each year.

The article said the two sides had met for three months and hoped to forge a new contract before the current one expired on February 27th. It stated that neither side expected any work stoppage and believed the deadline would come and go without a problem.

"This is just a bump in the road on our way to a new contract," Paulsey was quoted as saying. "These kinds of things happen all the time. We believe we will get a new contract soon, one we can all live with."

As Jimmy read through the item, his famous grin appeared and grew larger. Putting the paper down on his desk and reaching for the phone, the publisher couldn't help but laugh to himself at the thought of what was going through his mind.

Dialing Billy Dale's office number, Jimmy held the phone tight in one hand while tapping his pencil on his desk with the other. He even began humming a short tune to himself as the phone rang on the other end.

"Billy?" Jimmy said when his friend answered. "I've got it. I know what we need."

*　　*　　*

Two days later, Billy and Jimmy found themselves sitting in the darkest, most hidden table at Zuma's Cafe on Market Street as a blustery, cold wind whipped up outside. It was exactly 1 p.m. when the waitress came over and asked, again, what they wanted. For the fourth time in the last half-hour, Jimmy had to tell her they were waiting for someone.

Billy was getting antsy, and hungry, as he chewed on breadsticks and crackers and sipped his third Vodka martini. Jimmy remained calm but knew that his idea might be losing steam if Billy was getting impatient.

"Where is this bastard?" Billy asked his friend as the sound of a stick hitting the window next to the table made both men jump slightly. "Well, if he ain't here in another five minutes, we are eating."

Jimmy laughed at his friend's impatience for food. Just as he was about to comment back, the hulking figure of their tardy guest appeared. His face red from the seasonal cold and a coughing from the outside street dust, the large man walked up, leaned forward, and shook both men's' hands before sitting down.

"Hi Sal," Jimmy said. "You know Billy Dale. Billy, Sal Paulsey."

Paulsey greeted both men with hellos, speaking with a breath that reeked of cigarettes and cheap whiskey. His clothes were wrinkled and his hair strewn about in tufts. A day's stubble glazed his face, while a thick New York accent wrapped his speech.

"Hey guys, sorry I'm late," Paulsey said with a tired grin. "The traffic down Fillmore Street is always a fuckin' hassle."

Jimmy and Billy nodded, knowing that such a situation was likely, but probably not the complete reason for Paulsey's lateness. Nevertheless, the three men were there and Jimmy was ready to lay out his plan.

"Okay Sal, here's the deal," Jimmy said, sipping an iced tea. "You guys have not taken any public stance on this recall, correct?"

"No," Sal nodded, as he reached for a roll and began spreading the near-melted butter across it. "We've been too busy trying to get a fuckin' contract."

Both Jimmy and Billy smiled at the comment, as Paulsey chewed on the roll. Then they made their pitch.

"Well, we're not asking for your endorsement, but we do want to do something about the contract talks," Jimmy said.

"Yeah? What?" Paulsey said.

"We want them stalled," Jimmy began.

"And we want you guys to call a strike as soon as possible," Billy added, cutting off Jimmy's more-carefully selected wording.

Both men expected Paulsey to choke, spit out, or even yell at the two.

But not this man.

Paulsey was too well-versed in the art of political maneuvering. He'd cut his labor teeth as a representative in the New York City transit arena, often stuffing ballot boxes for political candidates backed by his union and marching in protests in sub-zero weather.

Two San Francisco hustlers asking him to call a strike for their political benefit was nothing new. Paulsey just gulped a sip of beer, grabbed another roll, and continued to eat.

"Keep talking," Paulsey said. "I'm listening."

"Well, it's like this," Jimmy said, cutting Billy off again. "You know about this recall campaign?"

Paulsey nodded

"Well, if we can get your guys to call a strike, even a short one, it can screw Callahan into the ground," Jimmy explained. "And, if he ends up losing, we can guarantee that the man replacing him will give you the nine percent raise you want."

Paulsey's eyes opened a little, but he remained skeptical.

"How can you ensure that?" Paulsey said. "You don't even know who is running."

"Yes we do," Billy said, breaking back into the conversation. "But we have to keep it hidden until the last filing deadline. We don't want to tip our hand, especially when that Alzeti broad is about to jump in."

Paulsey continued to eat, now stepping up to the salad with gobs of blue cheese dressing he'd ordered. Dipping bread into the salad dressing and shoving it into his mouth, Paulsey thought about it further.

As Jimmy and Billy listened intently, the union president asked about a few more specifics and, ultimately, the big question.

"How can we be sure?" Paulsey asked. "I can get my guys to strike and then knock Callahan out for you. But what's to make sure your man will give us what we want?"

"Look, if he doesn't come through, you can rattle him some more and strike again," Jimmy said. "I'll also put the *Advocate* behind it and vow to give as much editorial support for the union as possible from the beginning of the strike. If that doesn't convince you, you can end it and go back to work and the bargaining table."

Paulsey thought further.

As Jimmy and Billy began eating, they could see the idea was working its way through Paulsey's mechanical brain. He had a reputation for thinking things through carefully, but also for getting into action once a plan was laid out.

"Let me take it back to my board and see what they think," Paulsey said as he finished up lunch. "But I like it."

After shaking hands and wiping crumbs from his face, shirt, and arms, Paulsey left. Jimmy and Billy seemed confident as he walked away and they finished their meals. But they also knew that such a move would only work if it went into effect by the end of the week, when the union's contract ended on February 27th.

The next afternoon, February 25th, Jimmy Min got a call from Paulsey. He said he'd talked to his board of directors and they agreed to go along with the plan. He said they would push for a strike in meetings over the next two days and hold a vote to authorize it on Friday, February 27th—the day of the contract's end.

"But if we do this, you guys better hold up your end of the bargain," Paulsey said in a threatening tone. "Or else your asses will be dead meat."

As Jimmy hung up the phone he grinned with happiness, but also felt a tinge of concern. He knew this had to work. It had to knock the mayor out.

When Friday morning appeared, every newsroom in the city got a press release from the transportation workers union. Out of nowhere, the union had called for a strike vote to be held that afternoon. The notice said little about why such a move was coming just days after both sides had been quoted saying the contract talks were going well. The only word was that the vote would be taken starting at 4 p.m. and would continue until 11 p.m. to allow all shifts a chance to fill out a ballot.

Reporters were directed to come to a news conference at 3 p.m. at the steps of the Muni headquarters near City Hall. No other indication was given. Paulsey's phone began ringing off the hook just minutes after the press release went out, but he declined to comment.

"You'll hear it all at 3 O'clock," he told the inquiring callers. "It'll be short and sweet."

No one was more curious than Jack Callahan himself. He did not receive word of the strike vote until a reporter from one of the local TV stations asked for his comment during a morning press conference to announce a new child care center opening.

"I don't see the need for this," Callahan had said. "The negotiations, as far as I know, have been going smoothly."

But moments after the press event, the mayor raced to his office and began calling Carl Devins, Muni chief Eric Kleiger, and anyone else at City Hall who might have a notion of what was happening.

"I don't know," Kleiger said. "This is out of nowhere. We had a negotiation session just last night and things looked good. We will check it out."

When 3 p.m. rolled around, a horde of the press was situated at the steps leading up to the Muni headquarters. Three members of the union's board of directors—all well-versed in the Billy Dale–Jimmy Min deal—joined Paulsey on the steps.

No picket signs had been brought forth, but a large union banner stretched across the top of the steps, with another smaller sign stating, "Fair Treatment, Fair Deal."

Noticeably absent were Jimmy and Billy, who watched carefully on TV from Billy's office while a live camera crew broadcast the event over the local all-news channel.

"We are asking our workers to vote on a strike because we believe that negotiations for a new contract are going nowhere," Paulsey told the mass of press, who were slowly joined by passing residents and city employees curious about the event. "We have spent months on this issue and it is our belief that the Callahan administration is not willing to meet our demands. We have informed our membership of the situation and asked them to vote their conscience."

After the statement, Paulsey said there would be no further comments because he did not want to sway the vote. "I'll speak after the votes are counted, probably by Saturday afternoon."

With that, the press dispersed and the union leadership headed off to process the votes. Throughout the afternoon and evening, union members filed in and out of the union headquarters, some chatting about their support for a strike, while others said they did not believe one was necessary.

What no one commented on was the 22-page pamphlet that the *Advocate* had printed on its presses and Billy Dale had given to Paulsey to distribute to the union membership just a day earlier. The pamphlet was filled with stories written about Callahan's anti-union comments of the past, the trend in other cities away from higher raises for transit workers, and the growing need to remove Callahan.

Although the pamphlet did not directly indicate that the union was pushing for a strike so that Callahan would be recalled, it hinted that a walkout could help facilitate the mayor's removal.

Later in the day, one of the pamphlets made its way to the mayor's office when a union member anonymously slipped it under the front door. When the mayor saw the item and brought it to Devins's and Kleiger's attention, all three men realized exactly what was happening.

"That Billy Dale will not quit," Callahan told the two others. "The bastard is setting me up."

But as the three men talked in the mayor's office, the clock hit 8 p.m., leaving only a few hours of strike voting left and little chance for the mayor to take any stand against a strike. No vote count was being made until all the ballots were cast, but interviews by the press of those leaving the voting area seemed to show the group leaning toward a strike.

Billy and Jimmy's pamphlet did everything to urge the workers to walk out, all but promising them that the next mayor would give a nine percent raise or more.

"If you think Jack Callahan is going to give you the raise you deserve, after the way he has treated environmentalists, the homeless, and even his wife's memory, think again," the pamphlet ended. "Anyone is better than a mayor who can't stand up for himself."

By 11 p.m., about 88% of the union membership had voted, with the counting set to begin early the next morning. That night Billy and Jimmy had a quiet gathering of recall advisers in Billy's office, while Callahan, Devins, and Kleiger brainstormed in the mayor's office.

The next day, the vote count began with the press, union leaders, and all interested political heads waiting outside. At one point, one union member couldn't wait and stormed into the union headquarters to demand the count be completed.

The independent auditors hired to conduct the count, under the observance of representatives from Muni and the union, jumped up and began to run away when the transit worker entered. But before he could do anything, police took him away and the count resumed.

By noon, the counting ended, the results were confirmed, and the auditor addressed the media and other interested parties outside.

"The tabulation of the 2965 votes cast has 1435 opposing a strike and 1530 favoring a strike," the man said. "The vote indicates the union has approved a strike."

When the word went out, a loud cheer came from the 100 or so union members who'd remained to hear the count, along with a few boos and grunts mixed in. Again, Billy and Jimmy remained out of sight, as did Callahan, Devins, and Kleiger.

All five of them had been watching on television, in separate locations, when the strike word came through. Thirty minutes later, at a hastily prepared press conference, Paulsey announced that the strike was on.

The transit union president proclaimed that "the workers had spoken" and "the call was on for a fair contract and wage."

"We will walk off the job at midnight tonight," Paulsey told the crowd. "The negotiations may continue, but right now we want to wait for the city to come back with our requested nine percent annual raise over three years."

Then, unlike the previous day's event, Paulsey took questions. As reporters shouted their requests, cameras rolled, and some in the crowd chanted "Strike! Strike! Strike!"

After a few questions, one reporter asked Paulsey if the timing of the strike had anything to do with the approaching recall election.

"This is not about politics, this is about fairness," Paulsey said, looking straight into one of the cameras that carried the image through to a live broadcast. "We would never, ever jeopardize our workers in the name of backroom politics." ■

Chapter Twenty-Eight

The Surprise Deal

On Sunday morning, the trains and buses stopped promptly at one minute after midnight. Since the strike occurred on a Saturday night, many people out for a night on the town had trouble coming home.

Numerous residents, including some who were under severe alcohol influence, arrived at bus stops and train stations throughout town hoping for a late-night ride. Instead, many were greeted by transit workers leaving their buses and trains in droves, while Muni officials tacked up signs advising them that "A job action has stopped Muni service until further notice."

One bus driver, carrying a full load of passengers from busy North Beach to the Richmond District, stopped his bus in the middle of the street at the corner of Geary Boulevard and 18th Avenue and walked out the door precisely at 12:01 a.m. He even left the engine running and did nothing to advise the surprised passengers of where they could go.

"This is the worst," one passenger told a *Bulletin* reporter, one of dozens of journalists scrambling around the city in the early morning hours of March 1 to cover the breaking story. "What happened? This came out of nowhere!"

During the night, Muni officials frantically dispatched emergency buses to pick up stranded riders at train stations and bus stops around the city. By 3 a.m., all of the would-be passengers caught off guard had been rescued and taken to central locations.

But that didn't stop the expected criticism that Billy Dale and Jack Callahan both knew was coming. The Sunday newspapers and television and radio news broadcasts all focused on the strike, with most attacking the city for not knowing that it was coming.

The Sunday *Bulletin*, whose editors and publisher were still mad at the mayor over the Hunter's Point development vote, slammed him with a Page One Headline that stated "Muni Strike Hits." Underneath the headline, the paper declared "Surprised Mayor Has Little Explanation."

Inside the *Bulletin*, an editorial written by J.C. Townsend himself called Callahan's leadership "a failure and the key cause of a good negotiation turning bad."

Although Callahan had about as much to do with the negotiations as Townsend himself, the *Bulletin* editor saw the strike as a chance to skewer Callahan well.

"This is where we get him back," Townsend told one of his deputy editors late Saturday. "See how he likes being put out to dry."

But, of course, the editorial directive had come, as usual, from Emily Ingle. She called Townsend on Friday afternoon after hearing about the strike vote and ordered him to prepare the editorial in the event of a walkout.

"Nail 'em to the wall," she'd stated.

At the *Journal*, which remained grateful to Callahan for his Hunter's Point vote, coverage was a bit more slanted against the strikers. Stories were balanced, as usual, with a mix of comments from union members, city negotiators, and passengers. But the *Journal* editorial placed more of the blame on the union.

The editorial attacked Paulsey and his membership for launching a strike too quickly and "failing to give the negotiating process a chance.

"For the city's transit workers to refuse to come to a middle ground between their requested nine percent raise and the city's proposed four percent hike is unfair and flies in the face of every rule of collective bargaining," the editorial continued. "The key to union support is wage bargaining and a fair give-and-take."

Since neither the *Advocate* nor the *Reader* was due out for three more days, they had yet to weigh in. But both Jimmy Min and Danny Dugan dispatched reporters around the city that Sunday to get a different edge on the story, most likely one opposing the mayor.

"Get everything you can, especially anything that makes the union look like victims," Min had told Tammy Sharp, his ace reporter. "Get some real profile stories about union workers with big families having a tough time without money coming in. Good tear-jerker stuff."

Jimmy and Billy both knew that the way to win at this strike was to portray the union as the victim and Kleiger and Callahan as the unfair city officials. It would be tough since the last indication before the strike vote was that negotiations were going well and Callahan was already portraying himself as some kind of victim because the strike had virtually come out of nowhere.

The mayor remained baffled as Sunday unfolded with strikers on picket lines, press roaming the streets, and residents clamoring for City Hall action. During a brief press conference in his office Sunday afternoon, Callahan tried to put the blame on the union, saying, "I was given no warning of this job action or a strike vote until Friday morning. I see this as an unfair stand being taken by the union for no good reason and without proper preventative measures."

But, in this case, Callahan's efforts to deflect blame were not working. Even he realized that when it came to city politics, the mayor was the man in charge and the one who took blame when a major city service like the transit system stopped.

Callahan could try as hard as he wanted to blame Paulsey and the union, and to a degree it worked. But for most people needing a bus or a train that Sunday, all they knew was that the system was down and they couldn't get a ride. In the end, it would have to be the mayor who would take the heat.

"I will make every effort to return both sides to the bargaining table and end this job action as quickly as possible," Callahan said to the press corps gathered in his office, many in sport shirts and casual slacks due to the weekend timing. "I am seeking a meeting with Sal Paulsey and his executive board today."

On that hopeful note, the press conference ended and Callahan went to his private office to phone Paulsey. After getting through, a secretary put the mayor on hold and found Paulsey, who was with two other members of the union board, and Billy Dale.

Before taking the call, Paulsey asked Billy what to do.

"We can't look like we are completely unreasonable," Paulsey told Billy. "Shouldn't we at least meet with the guy?" Billy just grinned and shook his head.

"No way," he said. "The key to this is to make Callahan completely powerless to stop things. I guarantee you that when our candidate comes in, you can cut the deal that will ensure that Callahan is recalled and our man is elected."

Paulsey remained a bit unsure but decided to follow Billy. He realized if he was going to go through with this, he had to go all the way.

"Hello? Mayor?" Paulsey said into the receiver. "How are you? What can we do for you?"

On the other end, Callahan remained calm and simply stated his regret about the strike, asking why something could not have been done sooner to avoid it.

"Sal, we could have worked this out. You guys really undercut me by jumping the gun," the mayor said. "Why go so fast? I thought you and Kleiger were coming to terms. A five percent difference in raise proposals isn't much; you guys could have knocked that down. What gives?"

Paulsey clenched the phone with his hand and held his breath. He then let out a deep sigh and turned to look at Billy, as if seeking guidance. Billy nodded and waved his hands like a father prodding a child to take his first steps.

"Mayor, I'm sorry, but we had to do what was necessary," Paulsey said. "We did not think that you or Kleiger were willing to negotiate fairly. I'm sorry. Goodbye."

Paulsey then hung up the phone and turned to Billy, who applauded. "Great fuckin' work," Billy said. "We are moving closer and closer."

On the other end, Callahan was shocked. This made no sense to him. Why would the union back down and put itself in the middle of a strike situation when it was clear such a move was not needed. He was more and more certain as Sunday went along that Billy Dale had something to do with it and had been behind the pamphlets he'd seen being given to transit workers.

Sitting quietly in his office chair, Callahan considered his next move calmly. He knew that this strike could kill him as the recall came closer. And he realized that Billy Dale was not the kind of man to take such a fight lightly.

Quickly, the mayor called Carl Devins and asked for his advice. All Devins could think to do was fight back, possibly in court, where some kind of court order or injunction might be used to keep the strikers from staying off the job.

"The only problem there, mayor, is that that could make you out as the bad guy to those people who support the union," Devins told him. "Remember, this is still a big union town and you can't come off looking like the troublemaker here."

Callahan realized that, but he also realized that a strike would hurt worse. He quickly called his legal advisors and had them prepare a request for a court order the next day.

Meanwhile, the pickets and strike lines continued Sunday evening, with TV, radio, and print reporters everywhere. No major disruptions or violence occurred. Paulsey had been clear to the strikers that the only way they'd win was to peacefully assert their cause.

"You get into any kind of trouble or underhanded behavior and we are through," Paulsey had warned a group of picketers outside the Church Street Muni station near Market Street. "Just be patient, do what you can legally, and don't get caught up in it."

Throughout Sunday's demonstrations, which included a rally at Union Square, the union members were calm and peaceful. Even when one person threw eggs at a crowd of strikers, the picketers remained still and simply pointed the person out to police, who arrested him.

"If we keep going patiently, this will work," Billy told Paulsey late Sunday. "It's coming right down our path to success."

Billy wasn't the only one seeing the impact the strike was having on Callahan and the recall effort. Marie Alzeti, who had made her feelings clear with her last-minute petition move, also saw the strike as a blow to the mayor.

During a meeting Sunday night with some political advisors, Alzeti decided that this would be the time for her to jump into the race. Although she still had nearly two weeks to file for the recall election on March 13th, she saw this as an opportunity to get in and, maybe, have the strike work to her advantage.

"What if I got in and was able to negotiate with the union?" Alzeti asked her close-knit group. "This could work. Maybe they just want another open voice to reason with."

Her advisers were skeptical, but saw the logic. If Alzeti was going to make a move, this might as well be it. The next day, March 2nd, Alzeti had been scheduled to appear on a morning news show to discuss the recall.

Ever since she'd joined the recall campaign, reporters were constantly asking her about whether she would run, but she had refused to say either way. On this morning, Alzeti surprised everyone—including Billy and Callahan—with her simple, quick announcement.

"I have decided to enter the recall election race as a candidate for mayor because I believe I have the experience and reasonable outlook to run this city," she told the TV audience. "Mayor Callahan has done his best, but it is obvious he has alienated certain important groups while tainting his own reputation with a number of questionable actions during the past year."

After the show, Alzeti immediately went to the Director of Elections to file for a ballot spot and began collecting the signatures that would be needed. Unlike the recall petition, which required 55,000 signatures, candidates who sought to run in the election needed only 15,000 signatures, an easy move for Alzeti and her staff.

Once she filed and sent her volunteers out to gather signatures, Alzeti headed straight to the transit union headquarters to confront Sal Paulsey and his board of directors. Believing such a move would bring her good publicity, Alzeti also invited a half-dozen camera crews and a handful of newspaper reporters to follow her.

Not wanting to miss such an unusual moment in the strike, the press obediently followed as Alzeti drove to the union offices at Noon on Monday. She knew that Sal Paulsey would be inside strategizing and wanted to grab him at this vulnerable moment.

Inside, the union president and several board members were going over the different aspects of the strike—planning protest lines, pamphlet circulation, and press releases—while sharing a Paulsey favorite, Chinese take-out food.

Billy Dale had been in the offices earlier but had left to take his own lunch with Jimmy Min at Tiger's Diner. When Paulsey saw Alzeti approaching, he had an idea what was happening, having seen her morning announcement on a late morning newscast.

Just as Alzeti and the reporters approached the door, her hand about to knock, Paulsey opened the door and greeted her with a firm, but friendly smile.

"Supervisor," Paulsey said. "How good of you to come. What can we do for you?"

With cameras rolling, lights shining, and reporters' pens scribbling behind her, Alzeti put forth her request.

"President Paulsey, I believe that we need to talk," Alzeti said, keeping a firm stance and trying not to stutter in her nervousness. "We both have been involved in City Hall issues for a long time and I believe we can work out an agreement to end this strike. If you don't want to negotiate with the mayor, I understand. I believe you should negotiate with me."

Paulsey, still holding a cup of chop suey in his hand, reached his chopsticks down and raised a large chunk of the saucy substance to his lips as he thought about Alzeti's offer. The Board of Supervisors' president, who stood about a foot shorter than Paulsey, remained quiet, but nervous.

Chewing the chunks of food slowly and looking over the crowd behind Alzeti, Paulsey smiled a broad smile as he swallowed and made his answer firm.

"I'm sorry, Madam President," he said. "But I don't think that would work. You're not quite our kind of people. Thanks for the offer, though."

With that, Paulsey closed the door, leaving Alzeti there to wonder if she had made a mistake. As she turned around, the blare of the camera lights and flashing photographer's bulbs caught her weak, defeated expression.

*   *   *

That night, all the TV and radio news reports opened with two stories. The first was on Alzeti entering the race, while the second focused heavily on her failure to convince the union to negotiate with her. Most broadcasts had a complete videotape of Paulsey coming to the door and slamming it in her face, as well as Alzeti turning around in defeat.

On Tuesday morning, her defeated expression also covered both daily newspapers, with headlines that read, "Alzeti jumps into recall race, but misses strike talks," in the *Journal* and the *Bulletin*'s "Alzeti throws hat in ring, but gets slammed by transit negotiations."

Both newspapers played up the news that Alzeti had joined the race, but even more so clearly reported her failed attempt to engage Paulsey in negotiations. Such a move just one day into the campaign would hurt her. But as she and Callahan both knew, without another candidate in the race, Alzeti could still remain a favorable choice if the strike continued and no one else joined the recall.

Billy Dale was not about to let that situation remain for long. Without realizing it, Alzeti had actually moved up Billy's plans. He knew that her boondoggle with Paulsey had opened the gate clearer and wider for Walter Beard.

After reading the Tuesday morning papers with glee, Billy set up a conference call with Beard and Paulsey on Tuesday afternoon, swearing both men to secrecy as he placed them on the line. Also listening was Jimmy Min, who engaged in the phone call with Billy from the *Advocate* offices.

"Here is the situation, gentleman, we are ready to roll," Billy said. "Walter, you know Sal Paulsey and Sal, I'm sure you've been in touch with Senator Beard on many occasions."

Both men responded affirmatively through the phone lines.

"Okay, here is the plan. Jimmy is going to run a major editorial on Wednesday urging Walter Beard to come in and fix the negotiations. It will not mention him as a mayoral candidate at all, only as a man known for bringing two sides together," Billy said, knowing Beard's reputation as a dealmaker in Sacramento. "Along with that, Mike McLean will write a column also urging such a move.

"Then, sometime Wednesday, Sal will agree to allow Beard to negotiate on behalf of the city, and, after a day or so of talks, you will agree to a new three-year contract for a six percent raise each year," Billy instructed as the parties listened. "But, the contract will include a small provision allowing it to be reopened after six months."

As Billy caught his breath, the other men remained quiet, soaking in all of the information.

"One week later, on March 13th, the last day to file for a spot in the recall, Beard will announce his candidacy," Billy said. "With our support, and Alzeti and Callahan looking like losers, we can make him win. Then, once he is in, he will work to reopen the contract and bring the raises up to nine percent per year."

"How does that sound?" Billy said with a smile. "Does that work?"

"Are you sure this can work?" Paulsey said, still nervous about putting his membership on the line. "Can you be certain?"

At the same time, both Beard and Jimmy Min gave the same answer. "When Billy Dale says he is sure, he is sure."

With that, all sides hung up the phones. Beard went off to cancel some appointments for Wednesday to make himself available for the press, while Paulsey met with his executive board to give them the update.

At the same time, Jimmy Min went back to work to write his editorial and Mike McLean began work on a column that would be entitled, "Senator Beard, Come To The Rescue."

*   *   *

On Wednesday morning, the picketers were out in force again as the fourth full day of the strike began, while thousands of commuters braved the walk, bicycle ride, and drive to work, with most getting there later than usual and continuing to grumble about it.

Both daily papers kept up with regular updates of the strike and continued coverage that showed no progress in contract talks. The *Reader*, which had yet to weigh in on the strike effort in print, launched its first attack on Callahan with a front-page headline that said, "Strike hits, Mayor misses."

The lengthy story by the *Reader*'s Penny Atkins detailed how the strike had evolved and how Callahan and Alzeti had each failed to engage the union in talks. The paper also took a mixed slam against both the union and the mayor.

"The unusual circumstances of this job action make clear that the transit workers are partly to blame for not using every negotiating tool to avoid a strike," the story said. "Meanwhile, Mayor Callahan, obviously stung politically by the refusal to bargain, shows his weak side at a time when voters are re-evaluating his ability."

But it was the *Advocate*'s coverage that day that would cause the most stir.

Across the top of the paper, above the nameplate, ran the editorial that would grab attention citywide. Titled, "Someone Help Us," the editorial urged Walter Beard to step forward and put his negotiating abilities to work.

"Senator Beard has spent two decades in Sacramento working deals for everything from health care to votes on legislative raises," the editorial stated. "If no one in San Francisco, especially the weak mayor, can't end this strike, perhaps he can."

From McLean, the message was similar. His front-page column demanded that Beard "Come forth and lend your abilities to the city you represent before the strike does further damage."

The *Advocate* also included several stories on the strike, Alzeti's candidacy, and her failed attempt to get involved in the negotiations. The photo of Alzeti being turned away by Paulsey also appeared prominently on Page One.

"This is it," Billy told Jimmy and McLean on Wednesday morning as the trio shared breakfast in the *Advocate* offices. "Now the action begins."

But responses to the *Advocate*'s calls for Beard were slow in coming. All day Wednesday, no one responded to the *Advocate*, and Beard himself received only a few calls from friends and supporters in San Francisco who had seen the paper. Most were just curious and a few urged Beard to come forward.

But that didn't worry Billy Dale. "Be patient," the veteran political operative told his volunteers. "Give them some time to do something with this."

Then on Thursday, it began.

Several callers to some local talk radio shows began to muse about the strike, the failed attempts by Callahan and Alzeti to negotiate, and the need for the strike to end. Most also commented on the *Advocate*'s push for Beard to come in.

By noon, the idea of Beard negotiating had become the hot topic of the day for the radio shows, as well as several online political chat rooms. By 1 p.m., one radio talk show host—Gary Deener—had taken the liberty of calling Beard's Sacramento office to get some response from him.

"We are trying to get the senator on the line," Deener told his audience as the secretary put him on hold while she asked Beard. "Hopefully, we can get some opinion from him on this strange twist and turn of events."

After a minute, Beard came on the line but remained reluctant. When Deener asked him about lending his efforts, he said simply, "I haven't done anything because I haven't been asked."

"But, sir, if you were asked, would you be willing to do something to help end the strike?" Deener asked on the air.

"Of course," the state senator said. "I would do anything to help the people of San Francisco, you know that."

After some more chatter, the interview ended and Deener put the message out.

"It looks like it is up to the city's management to bring Senator Beard into the mix," he told his audience. "But what of the union? Would they let him negotiate? We have to see."

At that moment, Deener's switchboard received a call from none other than Sal Paulsey, who happened to be hearing the talk show interview in his car. Paulsey, driving back to strike headquarters from a round of visits to the striking members, had pulled over and gotten on his cell phone the moment he'd heard that Beard had offered his services.

"Gary, Sal Paulsey here," the union president said when he was put through. "I just wanted to call to tell you that we would be more than happy to negotiate if Senator Beard is the man doing the negotiations for the city."

Deener couldn't believe what he was hearing. His show was becoming the focal point for a deal to possibly end the strike. After the show was over, Paulsey phoned Beard's office and the two men announced that they would begin negotiating Friday morning in San Francisco at the Fairmont Hotel.

Beard, who had many connections in every corner of San Francisco business, had formed a special relationship with the Fairmont after giving the hotel a special exemption from city hotel taxes in exchange for allowing him to use the facilities for parties, fund-raisers, and emergency meetings like this at no cost.

The only thing left now was to get Muni's consent. Muni Director Eric Kleiger, a staunch Callahan supporter, was not likely to turn over the negotiating power of the city to Walter Beard just like that. Sure, Callahan and Beard had no real problems in the past two years, or even before that when Callahan was police chief.

At this critical time, though, with a recall looming and a serious strike on hand, the mayor needed every chance he could get to make up political ground. Ending the strike seemed to be Callahan's last, best hope.

But, even Kleiger saw how desperate things were. The union was willing to hold out on its strike as long as necessary, and Callahan was virtually powerless without being able to negotiate. Late Thursday, meanwhile, Callahan and Kleiger had gotten some more bad news when their attempt to get a court order stopping the strike and ordering the union to negotiate failed.

The federal judge, who happened to be an old college roommate of Walter Beard's, ruled that the city had not done enough to meet the requests for a new negotiator. Now that Paulsey had said Beard was the preferred person, the city almost had to let him try.

"I think we need to use him," Kleiger told the mayor during a late meeting Thursday. "If Beard can end this walkout, we can do more to salvage a fight against the recall. Otherwise, we're sunk."

But Callahan wasn't buying it. He hated the idea of letting someone else come in and do his job, especially when he was fighting to hold on to it. He would not give his support to Beard's negotiation.

"I can't do it, Eric," the mayor said. "I know I have no power to tell you who to use as a negotiator, but this I won't support."

That didn't stop Kleiger. The Muni chief, who had hugged Callahan when he appointed him to run the transit system just two years earlier, now saw that the mayor's star was falling. He could see that, even if the strike ended now, Callahan had come under so much attack and had lost so much credibility with the union that his recall was almost assured.

"I'm sorry, Mr. Mayor, but we have to do what's best for the city," Kleiger told Callahan. "I think this is the best way."

With that, Kleiger left the mayor's office and went to his own office at Muni headquarters. After a couple of quick calls to Beard's and Paulsey's offices, the negotiating session was set for 8 a.m. Friday at the Fairmont. Muni sent out a brief statement to all news outlets announcing the choice of Beard and the place for the first session.

Paulsey also sent out a press statement that made clear the strike would continue, but that the union "has high hopes that a man of Senator Beard's stature and experience can help us forge a proper deal."

Although Beard, Paulsey, and the rest of the union's executive board knew exactly what they were going to do, they spent hours behind closed doors at the hotel to make it at least appear to be a real negotiating session. After three hours, the group came out ready to announce a settlement.

With a bank of microphones set up in the Fairmont lobby and a dozen TV cameras rolling, Beard and Paulsey, joined by Eric Kleiger, announced the deal: a new three-year contract with a 6% raise each year and other benefit and health improvements.

No one mentioned the provision allowing the contract to be reopened in six months.

"Why spoil a good thing?" Beard had asked Paulsey. "We got what we needed."

After the press conference, reporters traveled to City Hall to confront Mayor Callahan. Would he blast Beard for butting in? Thank him? Say nothing?

The group waited to see.

Finally, the mayor came out and made only a short, brief statement. "I'm glad to see that both sides have been able to work out an arrangement for the Muni strike to end," he read off an index card in a somber, low voice. "It's good to know that the people of San Francisco can rely on the transit system to overcome these conflicts."

As the mayor turned to walk away, one reporter yelled out, "What about Senator Beard?"

Hearing the comment, Callahan turned halfway around and said simply, "Yeah? What about him?" Then Callahan walked back to his office and closed the door.

That night, the TV and radio newscasts were brimming with stories about the strike's end, interviews with residents and union members, as well as Beard, Paulsey, and Eric Kleiger. All praised the fact that the strike was over.

At one point, during an impromptu press conference at union headquarters, Paulsey made the calculated comment to several TV reporters that Walter Beard should run for mayor.

Billy Dale had not even discussed with his cohorts how to maneuver Beard from the role of savior negotiator to one of mayoral candidate. But when Paulsey made the remark, Billy realized it was the way to go.

"This man has shown he can work for this city in a crisis," Paulsey said before three rolling news cameras. "He should run for mayor and replace the useless man we have there now."

When the reporters shoved their microphones at Beard for a reaction, all the senator could do was give a modest response. "Wait a minute, first things first," Beard said with false surprise. "Let's get Muni back and running, then we can figure out what's next."

But Billy, Jimmy Min, Mike McLean, and Beard's staff were already figuring it out. By noon on Sunday, March 10th—three days before the recall deadline to file as a candidate—Muni was back at full capacity and the strike was officially ended.

By 3 p.m., Billy, Jimmy, and Walter Beard were already planning the announcement Beard would make on Tuesday of his intention to run. The Sunday papers were filled with stories about the Muni union deal, with both the *Journal* and the *Bulletin* editorializing in favor of Beard.

Neither daily paper had mentioned support for Beard as a mayoral candidate. But each stressed the efficient and thought-out way Beard had managed to end the walkout.

"Many San Franciscans may forget because he is 90 miles away in Sacramento, but Walter Beard is one of the city's best political assets," the *Bulletin* editorialized. In the *Journal*, a similar editorial proclaimed Beard "a master of negotiation and deal-making."

Each paper also printed a story about Paulsey's assertions that Beard could win the recall election. That was enough to get the talk radio shows on Sunday chatting about the prospect of a Beard mayoral candidacy.

By Monday afternoon, the talk was overwhelming and some supporters were already sporting "Draft Beard" shirts, buttons, and bumper stickers. While Callahan continued to ignore that Beard even existed, and Alzeti strategized with her advisors about how to get her own campaign back on track, a virtual wall of publicity and pressure for Beard to enter the race was taking over the city.

Wherever you went in San Francisco, from coffeehouses to parks to cable cars, people were buzzing about the moves Beard had made to end the strike and the calls for him to run for mayor.

"It is a bit overwhelming," Beard told Billy Dale and Jimmy Min when the three men dined Monday night at Moose's, the upper-crust North Beach restaurant. "This is more than I ever thought."

Then, on Tuesday at noon, just one day before the deadline to file, Walter Beard made it official. In a quick press conference held with just an hour's notice to the press, Beard threw his hat into the ring.

Walking out of the steps of City Hall just minutes after he formally filed his papers to run, and picked up the petition that would need to be filled out, Walter Beard told the people of San Francisco that he wanted to be mayor.

"During the last few days, I have been inundated with requests for me to enter the race for mayor," Beard said. "As I faced the prospect of term limits next year, I had planned to retire and enjoy the rest of my days with family and friends.

"But after seeing how much San Francisco needs a change at the top and a leader who can restore order and smarts, I changed my mind," Beard said. "I have taken the steps to place my name as a candidate for mayor of this fine city. Although I normally oppose recalls as a misused tool in many cases, this time, I believe it is warranted. I seek your support and I look forward to proving myself worthy."

Standing right behind Beard, Jimmy Min and Billy Dale exchanged sly grins, the small crowd of supporters cheered and waved, and Beard put on a smile larger than he had ever had before.

Just one floor above the cheering and celebration stood Jack Callahan. Peering out of his City Hall office, he could see the celebration and joy below. For him, however, it was the lowest of the low. Not only had he been backstabbed by the transit union, but his own Muni chief had allowed someone else to come in and take the glory that he believed was his. Slamming his fist down on the window sill, Callahan cursed under his breath and bit his lip as he watched Beard and the others cheer with happiness.

"Sons of bitches," the mayor said to himself. "Well, I'm not going down without a fight. Yes, Billy Dale, you know how to play this game and you may have pulled ahead. But don't forget, I am one of those you taught how to play, and I learned it very well." ∎

Chapter Twenty-Nine

"Nothing Can Stop Me"

The make-up man dabbed just a hint of color to Jack Callahan's face as the mayor tried to stand still on the stage of the San Francisco City College auditorium.

"Hold still, Mr. Mayor," the man asked as Callahan relaxed slightly and let his hands drop to his sides. "Just one more second."

On either side of Callahan stood Walter Beard, getting a last-minute powder touchup to his face, and Marie Alzeti, who used a compact to dab some improvements under her eyes, while a young woman fixed her large, dark mop of hair.

The three candidates tried to appear at ease. But for Alzeti and Callahan, at least, their nervousness showed. All around them, stagehands and camera crews made last-minute changes to the set, while the large, mobile control room outside bustled with activity that compared to that of a Broadway show opening or the preparations for a circus.

Billy Dale, who sat calmly backstage, had himself often referred to politics as theater or a circus, especially in San Francisco. As he stood in the wings while watching Beard prep for that night's television debate—the first of four scheduled Q&A sessions—he couldn't help but feel confident.

Here it was, a month since the campaign began, and Beard was blowing away both the mayor and Alzeti. Ironically, this first debate had been scheduled for April 13th, one month after the candidate's deadline for entry, and one month before Election Day.

Since they both had filed to run, Alzeti and Beard had had no trouble getting the requisite 15,000 signatures needed to make the ballot. Beard and Billy had utilized the services of Jerry Fields once again and obtained the signatures within several days. For Alzeti, it had taken a bit longer, but with the help of the many homeless volunteers and homeless rights groups who had always backed her, the names were obtained within a week.

But since the race had formally begun, neither Alzeti nor Callahan had been able to make any headway on Beard's lead. Fresh off his victory as the savior of the transit strike, Beard's polling numbers had given him a 20 point margin of victory over Alzeti and Callahan. The last poll, conducted by the *Bulletin* just three days earlier, gave Beard 45% of the vote, with Callahan receiving 25% and Alzeti a mere 19%. The rest were undecided, but likely leaning to either Beard or Callahan.

The poll's other question, which was almost more important, was simply whether voters would recall Callahan. Since they had to decide two questions—whether Callahan should be recalled, and who should replace him—the first question was even more telling.

The same *Bulletin* poll showed that that question brought a closer result. While a majority, 51%, said they would vote to recall Callahan, another 41% said they would not, with the remainder undecided. That poll remained a little too close for Billy Dale, and he knew that his hardest work remained in the last month of the campaign.

Still, as Billy stood watching Beard and the other two prepare to take questions from the panel of reporters, and the audience, he couldn't help but feel energized.

The latest poll results were no accident. They were, as usual, the result of Billy's knack for exposing his opponent's weaknesses, piling on the negative ads and innuendos, and promoting his candidate's best.

During the past four weeks, Billy engineered a mix of TV and radio commercials and pamphlet distributions that hammered both Callahan's record as mayor, and Alzeti's reputation for high taxes and off-the-cuff remarks.

Using some of the same messages that he'd invoked just two years earlier while running Callahan's campaign, Billy had focused on Alzeti's previous gaffes as supervisor.

The first was her proposed 10% city income tax to fund a string of homeless shelters and programs for the poor. The proposal, which went to the ballot and lost, made her seem like a far-left liberal willing to tax and spend for anything.

Billy also gladly repeated the comments she'd made prior to that ballot measure vote, when she said: "If the people of San Francisco are so selfish that they won't give up their expensive dinners, BMWs, and vacations so some downtrodden folks can have a decent life, then I am ashamed of this city."

At the same time, Billy also brought up Alzeti's suggestion during the final weeks of the last mayoral campaign that the city change its charter to assure that 15% of the city's budget would be set aside for funding programs in the city's worst neighborhoods.

When that idea came out, several neighborhood groups had jumped on Alzeti. Even some of her staunchest supporters pulled out, worried that she would radically change the city's budget process and might deny valuable resources such as police and fire protection, which are always hot-button issues.

Billy knew that harping on those items in campaign literature and on TV would knock Alzeti's numbers down.

As for Callahan, Billy took the same approach he had during the petition drive, only more so. Using the mayor's inability to stop the transit strike, mixed with Beard's efforts to end it, Billy had a simple one-versus-the-other approach. One pamphlet showed photos of Beard and Callahan, with a list of criteria under each and an example of how Beard had met such criteria, and Callahan had not.

For example, one section used the word Leadership. Under Beard's photo, the item said "Headed the California State Senate for 10 years, masterminded several state tax reductions, and single-handedly ended the Muni strike."

Under Callahan's photo, the pamphlet slammed the mayor hard, saying "Failed to implement heralded homeless plan, succumbed to pressure to approve environmentally questionable Hunter's Point development, and was unable to negotiate a settlement to the recent Muni strike."

The pamphlet's last comparison had been the most controversial, and had sparked Callahan to publicly call Billy a "scum without morals." It used the word Criminal and, under Beard's photo stated "Ethically spotless record of government service."

Below Callahan's image, however, the pamphlet read, "Questions remain over his role in the cover-up of Glenda Callahan's death."

"That is beneath contempt," Callahan told several TV stations when he received a copy of the pamphlet. "I was publicly exonerated after my wife's tragic death and never accused of anything. For Billy Dale to use this to obtain votes is inhumane."

But, as with so many of Billy's plots and ploys, the ethical standards were ignored and, as he predicted, the polls went down for the mayor. Now that the first debate approached, Billy sat confident that his man was in the right place.

Just after 7 p.m., the debate began. The crowd was filled with a mix of Alzeti, Beard, and Callahan supporters. All of them had been warned by Moderator Don Canton, a news anchor at KNSF–TV, to be civil and not applaud until the end.

The panel of reporters included Justin Swan of the *Bulletin*, Penny Atkins of the *Reader*, and KLSF Radio City Hall reporter Jane Leonard.

Callahan and Beard stood, both in dark, blue suits, well-combed hair, and smiles on their faces. But that was where the resemblance ended. While Beard was the picture of confidence and suave demeanor, Callahan was a nervous wreck.

The mayor had done well to hide his feelings. But inside he was suffering from a mix of anger at Billy Dale for his negative attacks and a sense of failure as he felt he was sitting idly by and watching the mayor's office slowly drift away.

As for Alzeti, she seemed to be glad that she was even in the race after two failed attempts at the city's highest office. She struck an attractive pose in a dark, yet colorful print dress and matching shoes. Looking out into the noisy and packed audience, she wished only that her father, the former mayor Carlo Alzeti, could see what she had accomplished. She'd originally gotten into politics at her father's insistence and always felt she had never measured up.

Alzeti hoped that she could make some kind of race out of this and prove his hopes right. She had taken many hits for her support of the poor and homeless and her efforts to provide more medical care, housing, and education to the downtrodden, all the time knowing that such proposals would make enemies of the rich and powerful, the business tycoons, and corporate power brokers who controlled the city's direction.

Still, she remained proud that she had done it all with her best intentions and with her conscience clean. "Whatever happens," she told a group of supporters during a fundraiser the night before. "I'll be glad that we did it for the right cause."

At precisely 7:02 p.m., the house lights went down and the cameras rolled. After a short introduction by Canton, the debate was on. The format had each reporter ask a question of one of the candidates, giving the other two the chance for rebuttal.

Over the next hour, Beard remained in control. When asked how he would handle issues from housing to Muni to crime, Beard was able to take an example from his legislative days and use it to offer a similar solution at the city level.

When asked about improving housing for the poor, Beard cited a bill he'd authored and shepherded through the legislature that took a percentage of the state's cigarette tax and set it aside for poor housing. The result had been more than $400 million in additional funding for low-income homes, resulting in about 10,000 new housing units statewide each year.

When Alzeti and Callahan were asked the same question, neither could offer a solution other than new taxes or, in Callahan's case, his homeless plan, which provided only more shelter beds and did nothing for new housing.

Such a response by Callahan brought Beard's stinging retort of "A shelter is not a home, a home is a place where you can feel family, love, and confidence. A shelter bed is nothing more than an army barracks."

The harsh comment drew a wave of applause from the audience.

By the end of the night, Beard had slammed both opponents hard, using only their records and his to fuel the fight.

Beard also managed to expound on several proposals he had made within the past month, all of which had also been promoted in TV commercials and pamphlets sent to voters. They targeted crime, housing, and jobs—the three most important issues to voters, according to research that Billy Dale had recently conducted.

Simply put, Beard's proposals would seek to cut spending on items he considered excessive, such as executive department benefits, city promotion of the arts and special events, and public relations. Beard even vowed to give up his chauffeured mayoral town car to make more money available.

With the extra funds, he had laid out a plan to boost teacher salaries and hire more of them, add 200 new police to the 2,000-member police force, and construct 1,000 new affordable housing units.

"I have shown in the past that I can lead legislation through and provide meaningful, worthwhile programs," Beard said in his closing statement. "Mayor Callahan and Supervisor Alzeti have shown they love this city, and I believe they do. But sometimes it takes more than love, it takes commitment and the ability to get the job done."

After that soliloquy, there was little Alzeti and Callahan could do but try to pick up the pieces of their campaigns. Each offered meaningless accolades to the city and attempts to show some of the minor accomplishments they had made during their respective terms, but they were no match for Beard.

When the debate ended, a rush of applause, cheers, and some boos swept through the auditorium and up to the stage. The three candidates met in the middle, shaking hands and talking, although Callahan kept a clear distance from Beard.

Each had a different spin on what the debate had meant.

For Alzeti, it still meant hope that her beliefs and drive for the underdog could mean something. For Callahan, it further drove him down into the pits of hopelessness. And for the always-confident Beard, it again reassured his belief that nothing could stop him.

But, as both Billy Dale and Jack Callahan had come to realize in the past few years, it is the unexpected in politics that can do the most damage.

*   *   *

In general, most newspapers exaggerate the importance of their endorsements. But that doesn't stop them from continuing to offer support for candidates, even though few voters give them any credence.

"Endorsements are just newspapers patting themselves on the back and trying to use their perceived power to get politicians on their side," Billy Dale had once told Callahan during the mayor's first campaign. "The truth is, they look good in print, but few voters give them any value."

Still, such political truths about endorsements did not stop the city's four major newspapers from offering theirs in the recall election.

One week had passed since the first mayoral debate when the last paper finally came forth with its editorial-page support. From almost the first day of the campaign, the *Advocate* had let it be known that it would back Walter Beard, while the *Reader* had made it clear that Alzeti was its candidate—just like two years earlier.

And, as most expected, the *Journal* paid back the mayor for his Hunter's Point approval by offering its support on the editorial page, but not until after the first debate. Donald Grossman hesitated only slightly on giving such backing to the mayor, until Callahan himself called to remind him what his priorities should be.

"After what I did for you, you should declare me the winner on Election Day no matter what the outcome," Callahan had told the *Journal* publisher. "I need to count on that backing or you may find some surprise loophole that blocks your project."

Just a day earlier, Grossman had driven past the Hunter's Point Shipyard site himself and nodded with approval when he saw the last of the toxic clean-up crews wrapping up. To everyone's surprise, the toxic removal had been done ahead of schedule—at least the removal that was required by law.

Callahan, still slightly nervous and irritated about his sudden opposition, the recall itself, and Beard's ability to rise in the polls out of nowhere, had taken it upon himself to ensure the endorsement was there. If this had been a regular election, the mild-mannered, politically-naive Callahan would likely have just waited for the *Journal*'s expected show of support.

But after the year he'd been through, the mayor grew impatient and weary, choosing to lay it on the line with Grossman as quickly as possible.

"Don't worry, mayor," a flustered and irritated Grossman said when the mayor put forth his demand. "We will be behind you 100%."

Sure enough, the next day, the *Journal* proclaimed Callahan, "the best man for the job," and derided Billy Dale's recall campaign as "mean-spirited and vengeful."

But, while the *Advocate*, the *Journal*, and the *Reader* had given out their choices for mayor, the *Bulletin* remained mum until just three weeks before the election. When the morning paper finally did support a candidate, there was little surprise about who it would be.

Ever since the whole Hunter's Point development fight, Emily Ingle had sent editor J.T. Townsend regular orders to press the negative aspects of the development, and later of Callahan himself when the recall officially began.

On this day, the *Bulletin* went so far as to place its endorsement on the top of the front page, a rare move for a newspaper. The editorial, written again by Townsend, declared Walter Beard "the man of action and the man with ideas for San Francisco," while describing the mayor as "someone who lost his chance and took the city down the wrong path."

As for Alzeti, the *Bulletin* editorial gave her only a passing nod, saying that she "showed great love for the people of San Francisco, but not enough serious planning or fiscal responsibility to make government work."

Now that the endorsements were public, the newspapers began the traditional dance of writing supportive stories for their candidates, while seeking to knock down the opposition. The *Bulletin* and the *Journal* had each done it two and a half years earlier when they supported William Carlson and took shots at Callahan, while the *Advocate* had had a field day slamming Carlson during its previous support of Callahan.

As for the *Reader*, Danny Dugan had gone after both Carlson and Callahan in his support of Alzeti during the previous election, but with few major blows.

This time, Dugan wanted things to be different.

He was glad to see Callahan falling down and out, but became ill at the thought of Beard taking over. Dugan had despised Beard from afar during Beard's years as a state senator and senate president, regularly hitting him on the editorial page for everything from his tight connections to the insurance industry and tobacco lobbyists to his taste for expensive clothes.

"Senator Beard has gained prominence in Sacramento as a dealmaker, and rightly so. He is the Monty Hall of the California State Senate," a recent editorial in the *Reader* had proclaimed. "But public service is not supposed to be about deals, it is supposed to be about people and serving them to the best of one's ability. Walter Beard can't deal with that one."

Two days after the last endorsement came out, Dugan began his pursuit of Beard, going through old boxes of campaign expenditure records, stories about Beard, and past issues of the *Reader*, the *Advocate*, the *Bulletin*, and the *Journal*, all of it in the hope that he could get something with which to nail him.

But, in addition to his deal-making and political maneuvering skills, Walter Beard also acquired the uncanny knack of never doing anything illegal, or even close to improper. For 20 years, newspaper reporters from Sacramento to San Diego had hunted through every corner of Beard's finances, voting records, and personal life in search of some nugget of scandal, but to no avail.

"Turn me inside out," Beard had once told reporters during a press conference prior to his last senatorial re-election campaign. "I'm an open book, but all the pages are clean."

That frustrated Dugan even more as he slumped down in his chair during the early morning hours of April 21st, wiped the sweat from his face, and let out a great sigh of frustration and exhaustion. Glancing up at the clock above his desk inside the *Reader* offices, he saw that it read 2:30 a.m. He knew he had been at this for a while, but didn't realize how late it had gotten.

Standing up with a grunt, Dugan leaned over and picked up one of the 35 or so boxes he had been lugging from the newspaper's archive and morgue room since 9 p.m. On this day—three weeks before the recall election—Dugan was busy doing research on all three mayoral candidates, but especially on Beard.

The boxes held little hope has he dug through the papers, documents, and reports in search of some morsel, some scrap, some whisper of trouble. But none were found.

Earlier in the day, *Journal* reporter Ty Davis—who normally held the investigative beat—had also begun digging up dirt on Beard. Although Donald Grossman and Tim Cross did not hold out hope that Callahan could overcome Beard's mountainous opposition, they knew that they had better do something if they wanted to keep their best city hall supporter alive.

Davis, who had shunned politics as frivolous—choosing to do stories on environmental scams, school district corruption, and the waste of government programs—had been chosen by Cross to take on the effort. But after more than 12 hours in the paper's clipping morgue, and on the phone with Beard political rivals in Sacramento and San Francisco, Davis had also drawn a blank.

"I would love to give you something, but the guy is as slippery as a fuckin' seal," one state senator known for his hatred of Beard had told Davis that morning. "I wish you luck."

But luck was not what Davis or Danny Dugan needed. They needed something to shoot at this rising star. Neither one, however, believed it would happen. It seemed that Callahan was sinking fast, Alzeti was still trying to tread water, and Walter Beard had smooth sailing ahead.

Beard was so confident of his victory that he nearly skipped the third and final debate, held two weeks before the election, opining confidentially to Billy Dale that his appearance could cause more harm than good if something unforeseen were to happen.

But Billy knew better. He knew from past experiences that no victory is final and no politician can afford to look too confident. "The worst thing is to appear like you think you've got it won," Billy told Beard. "The best thing is to appear humble enough to go to each debate, appearance, and community gathering. Voters love humble, they eat it up."

So Beard joined Callahan and Alzeti in the last debate, which proved to be even more triumphant than the first two. He pushed forth his various plans, took hidden shots at both opponents' failure to solve the transit strike, and even threw in a good jab at the mayor for his New Year's Eve attack on Billy Dale.

"I don't think the mayor should remain in office, but I think he does have a future in the boxing world," Beard had said during the debate when asked what he thought of Callahan's tenure. It received a rousing mix of boos and cheers.

After the debate, instead of huddling in their campaign headquarters to go over his performance, Beard, Billy Dale, Mike McLean, and Jimmy Min chose to take a night off and headed straight for the trendy South of Market neighborhood. Their jaunt spanned several nightclubs and restaurants, ending at Eddie's, one of the newer hot spots that gained some fame by allowing patrons to keep glasses behind the bar with their names on them.

When Beard and his cohorts entered, the bartender presented Beard with a glass with his name and the label "Mayor." Beard smiled, but knew that he could not be seen drinking out of the glass and asked the bartender to hold it until after the election.

But Beard's group still managed to take over a large table and celebrate into the wee morning hours. By midnight, the place was packed since it was a Friday night. Beard, not one to drink much in his day, had partaken of champagne and wine and became mellow enough to begin spouting his beliefs on many things.

His chatter, humor, and outlandish attacks on the mayor as he sipped his libations drew interest from patrons at other tables, who leaned or walked over to listen. After a while, Beard was surrounded and getting cheers and laughs for his comments from a large crowd of admirers.

"This is better than a TV commercial," Billy whispered to Jimmy Min. "The man is a magnet for voters."

At just after 1 a.m., a TV news crew from KBSA TV— which had been reporting on the debate all evening—stopped into Eddie's. Since they had finished their work for the evening and filed their final report, they decided to have a late dinner and a nightcap at the trendy spot.

The moment the crew walked in and saw Beard surrounded by cheering and supportive crowds, reporter Lange Jones saw the potential for getting a little extra perspective on the evening's activities. He knew that Beard was being portrayed as a humble candidate who did not believe he had the election won.

But, deep down, Jones knew that that was not Beard's style. He knew that the senator thought he was God's gift to San Francisco and might be more willing to speak freely about it as the late hours wore on.

Quickly returning to the news van to retrieve the camera and tape equipment they had just put away, Lange and his crew entered Eddie's and immediately approached Beard's table. Normally one to keep the press on their toes and masterfully talk around or avoid a question he didn't like, Beard would probably have simply had the news crew thrown out on any other occasion.

But tonight, as pending victory, alcohol, fatigue, and ego took control, Beard relished the attention the news crew was giving and agreed to let Lange Jones eavesdrop.

"Hey, Lange, long time," Beard said with a slight slur. "How'd we do to-night? Kicked some ass, right?"

As Beard laughed, Jones just smiled back and nodded, then hit Beard with every question he could that might catch him off guard. As usual, Beard deflected each with confidence, and gave thoughtful, provocative answers to those he chose to acknowledge.

For about 15 minutes, Beard was on, nailing every question, drawing more supporters to his table, and getting louder by the minute.

Then he hit one too many.

When Lange Jones asked Beard straight out why he thought his chances of beating Alzeti and Callahan were so good, his answer came out like a shotgun blast.

"Because this nigger is so good, nothing can stop me," Beard said.

"I beat'em all before and I'll beat'em now. That mick and that lasagna lady don't stand a chance."

With that, the crowd around Beard burst into applause, as did the rest of the half-empty bar. But Jones just turned around and looked at his cameraman with an amazed mix of glee and surprise.

Walter Beard had just slurred his own race and the ethnic backgrounds of his two opponents. In liberal, diverse, and often-P.C. San Francisco, that was among the worst missteps ever.

Even Billy Dale, who was sitting just across from the mayor, realized he had gone too far. But, in Billy's drunken state, he did little that night to react, just laughed along.

The next day, however, the fallout was just beginning. Although it was a Saturday, the story still blew out all over the city.

KBSA first launched it during its 6 a.m. Saturday news, then followed during a break in the network Saturday morning news. By 8 a.m., each radio station had taped the remarks from TV, while all other TV stations had gotten a copy from KBSA, with the simple requirement that they give credit to the station.

When Billy Dale woke up in a hangover stupor at around 11 a.m., the news was all over the city and both supporters and opponents were calling the campaign to complain. When he arrived at his office at about Noon, Billy had 50 phone messages, including 22 from supporters who wanted to know what the hell had happened.

"I was going to vote for Walter Beard, but now I don't want that kind of man in City Hall," one message from a woman in the Sunset District stated. "You can keep him and his mouth."

After hearing all of the messages, Billy was worried again. This was worse than any transit strike. Worse even, in some ways, than the mayor punching

Billy on New Year's Eve.

The first thing Billy did was call Beard at home. Although the senator had been out late, he always arose by at least 8 a.m., especially on Saturday. The campaign had only a half day's worth of events, but Beard still liked to rise and shine early.

When Billy called him, Beard had already gotten the bad news from several radio and TV broadcasts but didn't seem as nervous as Billy.

"I know, I know, but this can blow away, we can talk it away as just a humorous comment," Beard told his campaign manager. "Don't worry, we have enough on this guy and this broad to keep them out. I've got concrete plans, a record of achievement, and that transit strike settlement. People don't care about this."

But Billy knew better. He had been in San Francisco long enough to realize that anyone suspected of being anything other than a politician open to diversity and freedom of expression was doomed.

Billy told Beard that he would have to apologize and seek forgiveness from voters. He had seen how such an apology had helped Callahan after the punching incident. And, since the election was less than two weeks away, the chance for this incident to stick in peoples' minds at the polls was likely.

But Beard would not budge. Although he had mastered the art of appearing humble, he was all ego. He believed that he deserved this job, had earned it, and was not about to beg.

"No fuckin' way, Billy," Beard said. "If they don't like it, fuck 'em."

Billy tried to argue, but Beard wouldn't listen. After about 15 minutes of back-and-forth discussion, Beard said he wanted to get off the phone. He told Billy he would meet him 10 minutes before a scheduled 3 p.m. campaign appearance that day at a church group meeting in the Mission District.

That was the only campaign event of the day, other than a dinner before the local Rotary Club that night. Billy hemmed and hawed, but agreed.

"Okay, Senator," Billy said. "But think about what I said. You need to do this or it could be all over."

Beard muttered something about thinking about it, but hung up without a confirmed answer. Once Billy got off the phone with Beard, he immediately called Lange Jones and chewed him out for trying to ambush the mayor at a late-night bar.

"You son of a bitch, that was a cheap shot," Billy told Jones, who was working over the weekend on a lengthy campaign round-up story for Sunday night. "Where do you get off with that bullshit? We are going to sue your ass, and when we win, buy the station and fire you."

Jones, who was editing videotape when Billy called, just let him rant. He knew from experience that anyone with a complaint about a news story just needed to get it off his chest. He also knew that Billy wouldn't and couldn't sue over this. After Billy's bitching ended, Jones asked him if he was finished.

When Billy said yes, Jones thanked him for his comments and hung up.

Over the next few hours, the story grew more and more. Talk radio stations were jammed with callers both blasting the senator's comments and trying to defend them. Radio reports continued to play the sound bite from the bar over and over again.

For Billy Dale and Walter Beard, the incident meant non-stop phone calls from angry voters to campaign headquarters, Beard's apartment, Billy's house, and even the *Advocate* offices.

One message Jimmy Min found on his office voice mail said simply, "You fuckers can die for supporting that loud-mouth racist."

"That guy has to calm down and fix this," Jimmy told Billy over the phone that afternoon after hearing the messages.

Billy agreed but told Jimmy of Beard's refusal. "He won't back down," he said. "He thinks he is unstoppable."

Beard's mind changed slightly, however, when he appeared at the church group meeting at St. Anthony's Cathedral later that day. Outside of the church, a large group of protesters had formed, with picket signs that bashed Beard and his previous night's words.

The signs spouted attacks such as "Senator Big Mouth," "We don't want a bigot mayor," and "Walter lasagna–hater." As Beard stepped out of a limousine, the boos and yells began and grew louder as he entered the church.

A sea of microphones and inquiring reporters with pads and pens leaped on Beard as he walked up the steps to the church. For a moment, he tried to respond, but the noise from the crowd drowned out his words.

After five minutes, Beard just smiled, waved, and went inside. But once he entered the basement where the group of 30 church leaders, teens, and parishioners were waiting, things didn't get much better.

While Beard had come to talk about lowering taxes, improving schools, and public safety—and brag about his transit strike settlement—this group simply wanted to know why he had said what he did.

Beard tried to respond by claiming he was ambushed by the press and was only making jokes. But the crowd didn't buy it. Finally, after 20 minutes, Beard said, "Well, if you don't want to talk issues, maybe I should leave."

When the senator went outside, the protest crowd had almost doubled and was blocking half of Anza Street with noisy chants, horns, and even a few whistles. Some people had also brought bullhorns.

"Beard must go! Beard must go!" were among the chants. But the loudest bullhorn came from Marie Alzeti herself. In several of the news reports that day, Alzeti had been quoted as despising Beard's reference to her Italian ancestry and demanding an apology.

Now she stood next to Beard on the church steps and made her case again. Raising the bullhorn to her mouth and quieting the crowd with her hands, Alzeti took her shot.

"Senator, will you acknowledge that your comments were improper and out of line and apologize?" Alzeti bellowed. "Do you admit they were wrong and a sign of a racist nature, something that is unacceptable for a San Francisco mayor?"

Beard just ignored Alzeti and tried to take her bullhorn away. When she jerked it back in defiance, Beard gave her a mean stare, then cupped his hands around his mouth to shout to the crowd.

"I am not a racist or a prejudiced person," Beard yelled as the crowd continued to chant. "I said nothing wrong. I was ambushed and my words were taken out of context."

But the crowd didn't want to hear it. As the chanting and protesting continued, Billy Dale just took Beard and led him to the car. He could see the crowd and Alzeti were on top of this and Beard could not win. Better to get him out of there and regroup, Billy thought, than to make things worse.

As the limousine pulled away, Alzeti put her hand up in triumph and pumped the crowd up more. Inside the limo, Beard was cursing frantically.

Billy just hoped that this would prove to Beard that he needed to apologize and try to pick up the pieces of this incident. But the senator was still not ready to turn around.

"No Goddamn way!" he yelled as the car rumbled up Nob Hill toward Billy's offices on the other side of town. "I didn't do anything other than make a fuckin' joke. People know my record of equal rights, diversity, and fairness. For Christ's sake, I appointed more blacks, Italians, Jews, and Irish to posts in the senate than anyone."

Billy knew that, and made a mental note to get that out in the next campaign response and pamphlet. But he also knew that people's perceptions of a candidate were all that mattered. Billy had used perception to help his clients, and knew he needed to find a way to fight it for this one.

Saturday night at the Rotary Club dinner, things continued. Another loud crowd, led by Alzeti, was in front of the club's building when Beard pulled up that evening.

Inside, the Rotarians were a bit more civil than the picketing crowd outside, but they lodged the same questions that Beard had received at St. Anthony's. Although Beard threw in the information he had mentioned to Billy about the diversity of his past Senate appointees, the crowd still didn't care.

"That's like saying, 'Some of my best friends are Italians,'" one Rotarian stated. "We need to know that you will be fair to everyone, and so far your words don't show it."

Afterward, as Billy and Beard shared a ride home to their respective residences, Beard still refused to apologize. This was just 10 days before the election, and Billy knew it was getting down to the wire.

But Billy also knew that it might be better to let Beard sleep on it. He canceled all campaign appearances for Sunday, realizing that the campaign had to do something to get some damage control on this.

On Sunday morning, Billy went into high gear, appearing on three local public affairs shows and six radio interviews between 8 a.m. and noon. On each, he stated publicly that Beard's remarks were offensive, but meant only to be humorous. He also mentioned on each appearance that Beard's record of appointments was the most diverse in the Senate's history.

"Walter Beard has a distinguished career of public service, with a cornerstone of diversity and fair play," Billy told one radio interviewer. "He also has a sense of humor that, at times, might be misconstrued. But I stress that his leadership, plans, and experience are what's best for San Francisco."

But it still didn't work. Callers to radio and TV call-in shows remained divided about 4-to-1 against Beard, with many wondering why Beard had not spoken publicly himself on Sunday and had not apologized.

"This guy can't be so pompous that he won't say he's sorry when he should," one caller said. "At least the mayor admitted when he was wrong."

It was calls like that that worried Billy further. First Alzeti had begun to get good campaign mileage out of this by leading the protests and painting herself as a martyred Italian. Now some were comparing Beard's comments to Callahan's New Year's Eve incident, and giving the mayor more credit for admitting he was wrong.

The Sunday papers didn't help, either. Although the *Bulletin*, which had endorsed Beard, didn't editorialize against the comments, it did run a large Page One story on the statements, reaction, and calls for an apology.

At the *Journal*, where Donald Grossman was beginning to think Callahan might have a chance, the slam came hard in the form of a page-long editorial, a front-page story, and two columnist attacks on Beard.

The editorial called Beard's actions "unacceptable, mean-spirited, and representative of an opinion that is dangerous to city politics."

Neither the *Advocate* nor the *Reader* had published yet, and would not until Wednesday. But both Jimmy Min and Danny Dugan were busy figuring out how best to play the story to suit their needs.

In Jimmy's case, he needed some good damage control and met with Billy for several hours on Sunday afternoon to brainstorm. For Danny Dugan, deciding how best to blast Beard and boost Alzeti was the priority.

Beard, meanwhile, kept a low profile on Sunday under orders from Billy. He spent the day in Sacramento, playing golf, reading, and contemplating what to do. He was not ready to apologize, but he knew this would have to change.

Callahan also had offered little in the way of response, telling one radio reporter who caught up with him Sunday that Beard's comments "showed his true colors and should be seriously re-considered by voters."

But the mayor stopped short of calling for Beard to drop out of the race or apologize, choosing instead to throw some praise to voters by saying "San Franciscans are smart enough to decide if he deserves the job. They will make the right choice."

On Monday morning, the final fallout from Beard's comments came down. The *Journal*, still seeking to gain as much ground from the recent events for Callahan as possible, had commissioned a last-minute overnight poll during Saturday and Sunday morning. The paper had hired a pollster to do a quick survey of 1500 likely voters.

The results were partly what was expected and partly a complete surprise.

As anticipated, Beard's popularity had dropped severely. Instead of having a 20% lead over the mayor and nearly 30% over Alzeti, Beard now stood virtually even.

But, even more surprising: instead of Callahan reaping the benefit of Beard's demise, it was Alzeti who had benefitted from Beard's gaffe. The poll showed the mayor remaining at about 25%, with Beard pulled down to 28%. But for Alzeti, the poll had drawn her up to 27%, just under Beard and nearly twice as much as an earlier poll. The remaining 20% were undecided.

The poll had also asked those siding with either Callahan or Alzeti if they had previously planned to vote for Beard. More than half of the Alzeti voters, and a third of the Callahan voters, had said they would have voted for Beard prior to his comments at the bar.

"That is a confirmation that the senator's comments are having an effect," the *Journal* had written in an accompanying story. "It would seem that the public is not too fond of Senator Beard."

And Billy Dale knew it. With the poll results in hand, Billy went to visit Beard in Sacramento on Monday morning and cornered him in his palatial suburban home. Beard had expected Billy to use the poll against him and, despite his efforts to remain unapologetic, Beard realized that he had to make amends if he wanted to go forward.

That afternoon, Billy scheduled a press conference at his office for 3 p.m. sharp. At the appointed hour, the same press cameras, microphones, and scribbling reporters showed up.

At 3:15 p.m., Beard entered the room in one of his sharpest suits, with one of his most subdued ties, shined shoes, and smelling of his best cologne. His facial expression, however, was far from the usually cheerful and combative repose with which he usually greeted the press.

This appearance was one he had not wanted to make. As Beard approached the bank of microphones that had been placed on a long conference table in Billy's main meeting room, light bulbs flashed and video cameras whirred to life.

Beard offered only a shy wave of the hand, then pulled out a piece of paper.

"I have asked you here so that I can make a prepared statement," the senator said in a low, quiet tone. "On Friday, I made some comments about my two worthy opponents to a news crew that have been taken in an offensive matter. While I meant no harm by my words, and would never have sought to offend the ethnic background of anyone, I see why they might have been taken in the wrong context."

"Anyone who knows me knows that I have a boastful, outgoing nature and a strong sense of humor. Any comments I made were done simply in that vein," Beard continued, stopping shortly to cough. "However, if these comments did offend or put anyone in a bad light, I am profoundly sorry. I hope that we can put this matter behind us and get on with seeking to make San Francisco a better place. Thank you."

Once Beard ended his statement, he folded up the piece of paper and placed it in his pocket before walking away. Although the reporters tried to get more comments from the senator, shouting questions about what impact he thought the comments would have, and if he had seen the *Journal* poll, Beard ignored them, waved goodbye and left the building.

As his limousine rolled up Van Ness Avenue, Beard pulled the statement he had just made from his pocket, crumpled it up, and threw it out the window. Staring out at the passing street signs, buildings, and people walking about, he could only whisper his thoughts to himself.

"Shit!" he said under his breath. "Those idiots will eat up anything." ∎

Chapter Thirty

An About Face

For the final week of the campaign, all sides were in hot pursuit of votes, support, and money. Each campaign had raked in nearly $100,000 in the final month, with Beard pulling in close to $200,000 during the last four weeks.

Even after his bar commentary, the state senator had been able to average about $1,000 per day while Callahan and Alzeti each kept donations at a close rate themselves. No more debates were scheduled, but the candidates were on the road non-stop with appearances at bus and subway stops, neighborhood group meetings, and rallies from City Hall to Golden Gate Park.

Billy even resurrected his police bus tour, but with about 10 fewer cops. Some of those who had ridden before said they were still mad about Beard's comments at Eddie's and were jumping ship. Still, the support continued to grow in other areas as many of the undecided offered support to all three candidates.

Each of the major newspapers also put on the final attacks during the last week, with the *Reader* and the *Advocate* utilizing nearly all of the news space in their April 7 editions—published the Wednesday before Election Day—to slam Callahan and push their candidates' images.

The *Reader* reprinted its full-page endorsement of Alzeti, along with a full-page assault on Callahan and Beard. The Alzeti endorsement called her "the only candidate with a heart." The issue also included blown-up photos of Beard in the Eddie's Bar incident and Callahan punching Billy Dale.

"This city needs someone who will care about the people, not take improper action when put on the spot," an editorial by Danny Dugan stated. "Marie Alzeti has the courage, caring, and heart to do the job."

The *Advocate*, always more blunt and direct in its attacks, used a similar approach but ran the photo of Callahan punching Billy Dale smack dab on the front page, with the headline "Fight Back: The Real Reasons for Recalling Jack Callahan".

The issue contained another Jimmy Min editorial against the mayor, a story on the latest election news, polls, and anti-Callahan sentiment, plus a hard-slamming column by Mike McLean that called Callahan "a hood," Alzeti "a wimp," and Walter Beard "the best and brightest hope."

"San Francisco cannot put up with the poor performance of Jack Callahan or the politically naive beliefs of Marie Alzeti," McLean wrote. "Walter Beard is the only one who can do it. Don't let him get away."

The *Bulletin* and the *Journal* also offered daily coverage throughout the final week, with the *Journal* playing up Beard's embarrassing comments and the *Bulletin* focusing on Callahan's New Year's Eve actions and other negative moments during his term, including the mystery surrounding Glenda's death and the Hunter's Point Shipyard vote.

"Two key parts of Mayor Callahan's first term remain shrouded in mystery," a *Bulletin* editorial stated. "Although no evidence exists linking the mayor to his wife's death or any shenanigans at Hunter's Point, the uncertainty over both situations leaves enough of a question for voters to wonder if he can be trusted to remain in office."

A poll published in the *Bulletin* on Sunday, April 11th, two days before Election Day, showed Beard with a slight lead at 33%, Callahan at 31%, and Alzeti still contending with 29%, leaving only 7% undecided. While Beard's apology had helped lift him slightly, it had not gotten him out of the woods yet as the final vote approached.

More importantly, however, were the results from a second question in the same poll on recalling Callahan. When asked if the mayor should be removed, voters remained closely divided, with 45% responding yes, 46% saying no, and 9% undecided.

As Billy, Callahan, and Beard knew, Beard and Alzeti's popularity didn't mean anything unless voters first chose to recall Callahan under the two-question recall election format. Beard could get 99% of the vote on the selection of a replacement for Callahan, but if voters didn't first vote to remove the mayor, it didn't matter.

"That means we have to go full tilt for 48 hours," Billy told his campaign crew. "Every voter must be called, precincts covered with literature, door-knocking and ads, and a major TV and radio ad push."

Billy also planned his standard service of driving voters to the polls but made sure not to even hint that the free ride was in exchange for a vote. During the previous mayoral election, some of William Carlson's campaign team had accused Billy of offering rides to seniors and the disabled with the clear message that they had to vote for Callahan.

"We're not going to give the opposition any reason to question any vote," Billy told his volunteers on Monday morning. "I want no slip-ups and no potential votes lost."

All day Monday, Callahan, Alzeti, and Beard crisscrossed San Francisco, offering handshakes, donuts and coffee, and speeches to anyone who would listen.

Beard even took the chance to speak aboard a cable car as it ran up Powell Street. When the conductor advised him that most of the passengers were likely tourists who couldn't vote, Beard said simply, "Hey, I'll take any votes I can get. Maybe they will tell a friend."

Alzeti kept her bullhorn theme going by carrying the electronic device from appearances in the Bayview to a coffee klatch in Pacific Heights. In between, as she was driven around in her town car, she kept the window open and yelled out to pedestrians with the bullhorn, demanding that they "Vote for me, please!"

For Callahan, the final day also meant pressing the flesh and getting out the vote, but with the clear message to vote no on the recall question and no comment on his two opponents.

Although all three campaigns continued to run the same ads, Beard and Callahan surprised many with new TV spots that began Monday and ran for only one day. Callahan's ad, produced with help from Carl Devins, took a direct shot at Beard's bar tirade

Showing a freeze-frame from the video of Beard at Eddie's, which depicted a disheveled Beard slurring his words and obviously out of it, the ad asked viewers if they "wanted a mayor who doesn't care who he hurts."

In Beard's case, Billy Dale's classic mix of mudslinging and a go-for-the-jugular attack made no bones about his slam. The TV spot opened with a photo of Callahan on the podium at City Hall voting to approve the Hunter's Point shipyard development, then cut to a shot of Glenda Callahan's car wreck, followed by a group of homeless beggars and, finally, a freeze-frame of Callahan landing his New Year's Eve punch on Billy Dale.

Superimposed over each image was the question, "Can San Francisco trust this man?" At the end of the spot, the question was answered, "No...Vote to recall Mayor Callahan, and vote for Walter Beard."

Billy Dale had always prided himself on being able to deliver in a campaign. From day one, he had taken the attitude of pulling out all the stops, slamming all the doors, and landing all the blows possible until a rival candidate was demolished and his candidate was poised to sprint to the finish line first.

But, in this case, things remained too uncertain for Billy. With Beard locked in a three-way tie for popularity with Alzeti and Callahan, and the recall of Callahan still a big unknown, Billy was not pleased. On Monday, with just over 24 hours left in the recall race, he remained worried, irritated, and even physically ill due to the unsettled nature of the campaign.

"I hate this suspense," he told an aide Monday morning as he took a swallow of Pepto-Bismol to settle his stomach and chased it with black coffee. "We've done everything. What the fuck else is there?"

But even Billy had no idea what could be done to land the final blow to Callahan and give Beard cruise control into the mayor's chair. Short of paying off the Elections Department to rig the vote, Billy believed he had done everything possible.

As Billy pondered the fate of Walter Beard, Tim Cross was considering his own fate as he worked furiously in his office at the *Journal*, commanding reporters, checking story assignments, and reading and re-reading polls throughout the morning.

The uncertainty of the election was not only a hindrance for Billy Dale on this day before the big vote, but also for Cross, who had his own stake in the outcome. With *Journal* publisher Donald Grossman pinning many of his future plans on Callahan's ability to survive the recall, everyone in the *Journal* newsroom had been put on high alert to do everything possible to keep Callahan in office.

Since William Carlson had lost just over two years ago, despite the backing of both newspapers and Grossman's directive for them to push for his election, Cross had been on a teetering ledge in Grossman's view. Now that Callahan was the man the *Journal* needed to survive, Cross remained on the firing line.

It had been only four days since Grossman last visited Cross in the newsroom just after deadline and made it clear that the paper should pull out all the stops to blast the recall effort, Beard, and Alzeti.

"You are not doing enough to keep him in and knock them out," Grossman had yelled during their brief exchange days earlier. "You have less than a week to make something happen, dig something up, and blast away."

Grossman had been critical of Cross for not using the Eddie's Bar incident to the paper's advantage, and not assigning enough pro-Callahan stories that could recount his achievements or his support from various political factions.

"We can't make up the news," Cross had yelled back at Grossman in his defense. "We have to report it. This is news coverage, not creation."

But Grossman didn't care. He had gone through too much with the Hunter's Point development and the battles with the *Bulletin*—which had chosen to endorse Beard—to lose it now. He wanted to come out ahead and with a supportive mayor still in office.

"Well, the bottom line is, if you can't do what I need from an editor, I'll find someone after the election who can," Grossman had said. "You have four days to drum up something, and it had better be good."

When Grossman left, Cross had begun nervously to think of ways to skewer Beard over the weekend. But, just as he began making a list, he stopped.

This was the last straw for him.

Sure, he was willing to do critical stories about Beard, and even examine

Beard's record a little more closely than Callahan's. But going after a candidate because the damn owner wants him out was not enough.

Cross had had his fill of that kind of approach during the past three mayoral elections, almost quitting during the Callahan/Carlson race.

But this time, it was all over.

For the next four days following Grossman's visit, Cross assigned the same kinds of stories that he would have directed for any other election race. Profiles of the candidates, last-minute campaigning articles, and the typical round-up stories were done.

When Monday appeared, Cross was satisfied that his paper had done the right coverage. The Sunday paper had included profiles of all three candidates, which balanced critical review along with accomplishments. The *Journal* had also run a special article examining the history of recalls in California, with observers defending and attacking the process on both sides.

While Cross felt proud of his management abilities that weekend, Donald Grossman was angrier than ever. Just as Cross had finished reviewing the story assignments that Monday, he got a call from Grossman. The owner had been busy over the weekend tending to other business, as well as taking time off on Sunday to play golf with some state-level political operatives.

But when Monday rolled around, Grossman's attention was back on the *Journal* and the recall election, which he realized was in the same shape it had been four days earlier. With more anger in his voice than ever, Grossman called Cross and let him have it.

"Okay, you son of a bitch, that is it," Grossman yelled to his editor, who only half-listened to the tirade he had expected. "You obviously don't want to follow orders, so here is the final one. Unless the mayor survives this fiasco, you are out as of Wednesday morning. Got it?"

Cross listened, half-angered by such an ultimatum and half saddened by his employer's lack of respect for journalistic integrity. When Grossman ended his directive, Cross simply said, "Are you through?" and hung up when Grossman said he was.

During the rest of Monday, Cross focused his attention on covering the last day of campaigning. He placed his efforts on assigning reporters, getting photographers out, and the usual deadline pressures that come with the close of a campaign. He didn't mind being forced out if staying meant going against his beliefs.

Although Cross had played ball with Grossman for years on this issue, he had determined early in the campaign that the owner's approach was not what he wanted. As reporters came and went from his office, and the clock ticked away into the evening hours that day, Cross all but accepted the fact that Callahan would likely lose the recall and he would be fired.

By 8 p.m., as the first deadlines passed, Cross began to think about what he would do. He knew he could get some kind of job at one of the other papers, or maybe a local publishing house or radio station where he had plenty of connections. But the thought of losing his job and being put through another search for employment did not sound appetizing.

As the day turned into night, Cross kept Grossman's threat to himself, telling only some of his most trusted reporters the information. He figured that they would keep it to themselves.

But, as always, word got around the city and by 8 p.m. or so the message had been spreading even beyond the newsroom to campaign headquarters and newsrooms around town. Cross began getting calls from friends in both the city's political and news circles.

Since he had other things to tend to, Cross just acted as if the threats were rumors and he was focused on the election.

"You know how rumors get started," Cross told an Alzeti campaigner and former reporter with whom he'd worked years earlier. "The way this campaign has been, you can't believe anything."

But having others call to remind him of his likely fate made Cross's day that much more difficult. He continued to do his best to be a professional, but slowly felt his heart giving in to the inevitable loss.

By 9:30 p.m., sadness and despair began to turn to anger as he proofed the opinion pages that contained the paper's editorials and various columns. This edition would include a reprint of the paper's earlier editorial supporting Callahan and opposing the recall.

Ironically, it had been Cross himself who had written the editorial attacking the recall supporters and Billy Dale as "low-minded hacks" who were only pushing the recall to "enact some vicious revenge." The editorial also called Callahan "an important leader, full of heart, who was trying to do his best for the city and deserved a full term in which to do it."

As Cross looked over the page, one of several that needed his final approval before being printed, he began to seethe with a wave of anger for Grossman that he had never before felt. He had done everything his boss had wanted, aside from outright criminal activity, and it was still not enough.

After a few minutes, Cross felt his face turn hotter and red, while his heart began to pound. "That bastard has no right to tell me what to do," he said to himself. "That fuck shouldn't even be in a newsroom, let alone be in charge of one."

Cross looked up at the clock, which had just struck 9:45 p.m. Wiping sweat from his forehead and pushing his chair back from the desk, he reached into his pocket and pulled out a cigarette.

Lighting quickly and drawing a fast puff, he shoved the pack of cigarettes back in his pocket and moved his chair forward under the desk. Another glance at the clock told Cross that he had just over an hour until the final deadline.

Rolling up his sleeves and taking a longer drag on the cigarette, he called down to the production room and told them the editorial page would be a little later than usual, but would make the 11 p.m. deadline.

"I've got some fine-tuning to do," Cross said, his lips still clasping the cigarette in his mouth. "It needs some changes."

With that, Cross began pecking away at the keyboard. As cigarette smoke encircled his head, he felt more sweat begin to roll down his face while he pounded out the words. Brushing away a fly that had flown through the room, Cross concentrated only on the symbols the machine in front of him was forming at his command.

"So, you want to get rid of me?" Cross said to himself. "Well, let's make it worth your while!"

Soon, he felt a smile appear on his face that turned almost to laughter as his fingers dashed along the keyboard and his mind took control. He was taking action, and he knew it was right.

After about 40 minutes, Cross had completed his task and sent the finished editorial onward to production. Since the editorial page had been laid out, all the production crew had to do was place the final version in the space. They didn't even notice that it had been altered.

Once he got the word that the final version had been sent forth from production, Cross shut off his computer and headed from his office into the newsroom. Since it was past 11 p.m., most of the staff was gone, but Cross still reminded those who remained that the next day—Election Day—would require them to stay later, so they needn't come in until late afternoon.

Then the editor went downstairs, outside, and down to the nearest bar. For the next few hours, he soaked his sorrows in gin and tonics and left his problems behind.

*　　*　　*

When Tuesday dawned in San Francisco that Election Day morning, the fog was thicker than ever. Although most natives and longtime residents were used to seeing the rolling wisps of cotton-like clouds scramble across the city, many considered this day's helping of billowy mist to be unusually thick and dark.

It was a clear sign that this would not be a normal day in the city by the bay.

For the political and journalistic elite—who had been waiting months for this dawn—the cascading clouds were barely noticeable. All their thoughts turned to the recall election and what would happen.

No one was more curious and nervous than Donald Grossman himself. He was still irritated that Tim Cross had not been able to light some fire under Callahan's campaign or print something to knock down the recall.

As the *Journal* owner awoke, went to his kitchen and made coffee, he grew even angrier at the thought that the potential recall of Callahan could have been averted if Cross or someone else on his staff had done something.

Looking out of his window toward the mist-strewn morning, Grossman felt a terrible feeling of dread overtake his mind. He knew that his whole political and business career could hinge on this election, and he didn't like the way it was going.

Trying to take his mind off his fears, he headed toward the door to get the newspaper, and on his way, turned on the radio in his kitchen. Then Grossman stopped cold.

He couldn't believe what he was hearing.

"Everyone in San Francisco politics is talking about the unusual about-face that The San Francisco *Journal* has taken in today's recall election," the newscaster explained. "The *Journal*, which had been the only major newspaper in the city to support Mayor Callahan and oppose the recall effort, announced today that it was switching its endorsement to back Senator Walter Beard."

Fear run through Grossman's veins and he had to hold his heart as it began to beat faster. He didn't fully grasp what he heard right away, but he forced himself to listen more.

"In a surprise editorial today," the radio newscaster continued, "The *Journal* stated that it was changing its support from Callahan to Beard after feeling 'a strong desire to do the right thing'. The editorial went on to cite reasons for supporting Beard that included 'his longtime commitment to the city and his ability to find solutions and solve problems.'"

As the newscaster read on, Grossman dropped into a chair at his kitchen table and put his hands to his face. Grossman slowly realized what had happened.

His threats to fire Tim Cross had done the exact opposite of his intentions. His editor had taken his last probable day on the job and stuck it to him. As the radio announcer offered more and more from the editorial, Grossman jumped up and ran to the front door. Fumbling with the lock for a moment, he finally clicked it open, leaned over, and grabbed for the newspaper.

Although the *Journal* was an afternoon newspaper—with its first edition not hitting most newsstands until 11 a.m.—Grossman, as owner, got his paper delivered just after 10 a.m. By the time he had awakened that day it was 11:30 a.m., which meant the paper likely had been out on newsstands for at least half an hour, giving the radio and TV stations ample time to see what had happened.

Snatching the paper from his front stoop and ripping it open to the editorial page, Grossman's eyes quickly scanned the pages and found the full-length endorsement, with a headline that said only, "The Right Thing to Do."

Reading further, Grossman felt his heart sink with helplessness and his stomach churn with anger. The editorial went straight down the line in its opposition to Callahan, calling him everything from a "sloppy politician" to a "hazardous liability for the city."

The harshest comments, however, came at the end, when Cross wrote that "San Francisco must do everything in its power to remove Mayor Callahan from office and bring in Walter Beard. Since his election more than two years ago, the mayor has embarrassed himself and this city and made us a laughing stock!"

Grossman just stood there, let the paper fall to the floor, and felt his mouth drop wide open.

"That motherfuck!" he said to himself as he closed the door slowly and went back to his kitchen. "I'll kill him!"

With that, Grossman threw the paper down on his couch and immediately grabbed his phone. First, he called Cross's home, but got no answer. When the editor's answering machine came on, Grossman left an angry but simple response.

"You are dead, you bastard," Grossman yelled as Cross's machine recorded his anger. "I will kick your ass and sue you so bad you'll need a lawyer just to get a paper route in this town."

Then Grossman slammed down the phone but quickly picked it up again to dial Cross's office at the *Journal*. The receptionist, however, told Grossman that no one had seen Cross all morning.

"He hasn't called in or anything," the receptionist said. "We have no idea. By the way, Mr. Grossman, what is going on with the editorial? We've gotten dozens of calls about it."

Grossman just made a grunting noise and hung up. His temper continued to rise as he showered, shaved, dressed, and headed toward the paper. But, first he stopped by his office at Mack Corp. to check messages.

And there were plenty.

The most glaring, though, was the note that Mayor Callahan had called.

That was the first one Grossman returned. After about an hour searching for the mayor, who was still out campaigning on this final day, Callahan's secretary tracked him down at a downtown restaurant where he was glad-handing voters.

Using a cell phone, Callahan got on the line and ripped into Grossman.

"What the fuck happened?" Callahan screamed into the phone. "You double-crossed me? For what?"

Grossman, still unable to speak very clearly, tried to defend himself.

"Mayor, I had nothing to do with this, honest! My editor did it on his own. We had a run-in and this, I guess, was his way of getting revenge or something. I'm trying to track him down. But we will get the word out that we are still behind you, I promise."

But Callahan remained hot and angry.

"Well, if this causes me to go down, or even to have a close call, you will not hear the end of it," the mayor barked. "Even if I win, I will not forget this."

Then Callahan hung up.

For the next two hours, Grossman tried to find Cross, while also fielding calls from business leaders, political activists, and just curious readers who wanted to know "Why?"

The most annoying message, however, came from Billy Dale, who had noticed the editorial during a quick lunch stop at a local deli as he led his troops out to give free rides to elderly voters and run phone banks to remind people to vote. He couldn't help but laugh as he read the Cross version of the endorsement and had to let Grossman know what he thought.

"Hey pal, thanks for the nice work," Billy's message said, with an undercurrent of laughter. "We can use all the help we can get!"

That just added to Grossman's fury. After listening to messages and calling people back for several hours, Grossman finally left his Mack office at 2 p.m. and headed to the *Journal*. He barreled into the newsroom like a cop chasing a criminal, but still couldn't find Tim Cross.

No one in the newsroom knew where he was, and the managing editor—Gloria Wilson—had been forced to organize election coverage herself and try to explain to all of the readers and advertisers who were calling in what the endorsement change was all about.

"I don't know what to tell them," Wilson told Grossman after finding him in his office. "What happened?"

Grossman didn't want to reveal too much information, so he simply told her that Cross had done it on his own. "He stabbed us in the back," Grossman told her. "Look, just tell people that it was a mistake and focus on election coverage."

Since it was still early in the afternoon, and most election action wouldn't occur until later that day, Wilson could handle things. She had already sent photographers to get the obligatory shots of Beard, Callahan, and Alzeti voting, along with some shots of voters and overall comment from those who were casting ballots.

The real action wouldn't begin until about 8 p.m. or 9 p.m. when the vote counting started at the Election Directors' office at City Hall. For now, Wilson just had to hold down the fort.

But while reporters, editors, and photographers were gearing up to cover the city's biggest story, no one could find Tim Cross.

Grossman began to believe that maybe he had just run off, not able to deal with the owner's ultimatum or the embarrassment of being fired after the election. He also thought that Cross just might not want to do his job if the uncertainty of his future at the *Journal* hung overhead.

Grossman eventually went by Cross's Bernal Heights' house, in the city's southeastern corner, late that afternoon to look for him. But he found no one there. Even the editor's car, a prized 1965 Mustang convertible—which Cross had bought at a police auction years earlier—was gone. That convinced Grossman that he had skipped town.

Heading back to the *Journal* at about 4 p.m., Grossman just gritted his teeth and braced himself for what was about to happen. Whether Callahan survived the recall or not really didn't matter to him at this point.

The mayor still thought that the *Journal* had double-crossed him and, if he lost, Walter Beard would remember who had supported him and who hadn't. All of Grossman's work to get the Hunter's Point Development approved and going could be for naught.

If Beard or Alzeti got in, either one would likely halt the project and demand further testing or something that would eventually slow or stop everything.

As Grossman pulled into the *Journal* parking lot and headed up the stairs to the newsroom to check on things, he was stopped suddenly by one of his police reporters.

"Mr. Grossman, I heard some horrible news," the reporter told him, with his lips trembling and eyes red with tears. "We know where Tim Cross is."

Grossman's eyes widened at the thought of getting back at his two-timing editor. He was already coming up with ways to fire him and see that he never worked again when he pressed the reporter for more.

"Well," Grossman said, grabbing the reporter's arm. "Where is that son of a bitch?"

"He's...he's...he's in the morgue," the reporter blurted out. "They found him dead early this morning. He had crashed into a tree in Golden Gate Park. Drunk driving, they think. We didn't find out until now because they couldn't identify him until about an hour ago. But I just got the call."

Then the reporter began to tear up and walk away. Grossman just froze and stood there in the stairwell of the *Journal* building for about 30 seconds. After finding a way to walk without falling, he climbed the steps and entered the newsroom. The place was dead silent, except for some light keyboard clatter.

The first person to approach him was Gloria Wilson, who wrapped her arms around the newspaper owner and began to cry. Other reporters just looked over at Grossman with helpless pain on their faces. Many had known what he had said to Cross, and why the editor had changed the endorsement editorial to get back at him.

But no one else spoke. Grossman just put his arms around Wilson and tried to comfort her. He had no idea what to do. ∎

Chapter Thirty-One

The Final Blow

As Election Day wore on, word of both the *Journal* endorsement change and Tim Cross's death spread through San Francisco with a fury. Although campaign efforts forged ahead, and reporters and editors went full tilt to cover the Election Day activities, a dull feeling lay over the city in the midst of the unusually thick fog.

Police held a brief press conference in the late afternoon to offer details of Cross's death while the *Journal* released a short statement from Grossman that called his demise "a tragedy and loss beyond comprehension."

Investigators said Cross's car had been found in the early morning hours of Election Day by a passing jogger, and that he'd been discovered at the steering wheel with wounds to the head and back. No skid marks were found, showing that he did not try to stop.

"We found traces of alcohol in his body, but further tests are needed," an investigator told reporters at the press conference. "At this point, we believe it was a case of driving under the influence, but we have to await further results. No one else was in the vehicle and no foul play is suspected."

Since election news was the priority for every TV and radio newscast, as well as the newspapers, Cross's death and the *Journal* endorsement switch remained only a strange side story. While the endorsement flip-flop had done some of the damage Cross wanted by putting out another anti-Callahan voice and embarrassing the *Journal*, Grossman was able to take some of the sting out of it.

At about noon, soon after he discovered the endorsement change, Grossman released a short statement saying that the switch was "a mistake," but offering little further explanation for it.

"We stand by our original endorsement of Jack Callahan and continue to oppose the recall effort," Grossman told a radio reporter that day. "This editorial that ran today was incorrect. The editorial board of the *Journal* continues to object to any recall of Mayor Callahan."

Meanwhile, Billy Dale, Jimmy Min, Mike McLean, J.T. Townsend, and the three candidates went about their usual Election Day routines, but with an eerie feeling of dread and loss that seemed to reduce the level of excitement.

Callahan was the most furious. Although Grossman swore that the endorsement was a mistake, the mayor knew that it could make a difference and vowed to exact his revenge on the newspaper later.

"That son of a bitch is going to pay. His goddamn shipyard development is the first to feel the ax," the mayor told Carl Devins as they walked along Geary Boulevard for some last-minute campaigning after lunch. "I can't believe it."

At the *Journal*, most staffers were forced to focus on the Election Day coverage, which usually piled on ten times as much work as a regular news day. But that didn't stop many from hitting both Grossman and Gloria Wilson with questions about Cross's death and the endorsement switch.

Grossman tried to alleviate concerns with a short staff meeting, in which he explained that Cross had changed the editorial on his own, but never mentioned the threats he had made if Callahan lost. Most of the staff knew what the reason was, and a few even asked about it. Grossman just denied everything.

"You can't believe rumors," Grossman said, his voice shaky. "That is not what our business is about. It's about facts and those are the facts. He did something wrong and, sadly, died a tragic death. But one has nothing to do with the other."

That didn't satisfy everyone. At one point, one reporter even quit in protest, while three others walked out, but eventually came back after Wilson begged them. "We need you now more than ever," she said. "Tim would have wanted it that way."

For Grossman, the situation became more and more unbearable. Not only did he have to contend with the potential loss to his political and power positions in town, regardless of who won, but he also began to feel a pang of slow, creeping guilt over Tim Cross's passing.

He knew that the reason Cross had gotten drunk that night was because of him. He also knew that he had changed the endorsement on his own because Grossman had threatened him. But he refused to let it change his feelings.

"I have to run this place the way I run it," Grossman told himself as he smoked yet another cigarette inside his *Journal* office. "I've come this far this way and I had to do what I had to do."

But his worries remained. He knew that Jack Callahan would oppose him no matter what, and that the other two candidates would remember that he had not endorsed them. He just shook his head and braced for the worst.

For Billy Dale, however, life was completely different as he reveled in the Election Day fervor. From the first day he was in prison at the hands of Jack Callahan's testimony, he had been savoring the moment when he could take his revenge.

Now that Tim Cross put what would likely be a final nail in the coffin of Callahan's mayoral administration, Billy put his own final screws to work that day, directing staff to get out the vote by phone, drive seniors and others to the polls, and work the press line with comments to reporters who scoured the city all day.

"This is what we needed," Billy had told Jimmy Min during a short sandwich break inside Billy's car as they went from one voter precinct to another to keep an eye on campaign volunteers. "Even if those fucks at the *Journal* try to correct it, the damage is done."

Jimmy agreed, smiling his trademark grin and taking a bite of a turkey roll as Billy steered them through the Mission District toward The Castro. Nodding his head, Jimmy pulled out his cell phone and called several reporters, directing them to make the most of the *Journal* screw-up for the *Advocate*'s next issue.

"Get it all and play it big," Jimmy told reporter Tammy Sharp, who was running from campaign headquarters to City Hall to the police station trying to cover all of the weird aspects of the day's news. "We have plenty of time, so don't panic, but don't lose anything."

The *Reader*, which also would publish the next day, put its own efforts into overdrive to highlight the *Journal* screw-up and cover the election results.

"Make the most of it," Danny Dugan told his staff. "We must get it down to the wire. Otherwise, all people will see is the slanted coverage in the dailies."

As the newspapers pressed forward, Callahan, Alzeti, and Walter Beard did their final tours of campaign duty as voters went to the polls. Although most of the convincing had ended, each candidate still made appearances, cast their ballots, and bided their time as the day wore on.

While the fog continued to roll over the city, moderate temperatures and a lack of rain made for a larger voter turnout. By about 6 p.m.—two hours before the polls closed—Elections Director Susan Rover reported that turnout would likely be about 70%, a remarkable number, especially for a special election.

"I don't know what it is," she told a radio reporter during the evening newscast. "But people are coming out in droves."

By 7 p.m., political supporters and other campaign workers began to show up at Rover's office. While no worthwhile results would be ready until well after 9 p.m., this ritual of arriving and waiting with others for election tabulations had become a San Francisco tradition. Reporters, campaign managers, and usually near the end candidates, would chat, listen, and wait for the returns.

"It was like the Oscars for San Francisco," Carl Devins once said to a friend. "If you are not there, you are missing out."

Although each candidate also had "victory" parties planned at restaurants or hotels nearby, most would at least drop by or show up at City Hall later to get the most timely count. On this night, Callahan had a party planned for the Fairmont Hotel; Walter Beard set up his soiree at the St. Francis Hotel; and Alzeti—always the favorite of Italian North Beach—celebrated at The Stinking Rose, a popular and beloved garlic restaurant.

During the day, the only information that had been given out from the *Journal* about Cross and the endorsement suggested that neither had anything to do with the other. As far as the *Journal's* official reports, the endorsement had been changed mistakenly, but no word had been given about who had changed it or why.

As for Cross's death, nothing had been released by the paper or the police about what had caused him to get drunk and crash his car. As far as most people knew, the two were unrelated.

But, just after 7 p.m., all of that changed. During the last dash of election coverage planning, one report came out that told the entire story. At about 7:10 p.m., KKSF Radio broadcast a report telling the entire story of Grossman's threat and Cross's endorsement revenge.

"Following interviews with several *Journal* staff members, including many who talked to Cross during the day Monday, we have learned that *Journal* owner Donald Grossman had threatened the editor with the loss of his job if Mayor Callahan lost the recall election," the radio report blared. "According to sources at the *Journal* and among others who knew Cross, the editor had been ordered to print inflammatory stories about Walter Beard over several days, but refused. Many speculate that the threat of losing his job drove him to change the endorsement."

"What other reason could there be?" asked one *Journal* reporter, whose name was withheld and whose voice was altered electronically for the news report. "He was driven to this by our inhumane owner, who cared only about getting what he could out of this campaign, and not about journalistic quality. Mr. Grossman, the blood of Tim Cross is on your hands."

Within the hour, the news report had spread by mouth and broadcast replays, but still stayed a side event against the main election news. As more and more people gathered at City Hall to begin the result count, whispers grew about the entire *Journal*/Cross incident.

Most of the TV and radio newscasts updating the election results that night included the *Journal* endorsement story and its link to Cross's death, but without much more explanation.

Grossman was found at about 8:30 p.m. by a group of broadcast reporters waiting outside the *Journal* building. But he merely denied the reports.

"You must be savages to take something like the tragic death of this man and try to turn it into some kind of gossipy revenge report," Grossman said while getting into his car to head to City Hall. "This is untrue."

When Grossman reached Rover's office a few minutes later, the questions continued to come at him from both reporters and interested spectators. But he calmed the fire somewhat by denying everything again.

Eventually, at just before 9 p.m., the first results were released. With only 10% of the precincts reported, and the absentee ballots counted, the Yes on Recall vote was marginally ahead of the No on Recall vote, 55% to 45%, almost exactly in line with the last polls before the election.

On the question of who should replace Callahan if he is recalled, Beard was blowing away Alzeti, 61% to 39%. Not exactly a surprise.

Still, the veteran politicos knew that they had to wait it out, and that nothing would matter unless the recall succeeded. Slowly, but surely, the tally continued, as did the arrival of more and more reporters, candidates, political operatives, and the usual campaign-curious who always showed up at such events.

Among the major players, Mayor Callahan arrived first, at about 10 p.m., followed by Alzeti at 10:15 and Walter Beard—his usual fashionably late self—at 10:45 p.m.

Danny Dugan showed up shortly after Beard, while Emily Ingle—usually one to favor the fancy parties at a penthouse on Election Night over the City Hall waiting—entered Rover's jammed office at 11:05 p.m.

The last ones to show up, as usual, were Billy Dale and Jimmy Min. The two had been soaking up the gossip, food, and booze at Beard's St. Francis Hotel party, and could barely wobble in.

As usual, the drinking heightened Billy's overly-driven emotions. In this case, those emotions were way up. Billy relished the prospects for victory, not only from the initial vote count, but also from the feeling he had that the *Journal* had been slammed hard that day by Tim Cross's actions.

From the time that the *Journal* had first endorsed William Carlson nearly three years earlier, Billy had the newspaper's owner on his list of people to screw over, and now it was happening.

As the crowd milled about and talked politics, Billy—always one to find a fight or cause one—dug his way through the throng of people toward Grossman and immediately grabbed his arm.

"Hey, Donny boy, how do you feel?" he said, slurring his speech and spilling gin from his glass onto his sleeve. "You guys look like you lost it all."

Grossman, knowing Billy's helpless bent for booze, just jerked his arm away and turned his back. But that didn't stop Billy. He was going to enjoy this moment.

"Say, Don," Billy said, tapping the news executive on the shoulder. "How does it feel to be a laughing stock of the city's newspapers? You like it?"

As Billy grinned at his own commentary, Grossman slowly turned around and shot back. "You should talk about laughing stocks," Grossman said to the political consultant. "Look at you, a fucking disgrace."

"Yeah, well, at least I didn't kill anyone this week," Billy said, taking another sip from his drink and wiping his face. "Go live with that."

At that moment, Grossman could no longer hold back. The day's mix of aggravating and tragic events had finally taken hold with Billy's snide remark. Feeling an unstoppable wave of anger, frustration, and outright emotional explosion, Grossman let his days of irritation cut loose.

In a split second, Grossman swung around, grabbed Billy by the arm, and shoved him against a wall, knocking the drink out of his hands and spilling gin all over the floor. Then, walking toward Billy with the intention of punching him just as Jack Callahan had done months earlier, Grossman reared back his fist, ready to strike.

Just then, however, both Marie Alzeti and Danny Dugan stepped in, grabbed Grossman by each arm and held on.

"Don't do it," Dugan whispered, slowly walking Grossman in the other direction and patting him on the back to calm him down. "That idiot isn't worth it. Calm down."

Alzeti held Grossman's other arm. "C'mon, Don," she urged. "Forget about that loudmouth."

But Grossman's temper went into overdrive. Pushing both Alzeti and Dugan aside, Grossman felt as though he couldn't stop himself and went at Billy full throttle, running up to the drunken campaign manager, grabbing him with both arms, and throwing him into another wall.

As Billy's overweight body slammed against the heavy concrete, the force knocked Billy out cold. Blood then began to stream from his mouth as he toppled over onto his back.

At that second, Jimmy Min went after Grossman himself, jumping on him from behind and pulling him into a neck lock. Since Jimmy weighed about 75 pounds less than Grossman, he had little advantage over him in a normal fight. But with the element of surprise from behind, Jimmy brought Grossman to his knees.

After a few seconds, Danny Dugan got into the act, grabbing at Jimmy in an attempt to pull him off Grossman, while several people tended to the injured Billy Dale.

"Hey, Jimmy, Don, knock it off, knock it off," Dugan pleaded as he tried to untangle the two. But it didn't stop, causing Jimmy and Grossman to roll around on the floor, as several others jumped into the fray and tried to stop them.

After several minutes, the brawl spread as friends and employees of Grossman got into it with several Jimmy Min reporters and other Beard supporters. Eventually, Dugan was defending himself against punches from all sides, while Jimmy Min and Donald Grossman continued to wrestle.

At one point, Mike McLean, who had entered the office just as Grossman was punching Billy Dale, dove into the madness to help his boss and friend.

Soon, half of the people in the Elections Director's office were fighting. Punches flew, pieces of furniture were thrown, and at least one knife was pulled and stuck in someone's leg. It was a rolling, fist-flying, old-fashioned brawl that could have come from a scene in an old western movie.

"I'm going to kick your fuckin' ass, you son of a bitch," Grossman was overheard telling Jimmy Min. "Your fucking paper has done more to screw us than anyone."

But Jimmy didn't respond, he just threw punches wildly and tried to see if Billy was all right. Billy regained consciousness and jumped back in the fray, slamming fists at both Grossman and Danny Dugan.

The entire incident took place over a span of about five minutes, but it seemed much longer as the fisticuffs, curses, and flying objects were tossed about. Susan Rover, who emerged from the back offices where the vote-counting continued, was aghast when she saw the behavior, and quickly called the police when she realized it was out of control.

Others in the room either jumped into the fray or backed away to give those in the melee more room. Jimmy felt a piece of glass slice his head and saw blood trickle over one eye, but kept punching. Billy also tasted blood in his mouth but didn't let it stop him from landing punches on both Grossman and Danny Dugan, as more people jumped into the insanity.

Then, about six minutes after the riot began, everyone stopped.

Almost in unison, the punching ended as each person felt that ominous movement of the ground beneath them.

With a simple, slow shift, the floor began to rumble and the walls to shake. The 100-year-old chandeliers above began to sway, causing a slight clinking of crystal, while several chairs and tables visibly shifted.

For anyone who has ever lived in California for any major stretch of time, all of the signs were obvious.

It was an earthquake, and it was rolling.

Quickly, everyone stood up and looked around—the usual response when an earthquake strikes. But, for some reason, everyone knew this was bigger than most. Instead of seeking shelter under something, almost the entire roomful of people headed for the exits as the rumble of the shaker grew louder and stronger.

Little by little, items such as computers, books, and files were knocked off desks and tables as the shaking turned more violent, sounding and feeling like a freight train rumbling by. About ten seconds later, the walls began to crack, while the few windows in the room shattered or blew out completely and fire alarms were set off from the vibrations.

People continued to rush toward the door, but were either trampled by others or knocked out of the way. As the shaking grew more intense and the noise louder, pieces of the wall began to fall, along with several beams and tiles from the ceiling. One of the first struck by falling debris was Donald Grossman, who did not even have the chance to get up when the quake hit. Out of nowhere, a large piece of steel landed on his head, killing him instantly.

A few feet away, one of the large chandeliers that began to sway when the shaking began became disconnected from the holding wire and crashed to the ground, landing just over Marie Alzeti's shoulder. Her cries for help went unnoticed by the escaping crowd, and her life faded out just moments later.

For Walter Beard, who was closest to the door, the quake had caused him to head toward a window and attempt to open it. But, just as he lifted the large, wooden windowpane, a crumbling piece of the ceiling slammed him in the back, knocking him over. As he fell, his head slammed hard on an old-fashioned iron heater, knocking him down and ending his life.

The mayor, who was on the other side of the room waiting calmly for the results, had never even gotten into the fighting, choosing instead to let others get out their frustrations as he waited. But that placed him at the exact opposite end of the room from the exit, forcing him to run as soon as the tremors started.

Jack Callahan's life ended when one of the clear glass panels that created a skylight for the room crashed down, slamming shattered glass all over him, including a large dagger-like chunk that pierced his chest.

When the 30 seconds of quake madness, shaking, and terror was over, at least 55 people were dead inside Rover's office—including the Elections Director herself, Jimmy Min, Danny Dugan, and Emily Ingle. Since it was nearly midnight, the rest of City Hall had been virtually empty so most of the casualties involved those inside Rover's office.

But, the intensity of the quake had almost completely destroyed City Hall. The rumbling had sparked a chain reaction throughout the historic building, which began in the offices opposite from Rover's and spread, like a collapsing house of cards, to the Elections Director's side.

Police had just started to arrive when the quake struck, having been called by Rover as the fist-fighting broke out. But none of the officers had entered the building when the tragedy took hold. As the last rumblings of the quake ceased, small fires began to break out all through City Hall, forcing a slow, thick stream of smoke to rise from the collapsed rubble. Every room in the building had been destroyed.

Outside, police and fire units responded, but had no idea what to do. The dead bodies lay trapped inside under tons of concrete, steel, and stone, while frightened and scared survivors cried, yelled, or fainted outside.

Among those who managed to escape was Billy Dale.

Still feeling the effects of alcohol and the late hour in his body, and continuing to drip blood from his mouth, forehead, and hand, Billy just sat on a curb across the street as sirens wailed, people screamed, and rescue workers raced about.

Just five minutes after Billy had gotten out, and about two minutes after the small fires had begun, a thundering boom was heard that shook the area almost as much as the earthquake itself. Fire officials knew that it was a main gas line underneath the giant structure that they had been trying unsuccessfully to shut off.

But, once the smaller flames had ignited it, a giant fireball erupted up through the building's giant dome top, and eventually spread over most of the structure. Within about 10 minutes, the entire City Hall was engulfed in flames. The fire slowly burned the dead bodies of those inside, along with all of the city's records—including that day's election results.

*   *   *

Although at the time, voting results seemed meaningless in the face of such death and destruction, several days later—when a moment of order was regained—city officials who had survived realized that such a loss of tabulated votes required that a mayoral election be held again. Since Callahan, Beard, and Alzeti had all perished, somehow, some way, the city had to find a new mayor.

In her post as the Board of Supervisors' president, Alzeti would have been the successor to Callahan. But since she had died, the board had to appoint an interim mayor—choosing Supervisor Mary Menning to temporarily take the post.

If no recall election had occurred, Menning would simply serve out Callahan's term and be in line to run for it permanently in another two years. But because Callahan had died during a recall election, city charter rules required a special election to be held within six months.

Two weeks after the earthquake, when the city began to return to slight normalcy, it was announced that the special election would be held 90 days later. Within an hour of the announcement, Billy Dale was on the phone to none other than William Carlson.

"Carlson?" he said when the former mayor answered the phone. "I have an idea. Ya got a minute?" ■

ABOUT THE AUTHOR

Joe Strupp is an award-winning journalist with 30 years' experience spanning newspapers, magazines, radio, television, cable and the web. He has spent the past 18 years covering media and news issues for *Editor & Publisher* magazine and Media Matters for America.

He spent eight years in San Francisco during the 1990's covering city and political topics for *The Independent*, a citywide newspaper that covered all aspects of the City by the Bay.

Joe's work has also appeared in *Salon.com*, *San Francisco* magazine, *MediaWeek* and *New Jersey Monthly*. He has received honors from the New Jersey Press Association, Society of Professional Journalists, Syracuse University's Mirror Awards, The Jesse H. Neal Business Journalism Awards and Folio.

Joe is currently a reporter at the *Asbury Park Press* in New Jersey, a freelance writer and adjunct professor in media at Fairleigh Dickinson University and Rutgers University. He is also the author of *Killing Journalism: How Greed, Laziness (and Donald Trump) Are Destroying News and How We Can Save It*. Joe lives in New Jersey with his wife, Claire, and his children, Cloey and Cole.

ACKNOWLEDGMENTS

Sincere thanks and gratitude to my wonderful editor and publisher, Thomas West, who took on this project and made it that much better. Thanks to Ted Fang, John Moses, Susan Herbert, Zoran Basich, Tom Borromeo and all of those San Francisco journalists who guided me and supported my work that helped lead to this book. For support and friendship during the writing and editing, thanks to Eric Carlson, Nina Leone, Marilee Strong, Sam Delson, Steve Seeman, and Lou DeRossi. For guidance and positive views, James Brady, Nat Hentoff and Patricia Leasure. And most of all, thanks to my wonderful wife, Claire, and my children, Cloey and Cole, who support my writing and put up with losing me to long hours at the computer, on the phone and ranting about deadlines.